LOUISA GENE MORIYAMA

THE
OBSIDIAN
CROWN

children
of fate

For my family.

"Avaunt! to-night my heart is light. No dirge will I upraise,
"But waft the angel on her flight with a Pæan of old days!
"Let no bell toll!—lest her sweet soul, amid its hallowed
mirth,
"Should catch the note, as it doth float up from the damnéd
Earth.
"To friends above, from fiends below, the indignant ghost is
riven—
"From Hell unto a high estate far up within the Heaven—
"From grief and groan, to a golden throne, beside the King
of Heaven."

—Edgar Allen Poe, "Lenore"

PROLOGUE

I'M NOT SURE when it began for me. There are moments that stand out more than others, but the progression it took almost seemed insignificant at first—like watching paint dry on a canvas. The full scope of what was created and happened isn't realized until the paint completely dries. A single stroke of the brush could have wider implications to a greater whole. But then what determines its significance? What determines that a single brush stroke becomes a detail of something greater or something that is abstract without any clear meaning?

When does something become important? When do colors blend or form lines to define a masterpiece? When does it become a da Vinci or a Monet?

I'm not trying to say that these moments of my life form some sort of masterpiece. Far from it. But it is significant to me and maybe important for others.

Maybe it's just a horrible misrepresentation of something like a masterpiece. Even a painting of something dripping in death and despair can be considered something beautiful. It's all about how the colors blend and the lines form in exactly the right moment.

I'm not sure when I realized that something was different about me. I never had the consolation of someone telling me that I was "just unique" or "just different." Because I kept this thing about me hidden.

CHAPTER ONE
A SMALL BUTTERFLY

I NEVER THOUGHT that I would end up working in a hospital. Especially not one of the world's leading hospitals in research medicine for all the cancers you could ever imagine. The bad cancers, though. Not that any cancer is a good cancer. But these kinds of cancers don't go away with a couple treatments of chemotherapy and radiation. These are not the kinds of cancers that you can even excise with the finality of a scalpel and then hope that it's gone or that remission is a good and long time.

But here I am now, wearing an impressive white coat that is just a little too long in the sleeves and stitched like it's meant to make you feel as uncomfortable as possible—like when you cross paths in the hospital corridor with a patient's family member who has honed in on you as "The Doctor" taking care of their critically ill loved one, which is about to happen to me now.

"Ahh…um…doctor?" An elderly gentleman walking as fast as his arthritic knees will allow somehow catches up to me while I am taking a turn in the hallway, which is pretty impressive. I have one speed when walking, and it's barely short of jogging. I actually feel like a rope is being pulled around my middle as I jerk to a complete standstill.

"Er…doctor…Dr. Hashimo—" The gentleman pushes his glasses up the bridge of his nose, only to have them fall right back down as he squints at my name badge.

"Evie," I am quick to respond with a smile. "Just Evie, sir. Can I help you?" I resist the urge to look down at the little timepiece on my left wrist, but then I realize that my impressive coat sleeve is too long for me to see it anyway.

"Ah, Evie." The gentleman becomes nervous, holding his hands in front of him, his shoulders stooped over. "My wife, she's had some tests done today. We were hoping to know if the results are back. If the cancer…is…is gone now."

I get ready to deliver my usual explanation: *I'm not this patient's doctor, and the doctor assigned to the patient will be the best one to address any concerns or questions that you might have.*

Also, have you called your nurse? He or she would definitely know more than me.

You know, that sort of explanation.

But something stops the words from leaving my mouth. Is it the way he's holding his hands as his long, thin fingers twist a gold wedding band? Maybe it's the way he keeps pushing up on his glasses, as if to have something to do other than squint away the burning sensation of salty tears. Maybe it's because it is just the right turn in the hallway to slow me down enough for him to catch up to me. I'm not sure what it is, but eventually I find myself following this elderly man down the opposite hall of my original path and standing at the bedside of his dying wife.

I suddenly find myself remembering a moment when I was a very young girl. I think I was barely two years of age. I'm not sure if it's a true memory. I might've been too young to remember something that early on in my cognitive development. At least, that's what some textbook on psychology might say.

But this memory feels real.

My Grandpa Takeo holds a small white butterfly, the size of a dime, in the palm of his hand. He holds it out to me and my brother, Kiran, who is standing next to me.

"It's not moving, Grandpa." Kiran sounds so sad in his small, young voice. "It should be flying away."

"That's because it is dying," Grandpa Takeo says, and as he says it, the butterfly's wings freeze and become still in his hands. "It is the curse of something so small, that it should have a life that is so fleeting." He sighs, and we can both see how tired and old Grandpa Takeo has become.

He was in his seventies at this time, still working at a small-town doctor's office. It never occurred to my parents to ask him to stop working, to retire and enjoy his old age. They knew that he loved his work too much.

I remember reaching my very small fingers out and just barely brushing the butterfly's small wings. But then my fingers flutter back quickly as the butterfly's wings move just slightly. I'm not sure if it is because I had moved them. I look at Kiran to see if he noticed, but he is already looking down at the grass for more insects, preferably of the more lively variety.

Then I look up at Grandpa Takeo, who is looking right at me. The corners of his eyes lift up as he smiles. "Maybe this butterfly had one little heartbeat left for this life."

So here I am.

I find myself looking down at this dying woman, her husband holding her hand and watching me expectantly. His eyes are bleary and hopeful, the wrinkles around them drooping downward. I try to keep myself from forming any expression. I try to keep my forehead as flat as possible.

Because she looks terrible.

Her eyes are closed, and her mouth is slightly open at the corners. The muscles are completely relaxed in her face, and her skin has a dusky, gray pallor. Her eyes have completely sunken into their sockets. She looks like a skeleton with a fine sheet of skin pulled over the bones. I wish I could just walk away. I wish that a nurse would come in, a whirlwind of motion. Enough time for me to escape as he or she took the weight of this man's grief and this woman's suffering off of my shoulders.

I quietly pull the sleeve of my right arm above my wrist. I reach my hand down and just very slightly press my left ring finger to her wrist—at the radial area where the pulse whispers a song, skipping notes as it tries to be heard.

"Dr. Hashimoto?"

I jump back as if shocked with static. My fingers find

themselves hidden in my too-long sleeves. I turn around and notice the familiar face of a nurse wearing dark blue scrubs and holding at least five bags of intravenous medications in his arms.

"Oh! Dr. Hashimoto, I'm glad I ran into you. Dr. Mendez was looking for you just a minute ago."

"Right. Thanks, Clark."

I glance apologetically at the old man. My eyes land on his fingers clasping his wife's cold hand with both of his. I feel out of place, as if I shouldn't be there standing in this room. I think he realizes it, but at the same time, he seems relieved to have done something. Even if it was just to move his feet and to have found anyone at all who might've had at least one word to say. Any words. Or maybe even nothing.

I sincerely hope it was the latter reason, because I had said absolutely nothing.

"Dr. Hashimoto?"

I jump again. I'm sure I seem like I'm either incredibly nervous or overcaffeinated at this point.

"Yes, right. Dr. Mendez. And, Clark, please, it's just Evie."

CHAPTER TWO

SPINNERS AND SHINING SHEARS

"You're exactly ten minutes late."

After I take a seat, a stern-faced man greets me by looking up from a pile of documents, many of which happen to be spread out all over the table in front of him. I resist the urge to collect them, stacking each piece of paper on top of one another into one neat stack.

"Good morning to you, too, Dr. Mendez."

Dr. Mendez peers above his sharply framed glasses, his eyebrows shooting up over the rims. He has the most remarkable way of shouting out disapproval without actually shouting it. He has the loudest eyebrows of anyone I know. He snaps the current document in his hands and continues to look, if at all possible, even sterner. He might not look it, barely taller than me (even with shoes), but most of the resident doctors would agree that Dr. Julian Mendez is perhaps the most draconian on this side of the Cascade Mountains (minus the fire breathing—although, that has been disputed).

So it was quite a bit of a shock to everyone, myself included, that after completing my residency, Dr. Mendez personally offered me a job on his hematology-oncology floor, while promptly ignoring all twelve of my fellow peers. (They were not heartbroken, I can assure you.)

My hair, which was artificially colored a particularly bright neon yellow at the time, may have turned an even more shocking shade when this happened. After providing me this offer, Dr. Mendez then proceeded to deliver his manifesto on the honors of working at one of the finest leading facilities in cancer research in the world, etcetera…*but your hair is a shocking color for a professional of your aptitude*…etcetera.

Not that he needed to convince me. I already knew that I wanted to be an oncologist specializing in hematology.

However, when it came to my hair, that was a different story.

I promptly took his advice, arriving today, on the first day of my rotation as a full-fledged and fresh-off-residency doctor, with my hair a lovely dusty lavender color.

I assume Dr. Mendez doesn't mind the recent change in hair color, since he avoids making any further comments that might initiate a more unique hue change on my part.

"The Plaits will be arriving shortly."

"The Plaits," I repeat carefully as I lean over a few documents, trying to place the name with the unfortunate circumstance that is bound to follow—a natural reflex when you work in a major hospital that treats very sick people.

Dr. Mendez shoves aside a stack of papers, pulls out a slim tablet, and hands it to me. On the tablet is a glowing image of a skeleton. However, you don't have to be someone with eight years of medical-related schooling to realize that something is horribly wrong with this particular image.

Where there should be a brilliant image of glowing white bones, this particular skeleton has a sprinkling of large, gaping black spots scattered throughout; the darker spots seem to concentrate heavily at nearly every joint.

"Sylvia Plait, nine years old. Osteosarcoma," Dr. Mendez mumbles under his breath as he snaps one document and glances at another that he is simultaneously looking at in his other hand. "Swipe right."

As I start to move my finger across the tablet's screen, I immediately recognize the name— associating it with little strawberry earrings and glittery green nail polish. I remember her parents sitting at her hospital bed, both on either side, holding her very small hands. By this time, Sylvia had already received multiple rounds of chemotherapy. Her dark curling hair had already fallen out in little patches. Her mother had brought her a gray hat knitted with pink metallic yarn. Sylvia absolutely adored this hat.

The image on the tablet's screen is of a skeleton, with noticeably fewer black gaps scattered through it. I read the information under Sylvia's medical record number and note that this is an earlier bone scan that was completed just two months prior to the first one Dr. Mendez had me view. Obviously, this is an aggressively spreading cancer.

"If you can recall, Sylvia was receiving an experimental chemotherapy medication. Now swipe forward to the newest image."

I am already in the process of sliding my finger across the screen. I feel my pupils dilate and my eyes widen. This new bone scan is dated exactly one month from the newest image, but with one crucial difference. Instead of the image with all the gaping black holes throughout, I find myself holding the image of a perfectly pristine skeleton, glowing white with not a single imperfection.

I confirm that this is indeed Sylvia Plait's bone scan, even matching up the medical record numbers. The most successful cancer treatments are unlikely to result in something so drastic. Especially one month after treatment. I swipe back and forth between the images.

Before I can look up from the image, though, Dr. Mendez has already set his documents down and stood up. A gentle knock at the door quickly has me on my feet as well, still holding the tablet in my hand.

The door opens, and standing in the doorway is a young black couple. In between them is a little girl holding one of her parents' hands in each of hers. She has a knitted gray cap on her head with shiny pink yarn sparkling in the fluorescent hospital lights.

"Hello, Mr. and Mrs. Plait." Dr. Mendez strides across the room, reaching his hand out to shake each of theirs. He then kneels, leaning an elbow down on one knee, and with his sternest face, holds his hand out to Sylvia. "And you, young lady? Staying out of trouble, I assume?"

Sylvia, with an expression of seriousness only a nine-year-old could have after being told that she has a type of bone cancer that is likely going to end her life within the next twelve months, takes Dr. Mendez's hand firmly. Her fingers barely wrap around his palm.

Then the stern Dr. Mendez does something that no one (doctor, nurse, pharmacy technician, or cafeteria worker) would ever believe if I told them. He raises his extremely large left eyebrow and brings the right eyelid down for a very small wink.

Sylvia must be familiar with this uncharacteristic gesture, because she raises her own left eyebrow and very exaggeratedly brings her own right eyelid down for a wink. And then her serious expression relaxes into an enormous smile that matches her parents'.

Dr. Mendez stands up, pulling his shoulders back and gesturing toward me. "You may remember Dr. Hashimoto. She has graduated from residency and accepted a position here at this hospital."

I realize that my mouth is hanging slightly open, still shocked by Dr. Mendez's bizarre behavior. I am ready for his hair to suddenly turn a shocking neon pink color. I quickly close my mouth and wave in a silly way, which makes Sylvia grin.

"Hello, Evie." Mrs. Plait smiles. "We should let you know that Sylvia has informed us that she is absolutely determined to dye her hair green."

Mr. Plait grimaces slightly but smiles down at his daughter indulgently.

"Once all my hair grows back!" Sylvia whips off her hat in a grand flourish to show off her new hair-do, which is fantastically bald.

"She asked us to shave it off because apparently patchy baldness was not fashionable enough for her tastes." Mr. Plait laughs.

I can't help but feel a little spark of warmth in my heart when I observe the Plaits smiling in such a carefree way. Something that they haven't been able to do since approximately two years ago, when Sylvia broke her leg from a misstep down the very last stair of their home. The first X-ray showed the osteosarcoma at its earliest stage—a big gaping hole where healthy bone should've been. Besides the baldness (which Sylvia pulls off extremely well), you may have never guessed that this little girl and her family had literally been through hell for nearly twenty-four months. It was only in their very last breath of hope and a stretch of the imagination (with some help from intense internet searches) that they came to Seattle, Washington, completely relocating from their home in Santa Fe, New Mexico, in a desperate attempt to save their little girl from dying.

"Wow, Sylvia. You have one awesomely shaped head!" I put my fingers under my chin in mock concentration. "But I recommend you going red. Like, strawberry red."

"Hmmm." Sylvia presses her lips together in deep thought. "I might consider it."

Dr. Mendez harrumphs in his characteristic way and gestures toward the table with all the documents spread out. He immediately picks up one and hands it to Mr. and Mrs. Plait, who eagerly reach for it and start to skim over it, heads pressed closely together. I can see their eyes welling up, and they hold each other's hands even tighter as they both try to read the words. Even though they probably know what it all means in the first few lines, they continue to read it, not daring to hope too soon.

"Remission," Dr. Mendez confirms firmly and quietly—a tone that everyone takes to mean that you either passed or failed his latest test of clinical knowledge or strength of will (something along those lines).

"Yes, yes, yes." Mrs. Plait pulls Sylvia closer to her and cradles her upper torso somewhat awkwardly in her arms.

Sylvia, having definitely experienced more awkward discomfort in her short nine years of life, allows her mother to do this while also giving her dad the thumbs up.

"Does this mean I get to go back to school and play the drums?" Sylvia asks in a muffled voice as she tries speaking through her mom's armpit.

Mrs. Plait half sobs and laughs at the same time. "Oh, good lord. You beat cancer, and the first thing you think of is starting a garage band?"

Once the Plaits have walked out the door, and even before we can celebrate with a "kicked cancer's ass" cupcake, Dr. Mendez hands me the tablet again.

There is another computerized tomography (or CT) scan on the screen lit up with a skeleton that could've been mistaken for Sylvia's, but there are slight deviations from the image I reviewed earlier. I quickly note a different patient's information on the top of the screen: Philip Hart, eight years old. Dr. Mendez gestures for me to swipe the image over again where there is another CT scan of a skeleton riddled with gaping holes like the previous one, only this one belongs to Dayvon Pierre, twelve years old.

"Dr. Chien and Dr. Schmidt's patients, respectively." Dr. Mendez is already digging through his pile of papers, which apparently seem to be organized in some way, because he is already reviewing a different set of documents in a purposeful manner. "These two young boys were also undergoing the same experimental course of treatment that Sylvia Plait was."

I swipe the images back and forth. "Did they just start it?"

I hear the smack of papers hitting the table as Dr. Mendez removes his glasses and massages the bridge of his nose.

"No, they have been on the treatment for exactly one month. The same time we started Sylvia on her treatment course."

I nod slowly and gently set the tablet down on the table.

"Dayvon Pierre died two weeks ago, and Philip Hart yesterday. Both from advanced and aggressively spreading osteosarcoma, with little response from previous treatments along with the experimental treatment that Sylvia had been receiving."

I close my eyes and feel the all-too-familiar tug of helplessness, and something else. Guilt. I shove my hands into my coat pockets, clenching my fingers tightly and feeling my heart drop heavily.

"Dr. Chien and Dr. Schmidt are curious about Sylvia's results. Although successful, her response was extremely atypical from the test group, who all showed little improvements in their already advanced diagnoses. Sylvia was just as advanced, if not one of the worse cases in the group. However, it cannot be deniable that there was absolutely no extraneous factors other than the fact that she was also on this experimental treatment course. And now for the foreseeable future—Sylvia is cancer-free."

I feel like I am listening to a recitation of a research article from a medical journal, which somehow can make the most heartbreaking and depressing issues such as pediatric bone cancer treatments extremely academic and maybe a little insensitive.

"So maybe Sylvia had some genetic anomaly? Super blood and bone marrow powers that somehow were activated by the stresses of chemotherapy," I joke, but only half-heartedly. I am still learning about when humor actually fits into the world of cancer, especially when it comes to people's children. (FYI: Not terribly often. Sick kids are just not funny.)

Dr. Mendez frowns at me but then simply shrugs. "More testing will be needed."

It's not that all people in health care are cynical. Although one of our more endearing qualities, I would only place it in the top twenty-five key descriptive words for an individual working in health care. Other descriptive words that I like to include are rational, hopeful, and a little morbid.

The word "miracle" in medicine is not a term used willingly, especially to describe any unexpected or expected result when it comes to a life-or-death situation. This is why it's usually used sardonically among most healthcare providers.

But Dr. Mendez discussing Sylvia's case had none of the sardonic quality to it. If anything, he simply sounded, well, tired.

Being a research professional working hard to understand the disease process and what can impossibly or improbably amount to a cure is something both exciting and extremely frustrating. Sometimes cures are just a chance of fate for someone's DNA to decide whether it really wants to stretch itself into a longer string. I feel like professionals in the health-care field have an interesting role in standing on the other side of that string. Trying to spin it out as long as possible.

I'm always reminded of the three fates, or Moirai, of ancient Greek mythology. Rather than picture the Moirai as elderly wrinkled women, which they are typically portrayed as, for some reason, I imagine them as young and beautiful. The type of beautiful youth that is untouched by pain and suffering. Their only concern is of how the strings that they spin out feel between their smooth fingertips. Is the texture as soft as silk? Or can they feel the ridges and textures of a string that has been repaired and weathered over a person's lifetime?

I imagine them as carefree and radiant, smiling to each other as they giggle and pull their fingers through their hair. I imagine that the sharp metallic blades on their shears flash in the light as they gently slide them around the string of a person's life. And with one small movement of their soft-skinned hands...*snip*.

Yes, a little morbid maybe.

CHAPTER THREE
BLACK SMOKE

"MAYBE YOU READ too much fiction."

I barely raise my eyes over the top of my book, which is in fact a fine memoir detailing the intricacies of eating what the author classified as "unique" and "strange" foods from different cultures. The title is *What Are Strange Foods?* by an author's name that I can't quite pronounce because of the lack of vowels present.

I know that there are other books or research materials that a medical professional could be reading. Such as the latest books on the meaning of life or how many ways you can destroy a sterile field when inserting a central line into someone's jugular. Things like that.

However, I would like to think that the exploration of what comprises strange foods is in itself a good way to understand human nature.

"That was a statement, not a question by the way." Estelle sinks down into the couch across from me and immediately elevates her legs onto the coffee table. She is still in her scrubs, which look like they are covered in relatively dry but most definitely human blood.

"Maybe you're an orthopedic surgeon specializing in trauma who decided to work in the emergency department so that you could be covered in blood and spend all her free time doing laundry," I say, lowering my book, but just barely.

Estelle starts to run her fingers through her thick and knotted braids, and then stops to observe what is most likely some sort of dried blood clot sticking to the ends. "Good point."

Since attending our classes in medical school, this exchange of observations about why we are both single at twenty-six years of age is one of our customary greeting methods after a long day on the job. As busy and studious patrons of American higher learning, we are always exchanging slightly different observations about our individual relationship statuses as we get older. Basically, our relationship statuses never deviate from not being single.

"Maybe you're turning thirty years old soon and still haven't figured out that the most appropriate hair color to be changing to is gray."

"You win." I carefully place my bookmark and then set my book down.

"Awesome, so does that mean Thai food tonight courtesy of the Hashimoto generosity fund?"

"Actually, Kiran invited us to feast at his new restaurant. It's opening night."

Estelle nearly jumps off of the couch with as much excitement as a beagle when it realizes there's food somewhere in the house. "What? When? Tonight? O-M-G! I've been dreaming about your brother's stuffed bell peppers and placki ziemniaczane."

I am immediately annoyed that, while I'm struggling to pronounce the name of the author of my exotic foods book, Estelle is the only person I know who can pronounce everything food-related absolutely perfectly. But it has to be food-related.

(In case you're wondering, it's pronounced: "PLAHT-ski zhem-nyah-CHAH-neh." Yeah, I know, not very helpful to me either.)

"Yes, I told him we'd be there in a couple of—"

But before I can complete my sentence, Estelle is already running to her bedroom.

I try really hard not to roll my eyes and instead pick up my food-related memoir and continue to read.

Placki ziemniaczane is a Polish potato pancake dish, which my brother, like most dishes involving food, absolutely excels at making, and which Estelle Kagwe excels at eating.

A skill she is currently demonstrating with great zeal.

My mother, who is sitting across from us, is observing Estelle with some alarm, and I already know that she is having flashbacks of familiar scenarios of college students starving. Although an unlikely scenario in my case, this has always been one of the more popular maternal fears of hers.

My father, on the other hand, is gingerly handling a rather flowery sushi roll, brimming over with something yellowish green, which so happens to be his least favorite food-related color.

All around us are similar displays of zealous food

consumption from enthusiastic patrons. I can't help but feel incredibly proud of the result of Kiran's hard work. Grandpa Takeo left my brother and myself a sizeable inheritance after his death when we were small children, which my brother carefully used toward the opening of a small restaurant in Seattle.

"Welcome to the opening of the Hashimoto House!"

We all look up (except for Estelle, who is extremely preoccupied with eating her placki ziemniaczane) as Kiran greets us. He's dressed in a dark red apron embroidered with a white blossom. I assume this is a courtesy of our mother, who is extremely adept at crafts such as this. My brother is generally a very happy individual with the easiest smile, but at this moment, I feel like he is perhaps the happiest he's been in all twenty-eight years of his life.

"Oh, we are so proud of you!" My mom leaps up and throws her arms around my brother's neck. "Now you can get married and make us grandbabies!"

Estelle finally looks up from her impressively depleted meal and gives my brother an exaggerated gaze of absolute adoration. "My proposal is still on the table, dearest Kiran. You've already unlocked the key to my heart."

"Ah, which is the stomach!" My father nods approvingly as he finally decides to take a bite of his questionably colored sushi roll and instantly doesn't seem to regret it.

Kiran grins sheepishly—and to my amazement, he appears to either look exceptionally rosy from the success of his restaurant's grand opening or he's actually blushing.

"W-well, glad everyone is enjoying the food! I have something cool for dessert coming up, too!" He quickly grabs an impressively plumed chef's hat, the same reddish hue as the apron he's sporting, secures it to his head, and whisks off to the kitchens.

After an incredible dessert of crème brulee with fresh pineapples, and after congratulating my brother again on a successful grand opening, I'm looking forward to the nice brisk walk back home. The one-thousand-square-foot apartment that I share with Estelle happens to be just a few blocks from Kiran's new restaurant and only a seven-minute walk from the hospital. After completing our residencies nearly a year ago, the habit of convenience is something that Estelle and myself can't quite break.

Also, the rent in Seattle is ridiculous.

And we're still entertaining the relationship status of super single.

After entering our apartment, Estelle luxuriously stretches out on the couch, and with her legs kicked up on the coffee table, she promptly closes her eyes and begins to snore steadily.

I can't help but roll my eyes, but I'm also a little envious, too. Estelle is perhaps one of the most gorgeous human specimens on the planet. Even with her mouth hanging slightly open and her head rolled back, she never has to do so much as apply a skin moisturizer to her deep brown skin for it to glow effortlessly, and even with her braided hair occasionally caked with blood, she still looks ready to pose for the latest cover of *Vogue* or the Miss Orthopedic Trauma Surgeon Pageant.

Then there's the fact that Estelle Kagwe happens to be nearly a foot taller than me. She's not only intimidating as a Kenyan goddess with a fanatical preference for potatoes could be, but she's also incredibly intelligent and driven to her chosen specialty and profession.

I sigh loudly and grab the neon-pink neck pillow that I got for Estelle as her "congratulations, you're a doctor" present last year, and shove it under her head. The snoring immediately stops as her head is elevated and her airway is now able to obtain air unobstructed.

This is what friends are for.

I make my way to the bathroom and glimpse myself in the sink's mirror. Although I try religiously to get a minimum of six hours of sleep a night, it never seems to be quite enough. Faint gray shadows under my eyes that are really only noticeable to myself and my parents seem to always be there. However, it's my hair that concerns me the most.

For as long as I can remember, I've always been fascinated with different hair colors. Everyone always assumed it was to satisfy my own vanity, and I never felt the need to say otherwise. By the mature and responsible age of twelve, I decided to walk into a beauty supply store after watching extensive videos on YouTube on how to alter one's hair color without it melting off your head, and after approximately four hours, I walked out of our family's bathroom with hair that was the color of a coral reef (or "pink" if you had no imagination for the subtleties of the artist's color palette).

Both my parents were slightly shocked, but after spending many years encouraging my propensity toward drawing, photography, and finger painting, they allowed my creativity to flow freely.

I sigh and gently pull the bathroom sink mirror

forward. Rather than there being medicine or such items that you expect in your traditional bathroom medicine cabinet, there is only a small variety of lotions and hair creams. The rest of the cabinet is filled with boxes, bottles, and tubes of hair colors ranging from the deepest of plum colors to the more hazardous red colors that could compete with the red of a stop sign.

I grab a new tube filled with a slightly darker purple hair color. The name on the tube is "Amethyst Rocks!"

I'm not going to lie. I mostly purchase hair colors based on their pun quality. Although…amethysts are clearly gems, not rocks, but I'm not a geologist or anything.

I pull some latex gloves on (there are some benefits to working for a hospital…not that I snag a few pairs of gloves from the hospital on a frequent basis or anything), and coat the roots of my hair to the very tips with the thick and somewhat odorous paste.

I then turn on the shower and wait for it to warm up, thinking longingly of my bag of books that I set outside my bedroom door. Besides learning about the fascinating implications of food on one's psyche, I truly feel that the subject of learning about different chicken breeds has the potential to change my life…or turn me into a vegetarian. I might be open to either option.

"Wow, eggplants?"

As I emerge from my shower, feeling refreshed and absolutely glowing from my perspective, I am immediately faced with a bleary-eyed and annoyingly beautiful Estelle Kagwe, her neon-pink neck pillow still intact and hugging her neck.

"'Amethyst Rocks!' actually," I recite the actual name of my hair's new hue.

"Wait, isn't that a gem?"

"What are you? A geologist?" I'm wondering if I should consider sending a friendly letter to the creator of my hair-dye.

"Your hair reminds me of eggplants." Estelle stretches, and in a very coordinated move that has only taken us approximately sixteen months to master, we switch sides so that now she is in the bathroom. The first eight months had us running into each other on a continuous basis, so we have this particular movement down pretty well.

"You're probably hungry. Which is your natural state about 98.8 percent of the time. The other 1.2 percent is sleeping." I turn around and head to my room, impressed that Estelle can even think about anything related to food at this time. Kiran's meals are always enough to send me into a food coma that seems to last a full twenty-four hours.

"Astute observation. I'll be having dreams of Kiran's beautiful eggplant pie." Estelle gazes longingly into her distant food-related thoughts as she closes the bathroom door.

I vaguely wonder if she showered before we left for dinner since she seemed ready to leave pretty quickly. Perhaps she was able to scrub a few of the blood clots from her hair, but I'm sure she was in for a comparably longer shower than me. Even with washing purple hair-dye from one's hair, it takes just slightly longer to wash out dried blood clots—or whatever may have found its way into one's nest of hair when you're the type of surgeon cracking open ribs or sawing off horribly mangled legs caught in things like the wheels of some manufacturing machine...or whatever other trauma-related situation might call for.

Shrugging my shoulders, I grab my messenger bag full of books and make my way to my bedroom, where I eagerly fall back into my bed with a book titled *Chickens: Marvels of the Modern World* and feel the almost instantaneous relief that washes over my body after a day of trekking through the hospital or being slumped over a desk reviewing chart after chart of patient information through a bright computer screen.

But almost before I can really settle into this moment, my nearly perfect state of bliss is interrupted by a very sharp something sticking into my back.

Confused, I roll slightly onto my left hip and feel under me.

I can't imagine what it could be. I am a meticulous linen-smoother when making the bed every morning at exactly 5:45 a.m.

It breaks my heart seeing Estelle's unmade bed, but even after offering many well-cited sources on the benefits of quality sleep when pillows and blankets are positioned the right way, Estelle cites her own personal references in relation to her impressive ability to fall asleep anytime and anywhere. One example of this was when she found a towel room on a medical-surgical floor during a six-month clinical rotation. When interrupted from her precious naps, she would toss rolled-up towels at unsuspecting hospital workers committing the crime of trying to enter Estelle's towel room.

These unsuspecting hospital workers were pleased when they found out that she would be graduating and choosing a specialty that was well and very far away from their floor.

Now, on my bed, I feel my fingers brush the outline of

what feels like the shape of a book under my bedspread. I am even more confused when I realize that, although slim, this book is decently sized, and I can't quite understand how I had missed it while making my bed.

Hesitantly, I sit up and roll over. Sitting with my knees under me, I swipe my purple-hued hair behind my ears and lift up the faux-mink bedspread to reveal a black hard-covered book.

There is a moment that passes as I stare down at this book that I don't recognize. I hesitate before slowly reaching for it. When I have the book in my hands, though, I furrow my brow. It feels familiar, as if I have held it before.

Even though I firmly do not believe in déjà vu (which I consider suspicious hocus pocus; give me a peer-reviewed double-blind study any day), I can't shake the strange feeling that I have while holding this book.

It isn't so much the look of the book that seems to grab the very edges of this feeling. The book is black and in itself doesn't seem at all unique, but it is the feel of it in my hands. The book's texture beneath my fingertips is rough and grainy, with heavy ridges, as if it spent some time in water and was pulled out to be dried by the sun.

I flip the book over in my lap and notice the same texture on the back. I even slide my fingers down the spine of the book, which I can feel is strong, but it has none of the rippling texture of the front and back covers. It feels surprisingly smooth, like velvet.

Turning the book over again, I place my hand on the cover and slide my fingers down to the corner.

I'm expecting some sound from the book. Not screaming or something horrific like that (or whatever comes from strange black books in horror movies), but maybe a slight crack when a new or damaged book-binding breaks. Instead, the cover of the book literally falls open without a sound.

I find myself immediately and very oddly disappointed. Instead of some enlightening text or images of various chickens (which is what my original book of interest was arrayed with), I'm staring at a blank page, creamy and smooth. Back in my premedicine pursuits, this would've been ideal paper for sketching with.

I feel my fingers slide over the page like a paintbrush, and for the first time in many years, I surprise myself with a longing to grab some coal-tipped pencils, a watercolor brush, or even just a ballpoint pen.

Instead, I ball my fingers into a fist and slide my other hand under the cover to close it shut. I feel the familiar ache of wanting to draw or create something slowly leave my hands, but then I notice a small black smudge peeking out underneath the corner of the first page.

I immediately grab the corner of this page and slide it open, revealing a charcoal sketch.

I feel my eyes widen and refocus as I take in the image in front of me, which seems to be painstakingly drawn. The details are both soft and sharp. The lines and shapes of the sketch have the unique blurriness and clearness of drawing with charcoal. It's like throwing heavy black smoke into a vast and empty white jar.

I feel my heart pound, a feeling of horror and distant memories seem to surge forward. This drawing is familiar to me.

I trace the lines with my eyes and see what looks like a

spidery human-like form. Its spine is curved forward as it leans down, holding something in its fingers. But it can't be fingers. Instead the finger-like tips drip down into long points, which are painted in something metallic and silvery so that it almost looks wet. The effect is startling. I feel like I could lift the page and watch the silver slide off.

Before I realize it, my finger is lightly touching the silver, and I'm almost expecting it to come away wet or shining with silver paint. Of course, it is dry and my finger stays clean.

And then I see it.

Between the figure's pointed and silvery tipped fingers, there is a small white butterfly. And with its other claw-like hand, it is delicately pulling off one of the butterfly's wings.

I feel my breath catch, and I can suddenly hear the blood flowing in my ears as my heart pounds faster.

I slam the book shut.

CHAPTER FOUR
SECRETS

WHEN I WAS growing up, I resisted any thoughts of trying to be a doctor. Something about working in a designated, enclosed area for sick people just wasn't all that appealing to me. At some point in my life, though, I realized something—the fact that I was resisting so much was, in a way, guiding me to the ultimate direction my path took. I was aware that I was resisting it, which when you think about it, doesn't really make sense. After all, it wasn't like I was resisting the urge to be a drug dealer, or that I was trying to resist the urge to follow in the steps of my oh-so-successful and medically inclined parents.

Actually, my parents were never in the medical field at all. My mother is a financial analyst for a large tech company in Seattle, and my father is a high school band teacher. I can't even blame the stereotypical sibling for being so brilliant that I needed to shine brighter than the shadow that they cast over me. My older brother is a chef.

Not that being a financial analyst, a band teacher, or a

chef is lacking in ambition. I always thought of myself as extremely lucky, because my mom was an awesome math teacher, my dad allowed me to explore my "creative" side all the time, and my brother makes the best-ever yakisoba and green bean casserole you ever had.

So becoming an oncologist specializing in hematology, or cancers of the blood, definitely seemed to come out of nowhere.

I remember the evening it started. I sat down at the dinner table—it was my senior year of high school, and I had already lined up precisely three universities where I would be sending my applications to. Their names were on a little blue sticky note that I had carefully written out in three even, neat lines with a smudge-proof ballpoint pen.

This was something my parents had requested, but not in the overbearing type of way that some people may have experienced or assume occurs among all Asian-American households. I am always organized.

My dad looks at the sticky note and nods approvingly. My mom is absolutely delighted as she sits down.

"Oh, what wonderful choices, Evie!"

"Hey, two of those are local. Which means you won't be a starving college student!" Kiran lays a freshly made dish of vegan lasagna on the table. At this time, he was most definitely on a vegan-themed cooking phase.

My father eyes the lasagna and sighs resignedly. For the sake of not hindering my brother's amazing prowess with anything to do with food, he's been extremely indulgent. However, it has made for some extremely odd experiences. There was one particular experience with unripe bananas, chicken gizzards, and sour mustard that still has my dad to this day wary of anything that is even slightly yellow that lands on his plate.

"Kiran!" My mother frowns, her anxiety already showing as she thinks of all the horrible scenarios in which her youngest child would be found starving in a college dorm room. My mom quickly decides to change the subject. "Have you given thought to a major yet?"

So this is where my family starts to take bites of their food, as they await what is most certainly the obvious answer. Which in my case, was photography with a minor in something like women's studies and/or something to do with literature. Like my brother with a spatula and frying pans, I had a similar affinity with photography and writing.

My parents were proud to show off all the wonderful awards and written praises that I accumulated regarding this. And I mean *all* of them. Including a couple finger paintings that I did when I was, like, two years old.

They were pretty impressive finger paintings by the way.

I chew slowly and swallow the small bite of vegan lasagna before answering. (It is, of course, absolutely delicious).

"Medicine."

And this is the part where my family all stops, mid-chew, and stares at me. It's almost comical.

Surprisingly my ever-the-observer-first father is the first one to speak. "Oh."

"Well…well, Evie. That is really interesting. Of course, we support whatever decision you make." My mother smiles, as if translating my father's "Oh" into an acceptable explanation for their surprise.

"Wooow… Does that mean…free medical care from

now on?" My brother breaks out in a big grin. He has a way with making awkward moments more tolerable. Another affinity of his, besides his delicious pork dumpling stews.

"Kiran! This is a serious decision your sister is making!" my mother exclaims again.

My dad nods. "Your Grandpa Takeo was an entomologist."

"Ahh...he studied bugs?"

Again, my dad nods. He has quite the way with nods, but he also has a way with using simple sentences to form a very complete idea. An idea that would sometimes take me an essay's length of time to express.

"He was a very good entomologist. Even as a child himself, he was able to identify one fly from another. However, he decided to become an epidemiologist, to study diseases, and then became a doctor."

I found myself nodding this time, suddenly very appreciative of how unquestioning my family was regarding certain aspects of their children's lives. Everything from the hobbies that I participated in (as long as it didn't involve dealing drugs and stuff), the friends I hung out with, to the color of my hair (which happened to be bluish-gray during this moment in my life). They never were the ones to pry or to delve too deeply into matters that would affect the course of one's life. The reasons and decisions one makes was a matter of the heart.

I was appreciative of this, but I found myself taking advantage of my family's unquestioning faith in me for my own selfish reasons.

CHAPTER FIVE
CLAWS AND CRAYONS

ACCESS DENIED.

Access Denied.

Access Denied.

Please contact your hospital's security—"Uh…Evie?"

I whip around and suddenly find myself spitting out a mouthful of my hair as it flies up and into my face.

"Grapes?"

"Eggplants actually," I state just ever so forlornly as an individual approaches me. I recognize the voice but don't actually recognize the person until he's standing next to me.

"Oh, Clark!"

Clark stares down at his tennis shoes sheepishly. I'm trying to figure out why he looks so different. It's not that he's in "normal person" clothes that gets me, although that can really throw a hospital worker off when you encounter someone who you're used to seeing about 99.5 percent of the time in shapeless scrubs of varying colors or cat patterns. I guess I'm usually used to seeing Clark with a pile of medicine bags bundled in his arms.

His hands stuffed into his coat pocket, he shuffles his feet and a cloud of vapor forms in front of his face. The sun still hasn't risen quite yet, and all of a sudden I can feel the morning chill through my own jacket.

"Staff meeting at oh-seven-hundred." Clark looks down at me, and I feel how short I am. Not that I'm self-conscious about this, but I feel particularly stunted at the moment, especially since I can't seem to figure out how to get through the door's security keypad lock. I guess I could always get those clog-like shoes that are made for health-care workers to at least add a couple inches to my height, but I can't seem to catch the corners at my walk-run pace through the hospital halls as effectively with such heavy shoes weighing me down.

As I'm pondering my footwear, I don't realize that Clark happens to still be talking to me.

"I'm so sorry, Clark." I start jabbing at the buttons on the door's security panel again. "Could you repeat what you just said?"

"Did you forget the entry code?" Clark raises one eyebrow, and I immediately realize how haphazardly I'm pressing random buttons.

"Er, is it that obvious?" I huff and shove my frigid fingers into my pockets. "Isn't this the door that they change the entry code every other day or something like that?"

"Actually, it's every three months—and no. That particular door is at the West Tower, Maternity Wing."

"Oh…"

From his pocket, Clark pulls out his badge with his hospital ID on it. "This one…"

He slides the badge into a slit on the right side of the keypad, and I hear an annoyingly happy-sounding *click* as the door decides to unlock.

He shoves his badge back into his pocket and proceeds to open the door, letting me slide in. I'm immediately miffed at how every door in this hospital seems to have maddeningly secret ways of getting in. There's one door on the opposite side of the hospital that I swear, you have to tickle its handle just the right way or sacrifice your first-born child to proceed through it.

In a desperate attempt to make it to morning rounds, there's a few of us who have considered doing the sacrifice thing, but usually we end up running to the other door on the opposite end of the building (having a firstborn child has a longer timeframe attached to it). No one has measured the distance, but we're always out of breath by the time we reach it. Then there's the fact that we have to travel back to the other side of the hospital to get to our intended destination.

This is another reason why I opt for running shoes.

"Thanks, Clark." I start heading down the hall. Since it's one of the back entrances of the hospital, it's narrow and not as brightly lit as the main areas. The sound of plodding shoes carry down the corridor. It might be a little odd, but I appreciate the back entrances of hospitals. Widely underused and infrequently trafficked, I always find a little solace in pacing down such hallways. I rarely encounter other humans, since most tend to avoid empty, dimly lit corridors in the back of very large buildings. It could be considered the material of horror movies, or something along those lines.

"Are you working today?" Clark falls into stride next to me, which is pretty impressive since most people grudgingly jog to keep up with me—or don't even bother. However, Clark has the benefit of having proper leg anatomy to keep up at a steady and brisk pace.

"Actually, no." I slow my speed just slightly, as Clark is obviously making a very casual and friendly observation for the sake of conversation.

My current attire is devoid of my usual white coat with the too-long sleeves and clunking stethoscope around my neck. In fact, I'm pleased to note that under my jacket, I'm wearing my favorite and well-worn T-shirt with the words "Sci-Chan," which happens to be my favorite YouTube science-themed channel. I'm also wearing jeans. This combination of attire was random. My morning abilities are strictly limited to turning the alarm off, making the bed, brushing my teeth, and brewing/consuming coffee (in that precise order). Clothing coordination is not a priority in those precious forty-five minutes before I'm heading out the door.

"I forgot some personal notes on the Plait case that I wanted to take home with me yesterday evening so that I could compare and research some details regarding the impending courses of future treatments," I respond in an impressively verbose manner, which surprises not only myself judging from Clark's raised eyebrows.

"Oh." Clark nods.

I nod back. The thoroughness of my answer leaves all inquiries into further conversation on the topic somewhat unnecessary. But I also give Clark a smile to hopefully soften the fact that I ended this particular topic of discussion.

In what could only be described as an extremely timely manner, Clark and I have crossed into the main hospital lobby, taken an elevator to the sixth floor, whisked by the associated waiting room, and even waved enthusiastically at the nurses at their main station. All in all, this commute takes approximately twelve minutes.

"Well, hope your research is informative!" Clark waves as we approach the conference room where his meeting is going to be.

"Have an informative meeting!" I proceed past the conference room as Clark gives an exaggerated eye roll.

Heading for the doctor's office, I mumble a greeting to a very gray-haired Dr. Toyomi, who's sitting forward at his computer in a very peculiar manner, as if dozing off just slightly. He shakes his head awake, opens his eyes in a startled manner, and grunts in response to me as he determinedly resets his efforts to look at his computer intently.

I kneel down between his chair and the file cabinet next to his desk, my book bag just slightly hindering my attempts to effectively explore under the occupied desk. The unsuspecting Dr. Toyomi demonstrates even more startled reflexes as my book bag bumps into his chair—nearly half my body is under the desk, and I'm actively rummaging around.

After rearranging some unfortunately placed papers (along with an empty Cheetos bag), my hands close around a very rumpled and coffee-stained manila envelope. I grab ahold of it and back out triumphantly.

With Dr. Toyomi now staring at me in confusion,

echoes of slamming the strange black sketchbook closed from the night before seem to reverberate through my thoughts.

Still on my knees, I stuff the manila envelope into my book bag while giving Dr. Toyomi a less verbose explanation than I gave Clark earlier.

I stand up and very purposefully pivot out of the room at my usual pace, as if I had not just startled a particularly senior oncologist by digging around under his working area.

When I get home, I sit at the very edge of my bed. When exactly five seconds have passed, I start to remember something. It's not like the type of remembering that has you rushing to the kitchen to check if you left a burner on. It is the type of remembering that has been waiting patiently, like something sitting in the periphery of your vision.

Sitting cross-legged, I reach for my bag and empty it of exactly five hardcover books, including the *Mysteries of the Great Quahog*. Carefully avoiding a relatively soft but remarkably intact banana, I pull out the wrinkled manila envelope that I salvaged from under the desk of an unsuspecting Dr. Toyomi.

Holding the manila envelope, I am gripped with the sudden desire to throw it out the window.

It really seems to be an inconspicuous item. The corners are dog-eared and blotchy with what looks like a coffee stain. It is also dirty from being inadvertently stepped on under the desk. It is slim and lightweight with what I already know will be about a dozen pieces of paper.

Flipping the manila envelope, I see that the small metal fastening that holds the opening closed is secured in place. Taking my index finger and thumb, I very carefully pinch the fastening open. Its metal points, now straight up rather than flat, remind me of a bird getting ready to dive into water.

Lifting the flap of the envelope up, I carefully slide my fingers in, brushing the top of loosely stacked papers. Grasping the ends of these papers and tipping the envelope at an angle, I let them flow out. The pages are yellow and lined, the kind torn from one of those legal notepads.

However, instead of letters denoting some form of writing, these are drawings. The drawings are obviously doodles—the kind you would see being posted on a family's refrigerator with alphabet magnets. Some pages have colorful flowers and images of what could be either exotic safari animals, or maybe domestic cats. These are the obscure drawings of a child who is given something to do while she lay sick and dying in a hospital bed.

As I flip through a couple of these images, the paper crinkling in my hands, the drawings became noticeably sloppier. Less of the systematic abstractness of a child artist, and more of a child stubbornly trying to stay entertained as she becomes more fatigued from having medicine drip into her bloodstream that will indiscriminately kill the cells of her body with the hopes that it will eventually wipe out the cancer growing in it.

When I reach the final three pages, I already know what I'll find—it's what I was looking for and the reason I scrambled to find it under a work desk.

On these pages are the same image drawn in the dark, heavy, and imprecise lines of a black crayon.

It is of a dark creature, human-like in shape but distorted, as if it could only be recognized by its shadow. Its shape is familiar though.

The long limbs stretch out, and its back is hunched over. There is a large square box filled in with blue, with what look to be clouds. This clearly represents a window, which is positioned right next to the creature's head. My eyes trail up one of its long, pointed fingers as it reaches toward the window, as if to pierce through it with its nails.

The next two pages are of this same image, without much variation. My eyes are drawn toward its long fingers. Perhaps it is a coincidence, but this childlike drawing reminds me candidly of the dripping pointed claws of the strange charcoal sketch that I observed the night before.

My eyes flicker up to the shelves of books that are arranged across the room next to the door. They land immediately upon the exact location where I haphazardly shoved the black sketchbook. I can feel the familiar beat of my heart in my ears. Resisting the temptation to grab the sketchbook, I stack the yellow papers together and slide them back into the manila envelope; remembering the day that a sick little girl held them out to me as a gift, her face tired and her eyelids drooping closed in fatigue and exhaustion.

This sick little girl was Sylvia Plait.

CHAPTER SIX
A SILVER STRING

"Dr. Hashi—er, Evie?"

I turn around from the computer screen. My chair is conveniently the type to spin and stop right at ninety degrees, which forces me to shuffle the rest of the ninety degrees, so that I can complete the half-circle in my chair that I intend.

"Yes? Oh, hi, Clark." Clark is standing at the entryway for the doctor's office/lounge area. No one is ever sure what to call it. At some point it was meant to be a "break room" for doctors, but this got quickly converted to an office-type area, which just so happens to have a strategically placed vending machine. From my understanding, the unofficial name designated by the hospital staff has been the "Hole of Optimism."

Did I mention that people in health care can have a fantastically sarcastic side to them?

"Hi, Evie." Clark shifts a few bags of carefully packaged intravenous fluids in his arm and nods behind him. "Dr. Mendez is looking for you."

I immediately resist the urge to roll my eyes in a

profoundly unprofessional manner. It seems that Dr. Mendez spends 50 percent of his time in his office reviewing cases and meeting with patients, and the other 50 percent sending Clark to retrieve me.

"Location—his office," Clark says, a detail that he has taken to adding with a smirk.

"Designation noted." I quickly scan my ID badge to log out of the computer and surprise myself by just how cramped my calves are when I stand. I have a fleeting thought that I should be wearing compression stockings and preventing a thrombus from forming in the deep veins of my legs.

Sigh. The slightly hypochondriac musings of your typical health-care worker.

"Oh, and Evie?" Before shifting the weight of his IV bags in his arms, Clark says, "The Mickelsons were asking about you."

I raise my eyebrows as I try my hardest to acknowledge the fact that I might recognize the name…even though I don't.

Clark realizes this. "Room Twenty-Nine."

"Gracias, Clark."

"Your recommendation?"

I squint my eyes for what might be the 116th time at the image that Dr. Mendez had me refer to. Of course, I'm not necessarily counting. I've just been staring at this particular image for what *feels* like the 116th time for approximately the last thirty-seven minutes.

Not that this image isn't particularly interesting. Actually, it would be considered quite medically fascinating. Which means that it's actually terribly horrific at the same time. The parallel of what is considered interesting in the world of medicine is in its own category compared to the rest of the world.

This image is of a twelve-year-old named Ivan Kovalchuk. His CT scan is scattered with brightly glowing spots all over his body. Two weeks ago, he arrived with his parents in their local community hospital's emergency room with increasing weakness. This was the morning when the usually lively young boy with interests in lacrosse and playing the violin just couldn't get out of bed. After running multiple blood tests and procedures to prove otherwise, it was finally concluded that he had a rare form of multiple myeloma with metastasis to the lymph nodes.

I set the tablet down and immediately think of Sylvia Plait. The look on her parents' faces before burying them in their hands. If tears could have a sound, theirs would have been like glass shattering. As the doctors delivering the news that their only option was this single and experimental course of treatment, we were the ones holding the hammer precariously over their fragile hopes.

I stare down at the tablet (for the 117th time). Ivan's CT is getting darker as the screen's backlight dims. I look up at Dr. Mendez and he nods, already knowing what my recommendation is going to be.

The image of Sylvia's parents leaving this office with their daughter's hands in theirs pretty much makes up both our minds.

CHAPTER SEVEN
IVAN

IVAN OPENED HIS eyes and immediately regretted it. He felt a dull grogginess and pain pressing into his temples. Every movement, even one that involved repositioning his neck so that he could look away from the window's light, took so much effort.

He was so tired.

It was such a strange feeling for him. He always felt that his energy was endless and that there was no limit to how long he could run with his teammates and friends, playing lacrosse or a variation of ball and stick games (they became creative after an hour of practice, much to Coach Thea's chagrin).

Gradually he started feeling a little more winded at the end of practice. Instead of going to after-practice pizza, he found that he was more eager to go home and lay down for more frequent naps. Both his parents attributed this to his growth pattern.

"A growing boy needs to sleep!" his father would boast confidently as he acknowledged his wife's quiet concerns.

Without them knowing, Ivan's blood had started to weaken, unable to deliver enough oxygen to his organs; his bone marrow started leaching cancer into his body.

For the first time in his twelve years of life, Ivan wondered what it would feel like to die. Would it be painful? Would it feel like falling asleep?

"Hello, Ivan."

Ivan almost forgot that he had his eyes closed. Now that he was facing away from the light of the window, it bothered him less and he was able to open his eyes and blearily focus on the person standing in front of him. He was carrying what looked like plastic bags of water, but Ivan suspected that this must be the medicine that he would be receiving. It was the medicine that Dr. Mendez and Dr. Hashimoto, or "Evie," although she said it would be okay to call her "Señora Eggplant" if that was easier to remember (Ivan remembered smiling because he had thought that her hair looked precisely like that specific purple-colored fruit), had discussed with him and his parents.

"Hi," Ivan mumbled and then pushed his elbows behind him so that he could sit up in his bed. He was wearing a white gown with small blue dots printed all over it, with a tie in the back. He thought he should care about wearing something that kind of looked like doll's clothes, but he just couldn't seem to muster up the energy. It seemed that nothing mattered more than sleep for him lately.

"I'm Clark. I'll be your nurse today." Clark smiled and set the bags of medications down on Ivan's bedside table, which had a box of Legos and a small tablet that his parents had purchased for him when they admitted him into the hospital. He was grateful for these items and suddenly felt his stomach clench in on himself as he thought of his parents.

As Clark wrapped a blood pressure cuff around Ivan's right upper arm, he caught Ivan's eyes, his brows slightly furrowed. "Your parents just called. They're on their way right now."

It was as if Clark read his mind. Ivan nodded appreciatively as Clark turned the machine on, and the cuff around his arm started to tighten as air squeezed into it. Clark inspected Ivan's left arm, which was where another nurse from earlier had started an IV. She said that they would need to use this to administer medications until he was able to get something called a port, which would be something placed under the skin. This would allow him to bend his arm whenever he wanted, since it would be in his chest a little under his collar bone. He would eventually be able to go home with this thing.

When the blood pressure cuff deflated, Clark recorded the numbers in a tablet that he carried, which would in turn send it to the main computer system for the hospital. The previous nurse had explained all this to Ivan when she had noticed his own tablet sitting on his bedside table.

"Do you like to read?" Clark asked after he had finished listening to his heart and lungs, and feeling the pulses in his wrists and the tops of his feet.

Ivan shook his head. "Not really."

"Hm, how about comics or graphic novels?"

Ivan tilted his head as he averted his eyes from what Clark was doing—hanging the medicine bags on the IV pole and then opening small bags of long IV tubing.

"Not like the newspaper comic stuff." Clark stretched out the IV tubing and pierced one of the hanging bags with its sharp plastic end.

Looking down at the small IV line that was inserted into the crease of his inner arm where the elbow bent, Ivan felt his heart start to beat a little faster. He suddenly wished his parents were there right that second.

Clark had quickly spiked the other bag of fluid, letting them fill their small drip chambers as he turned on a small machine that was attached to the poles. He then inserted a small rectangular cassette into it, which was attached to the IV tubing. The machine beeped and lit up. Clark started pressing buttons, and once he was done he turned to Ivan, who looked more pale than usual as he glanced nervously at the bags of medication.

"Here, are you okay if I showed you?" Clark gestured toward Ivan's tablet.

Ivan blinked at Clark and nodded, realizing that he actually hadn't used the tablet very much. He had only just received it and was so exhausted after all the admission assessments and other procedures that were performed, it had sat untouched for the majority of his time in the hospital so far.

After turning the tablet on, Clark made short work, running his fingers expertly over the screen, before handing it back to Ivan.

Ivan stared at the tablet's screen, which had the image of an e-book. The cover had the elaborate illustration of a dark green dragon and a young boy standing in front of it. Ivan couldn't help but feel that the young boy looked remarkably like himself. He had the same light-colored hair that was of medium length, a slight build, and blue eyes.

The young boy had his hand extended out to the green dragon, which had long wisps of smoke curling out from its nose. The dragon had friendly eyes that seemed to smile. The title of the e-book was *The Ryuu Chronicles: Part I.*

"It's a good one. I won't spoil anything, but it's about a kid who explores the world to discover different mythological creatures. Oh, and it has a cool dragon that can turn into a beagle so that it can follow him around all the time."

Ivan felt a small laugh escape his lips as he thought of a dragon turning into a small dog, wagging its tail as it barked out little fireballs to chase around.

He barely even noticed as the medications started infusing into his arm; he had already started to flip through the pages of the book on his tablet.

"He has tolerated the first round of his treatment extremely well." I pull a chair out and sit down across from Mr. and Mrs. Kovalchuk. They are sitting as close to Ivan's hospital bed as they possibly can. Ivan has fallen asleep, his tablet resting on his chest, gently rising up and down along with his breathing.

"Clark, his nurse, has given me a great report. He will be tired, which will be normal, but we'll be watching him closely for the next couple of days. Hopefully we'll send him home for a good rest until his next appointment, where we'll have his chest wall port implanted."

Mr. and Mrs. Kovalchuk both nod as tears begin to well up in both of their eyes. Mr. Kovalchuk is holding his son's hand in his and gives it a firm but gentle squeeze. He then determinedly clears his throat and looks back at me.

"Thank you, doctor. We would like to stay with him tonight if that would be okay?"

"Of course. Dr. Mendez will want to have another meeting with you before we leave for the night." I give both of them a smile. "In the meantime, I'll let Clark know to tell the night nurse you'll be staying. We'll provide you the appropriate accommodations." I gesture toward the recliner and long, cushioned bench that will easily be able to fit the slender Mrs. Kovalchuk. The rooms on this floor, although not particularly large, are comfortable enough to accommodate a very small number of family members.

It is at the very moment I stand up that Clark enters the room.

"Oh, hey, Clark—"

Holding up a hand nonchalantly, he says, "Already got some pillows and extra blankets from housekeeping on their way."

Mrs. Kovalchuk looks up and smiles in appreciation.

"Thanks, Clark," I say as I'm heading out of the room. "Please, don't hesitate to call me if there are any changes. I'm rotating on-calls with Dr. Mendez. It's my turn tonight."

"Sure thing. And I'll let the night shift nurse know as well." Clark waves as he continues over to speak to Ivan's parents and take further vital signs.

CHAPTER EIGHT
UNRAVELING THREADS

"AH…EXCUSE ME? DOCTOR?"A quiet and familiar voice quickly has me at a standstill as I'm about to round a very familiar hallway corner at my usual pace of a gazelle skipping along the beautiful terrain of an African landscape, or away from a particularly hungry lion.

I am now face-to-face with a familiar elderly gentleman, his glasses sliding down his nose. He quickly pushes them up, his eyes glittering with the all-too-familiar look of unshed tears that is unique to the hospital setting.

"I'm sorry, doctor…?"

"Evie, please." I smile up at the elderly gentleman, who I recognize from the day before.

"Evie." He then smiles, something that is quite startling to me and extremely unexpected. I can literally count the times that I see a smile among occupants of a research hospital that specializes in treating terminal illnesses.

"I'm so sorry to disturb you, but I-I was wondering"—he looks uncomfortably hopeful as he holds his hands together—"if you would mind stopping by to see my wife again?"

"Oh." Now it's my turn to look uncomfortable. Only my method is to shove my hands in my pockets and look extremely awkward. "You should really wait for your wife's doctor to round. I don't know if there's anything that I can do, as I'm not her attending."

The gentleman has already started to nod his head before I'm halfway through my explanation, as if he is prepared for my answer. "I understand, but it's just...my wife has been asking for you personally."

I open my mouth slightly, but nothing that I intend to say comes out. I find myself remembering his wife yesterday, her skin pale and gray, her pulse barely whispering under my fingertip, her eyes nearly plastered closed; even the act of lifting an eyelid seemed impossible.

"She remembered me?"

"Yes." He looks at me intently. "She asked for a girl with silver hair. She opened her eyes—" I feel my heart stutter as his voice cracks, the inner corner of his eyes pooling with tears. "She opened her eyes for the first time in almost a week. Her first words were to ask for you."

I can't help but feel startled, but also a little relieved. "Are you sure she wasn't thinking of Dr. Toyomi?" I suggest one of the first Asian doctors that comes to my mind with "silver" hair. Not that I'm assuming that I would be confused for most Asian doctors, just that Dr. Toyomi is of a good age to have the appropriate hair color.

"No," he responds immediately. "Silver."

I then uncomfortably state the obvious, "Ah, my hair

color, though…it's not silver." In fact, it is a lovely shade of a non-silvery purple.

This time it's the gentleman who seems unsure. He repositions his glasses once again, and he looks confused. "But, your hair…it was a different color yesterday, wasn't it?"

I can see the uncomfortable shift in his body movement as he wrings his hands embarrassingly. "I'm so sorry to be a bother, Evie."

Smiling in what I hope is an understanding way that expresses my empathy toward the aging retinas of certain individuals, I say, "Not at all, sir. Would you like me to page your wife's doctor?"

The gentleman shakes his head and smiles again. "Oh, no. He'll be around shortly. Thank you, Evie."

I nod and am about to pick up my gazelle-being-chased-by-the-wind-or-hungry-lion pace when for some reason, I turn around. Over my shoulder, I notice him entering a room with the number twenty-nine above its door.

"Hi, Evie."

I'm about to swing my book-laden bag over my shoulders as Clark, once again encumbered by quite a few types of intravenous medications and other various bags of fluids, stops at the entrance of the doorway as if he is unsure if he should cross the threshold of the Hole of Optimism.

"Hi, Clark." I have a hard time disguising the exhaustion in my voice. The weight of my bag full of books somehow reminds me of the metaphorical weight of the world. Which I'm well aware sounds quite melodramatic. The weight of my book bag consists of quite a few titles specializing in different breeds of chickens actually.

Dr. Mendez and I had just completed another meeting with Ivan Kovalchuk's parents as he lay in a bed down the hallway, hooked up to various monitoring devices sending information to computers at the nurses' station on the pediatric oncology floor. Mrs. Kovalchuk needed the physical assistance of her husband to leave the office, her thin frame leaning heavily on her husband's stout one. We had discussed Ivan's prognosis as well as reviewing his treatment course and the results of other patients that have underwent this same treatment. They seemed to have the most questions about the exceptional case of Sylvia Plait's. Sylvia's case had something of the miraculous, something that tugged at the hopes of not just Ivan's parents, but also of ours as well. Dr. Mendez led the conversation discussing the details of the treatment, which entailed a lengthy hospital stay and possibly very poor outcomes, i.e. death despite all the efforts to prevent it, which is a detail that is unfortunately overlooked in most doctor-to-patient conversations.

However, the extensive results of Ivan's test and the cruel expedition of his clinical presentation that was leading him to the inevitable conclusion of death, led his parents to the decision that they had already made.

Which was anything to save their only child's life.

"Evie?"

I'm drawn back to the realization that I am carrying the weight of books hanging down my back. I close my eyes and shake out my wearisome thoughts and try focusing on the absolutely riveting subjects of my books.

"I'm sorry, Clark. Could you repeat the last thing you said after, 'Hi, Evie'?"

Clark displays an indulgent smile as the plastic encasing the medications and IV fluids in his arms makes a crackling sound. "The Mickelsons. Did you ever get a chance to stop by their room?"

"The Mickelsons?" I repeat guiltily, although I have the strangest feeling that he already knows I know whom he is referring to.

"Yes, Room Twenty-Nine."

"Well." I shift the weight of my backpack that is slung across my shoulders. "I ran into Mr. Mickelson actually, but I think he was looking for Dr. Toyomi."

Clark draws his eyebrows slightly down as he raises his chin thoughtfully. "Oh, they seemed pretty convinced that it was you. I'm sorry to have bothered you with that then."

I smile at Clark. "Well, they were looking for someone who I think was of an advanced age. You know, with the right hair color."

"Of course." I can see Clark's face turn slightly pink as he acknowledges this information. He seems eager to continue with what he is doing, which probably has something to do with the dozen or so bags of medications and miscellaneous things he is holding in his arms. "Right, your hair is definitely more noticeable than the typical provider."

I nod and steadily trudge toward the door, eager to leave the Hole of Optimism for the world of diverse chicken breeds.

CHAPTER NINE

A GOLD RING AND COLD CURRY

"—AND THEN HIS hand fell off." Estelle has been talking for the past thirty minutes nonstop about a case involving a patient of hers who had an unfortunate encounter with a piece of heavy machinery, which left him with a mangled hand that looks like "ground beef." (Leave it to Estelle to use inappropriate food descriptions to describe horrible cases of debilitating trauma.)

I am in the middle of pouring hot water into two mugs, which I have filled with our fantastically packaged powdered hot chocolate mix. Every Wednesday since starting our med school courses together, we memorialize our ability to make it halfway through the week with celebratory hot chocolate, which has these deliciously processed and dried marshmallows sprinkled in with the powder.

"Well, I guess that means we won't be having burgers tonight," I mumble, still thinking of Estelle's poor patient and his horribly ground-up hand.

Estelle blanches as she reaches for her now full cup of steaming hot chocolate. "Whatever could you mean? I thought we were having lasagna?"

I cringe. "I don't know if I'm really in the mood for a plate of gooey mangled-looking pasta dishes."

Pouting dramatically, Estelle leans back into her armchair. She has already taken her shower and is sporting a slouchy heather-gray sweater and leggings, which somehow on her makes loungewear look as if it belongs on a runway fashion show.

"I actually ordered us curry from Lois Thao's."

Estelle replaces her pout with a look of pure ecstasy. "Ohhh, Lois's takeout is one of the five things that make life worth living."

"The other things include saving people's lives…" I start to list off as I sip my hot chocolate, savoring the richness that can only come from a two-dollar box of hot chocolate packages.

"And Kiran's strawberry-glazed cinnamon wafers, chicken and waffles, and teriyaki salmon-kabobs."

"And the other two?"

Estelle raises her eyebrows. "What?"

"Oh." I roll my eyes as I realize that I made the mistake of counting Kiran's cooking as one of those five things. Apparently, Estelle meant those things to be three of the five things worth living for—besides saving lives and Lois Thao's takeout options.

Before I can take another sip of hot chocolate, there is an abrupt and violent rattling noise, which emanates from a pager sitting in the center of our coffee table.

Instinctively, both Estelle and myself dive for the pager.

Estelle, having the longer limbs in general, has the pager in her hand within seconds while at the same time bringing her hot chocolate mug to her lips.

"Oh, wait, this isn't my pager!"

I roll my eyes, setting my mug down. "That's because you're not on-call…and my pager looks like a pager, while yours looks like a glittering grenade of cuteness."

I reach for the pager, feeling my heart start to flutter. Although usually my pages are of abnormal lab results, they aren't always. My thoughts go immediately to Ivan Kovalchuk lying in his hospital bed while his parents try to get some semblance of sleep as they observe their only child. The thought that the only way to save him is to slowly poison him with medications in the hopes that it will target the cancer cells is something that would easily make any parent or loved one unable to get a good night's rest.

"You have something against my pager?" Estelle's eyes widen in great offense.

I press one of the pager's buttons to read the message that scrolls across the slim, dimly lit screen (for all the technical advances of a cutting-edge research hospital, it amazes me that pagers are still a thing).

Please call Onc 6. STAT. Clark, RN.

I frown. Even for a paged message, this is remarkably more vague than usual. I look at the clock hanging over the kitchen door and note that it is 8:15 at night, which is unusual for Clark, whose shift change is 7:00 p.m.

Grabbing my cell phone, neatly stacked atop of my latest reading venture (*Mysteries of the Great Quahog*), I open up my contacts list, which already has *Sixth Floor Oncology, Everline Hospital* at the very top.

After exactly one ring, the phone is picked up. "Hello, Oncology Six. This is Rene."

"Hi, Rene, it's Evie."

"Oh, hi, Dr. Hashi—er, Evie! Clark paged you; let me transfer you over to him."

"Thanks, Rene." There is a brief pause and another ring.

Barely halfway through the ring though, Clark picks up, sounding slightly breathless. "Evie?"

"Yes, this is Evie. Hello, Cla—"

"I'm so sorry to bother you, Evie. We're unable to get ahold of Dr. Toyomi."

"Okay, what's up?" I can't help but feel selfishly relieved when I realize that this call isn't referring to Ivan or any of my other patients.

"It's Mrs. Mickelson. She's in respiratory distress. We don't think she has much longer. Her husband is at the bedside and wanted a doctor here to assess her before he makes any other decisions related to possible intubation."

I close my eyes and gently whisper a silent admonishment to Dr. Toyomi for not answering his page.

"Okay, I'll be there in fifteen." I'm already standing up and heading over to the door. My messenger bag, already packed with my coat and a banana (because you never know if delivery curry will appear before a page comes in), is ready to go.

"Well, I'll consider leaving you some curry. But beware. I'm quite offended." Estelle stretches her long legs out, resting them on the coffee table, as she raises an eyebrow.

"Okay, okay. It's only slightly gross looking but mostly cute," I say in reference to Estelle's bedazzled and very pink pager.

"You're slightly forgiven then."

I dip my head in exaggerated supplication and head out the door.

Living just a short jog away from the hospital has its advantages, I've found. Although I don't quite make the fifteen-minute mark that I approximate over the phone. Once I've sprinted the block, crossed the hospital's lobby threshold, and taken the elevator, eighteen minutes have elapsed since I hung the phone up with Clark.

"Not bad," I murmur to myself as I swing my messenger bag around to pull out my doctor's coat. I barely have one arm in the sleeve when I see Clark making a beeline toward me, but I am already heading toward Room 29.

I only make brief eye contact with Clark. For some reason, my mind seems to focus on my memories of Mr. Mickelson twisting his gold wedding band around his left ring finger.

Walking into the room, I am met by almost the exact picture that I imagined in my head. Mr. Mickelson is standing over his wife, almost as if he is afraid to touch her. Instead he is rotating his wedding ring anxiously. Mrs. Mickelson looks to be gasping for air, her eyes closed and her hands clasped loosely over her chest where her heart, I am sure, is beating rapidly as she struggles for air. I still place a stethoscope gently over her rib cage, trying not to wince as I can feel every rib prominently under her hospital gown.

I then whip my stethoscope off and without even thinking close my own eyes, placing my right hand gently over her cold hands. They are so thin that I'm sure I can feel her beating heart through her fingers. It would soon be too tired to continue at such an accelerated pace.

I open my eyes and am almost startled to see Mrs. Mickelson's own eyes gazing right into mine, but I'm definitely not as surprised as her husband, who gives a small cry and lays a hand on her shoulder.

I see an image of a small white butterfly dying in the hands of my grandfather. My fingers jerk back as I remember the feel of a wing flutter under my small, child-sized fingers.

"I'm ready," she whispers. But the sound almost seems to be a huge roar in everyone's ears with how quiet the room is.

Mr. Mickelson suddenly collapses into the chair that Clark has quietly slid behind him, his tears flowing freely as his glasses become skewed across his face. He nods as he places his hands gently over his wife's. Mrs. Mickelson still has her eyes on mine though. I feel them pull at me, and I lean closer as she suddenly slides a hand out from under her husband's. I cannot imagine the effort it must take as her heart begins to slow down, barely able to pump the blood needed to reach her organs and muscles. I feel her hand rest on my collarbone as she lays two fingers on a strand of my hair.

Then just as the weight of her fingers starts to relax, they are already sliding away, falling to her side. Her eyes stare at the place they had been.

I can feel Clark as his shoulder brushes mine; he lifts his hand to gently close Mrs. Mickelson's eyelids.

"Evie?"

"Hm?"

Estelle is waving her hands in front of me. I blink and refocus my gaze, not realizing that I was staring blankly at my bowl of rice and green curry for long enough to concern Estelle, who cannot imagine what could possibly be distracting me from a bowl of food.

"Is something wrong with your curry? Because...you know...I could take care of that for you." Estelle raises her eyebrows expectantly but then leans back into her chair and folds her arms across her chest. "Are you okay?"

I look up when I realize that Estelle is using her serious voice, which she only utilizes when providing instructions for a patient undergoing chest compressions because their heart has stopped, or when she is trying to figure out where she has placed her lunch.

"Just...distracted."

"Did you end up coding that patient?"

"No, the patient didn't want that." I distractedly shove a spoonful of curry and rice into my mouth, chewing slowly. "She was ready to die."

Estelle nods, and without asking anymore questions (the nice thing about having friends who are health-care workers), she just says, "Okay."

Before Estelle can ask me anything else—which I'm sure has something to do with my curry that is already getting cold—there is a knock at the door.

"Ah...expecting visitors?" Estelle grudgingly stands but then perks up as she rushes to the door. "Maybe it's Kiran! With a special delivery of chicken pot pie?"

"I doubt that." Most likely Kiran is too busy managing his restaurant.

"Uh, Evie?"

"Hm?" I had just shoved a large spoonful of curry into my mouth.

Estelle is staring at me, a look of bewilderment on her face. "It's for you."

"Really?" I am definitely not expecting any visitors and wonder if it actually *is* Kiran with a chicken pot pie, but Estelle would have a different look on her face than this one of obvious confusion.

Estelle walks back to me and slouches into her recliner. "It's...a boy." Her eyes become wide. It is almost comical coming from a newly graduated orthopedic trauma surgeon. Her observation rings absurdly as that of a five-year-old in a grade school playground.

I quickly swallow the rest of the curry that I had nearly forgotten was in my mouth, and with the bowl of curry and rice still in my hands, I walk over to the door with what I'm sure is a similar look of bewilderment on my face.

When I approach the door, I notice the back of a relatively tall and familiar individual standing with his hands shoved into the pockets of his jacket. There is a cloud of cold air hovering above his head as he lets out a long breath.

"Hey, Clark."

Clark turns around, looking slightly embarrassed. "Oh, hey, Evie. I'm sorry. I hope I'm not bugging you at a bad time?"

"Oh, no." I hold the bowl of cold green curry up higher in front of me. "Just this. What's up?" I suddenly feel my heart beat faster, and my eyes fly open wide as I almost drop the bowl of curry, shoving my hand into my pockets frantically. "Did I forget my pager?!"

Clark looks startled as I thrust the bowl of curry into his hands.

Whipping back around, I see Estelle nonchalantly lift up a small un-bedazzled black pager, grinning ridiculously. "It's right here."

"Oh," I say sheepishly and look back at Clark. "Sorry about that. Long day."

Clark agrees, still holding the bowl of curry. "Me too. I stayed late to cover for Chandra. She got stuck in traffic heading into work. Which is why I was still with the Mickelsons."

"How is Mr. Mickelson doing?" I ask quietly.

"Well, considering he's devastated and heartbroken from losing his wife, who he's been married to for nearly the past fifty years…" Clark stares down at the bowl of curry. "He wanted me to thank you."

"Me?" I furrow my eyebrows. "But…I didn't do anything."

Clark shifts his weight uncomfortably, another cloud of cold air escaping his lips. "They…well, Mr. Mickelson felt that you did. Just by being there."

Looking down at my feet briefly, I see the flash of a golden wedding band flit across my memory. Then I glance back up at Clark, who seems to have a strange look in his eyes that I can't quite interpret, but before I can put any more thought into it, it disappears.

"But, actually there's something else…uh…" He lifts the bowl of curry, which I had completely forgotten about.

"Ah, I'll, um, take that back now."

Clark, relieved of his delicious burden, finally swings something off of his shoulder, and I realize immediately that it is my messenger bag (which I'm sure has a pretty squished banana somewhere in it).

"You forgot this." Clark transfers the bag to me, which I gratefully take back, setting the bowl of curry aside on a bookshelf in the entryway.

"Thanks, Clark!" It is at that moment that I remember setting it down at the nurses' station when I was en route to see the Mickelsons.

"No problem. I hope you don't mind. Rene said that you two used to ride the same bus into downtown, so she knew what building you lived in." Clark seems almost apologetic for having gleaned this information. "I just remember that you might've had important case information that you wanted to review from the other day. Oh, and your place was on the way to where I actually live, too," he adds this last part quickly, apparently not wanting to sound like a stalker, or something concerning like that.

"Yeah, I did…and an old banana," I mumble a little distractedly as I clutch my messenger bag in my hands.

"Huh?"

"Nothing!" I jerk my eyes up, meeting Clark's.

"Sure." Clark rocks to the balls of his feet and then back to the heels. "Um, I'll see you later then!" He quickly turns around.

Feeling my face flush, I call out, "Clark?"

He turns around slowly. I realize how dark the night sky is, the streetlights contrasting against the inky blackness of a city sky that stars can never quite penetrate. There is no moon visible tonight.

"Thanks, I really appreciate it."

Clark pulls a hand out of his pocket and gestures a casual acknowledgement as he continues to the street. I am just able to glimpse him placing his hand back into his jacket pocket as I close the door.

"So!"

Jumping in surprise and effectively dropping my messenger bag onto my toes, which besides having some other lightweight papers also has about four or five hardcover books in it, I see Estelle now standing up from her comfortably reclined position with her hands on her hips. "Ouch."

I grab my bag and swing it across my shoulder. I reach for my bowl of cold curry and look up at Estelle in mock innocence before rolling my eyes when I catch a look of hopeful annoyance on her face.

"No."

"What do you mean, 'No'?" Estelle absolutely bubbles with excitement. "Who was that?"

Clutching the curry bowl in my hands, I contemplate immediately heading to my room. "Clark."

"He's a boy."

"Yes, he is anatomically and physiologically a boy." I pause, thinking carefully. "Well, physiologically at least. I don't know about the first part, personally. I also work with him. He brought my book bag, which I left at the hospital." I pronounce slowly and clearly, hoping that will end any further inquiry. Inspecting my bowl of cold curry, I decidedly shove another spoonful into my mouth.

"Anatomically or not. He's cute." Estelle smiles mischievously. "Kind of reminds me of…one of those pretty boy vampires from that TV show. Tortured and gorgeous at the same time."

"Maybe you watch too many silly paranormal romance sitcom things," I say through my mouthful of curry. Thinking of Clark as a tortured vampire somehow conflicts with my image of him administering armfuls of complex medications and downloading graphic novels for a sick kid as he lay stuck in a hospital bed.

Estelle drops her mouth open, obviously offended. "It's not a sitcom! It's based on a great novel series with a meaningful plot and great character development."

"Yes, and obvious sexual tension."

"I don't know what you're talking about," Estelle mumbles, giving up on the discussion at this point.

Dejected at my lack of steamy details related to nonexistent work-related romances, Estelle drops down into her recliner, kicking her feet up on the coffee table, and then continues to mope.

"Don't forget your pager." She tosses it over her shoulder, and I reflexively grab it, which is impressive considering that I now have my bag of books slung across one shoulder and a bowl of curry in my dominant hand.

I look at the bowl of curry one last time, already feeling more than distracted. I can't seem to muster up any more energy—for what started out as a meager appetite to begin with—to finish my meal. (Maybe it has something to do with the ground beef hand story.)

"I still have half a bowl of curry left. Do you—"

Estelle whips up to attention, practically glowing with forgiveness and glee. "Yes!" And before I realize it, the bowl of curry is in her hands and being graciously consumed.

CHAPTER TEN

DREAMS AND MEMORIES

IVAN SUDDENLY SAT up in bed, clutching his hands to his stomach. He had woken up from a deep sleep, feeling a heavy wave of nausea grip him. Tired, he hadn't been able to eat very much since his treatment, just a small cup of green Jell-O. He felt a cold sweat behind his neck as he squeezed his eyes shut, taking deep breaths in through his nose and out through his mouth. Although not very far away, the snoring of his father sitting in a chair sounded so distant to him as his heartbeat pounded in his ears. His mother lay curled up on the bench by the window across the room.

He resisted the urge to cry out, not wanting to scare his parents.

Suddenly he felt a weight resting on his shoulder—it was cool and soft. Without opening his eyes, he knew it was someone's hand, the palm lightly touching his neck where he could feel his own pulse pound against it.

He gasped, feeling an odd sensation fill his chest. It

was as if it had begun from where the hand lay resting and somehow flowed like water down a creek, sliding over smooth rocks. It was cold but kind, a caress that reminded him of his mother touching his cheek when he lay in bed falling asleep. He opened his eyes slowly, blinking as the wave of nausea receded.

The first thing he saw as his blue eyes focused was a shimmering silver color that seemed to glimmer with movement, like light reflecting off of water. It was draped around the shadowy shape of a person, but even though the room was lit by the soft light of dawn as the sun broke above the horizon, he was unable to make out any facial features or characteristics. Only that the strange silvery color was this person's hair. It was long and seemed to move with air brushing through it, but he couldn't feel a breeze anywhere in the room.

Ivan had a fleeting thought that he should say something to whoever it was, or maybe even to his parents, who were still sleeping. But something seemed to stop him. A thought whispering quietly through his mind, comforting but without any clear words.

The beat of his pounding heart started to steady. As if cued, his eyelids started to droop downward. Without even realizing it, he drifted into a silent and dreamless sleep.

When he awoke just a couple of hours later with his father holding out a cold cup of orange juice for him, he had no recollection of what had happened other than a faint glimmer of silver that seemed to linger behind his eyelids right before he opened them.

CHAPTER ELEVEN
BROTHERS IN SHADOWS

TAP. TAP. TAP.

Long, thin nails belonging to slender fingers gently tapped the hard railing of a balcony overlooking a quiet city, shrouded in night, blinking with soft lights and the occasional car passing through.

The fingers belonged to someone tall and cloaked in a dark material that fell like silk over broad shoulders. It was hard to tell if this shadowed silhouette belonged to a man or a woman, young or old. Long straight hair flowed heavily down this person's back. It was the color of smoke streaked with inky black. It fell in long curtains, framing an angular face where piercing eyes that glinted a strange gray color—but at a certain angle, looked almost colorless—stared out ahead, unblinking. The only movement came from fingers tapping away, slowly almost lazily. A breeze stirred a strand of smoky hair across the person's cheekbone.

One finger stopped midway down, and then using this same finger, the person tapped firmly and purposefully three times against the cold metal railing.

Another breeze, this time strong enough to lift the silken cloak, its fabric rippling like an octopus's ink forming clouds deep underwater.

"Neko." a voice broke the still night air. It belonged to another individual, who suddenly appeared behind the first, standing off to the side as if only wanting to be seen in the periphery. "To what do I owe this pleasure?" the voice uttered, words subtly accented with annoyance.

The first person's lips turned upward, revealing canines that were just slightly elongated, points shining. The strange, colorless eyes still gazed out at the sleeping city below.

"I see why you've grown fond of this particular location, my dearest Cerin," the first figure called Neko breathed out in a sonorous voice.

The shape of the second figure named Cerin did not move. He seemed to be waiting.

Not needing further acknowledgment, Neko continued, "I always enjoy visiting the cities. The closeness of shadows at every corner is…comforting."

Cerin remained silent.

Neko frowned, obviously awaiting some sort of response. "Well. I see you're not in a generous mood for conversation."

With a slight tilt of the head and a lazy tap of a single long fingernail, Neko held out a small white flower. Its petals shone beautiful even in the dark, moonless sky, the city glow sufficient enough to illuminate it.

"A message from our father."

As if cued, another breeze blew, catching the flower from the slender fingers holding it loosely.

Already holding a hand out, Cerin caught the flower and his hand enclosed around the delicate blossom, his fingers encircling it gently. Opening his fingers and holding the blossom in his palm, his face hidden in shadows, Cerin went still.

Suddenly the flower burst violently into blue flames, the petals curled and blackened. The flames licked Cerin's hands, wrapping around his wrist, but rather than flinch away, he remained frozen as he stared down at it.

The flower continued to burn and turn into ash; however, the flames remarkably lingered until they too disappeared, leaving the hand holding it unscathed.

"You know father." Neko sighed, looking over his shoulder. "Not one for details or subtlety. But I think he might be unhappy with you."

There was barely a whisper signifying any movement, but with a stirring of the shadows surrounding them, the figure of Cerin disappeared.

Tap. Tap. Tap.

"So much like father when it comes to holding a conversation." Neko rolled his strange gray eyes, annoyed. He scanned the cityscape, his eyes trailing across the glassy surface of the buildings before him. He could just barely make out a dark blue color gradually breaking through the black of the night sky.

A light flashed on over the balcony. A person cracked open the door and peered out, blinking bleary-eyed, no doubt trying to locate the source of the rhythmic tapping that had awoken her.

But there was no one there.

CHAPTER TWELVE
MIRACLES AND GOLD THREADS

"Hrrrum.... Hrrrm.... Hmmm..."

"Treebeard."

"Hrm?" Dr. Mendez appeared startled as he looked up from his papers and tablet, his thick black eyebrows arching over his eyeglasses.

"You know, from *Lord of the Rings*? The Ent things. They kind of look like trees, but they aren't really trees." I have been sitting across from Dr. Mendez, who called me in, for about ten minutes, but he hasn't seemed to notice. I was sitting here observing him the whole time, waiting for him to take notice of my presence, when the sudden realization dawned on me.

"You make the same noises that they make." I nod enthusiastically, extremely proud of my assessment skills so early in the morning.

Dr. Mendez squinted at me, as if I'm some kind of

apparition that he can't quite fathom, then after deciding to ignore my comment, he pushes his tablet toward me.

Feeling slightly affronted for my well-intended (and really quite brilliant) observation, I sigh and whisk the tablet off of the table. I stare at what looks like an unremarkable CT scan image of a skeleton. "Unremarkable" in health care meaning "nothing appears to be wrong." In fact, the skeleton looks absolutely healthy without a single abnormality.

"Hrmmmhm," I say under my breath. Unfortunately, it seems that Dr. Mendez doesn't get the jest. Instead he sits back in his chair abruptly, swipes his glasses off, drops them on the table, and pinches the bridge of his nose. I stare, completely caught by surprise. This is as uncharacteristic as Dr. Mendez wearing pink polka-dotted lederhosen, or winking. (Only one of these two things can I personally attest to as being truly uncharacteristic.) "Dr. Evelyn Hashimoto."

I sit up straighter at the referral to my full professional-sounding name. Without realizing it, I am effectively squeezing the tablet to the point that I'm surprised that I haven't done some harm to it. (A testament to their sturdiness, unless you drop it of course.)

"I don't quite understand this."

Furrowing my brow, I hold up the tablet. "Er, *this*, Dr. Mendez? It looks to me like a perfectly healthy and normal image of a skeleton." Glancing back down at the tablet, I look at it again, trying to see if maybe I missed something. "No, Dr. Hashimoto." Dr. Mendez interlocks his fingers together and shakes his head slowly. At the same time, he looks like someone who has just found out that the moon is made of a specific type of dairy product. "This is not a normal image of a skeleton. Healthy, yes, but normal? No."

I feel my eyes widen. I swipe at the tablet quickly, dragging my finger across its glassy surface, and then I see it. The image before it is unmistakably a horrible, bright, and discolored image of a skeleton that shows the spots of a rapidly spreading cancer. I look at the very top of the tablet where a small line describes the person both of these images belong to.

Ivan Kovalchuk.

"This—is this…?" I stare at the image, swiping back and forth. Suddenly the image of a little white butterfly flashes across my eyes, the butterfly moving its wings slowly, as if testing its strength and ability to fly.

I feel my face flush as I look up at Dr. Mendez, who is looking down at his interlocked hands. I find myself looking at them to. It's the first time that I have noticed a silver-colored band on his ring finger, and set in the center shines a small yellowish-brown stone.

"Many years ago, my wife died." Dr. Mendez looks up at me. Maybe it is because he doesn't have the sharp edges of his glasses framing them at the moment, but his eyes look noticeably sadder. "But not of cancer, which is what most people will assume when they consider that I am an oncologist. However, I have been an oncologist for much longer. Since I was your age, Dr. Hashimoto."

Nodding, I vaguely acknowledge the fact that I must look surprised. My mouth is hanging slightly open as I'm listening to Dr. Mendez, who has never uttered more than the general statements referring to medical diagnoses and the applicable treatments to me. For some reason, he has chosen this moment to recount important facts and events in his life.

"She died in a car accident." Dr. Mendez releases his interlocked fingers and points to what I now assume to be his wedding band. "I had this stone placed here a week after her funeral. It is a topaz, but it is not her birthstone. Rather, it represents the month that she died. It is also a reminder."

Uncomfortable, I find myself staring back down at the tablet. Staring down at Ivan's name at the top of his skeleton's image.

"It reminds me that I am a doctor. I am also a human with the qualifications to help decrease suffering and possibly defer death for a later time. Perhaps that time is sooner than expected. But in the face of the unexpected, death is always ahead, and it will always remain the clear winner."With that being said, miracles are for the hopeful, optimistic—and the living. They are not for the dying. For the dying, miracles are promises that are impossible to keep. For death is inevitable. I do not believe in miracles, Dr. Hashimoto." This time he points at the tablet. "But this…"

Dr. Mendez then stands up. "Dr. Hashimoto. We have good news to deliver to this young man and his parents." Taking his glasses back into his hands, he carefully replaces them, straightening them over his ears and nose.

For the second time since I have known Dr. Mendez, he looks at me and smiles.

The city was illuminated by the morning light as it cast a gentle glow that swept across the buildings below. It was the sky that caught the attention though, as the contrasting blackness of the night gave way to the deep blue of day.

Atop one of these tall buildings stood a dark figure. It was hard to make out any colors or features of this shape, because from a distance it looked as if only a shadow remained, lingering. If one were to focus, though, the figure could be seen staring up at the sky.

The sky reflected into colorless eyes, the pupils almost invisible. They seemed empty and vast—and terribly tragic, for they reflected not just the sky's light, but something more. Something unknowable and cold.

"Cerin," a voice whispered into the chilled morning air.

A person appeared next to the shadow named Cerin as he continued to stare up into the sky. Cerin was always struck by how different his sister looked in comparison to his brother, Neko. Even though they were twins, she was the complete opposite in appearance. Her face, rather than being sharp and mischievous, was flat and void of expression. It was also beautiful and terrible in its coldness. Her hair was long and fair, where both Neko and Cerin were dark. Tied to the ends of her hair were thin golden threads that sparkled in the light. They dripped down her back as if woven from heavy metals.

"Neko sent me," she said as cold wisps of air escaped her lips. Despite the morning's chill, she wore nothing but a simple white dress that appeared weighed down by heavy black ink, the hem dragging across her feet, and the collar just low enough to see black veins slithering up toward her neck.

Cerin finally stirred, tilting his eyes down from the sky.

"He is faster than even the swiftest shadows at delivering messages. I just spoke to him last night, Auriel."

Auriel narrowed her eyes, the same gray colorless shade as Neko's and Cerin's. "Neko is my twin. A fact that you are well aware of, dear brother. We are afforded different methods of communication."

"Yes," Cerin stated plainly. "I am aware."

"Cerin, this has been going on long enough. Father is displeased."

"I'm also aware of this. He sent me a rather beautiful and rare white flower, which then proceeded to burst into hell-fire."

"Father does not waste time with explanation," Auriel intoned flatly.

"I cannot agree more, dear sister."

"Then you know that this...creature...needs to be taken care of."

For the first time, he looked at his sister. Despite her careless demeanor, she had the subtle look of quiet concern, though she was unwilling to express it completely—her face remained almost frozen.

"Creature? This creature could quite possibly be the strongest of Maluna's children born to this mortal realm."

This time Auriel raised her dark eyebrows, which contrasted sharply against the paleness of her hair and skin. "Impossible, Cerin."

Cerin's response was slow. "Perhaps."

Auriel opened her mouth, but uncharacteristically nothing came out. She pressed her lips together in thoughtful silence instead.

"Then it's even more critical that you take care of this." Auriel turned away from Cerin just as the sun began to set the top of the building alight. This had the effect of completely *washing out the color of her hair, making the many layers of heavy golden thread shine even brighter. "Or Neko and I will."*

Without a glance back, her whisper echoed into the morning air, "Before father finds out." She disappeared.

Cerin's face froze in a blank expression. He looked down at his hand, the image of a white flower bursting into flames imprinted into his memory.

Closing his fist, he walked forward, to the very edge of the building's roof. Just before he would have stepped off the edge, his figure vanished like a morning cloud dissolving into mist.

The remaining wisps of cloud blew across the name of the building:

Everline Hospital.

"Hi, Ivan."

Ivan looked up from his tablet and a big smile appeared. His blue eyes were bright and his face pink with the color of healthy blood cells circulating through his body. Rather than sitting feverishly wrapped up in blankets, he had the covers turned to the side as he sat at the edge of the bed.

"Hey, Clark! Check this out." Ivan whipped the tablet around. "I'm already on the third volume! Ryuu and his dragon-beagle, Jeffrey, are heading to India to speak to Saraswati to find a book about magic star opals."

Clark smiled as he placed the blood pressure cuff on Ivan's arm. "I think that's one of my favorite parts."

"Oh! And Dr. Mendez and Evie said that I don't have cancer anymore!" Ivan, although ecstatic a second ago, became quiet in an instant, just as Clark deflated the blood pressure cuff.

Setting the cuff and his stethoscope down, Clark sat down in a chair across from where Ivan sat in bed. Ivan stared down at the screen of his tablet, which had the image of a green dragon and young boy flying through cloudy skies, his blue eyes unblinking.

"Ivan, you okay?" Clark asked gently, concerned at Ivan's sudden silence.

Ivan flinched, and his shoulders shuddered as he took in a deep breath. "I thought I was going to die."

Clark remained quiet as he looked at Ivan, hunched over, his shoulders seeming heavy with this knowledge—death had come so close to ending his life at twelve years old. He looked up, and Clark was startled by the haunted look in his eyes.

"The doctors are not sure what happened. They said it was good, obviously…but 'unexpected.'" Ivan continued, as if trying to comprehend the words that had been spoken earlier by repeating them. "They asked if it would be okay if they ran more studies on me, just to see what was different. They said that for other kids, it took more treatments. And even then…it still might not have worked. My parents said it would be up to me, but that I would still be able to go home and back to school."

Ivan averted his eyes before whispering, "I said yes. I want to be able to help other kids, but…"

For some reason, Clark found himself growing still as he listened to Ivan.

"I think it was something besides the medicine. Something else that helped me, too."

Clark furrowed his brow, not quite understanding. Ivan seemed to notice this, because he started to tighten his fingers on the tablet, as if he didn't want to say anything else. His face became flushed, obviously embarrassed.

Standing up, Clark smiled down at Ivan, trying to reassure him that whatever he was thinking was okay. "Well, one thing is for certain! You might be getting a puppy. Your parents may have mentioned that before leaving the nurses' station." Clark frowned, as if realizing that he said something that he probably shouldn't have. "Ahh, maybe don't tell them I told you. I think it was supposed to be a surprise."

This didn't quite have the effect that Clark was hoping for, though. Ivan still remained at the edge of the bed, unmoving.

He couldn't know that in the back of Ivan's memory was something trying to reach out to him. Something silvery and beautiful. Something that lingered and drew him to that glowing spot in his thoughts.

Ivan knew that whatever "it" was had somehow cured him—had saved him from an early death. He didn't understand how, though. Even at twelve years old, he wasn't quite sure if miracles could be manifested in such a way. He wasn't even sure if he was praying the right way in church. His parents had always told him there was a reason for everything.

He continued to stare down at his tablet, realizing for the first time that the screen had timed out and he was now staring down at its blank surface. The glassy surface reflected his own face, as if he were staring down at his reflection in dark water. His eyes stared up at him, almost knowingly, and at the same time reassuringly. Maybe this reflection could remember what he couldn't.

Suddenly there was a rustle of movement that startled him from his thoughts. Ivan and Clark both looked toward the doorway as Ivan's parents entered. They stood next to each other in a very awkward way, their shoulders touching as they both held either side of an open-ended box. They were looking at Ivan and Clark enthusiastically, matching smiles on their faces.

Setting the tablet aside, Ivan walked over to his parents, who waited expectantly for him to approach. Before he had crossed the small distance, he saw a furry head peeking out of the box. Its ears were long and floppy, and it whimpered as it tried to climb out.

Ivan leapt toward the box and felt his face break out into a huge smile. Although he still had lingering thoughts in the back of his mind—thoughts of what could have been his impending death if he had not been miraculously saved—he couldn't help but feel a rush of affection for the furry little animal he now held in his arms.

"It's not exactly a beagle, Ivan, but we thought you would enjoy a new friend to grow up with." Ivan's parents watched happily as their son nuzzled his face into the puppy's soft brown fur.

"Thank you." Ivan was surprised to find his voice cracking slightly as he tried to hold back tears.

CHAPTER THIRTEEN

CHANCE ENCOUNTERS

"Do you think Kiran will have his eggplant casserole on the menu?" Estelle jaunts merrily next to me, her arms swinging and her eyes slightly glazed over with that dream-like look she gets when she's thinking of meals prepared by Kiran (or whenever she has thoughts of food).

Walking next to her, I'm only slightly worried that she might walk into a signpost or another human being as her attention seems to be focused on things other than the sidewalk. I carefully readjust my bag across my shoulders. I have a fleeting moment of regret for accidentally stuffing an extra book in my bag along with the three other sizable books already in there to begin with.

"Honestly, I think you're the only one that actually likes Kiran's eggplant casserole." I can remember when Kiran was in high school during his eggplant experimental phase. This was one of those lovingly indulgent moments in our childhoods that my parents try not to remember.

Noticing a light pole fast approaching us, I

automatically nudge Estelle out of the way with the bump of my shoulder. At the very instant that we're passing the light pole (and Estelle has successfully averted running into it), I collide into someone.

Shocked, I find myself sitting on the concrete, while the other person, who I honestly cannot remember ever being in my path, is looking down at me with eyes of a startling color.

I feel my face start to burn bright red with the fact that I've taken to noticing this person's eyes while I'm still sitting on the concrete in the middle of a busy sidewalk.

As if recovering from the fact that he just knocked over another human being, the man with stunning eyes quickly extends a hand down toward me.

"I'm so sorry!"

It is at this moment that I realize his eyes are actually two different colors—one a pale blue color and the other an amber brown.

Heterochromia.

I find myself reciting the medical term in my head. Then I immediately feel less embarrassed. This is obviously a good enough reason to still be staring at this person's eyes. Genetics are a fascinating thing.

Right. Genetics.

He smiles, and I notice that the corners of his mouth turn up in a curious but pleasant way.

At this point, I realize that I might be staring at him for other reasons, which is probably why Estelle is standing there next to me with her eyes wide, her mouth open slightly. Like me, she has yet to be deterred by the fact that I'm still sitting on the sidewalk.

Without really knowing how it got there, I find my hand already in his.

"I must not have been paying attention. My sincere apologies." He pulls me up to a standing position without much effort. He's stopped grinning, but the corners of his mouth are still lifted upward. His hair, dark and shining, is messily tucked behind his ears and the ends brush the collar of his coat. I can't help but notice that the color of his hair contrasts exceptionally well with his interesting eyes.

Feeling the flush slowly start to leave my face, I shove my hands into the pockets of my coat for the sole reason to have something to do rather than marvel unbecomingly at this stranger's heterochromatic genetics.

"I should apologize as well. I must've been distracted." I look pointedly at Estelle and the light pole that I was saving her from. She blinks and closes her mouth, but that's pretty much it.

He turns his grin back on, and then as if on cue there is a sudden and loud cry that seems to pierce through the crowded sidewalk. All three of us turn toward the sound. Just a short distance away, a small crowd stands around a person lying on the ground. This person looks like he isn't moving.

Reflexively, and without even a glance at one another, Estelle and I are rushing over to the person. Approaching, I notice that the man lying on the ground is perhaps middle-aged and in a business suit. He is lying on his side, a briefcase next to his hand.

"He just yelled out and collapsed," a concerned and nervous bystander explains while pulling out his cell phone. "Should I call nine-one-one?"

"Yes," Estelle answers automatically, already on her knees and pressing her fingers alongside his neck, searching for the steady beating of blood pulsing through a carotid artery under the skin. She looks at me, and I can already read it in her eyes before she says it. "Nothing."

There is no pulse, which means that this person's heart has stopped and is no longer oxygenating the rest of his body, including his brain.

Within fractions of a second, we're already turning him carefully to his back. My knees scrape against the concrete as I help Estelle by rolling his shoulder toward me. I barely notice that the crowd has quickly gotten larger. Shocked gasps and concerned chattering seem to register as nothing but a slight buzz in the back of my mind.

Estelle immediately stacks her hands one on top of the other and presses them to the man's chest. With her arms straight, she pushes all her weight down into her hands as she attempts to physically pump blood through his heart. She repeats this, compressing at a steady and purposeful rate.

I'm kneeling down at the top of the man's head. For some reason, I feel as if everything were moving in slow motion at this very instant. I look down into his face. His eyes are closed and his jaw slack. His skin is pale.

I feel my own blood pumping into my heart, the loudness of my pulse seems to cause a rushing sound in my ears, blocking everything else out. Reaching my hands out to either side of his face, I pause, blinking slowly. My gaze shifts to my hands.

I feel a sudden coolness flow into them, like water sliding down to the very tips of my fingers. It's a sensation that feels strange, but also comforting. Closing my eyes, I breathe out and press the fingers down along either side of the person's jaw.

It's as if time finally decided to pick up when I feel my fingers touch his skin. I quickly press firmly against his jaw and pull up gently so that his trachea is straight and oxygen can flow unobstructed down into his lungs.

Over Estelle's shoulder, I'm surprised to find myself making eye contact with a pair of mismatched eyes belonging to the stranger who I had walked into. He's standing in the crowd, but I can still spot him easily, even in the split second that I've brought my eyes up. He seems to be observing intently as the surrounding people watch and talk to one another. I can't help but notice his lips. They seemed to be perpetually turned up, as if he's always on the verge of a smile even during an unexpected situation.

Estelle suddenly stops, and I can hear a small exclamation of surprise as she stares down at her hands. She looks at me, her eyes bright with surprise.

"Cold," is the only word that she's able to express.

I frown in confusion. "What?" At the same time, I slide my right hand down from his jaw and place my finger on his carotid. I can feel a gentle pulse beating against my fingertip. I can't help but sigh in relief, which is quickly drowned out by the approaching sounds of a siren. A vehicle door slams, and I can hear the fast-approaching footsteps of what I already know to be paramedics. The crowd is already parting as they make their way toward us.

Lifting my hands and starting to move away so the paramedics can take over, I glance down and notice that the man has opened his eyes.

He looks up at me, and my breath catches as I see a flicker of silver flit across his eyes. I blink and refocus, wondering if I had imagined this.

Through his dazed look, I can just make out a semblance of recognition—something he's trying to understand—which isn't surprising, considering the fact that he just experienced cardiac arrest. He blinks slowly and decides to close his eyes again; perhaps the effort of having his body shocked back into life is enough for him, and his brain has decided to encourage a moment of rest.

"Thank you, ma'am." A woman in a navy-colored uniform, with emergency medical personnel patches emblazoned across the chest and sleeves, places her hand firmly on my shoulder. She motions a gloved hand over her own shoulder toward Estelle and the man who called 911, now talking to another paramedic in a similar uniform, apparently providing details on what had happened. Nodding, the paramedic walks over to his partner and me.

This paramedic places a machine on the ground and starts untangling cords connected to an electrocardiogram, or ECG, monitor for the heart. He looks at me and smiles. "Perfect timing, doctor."

I stand up, brushing the knees of my pants. Sheepishly, I shrug and watch as Estelle joins us. "It was Dr. Estelle Kagwe here that did the actual work. I just kept his tongue from blocking his airway."

"Still, impressive response time and chest compressions." The male paramedic kneels down next to the person on the ground. His partner is already attaching the sticky monitor leads to the man's chest.

"It's a good thing you two were here," the female

paramedic says with a serious expression on her face as they prepare to slide the man onto the gurney.

As the crowd starts to disperse, Estelle glances over at me with a tragic expression on her face. "I think we're late for dinner."

Rolling my eyes, I say, "Yes, but you also participated in a particularly important event in another human's life… preventing their untimely death."

The paramedics are already wheeling the man away toward their ambulance. I can't help but notice that the male paramedic has the man's briefcase in his hand while he helps guide the gurney. This immediately reminds me of my own personal bag full of my important reading selections.

"My bag." I frantically glance around as the crowd begins to disperse. I jog back to the light pole and search the area where earlier I had found myself in an uncomfortable seating arrangement with the hard concrete of the sidewalk.

Turning around a little too quickly in the same spot, I end up tripping over my feet—and find myself backing into another person. Then I realize that it's the rather interesting person with the heterochromatic eyes and distractedly absorbing grin.

"Oh, not again!" I feel myself flush with immediate regret at the rude response that has just escaped my mouth. I just vaguely make out the look of horror, reflecting my own thoughts, on Estelle's face as she catches my eyes and stops right behind this person.

He puts up his hands in an exaggerated gesture of surprise, raising his eyebrows. "Wow, is this a typical form of interaction for locals here?"

For this first time since our impromptu meeting, I recognize a subtle accent that I can't quite place and find myself staring at his brown and blue eyes. Immediately I feel frustrated with myself for getting so easily distracted. I mean, just because a person has interesting eyes doesn't necessarily make *them* interesting.

However, Estelle seems to find him interesting enough with the way she continues to gawk. Although an excellent first responder in life-or-death situations and/or situations dealing with mangled limbs, she has yet to form a coherent sentence when it comes to certain attractive individuals.

"Only for the clumsier sort," I mumble a bit, breaking my gaze, and immediately continuing my search alongside the sidewalk.

"Hm, I guess there might be a learning curve." He holds up a brown messenger bag that is unmistakably filled with what might be one too many books.

"My bag!" Although lacking my usual cleverness or wit, I can't help but feel relieved. As I reach for my bag, I stop myself just in time to mutter a contrite, "Thank you."

Despite my lackluster gesture of gratitude, the corners of his mouth turn up in that curious way of his. He gingerly passes my messenger bag into my hands, and before taking his leave, he nods his head modestly. "It was an absolute pleasure."

With my arms wrapped awkwardly around my book bag, I find myself trying not to stare at his retreating figure. At the time same, Estelle dives toward me and starts digging around in my book bag.

"In the mood for some light reading, I assume?"

Estelle continues her rummaging in my bag, obviously

searching for something. She then stops abruptly, and with a resigned sigh, she looks at me.

"There must be something about this bag that I'm just not getting."

Defensively, I hug my bag tighter. "Huh?"

"I think this bag somehow draws attractive individuals to you like moths to an eggplant-colored flame."

"It's actually Amethyst—" I begin to say before she pulls out a book while emphatically shaking her head.

"And that's another thing. It really *is* the color of eggplants."

"Do you have something against eggplants?" It's surprising how defensive I've become for this particular fruit lately.

"I love eggplants. I just didn't realize that it had such an attractive application as a hair color." She then looks down at the book she's holding, which happens to be titled, *The Colorful Lives of Bacteria*.

"Your reading material is inspiring," she states rather bluntly and places it back into my bag. She then pulls out an old banana, soggy yet surprisingly intact.

Oh, forgot about that.

"That must be the source of my strange magnetism," I observe.

Estelle wrinkles her nose and tosses it in the waste bin that happens to be conveniently placed next to us. "Apparently." She straightens her back and smiles as if a pleasant thought just so happened to cross her mind right then.

"It's not too late for dinner!"

CHAPTER FOURTEEN
A PAGE TORN

"You're late."

Kiran looks slightly flustered as Estelle and I follow him to a table next to the kitchens. The restaurant is already empty, with the last patrons just now leaving and looking pleasantly satisfied. Kiran has our table set for three, since he'll be joining us for his own dinner as well.

"It was completely unintentional, I can assure you, dearest Kiran." Estelle brandishes her white cloth napkin and lays it across her lap neatly while fluttering her gray-green eyes up at my brother.

Once again, I swear I see Kiran's face redden just slightly. I find myself entertained by this new onset of shyness, uncharacteristic of my twenty-eight-year-old brother.

He's already removed his fancy red chef's hat and apron and was about to take his seat when he immediately straightens up, slightly alarmed. "Oh, right, the food!"

Avoiding eye contact with either of us, he runs back to

the kitchen. In what has to be less than thirty seconds, he returns balancing two large and still-warm dishes of food.

"Zucchini lasagna and—" Kiran starts when Estelle jumps in, reaching for the dishes to help set them down on the table.

"Beef and pea dumplings!" Estelle completes an accurate description of Kiran's dishes. Impressed, I look at the dumplings. Personally, I can't tell what's in them, but somehow Estelle has developed something of a sixth sense when it comes to Kiran's cooking.

She wastes no time in serving out everyone's portions. By the time Kiran is sitting down, Estelle is already handing me a heaping plate of food.

"So what was the event? Usually you're never late when Estelle is coming." Kiran sits back comfortably, stretching the muscles in his neck and arms in his routine way after spending a full day cooking.

"Saving lives." I take a bite of my zucchini lasagna and instantly feel a great affection for my big brother. He takes such good care of my dietary needs. "You know, that sort of thing."

Kiran laughs. "Of course, just a small sorta' thing."

As Estelle luxuriates in her meal, I recount the details of our eventful delay, leaving out the distracting stranger and his different-colored eyes. I wait for Estelle to interrupt me regarding this detail, but she is well preoccupied with devouring her delicious dinner.

Kiran nods thoughtfully while I'm speaking, but at the same time, I can tell his mind is on something else.

However, something about the way his gaze loses focus every so often makes me realize that it might not be Estelle he's thinking about. Although, she is quite distracting at the moment, since she is already working on her third helping.

It's only after the last dumpling and piece of zucchini has disappeared off the table that Kiran finally seems less distracted. Estelle hops up from her chair, but rather than appearing like she's just eaten three times her allotted calories for the day, she looks spry and refreshed. I'm only slightly annoyed that she looks ready to run a marathon and I'm ready for twelve hours of uninterrupted sleep.

I follow Kiran to the kitchen with a small assortment of empty dishes in my arms. When the doors close behind us, he turns to me, a serious look on his face.

"Evie…" He looks almost unsure how to begin, but after just a moment's pause, he reaches into his pants pocket and hands me a neatly folded piece of paper. "I found this. It was just lying in my chef's hat the other day. I've been waiting for dinner tonight to give it to you."

Confused, I stare at the folded piece of paper. "Why?"

Kiran looks uncomfortable. "I-I just had a feeling." He then looks down at his feet. "It reminds me of your drawings from when we were younger."

My eyes sharpen as I look at him. I lift my hand in what feels like a weirdly mechanical reflex. Although he is maybe one of two people who knows why I stopped drawing, it was so long ago, I am surprised he remembers it. It seemed so insignificant at the time. At least, that's what my intentions had been.

Silently, I take the piece of paper from him. I feel an involuntary shivering sensation travel up my arm. The texture of the paper is so familiar to me. It has the unique quality of soft, creamy sketch paper. With a creeping sensation in my fingertips, I begin to unfold the paper carefully.

The first thing that catches my eyes is a gleaming silver color. It's almost overwhelming at first. I then notice the soft blurred lines of black and gray charcoal. Its lines form into the slender figure of a woman. The silver color is her hair, which is long and swirls around the figure as if wind is blowing through the strands. I almost expect the paper to flutter in my hands, but it stays cold and static between my fingertips.

Although beautiful, something about the image is unsettling. Perhaps it's the way sharp lines can be seen where the charcoal smudged. As if someone had drawn it hastily. Angrily.

The features of the person are also hard to make out. Any defining details of her face are obscured by a smudge of charcoal that looks like smoke.

Her wrists are hanging in front of her. It takes me a moment to realize that they are bound together by what almost looks like the silver strands of her own hair, but then I realize that the ends of the silver bindings are weighed down and tied to a rocklike shape at her feet.

I suddenly remember Kiran standing in front of me. He is watching me carefully, an unsure look shadowing the angular features of his face.

Glancing up, I make eye contact, not sure what to say myself. "Well, it's definitely unique." I try to say this lightly, but it comes out sounding strained and quieter than I meant it to.

"I know you stopped drawing for a reason, Evie. I didn't mean to bring up anything that you didn't want to remember. I just thought—" Kiran looked pointedly at the drawing in my hands. "I thought it would mean something to you."

I look at him, not sure if I understand, or if he does either. I fold the paper carefully and place it in my own pocket. Even though the paper is light, I still feel its weight against my skin.

"Do you know how it got into your hat?" I ask, although I already know the answer.

Kiran shakes his head. "No. It was at the beginning of the day, when I just opened the restaurant. Jeff, Regina, and Mel hadn't shown up yet. And I'm usually the last one out to close shop."

Nodding, I feel my mind going blank. "It's just a drawing." I then add after a brief pause, "Thank you."

Kiran follows me out of the kitchen. Estelle is waiting for us at the front of the restaurant. She's already pulled her jacket on, and she's holding out my precious book bag.

Before we reach Estelle, Kiran touches my shoulder. The weight of his hand is unexpected, but comforting.

"Evie." I turn to him and am reminded how alike we look at times. It's almost like looking into a mirror, our eyes are so similar. "Be careful."

This catches me off guard. "What do you mean?"

He nudges his shoulders up, pulling his jacket closer around him, but he doesn't say anything. Estelle suddenly decides to meet us halfway—apparently we're not walking to her fast enough. She pushes my book bag toward me with a big and satisfied smile.

"Kiran, dear, you are a dream come true! Until next time. And next time better be soon!"

Looking away from me, Kiran responds to Estelle with a laugh and leads us out of the restaurant.

Making our way back to our apartment, Estelle is too engrossed in her retelling of Kiran's delicious dinner to notice that I haven't said a word except for the appropriate "mhm" and agreements related to the fantastic edibleness of our food.

My mind keeps drifting back to the drawing. It's like I can feel it in my pocket, its weight significant and burdensome. I'm impatient to be alone so I can look at it again. I resist a sigh of relief when we're finally walking through our front door.

"Sweet dreams, my eggplant-inspired paramour." Estelle waves her fingers at me as I mutter a good night.

Closing my bedroom door behind me, I find myself standing in the dark for just a moment. Before turning on the light, I'm already heading straight to my bookcase, knowing exactly where my hands need to go without the light to guide me. My fingers brush along the smooth velvety binding of the mysterious sketchbook that I shoved into an obscure section of my bookshelves. Pulling it out, I walk over to my bed and turn the lamp on at my bedside table.

The dim orange-yellow light isn't the brightest, but it's enough.

Sitting on the edge of my bed, I pull the drawing out of my coat pocket and start to unfold it slowly.

The silver and smoke-colored image is already familiar to me, since it is the only thing I thought of as we walked back home. It is already seared into my memory.

I notice that one side of the drawing is subtly serrated—a detail that I hadn't noticed standing in my brother's restaurant kitchen. I can barely feel it as I slide my finger carefully down its side.

My gaze then falls onto the black book in my lap. Its rippling texture seems to capture the orange light in such a way that it almost looks like the sun's reflection in water gently rolling over the surface—or burning flames.

Maybe it is the coincidence of the charcoal or perhaps the uncommon use of the silver (which I still can't figure out—is it ink, paint?), but I can feel something pulling me toward this mysterious black book.

Setting the drawing down, I take a slow, deep breath, not realizing that I was holding it up to this point. Lifting the book and setting it along its spine, I prepare to open it up, but somehow the covers slip between my fingers and the book falls open and heavy on my bedspread. Without even a flutter of a page, it lays there like a rock that has sunk down into a pool of water.

The pages that lay open in front of me are blank. Looking closely, though, I see something in between the pages where they are bound. I run my finger in between the pages, and a buzzing fills my mind as I inhale sharply.

There is a subtle and jagged edge as I slide my fingers down between the pages. It is unmistakable. A page of this book has been cleanly torn away.

Without even thinking, I'm already reaching for the drawing lying at my side.

Gently I fit it between the pages where the torn ends meet perfectly. The color of the paper, the texture, the size, everything fits perfectly, like a puzzle that's missing all but one piece.

When I try to lift the drawing again to inspect the torn side, I feel my hands twitch with surprise. The page is stuck as if super-glued.

Bringing the book closer to my face, I stare in disbelief. The page has somehow sealed itself back to the book. I lower it and lift the one page up. It's as if it had never been torn from the book in the first place.

Removing my hands from the book, my eyes unblinking, I suddenly feel as if ice has filled my chest. My brain seems to be moving sluggishly through memories, desperately trudging through many years, days, hours, minutes, and seconds. My thoughts feel so disorganized as they flit between details that I've tried forgetting over the years.

The images flashing through my mind are like pages sticking together in a book that hasn't been opened in a long time.

I suddenly see myself as a young girl, my small fingers wrapped around markers, pens, pencils, and other such drawing utensils. I'm frantically dragging them across pages and pages of blank pieces of paper. Shades of black and gray, with shots of blue, fill the pages. Hastily scrawled and then crumpled up to be thrown away.

The images flutter by as I get older. I'm now looking at my twelve-year-old self in the mirror—staring into scared, young eyes as I lift a layer of my dark brown hair up and see a streak of pure white hair hidden underneath.

This image shifts to my hands as they compulsively start drawing dark shadows with claws that drip ribbons of blood and eyes that peer out from the pages, gray and empty with no pupils visible in their depths.

Now I'm throwing all the pens and papers away, throwing them into storage bins and dragging them down the stairs. Locking them away, and resisting the temptation that I feel so viscerally in the very bones of my body to draw and draw. Somehow, I feel that just by keeping myself away from drawing, it will prevent me from having the compulsive need to draw such dark and forbidding images.

And then I'm back to being a small girl with the little white butterfly. My grandfather, sitting on his knees, looks up at me with his tired and gentle eyes. This time he hands me the unmoving butterfly. With a flutter in my heart, my fingertips suddenly going cold… the butterfly moves and flies away.

He smiles down at me, but his eyes are so sad.

Even though I'm young, I can understand the sadness on my grandfather's face. Something has gone terribly wrong. Even though the butterfly flew away.

It had been dead.

CHAPTER FIFTEEN

OBSIDIAN THRONES

WHEN I WAKE up in the morning, I feel slightly dazed, not quite remembering exactly when I had fallen asleep. My last memory was of closing the book and laying my head down on the pillow; my thoughts lingering on who was responsible for the drawings.

The black book is still lying there beside me. I rest my hand on top of it and imagine myself throwing it out of the window, or into a body of water somewhere.

At the same time, I know that I wouldn't be able to. Something about the book seems both unnatural and dangerous—but beautiful and mysterious too.

Pushing the covers aside and getting out of bed, I take the book in both hands. Walking toward my messenger bag, I take out one of the books already in there and replace it with this one. It slides in between the other books, unassuming and quiet looking. Slimmer compared to the others. Its velvety binding looks discreet against the thicker and more colorful ones next to it.

Closing the flap of the messenger bag, I continue with my usual morning routine.

Twisting the metallic threads woven throughout her long hair, Auriel admired their weight, her straight, dark eyebrows and colorless eyes blank and void of emotion.

She sat in a hard high-backed chair, made of a material that shone black and sharp. The edges that shaped the chair were like knives, but rather than fearing they would slice her pale skin, she appeared comfortable, reclining as she continued to twist the golden strands around her fingers in a repetitive motion. They twirled and slipped between her fingertips like a snake's tongue.

Beside her was a similar high-backed chair, and sitting in it was Neko. He sat there, leaning slightly forward, a look of boredom on his face as he gripped the armrests lazily, tapping his long-nailed fingers against them.

"Cerin is being foolish," Auriel finally said. "He is easily distracted."

Neko glanced over at his sister, smirking slightly but tilting his head in agreement. "He has been distracted for many years, dear sister."

"He claims that this particular creature is a child of Maluna." Auriel blinked slowly.

Neko's finger froze in mid-tap.

"It happens every so often. They appear in the mortal lands," Neko stated plainly, but his voice intoned a subtle interest.

Auriel's eyebrows shifted downward. "Cerin thinks she is not what she seems, even for a child of Maluna... He's convinced of something greater."

Now Neko's whole body turned toward Auriel, his interest unconcealed.

"That would be quite impos—"

"Impossible?" Auriel interrupted Neko abruptly.

"But if father were to find out, he would be…" Neko paused, as if thinking of the right words. "Well, displeased would be putting it rather mildly."

Auriel nodded, and now she looked at her brother. There was a moment of silence that passed between them, but it was quick, as if they had uttered a string of thoughts between them without speaking.

"To think that Cerin could possibly do something that would risk incurring father's anger… What has he gotten himself into?" Auriel frowned, her eyes darting away from her twin brother's.

"Cerin has always been the more foolish one." Neko raised his eyebrow at his sister in response, shifting his body forward as he readied to stand.

"He may require our assistance." Auriel tightened her free hand on her black armrest, the other fingers of her hand still mechanically wrapping around the metallic threads in her hair.

Neko closed his eyes, and when he opened them, a strange look of mischievousness brightened his face right before he was enveloped in a cloud of black smoke and disappeared from his obsidian throne.

His sister barely acknowledged that he'd left. Instead, she continued to stare blankly ahead, the only movement from her person was the twirling of gold in her fingers.

CHAPTER SIXTEEN
DROWNING WATERS

"DR. HASHIMO—AHHH…EVIE? DR. EVIE?"

As I'm rounding the corner of the hospital hallway, a tablet in one hand and a paper cup filled with precious coffee—emitting wondrous, steamy, energetic promises—in the other, I immediately find myself face-to-face with a nurse, her cheeks flushed and her curly hair arranged in a long ponytail.

"Chandra?" I eye the sloshing coffee in my cup, realizing perhaps too late that it might've been a good idea to obtain a lid for it at some point.

"Yeah, Clark called in for a family emergency of some sort. Since I had the last few nights off, they asked if I would mind picking up his day shift this time," she said in response to what I suppose was an obvious look of confusion and surprise on my face at seeing her so early in the day. She normally works night shifts, so I usually run into her when I end up staying late researching cases for Dr. Mendez or following up on some other responsible healthcare provider activities.

"It's June Reese." Chandra furrows her otherwise smooth forehead. "She's not doing all that great. Heart rate is in the one-sixties, and her work of breathing has been increasing gradually over night. We don't think she'll last much longer unless we intubate her." She gestures with her hands and, rather impressively, pantomimes inserting a breathing tube into the lungs of another person. In this case, the person is June Reese.

I'm about to ask questions, but before I can form the words, Chandra is already answering them for me.

"Chest X-ray was already done, labs drawn, her dad has been notified, and Dr. Mendez is on his way into the office right now."

I nod and follow Chandra to the patient's room. Inside, I'm immediately met with a young girl who looks to be about fifteen years old. She's sitting up and leaning forward in bed, her arms straight out as her hands clutch her knees tightly. She has an oxygen mask strapped to her face. I can hear air blowing loudly through the mask as she gasps, her collarbone moving up and down in shallow breaths. Next to her, monitor alarms are blinking and pinging abnormal numbers regarding her vital signs.

She glances up at me with wide eyes and then squeezes them shut, unable to form any words or sounds.

"Crash cart now." I say quickly and calmly as Chandra runs out of the room, leaving me and the teenage girl alone. The oxygen blowing into her face from her mask and her short gasping breaths seem louder all of a sudden.

I rush over to her and hold my stethoscope out, pressing it against the skin of her back. I can barely hear anything. The tightness and crackling noises in her lungs ring disturbingly in my ears.

As I take the stethoscope away, her eyes meet mine. I see a look of fear and of questions that she's unable to ask.

I can hear the rumbling of Chandra pushing the crash cart down the hallway, and I know the large red tool-box-type cart with drawers stacked on top of each other, full of potentially life-saving medications and different-sized breathing tubes, is rushing over to us.

I grab the girl's hand. She looks startled, but I can feel her fingers tighten around mine.

A brief moment that feels like hours seems to pass, and then her gasping suddenly stops, the bones in her fingers relaxing. She leans back into the pillows of her bed, eyes closed.

Then I feel it. A strange sensation at the back of my neck, as if someone were brushing their fingers against my skin. I whip around, not sure what I am expecting, but all I see is an empty doorway. My eyes scan the room, the sensation lingering.

Chandra appears, the large red cart in front of her as she pushes it into the room.

Startled she looks from me to June, and then once again back to June.

"Is she—?" With quick steps, she stands at June's bedside. At that very moment, June takes a long, deep breath, and the alarms become quiet, her breathing unlabored and easy.

"What—how—?" Chandra begins to ask, observing the numbers blinking away on the machine as if nothing had been going disastrously wrong mere seconds ago.

The small hospital room fills with three more additional people. Teresa, a short-haired and middle-aged woman whom I recognize from respiratory therapy, Dr. Mendez in a dark gray sweater with his white coat slung over one arm, and finally a frantic-looking man, who rather than stopping at the door way with the other two, rushes over to the bedside.

"My daughter—this is my daughter." He stares down at her, his eyes already filled with tears. He hasn't taken his eyes off of her, repeating those words over and over again, unable to do anything but fear the worst as his daughter lays still before him, eyelids closed heavily.

"She's okay, just resting for now." I catch Chandra's eyes. "Please order a repeat chest X-ray."

Chandra nods, and the shock that was evident on her face is replaced with concentration as she springs to the computer mounted against the room's wall, picking up the phone to call radiology at the same time.

Dr. Mendez gives me a quick nod as he walks over to Chandra to discuss the recent events related to June. Teresa also replaces me at June's bedside to swap the oxygen mask out for a different one that will be ready for administering vaporized medicine.

Quietly but quickly leaving the room, I take a deep breath in. I then remember that I left my tablet and coffee at the nurses' station. Turning around abruptly, I find myself colliding into someone.

Immediately, I am flooded by horrified thoughts that this is an ill patient, minding their own business as they ambulate their way through the hospital hallway. I feel my body respond instinctively, though, as I lean forward, bringing my arms out and wrapping them around the other person. Repositioning my feet, I prepare to shift my weight to keep the other person from landing backward on a fragile hip or fragile head.

Ooof! The person lets out a startled breath as my arms tighten around their torso.

A flash of annoyance crosses my mind that hospital hallways are not lined with crash pads.

After realizing that the other person isn't going to fall over, I ask, "Are you steady? Is your footing stable?"

"Uh, I think so actually." The amused, and somehow familiar, voice startles me. Tilting my head up, I find myself looking into a pair of dual-colored eyes, one light blue and the other an amber brown.

Realizing that my arms are still tight around his waist, I immediately unwrap my arms and bounce back as if from an electric shock.

"I-I thought you were a patient!" Of course, after saying this, I notice that he's wearing what is unmistakably a white coat. I can't help but also notice that this coat fits him in quite a flattering way.

Immediately disturbed by this inappropriate observation, I shove my hands into my own white coat pockets and glance around for my coffee, or anything that will avert my gaze from staring at this particular individual standing in front of me with his interesting eyes.

"I suppose this really *is* a welcoming gesture in the area." He grins and bounces forward on the balls of his feet in a charming way. "My name is Ian, by the way. Ian Nakano. Your new cardiologist on board." He dips his head humbly, his eyes glittering as the corner of his mouth perks up.

"Evelyn Hashimoto. Or just Evie, please. Oncology-hematology," I say in such a brisk way that Dr. Mendez would be proud of me.

"Absolutely lovely." Dr. Ian Nakano nods thoughtfully. "I must say. I would assume otherwise. Your ability to restart a heart was... miraculous."

"Well, it really was my friend who should get the credit. Estelle Kagwe. Emergencies are her thing. She works in trauma-orthopedics. And she was the one doing the compressions."

Dr. Nakano raises an eyebrow appreciatively, and just before he is able to say anything else, Dr. Mendez emerges from June's room.

"Dr. Hashimoto!"

I jump as Dr. Mendez walks briskly past us. "To my office, please!"

Thinking longingly of my coffee, I give Dr. Ian Nakano a brief glance. He responds with a smile of understanding, and without really needing to because the hallways are already wide enough, he steps to the side as if clearing the way for me to follow Dr. Mendez.

Walking into his office, I find myself facing an intent Dr. Mendez, staring into the screen of his computer. He's running the computer's mouse back and forth across the pad, clicking continuously at an alarming speed.

"I just spoke to Dr. Lane, the radiologist. She personally

wanted to speak to me regarding Miss Reese's chest X-ray before reporting her findings."

"Before placing the report?" I raise my eyebrows and sit down across from him. "Well, we would expect that in an emergent situation." Usually, the only time Dr. Lane called before making a report would be to let us know of an emergent life-threatening finding. However, in June Reese's case, we already knew that the results would be critical, so it wasn't all that unexpected.

"Dr. Lane is very familiar with Ms. Reese, Dr. Hashimoto. She has been following her for several months now, since she has been diagnosed with an aggressive form of lung cancer. She has been needing frequent X-rays."

I am easily able to detect a subtle tone that sounds remarkably like bewilderment in Dr. Mendez's voice.

"An aggressive form of lung cancer with a very poor prognosis," Dr. Mendez reiterates and swivels his computer screen toward me. I can immediately identify a black, gray, and white image of what is apparently June's lungs splotched with opaque clouds—the ugly nodules and tumors of cancer scattered throughout.

"This image was taken just last night when Jay, the night shift nurse, noted a decline in her respiratory status. This X-ray was unremarkable in June's case. She has not been responding well to treatments. And then, prior to your arrival, Chandra had ordered another X-ray when it was noted that Ms. Reese was declining even further."

With a swipe of his mouse and a precise click, another image flashes over the screen. My eyes widen as I observe June's lungs, which are completely white. The nodules and tumors that were prominent before have now disappeared in a sea of eerie and cloudy whiteness, which represents fluid completely filling up her lungs.

"Pulmonary edema," I mutter under my breath, and the image of June's wide, round, and terrified eyes staring at me flashes across my vision. The fact that she was still conscious shocks me now that I see her X-ray before my eyes. Her ability to compensate after months of declining health must've finally reached its tipping point.

Dr. Mendez then pauses; his hand on the mouse is still as he stares at the image in front of us both. He then brings his pointer finger down firmly, the mouse clicks, and a new image appears in front of us.

It's as if time slows down, and my pupils dilate as I refocus my eyes on the new image before me.

"This is why Dr. Lane wanted to speak to me in person." Dr. Mendez continues to stare at the image.

Like the previous ones, this new X-ray image in front of us shows a pair of lungs. The opaque whiteness of fluid is completely gone, despite the lack of medications at the time—but it's apparent why Dr. Lane wanted to speak to Dr. Mendez before filing her report. This image is obviously something that would be described as remarkable.

The heavy opaque clouds of cancerous tumors and nodules are gone.

CHAPTER SEVENTEEN

FLOWERS OF INK

I leave Dr. Mendez staring at his computer screen, clicking back and forth between June's X-ray images as if trying to make sense of the impossible, which is understandable, given the situation.

I find myself walking into the Hole of Optimism, which is vacant except for the soft dim light of a cloudy sky from the window. Walking over to the window with my hands hanging loosely at my sides, I can still see the images of June's lungs impossibly and miraculously free of cancerous tumors.

A miracle?

Staring down at my hands, I suddenly feel tired. And something else.

I imagine a dead white butterfly sitting in my hand.

And then flying away.

"Excuse me? Doctor?"

I blink and turn my head slowly.

"My apologies for bothering you. For some reason, I

couldn't seem to find anyone who didn't seem occupied with hospital-related activities."

"Probably because you're in a hospital." My mouth turns up in a smile as I address the person standing in the doorway.

The woman standing there responds with an appreciative grin as she catches onto my lighthearted sarcasm. The first thing that I notice is that she's dressed in a stunning and professional-looking white suit. Her pale blonde hair is pulled back in a bun, and her black-framed glasses seem to contrast sharply with her pale but pretty face.

She walks over to me in even and graceful strides. In one hand is a medium-sized case, which hangs down at her side. As she extends her other hand out to me, I can just make out the black swirling shapes of vines and flowers wrapping their way down her wrist and toward her fingers. Before I find myself staring too long, I shake her hand and look up, noticing the same tattooed pattern peeking out from the collar of her suit coat—elegant flowers, leaves, and vines can be seen coiling up her collarbone to her neck. Up close, I can see small glints of gold tracing the outer edges of her ears where they are neatly pierced, and a small golden hoop pierces one of her nostrils.

"Ness Rose." She introduces herself as I release her hand.

My head clears from my previous thoughts, I can now pick up a very pleasant and melodic tone to her voice.

"Evie. I'm a doctor here," I explain, but then realize that this is probably unnecessary since I happen to be wearing the white coat and all.

"Music therapist." Ness nods and lifts up her case, which I assume contains her instrument.

"Oh, I didn't know we had a music therapy program." This is genuinely interesting to me, but before I can rattle off a few dozen research articles on complementary medicine, which highlights the benefits of music therapy in acute care settings, we find ourselves interrupted by a flurry of activity entering the room.

Actually "entering the room" might be somewhat of an understatement. This person practically hurls himself like a cannonball through the doorway.

"Oh, hey, Clark!"

Clark straightens himself up, his eyes wide and his face flushed. He smooths down the fabric of his dark blue scrubs.

"Hey, Evie." He holds up a hand, and his eyes dart toward Ness in brief acknowledgement.

"I thought you were out for a family emergency?" I shove my hands into my pockets as I recall Chandra's explanation of why she was covering his shift earlier.

"The situation seemed to change a bit—and I found myself being able to pick up the rest of my shift anyway," Clark explains hurriedly.

"Ah." I then glance over at Ness. "Oh! By the way, Clark, this is Ness. She's our new music therapist," I explain enthusiastically. "You know, according to the *World Journal of Complementary Medicine*, implementing music in the acute care setting—"

"Right, right! Music therapy is good." Clark purposefully rushes past me and grabs a pen and blank piece of paper lying on the desk between me and Ness.

"Well, yes, to sum it up I suppose," I concede, rather

disappointed at the interruption. "Sorry, Evie. I need to relieve Chandra and get a change of shift report. I forgot my supply of pens at home." He holds up his newly found writing utensil. "I couldn't seem to locate one at the nurses' station. Rare items for some reason."

Before I can respond in likewise commiseration, ready to cite some of my own personal incidences of stolen pens from fellow colleagues, Clark pivots toward Ness.

"Hello, Ness," Clark greets her in a rather perfunctory tone, in my opinion.

"Hello, er—Clark, is it?" Ness shifts the weight of her briefcase and holds out her hand. Her mouth is turned up in a curious smirk, which has more of a mischievous than flirtatious quality to it.

Clark takes her hand and releases it after what hardly seems like a second, but then in general his actions are sped up as he seems ready to head out the doorway as quickly as he possibly can. With a quick duck of his head at us, he rushes out of the room, leaving a cool breeze in his wake.

Ness, appearing amused, raises her eyebrows and looks back at me.

"Well, let me show you around the floor then," I say.

Neko looked up, his glassy, nearly colorless eyes reflecting the movements of a small bird fluttering toward him. He stood in the middle of a dark copse of trees belonging to a city park. The distant orange glow of park lamps illuminated the branches of the evergreen trees, which in turn threw shadows across the small clearing.

Just as the small bird was about to land on the tips of his fingers, which were patiently stretched out, there was a whisper as something golden and sharp slid through the air. It skimmed the tip of Neko's ear as it flew past and pierced one of the brown-feathered wings, pinning the bird to the nearest tree.

Neko turned around, unsurprised, as a small trickle of something silvery slid down his ear from a fine cut left by the dart. The dart shone with a smooth and golden glow; it appeared delicate, but its sleek design held deadly precision.

Auriel walked forward, passing Neko and heading straight over to the little brown bird, which fluttered its wings frantically against the tree.

After a moment, as Neko and Auriel both stared at the little bird, it became still. Its free wing wrapped up and over its head, curling itself into a ball before slowly unfolding.

Where the bird had been pinned, there was now a small scroll of paper the color of black satin, hanging where the golden dart had pierced a small brown wing.

Neko, standing next to his sister, blinked at the lettering. He didn't seem to notice a thin trail of silver now sliding down his neck and toward his collar bone. The lettering on the small black scroll was the same color as his blood.

"Leave now, brother and sister," Neko read under his breath.

Auriel's own colorless eyes skimmed the silver lettering swiftly. She barely moved her eyebrows, her lips pressed into a straight line as she reached her long, thin fingers toward the golden dart.

Grasping the end of the dart, she slid it from the tree with a twitch of her hand. The black scroll, with nothing to hold it against the tree, descended to the grassy ground to meet the tree roots. However, just before it touched the ground, it turned into heavy, inky black smoke. It coiled itself at the hem of

Auriel's white dress, which already hung heavy with something that gleamed black and dark, before finally disappearing.

"I think Cerin is officially unhappy with us." Neko let out an exaggerated sigh.

Auriel pulled the golden dart up to her eyes, inspecting its points carefully. She then gently wrapped a tendril of her own pale and golden hair around one of its sharp points. The golden dart melted into this strand of hair, slipping back to join the rest of the flexible pieces of metal hanging down her back.

"I don't understand his reluctance to accept our help." Auriel's tone held traces of subtle annoyance. "If father were to find out that he's been this close to a child of Maluna this whole time—"

"So, you think she's a true child of Maluna then?" Neko interrupted his sister, his own tone barely masking astonishment.

Auriel nodded her head carefully, the metallic strands of gold gently slithering from side-to-side with this movement. "You've seen it. She has the power to heal, and I suspect more than she herself is even aware of. Something that we haven't seen in the mortal world for a—"

"Very long time," Neko finished her sentence. "Which may be putting it rather lightly when you consider that a 'very long time' is equivalent to…oh, a couple of centuries or so."

Auriel tilted her chin as if to dismiss Neko's flippant tone. She then lowered her voice to just above a whisper. "We will observe her closely." She paused as she made eye contact with Neko. "And Cerin."

Neko nodded in agreement. The silvery trail of blood along his neck had turned black as the cut on his ear healed. Bringing up a finger, he gently wiped the inky blackness from his skin clean.

CHAPTER EIGHTEEN

THE THORNY HEART

"LET ME GUESS. Electric Blue Surge?"

A little over a week has passed since starting my first rotation as an independent provider, and I decided to mark the occasion with a new hair hue.

Looking up from my book (*The Tragic Story of Polar Bears*), I see Estelle observing me intently as she stands in my bedroom doorway.

"Actually, it's Turbulent Turquoise," I correct Estelle's inaccurate description of my new hair color.

Rolling her eyes dramatically, she crosses the threshold of my room and tosses a large piece of paper at me. Looking down at it, I realize that it's a sort of flyer emblazoned with shiny blue and gold flecks. In appealing calligraphic lettering, it happens to be advertising some sort of music concert at a local night club called the Thorny Heart.

Hardly even lowering my book a centimeter, I raise my eyes at Estelle.

"So...are you trying to tell me that you're going

through some sort of phase to relive the younger years of your life wasted away by studying to become a successful orthopedic surgeon in one of the leading trauma and research centers in the region?"

"Obviously." Estelle looks at me expectantly, her gray-green eyes hopeful as she watches me inspect the flyer over the top of my book again.

"No."

I settle determinedly back into my bed, admiring the soft fabric of my blanket against my skin as I shove my nose further into my book in an effort to obscure the flyer and most of Estelle's tall figure from my field of vision.

After a few seconds pass, I am admittedly disturbed by the lack of melodramatic sighs or complaints. I chance a glance back over my book to see that Estelle is still standing there with the same look of stubbornly sweet expectancy on her face.

Huffing, I slam the book closed. "Why tonight of all nights?"

"Because…" Taking a deep breath, Estelle launches into an extremely animated and happy explanation, "It's Friday!"

"So? Weekends don't exist for the laboring health-care worker." I cross my arms.

"But we're not on-call!" To illustrate this, Estelle holds up a glittery pink pager and a plain black one, both of which had the batteries removed as per the usual declaration of a provider who is indeed not on-call.

"Wait, why do you have my pager?"

Looking sheepish and mumbling something about going through a messenger bag that was definitely not hers,

Estelle then somberly shrugs her shoulders and continues to look at me imploringly.

"Well, then why don't you go yourself?" I glance at my book longingly and then grudgingly pick up the flyer.

"You don't just go to a club by yourself!" Estelle blanches, her eyes wide with amazement at my lack of knowledge regarding the decorum of night-related social outings.

"Obviously. Lord knows why you shouldn't go to a club called…the *Thorny Heart* by yourself." Frowning, I set the flyer down. "Where'd you get this by the way?" Although the flyer looks professional enough, I can't help but want to trace the published material back to its distribution source.

As if already expecting this, Estelle uses her formal research-based-and-well-cited-sources tone of voice that her graduate school education prepared her well for, and says, "A music therapist at the hospital—her name's Ness Rose. Apparently, she organizes music events in the area as well. She was handing out this flyer around the hospital floors that she was working on."

This time I look back at Estelle with interest. "Oh, I think I know who you're referring to. I met her last week."

"So, does that mean you'll come with me for a fun-filled night of revelry because my sources are reliable and the risk of being involved in a questionable situation is somewhat less likely?" Teetering on the very tips of her toes, Estelle clasps her hands expectantly.

Grudgingly, I sit up straighter in bed, and at the same time I catch my reflection in the mirror. Although I found my hair to be a lovely and flattering color of blue (in my opinion), it was also noticeably unkempt from lack of further maintenance other than the color-changing part.

"I guess I should brush my hair then."

Practically bouncing on her feet like I gave her a passing grade on an exam, Estelle heads out of the room to get ready for our night out.

After a few rounds of chastisement at my lack of proper club-going attire, Estelle hands me a flowy tunic of hers, which pretty much turns into a mini-dress on my smaller frame. It has a subtle metallic bluish-gray shimmer to it. With some decent black leggings (because I outright refuse to not have anything on my bare legs in the late autumn weather) and a pair of black ankle boots with a comfortable low heel, I feel half-way ready to go to the Thorny Heart.

"No. Evie, no books. Absolutely not." Although I might look semi-prepared to attend a night club, Estelle looks like she walked right out of a fashion magazine. She's standing in three-inch gladiator sandals, with the straps wrapping around her slim legs, and a black mini-dress with a flowing fringe at the ends that brushes lightly down at her mid-thigh. Her long braids hang loosely down her back and sway as she raises her eyebrows at me, her hands on her hips. To say the least, she looks absolutely gorgeous.

"What? What do you mean no books?" I tighten my grip on my messenger bag, which indeed has four hardcover literature pieces tucked into it comfortably. "You mean, they don't read at nightclubs?" I add the last part with a bit of sarcasm and just a tinge of anxiety right as Estelle stretches her arm out to take my messenger bag. She then promptly drops it unceremoniously onto the recliner.

"Tonight, we shall revel in the fine music of our

generation." Estelle opens the door with a flourish and gives me a mischievous smile, which is akin to the smile she once gave when we were caught raiding our attending physician's stash of coconut macaroons and assorted nut bars back as residents. (I don't think he was overly fond of us as his residents and did absolutely nothing to hide his relief when we moved off his floor.)

Contemplating what sort of "fine" music an establishment named the Thorny Heart could have, I exit the apartment resignedly as Estelle pretty much skips out in an impressively graceful way for someone wearing three-inch heels.

Conveniently, the destination for the Thorny Heart is a relatively short distance in proximity to our apartment building. Despite Estelle's enthusiasm, I can't help but feel distracted by the moonlit night, which in combination with the orange streetlights, has a strange calming effect to it. It's sometimes easy to forget that you're in the city at times like this. Even the trees seem more imposing than the tall buildings and skyscrapers that tower over them, their shadows stretching over the pavement before us.

I'm definitely caught off guard a bit when Estelle abruptly stops as we round a corner. Right past this corner is a discreet brick building with a door the color of dark lacquer. The doorknob could easily be missed since it is the same color as the door. The only noticeable indication that this is, indeed, the Thorny Heart nightclub is a pearlescent insignia engraved painstakingly into the door's surface. It is in the shape of an anatomical heart with thorny vines encasing it in a careful and elaborate design.

"Well, if this doesn't look strange and mysterious…"

I eye the establishment suspiciously. "Shouldn't it be more night-clubby, and loud?"

Estelle gives me a pained, harassed look and pushes the door open. With a sweeping motion of her other arm, she urges me on impatiently.

As we enter, I'm immediately hit by a wall of sound and music, the source of which isn't completely obvious because we've actually entered a smaller room that seems to be separating us from the actual music.

"Hello there!" Estelle and I both turn in sync as we're greeted by a boy with pixie-like features, his hair spiky and green and his tan skin covered in colorful tattoos of flowers. He smiles at us in an impish way. "Welcome to the Thorny Heart! I'm Dean, the door greeter."

Dean then holds up a wooden stamp, and although I'm sure he's supposed to ask for our IDs first, proceeds to stamp the insides of our right wrists with a scarlet-colored ink version of the club's insignia. He then gestures ahead to another door, which is identical to the one that led us inside.

"Is there a cover fee?" I ask, but Dean is already shaking his head in anticipation of my inquiry, his face bright with a smile.

"This is the grand opening for the Thorny Heart."

Estelle looks at me and smiles, her eyes alight with barely contained excitement.

As we push the door open, Estelle leading the way, we're immediately surrounded by loud music. I'm surprised at how deceptively spacious the building is compared to its discreet exterior. There's a band playing on the stage at the opposite end of the room, where a sea of people are moving in flickering and flowing patterns of different-colored lights. Nearby, there's a spiraling staircase leading to an upper floor where there is a balcony to look over the stage.

I can tell that the club, even dimly lit with patterns of moving lights appearing every so often, is artfully designed. The staircase is a shiny black color that contrasts appealingly with the dark, polished wooden floors. The walls are covered in a mosaic of different-colored fragments of glass, which catch the flicker of the lights in a way that is beautiful and mesmerizing.

My heart starts to pound with nervous excitement. The music, without me realizing it, has filled my body, and I can almost feel my fingers tingling with the buzz of sound bouncing off the walls.

Estelle is already eagerly weaving herself through the crowd, her hand wrapped around my wrist. We're making our way between people, the lights illuminating their faces for a brief second before flashing away. I catch myself trying in vain to focus on faces that I think I recognize from people I work with at the hospital. However, just before I can get a complete look, they've already disappeared in the shadows of moving bodies.

Just as Estelle and I somehow reach the front end of the crowd, the flickering and flashing lights dim and focus back on the stage. The singer, accompanied by a loud crashing of drums and guitars, reaches a final crescendo as the song ends. There's a rippling of movement and electric-filled excitement as people all turn their attention to each other, and some are already looking back to the stage, impatient and eager.

The current band politely thanks the club patrons and

the Thorny Heart for hosting them. The lead singer waves at the crowd, who respond in an appreciative chorus of excitement. I find myself, and Estelle beside me, shouting as well, rocking onto the balls of my feet and gravitating closer to the edge of the stage.

"Ladies, gentlemen…and all those in between…" The singer chuckles, his voice a soft and crooning tenor, as he winks at the crowd. He seems to be referring to himself as one of those "in between" as his bright red hair, curling with sweat, falls over eyes heavily shadowed with sparkling black and silver glitter. He gives off the vibe of being unabashedly androgynous. His features are both delicate in the fine curve of his nose and masculine with the sharp squaring of his jaw. He's wearing a shirt sparkling with multicolored sequins and very fitted black pants.

"It is my pleasure to introduce the headlining band of the night." He spreads his arms wide, his dark skin also shining with glitter and catching the stage light in a dazzling show with the flexing of his arm muscles. "Lenore's Wings."

His voice drops softly as he says the name of the band. His voice, although just above a whisper, is amplified by the microphone in front of him, and it echoes off the colored glass walls. The crowd suddenly becomes hushed in buzzing anticipation as the lights dim lower until the only thing that can be seen is the shadow of movements on the stage as the musicians change places.

Gradually the lights turn back on, flowing across the crowd of people, and then settling on the stage in a fuzzy glow of soft blue-gray light.

The previous band is completely replaced by a different set of musicians. Surprised, Estelle and I glance at each other as we both realize who the person occupying the center stage at the microphone is.

It happens to be our hospital's new music therapist.

No longer in her sharp white business suit, black-framed glasses, and tightly pulled-back hair, Ness looks much younger standing up there on the stage. Her thin frame is accentuated by a closely fitting and simple white dress. Her hair hangs long and loose, the ends brushing her waist. She is also wearing thick-soled black platform shoes that are at least five inches high, and still, you could tell that she was closer to my height without them.

The tall and muscular guitarist standing a little apart from her towers over her in an almost comical comparison. Her tattoos are especially noticeable now, and I'm surprised to see that 90 percent of her body appears tattooed. The black designs of flowers and vines twist around her limbs. The stage light bounces off of gold metal, glinting off the piercings on her face and ears.

The crowd begins to whisper as the drummer tests the snare, turning the sticks expertly in his hands. The bassist and guitarist also twitch a few strings, the sounds vibrating across the room. This whole time, Ness is standing there, her eyes turned down as if in deep thought. The only movement comes from her fingers, which twist around a thin golden bracelet on her wrist.

Suddenly her eyes flicker up, and her hands fall to her sides. As if this is the cue, her bandmates stand at attention and the drummer taps his sticks quietly three times before a slow rumbling and rolling sound of music begins. Compared to the loud and rattling music of the last band, this sound is almost haunting. When Ness starts to sing, her voice is surprisingly low and raspy. It's almost as if the crowd is holding their breath as they listen, mesmerized—some people even have their eyes closed as they stand, swaying slightly as the music washes over them.

The song ends on an abrupt note. Ness, whose eyes were closed the whole time during the song, opens them along with some other people in the crowd who look as if they have just awoken up from a dream, their eyelids fluttering upwards in the soft light.

Before the crowd is really able to comprehend the end of the music, the room goes completely dark for a split second. The only sound is a loud slap of the drummer's sticks as he strikes them together three times. The lights start to flash and flicker as the band begins to play again. The music that restarts is louder, and the crowd immediately responds in enthusiastic unison. The sound underlying it has a hollow and mysterious quality that carries over from the ballad sung before, but this time the music is pounding against the walls as the lights roam and blink across people in the crowd.

Less reserved, Ness dances across the stage as she sings, spinning and jumping around her bandmates, balancing on her platforms effortlessly.

It continues on in this thread, and I easily find myself losing track of the time. As the music continues, I'm startled as I find myself surrounded by people I'm unfamiliar with, their bodies moving fast and unrestrained in rhythm with the music.

I suddenly realize that I don't see Estelle anymore. An instant wave of guilt washes over me as I acknowledge the fact that my attention has been completely fixated on the music, and this is only shortly after Estelle told me the rule of not going to a club solo.

I start to push and squeeze between the people moving all around me, which is relatively easy, given my smaller size. But I realize quickly that there is absolutely no way that I will be able to navigate through the crowd to find a single person. If Estelle is still in this sea of people, she may well have found herself in another part of the room through the natural motion of many bodies eagerly trying to move closer and closer to the source of the music or in some other unforeseen direction. It feels like I'm moving against ocean waves crashing up against the rocks.

I reach around for my bag out of habit, but of course it's at home sitting on a recliner with all my books and my cell phone. I slap my hand on my forehead and wish, for once, that I had my pager—at least then I would be able to feel the vibration in case Estelle were trying to get ahold of me somehow.

Reaching the opposite end of the crowd, where the entrance is, my eyes catch the staircase spiraling up to the top floor. There're a few people lingering on the staircase, talking to one another. One couple is standing extremely close, their hands brushing each other's arms. Rushing over to the staircase, I breeze past these people somewhat clumsily, which doesn't seem to disrupt any romantic notions that they are having, because they begin kissing rather passionately.

Once I reach the top of the staircase, I'm a little startled by the change in scenery. It's an open area with lounge furniture, a busy bar in the corner where people are huddled around consuming an assortment of beverages, and two balconies on opposite ends separated behind thick glass windows—one balcony looks over the main part of the club and another looks down to the street outside of the club.

I quickly make my way to the balcony looking over the dance floor, dodging groups of people standing closer together to hear each other over the music and others who sip their drinks while admiring twisted pieces of metal artwork in many beautiful designs hanging on the walls. My eyes briefly scan these as I reach the balcony.

Looking down, I squint, trying to decipher Estelle's shape in the sea of bodies. Lenore's Wings is at the peak of their performance, and I can see Ness flying across the stage in graceful movements, her white dress making her stand out in the darkness of the club.

I'm feeling even more discouraged when I suddenly feel a hand rest on my shoulder. I spin around and immediately recognize the person standing there. Even half in shadow, as the lights flash across his face, I can see a blue and amber pair of eyes looking down at me.

"Dr. Nakano?" I shout over the music.

"Dr. Hashimoto?" He smiles as he gently mimics my surprised tone of voice.

A little embarrassed at how close I have moved toward him to hear his voice above the music, I step away, feeling the balcony rail press into my back.

"Ah, you can just call me Evie." Despite the redness of embarrassment that I feel creeping around my ears, I find myself smiling back at him.

"And you can just call me Ian," he responds in a humbled way. "I see that you received the flyer?"

I nod in confirmation. "Actually, it was my friend Estelle." Again, I catch myself guiltily distracted and slap my forehead. I wonder vaguely if there is a red mark there from the previous one. Quickly turning around, I lean over the balcony rail and scan the crowd, looking for the familiar figure of Estelle.

"I take it that you've lost her?" Ian walks over to me and leans against the railing as well.

"Yes," I admit reluctantly. "Apparently, you're not supposed to go to the club alone." I recite the rule that I just learned. "I think that means you should at least know where the person who stated the rule is in a crowd of strangers."

Ian nods in agreement. "I think that's a fair assumption." His eyes scan over the crowd, and I notice he's holding a clear iced drink in one hand, which I'm pretty sure is water.

"I'm actually here with my sister." He's close enough now that he doesn't have to shout.

"Oh, are you hoping to find her, too?" I respond, just a little distracted when I think I may have spotted Estelle, but then quickly the person spins around and I realize it isn't her. I sigh and feel myself grow a little nervous.

Ian glances over at me with a smile, his mouth turned up at the corners in that curious way. "Actually, I think she could probably take care of herself."

Before I can say anything in response, though, I hear a shout coming from the other side of the room, and the door leading to the other balcony opens and closes as someone rushes through.

Without thinking, I start to run over to the door, a

sense of dread filling my chest. I can see Ian following me in the periphery of my vision.

I throw my body against the door and my breath catches as cool air slams into my face. The temperature change from the inside of the warm, busy club almost feels like knives against my skin. My eyes widen as I see a person standing on the balcony railing, and I focus on the person's sharp heels, which are precariously balanced over the edge. The heels belong to gladiator sandals, the straps wrapping up long, thin legs.

It's Estelle.

CHAPTER NINETEEN
FALLING

"Estelle," I whisper under my breath, and I almost can't believe what I'm seeing.

There is a small crowd of people standing a short distance away from her as if worried that they will startle her into toppling over with any sudden movements.

I measure my paces toward Estelle and try to stay in her visual field so as not to startle her. As I approach, I can see her gently swaying in the cool wind, her skin glistening with a fine sheen of sweat, as if she had just left the dance floor.

However, I notice that she has the strangest expression on her face. It's completely blank, and her eyes seem to be unfocused. I wonder if maybe she has been drugged, but I shake my head, thinking that Estelle would never accept a beverage from a stranger.

"Estelle?" My pulse pounds rapidly in my ears, and I surprise myself at how steady my voice is, like I am standing at a patient's bedside or talking to distraught family members as they watch their loved ones struggling to live.

Estelle stops swaying, her body jerking to a standstill. She turns her head slowly, and I can feel panic start to push itself into my body as my muscles tense—the look on her face is still blank as if she doesn't recognize me.

And then she moves, spinning almost gracefully around so that her entire body is turned in the opposite direction. I feel a fleeting sense of relief, expecting her to step down from the railing, but the feeling vanishes when I see her slide her left heel out and over the railing in the direction of the city street.

No! I shout in my head as I launch forward just as Estelle's whole body leans back and she starts to fall. I crush myself against the railing, my torso hanging over and my feet leaving the ground. It's as if time slows down. My fingers barely graze her hand, and my heart leaps as I close my eyes, not wanting to watch her descent as she crashes to the cold concrete of the street below.

As I close my eyes, I feel a familiar cooling sensation across my skin, which is so different from the cold night air. The feeling seems to come from the very center of my chest and slides down like water to my fingertips. I open my eyes and a gasp escapes my lips as I see something glowing at the tips of my fingers—a silvery glow that forms into a soft web of threads.

Instead of feeling alarmed, though, a comforting lightness spreads throughout my body. The threads flow down and then tighten around Estelle's wrist, and I lean forward just an inch more as her own body lifts toward me. My fingers finally make contact with hers, and I'm able to slide them down and grasp her entire hand.

Just as my fingers clasp around her wrist, time seems to return to a normal speed. Estelle's eyes, which were blank mere seconds before she started her descent, blink and fill with shock and confusion as she makes contact with my own wide and scared eyes.

She lets out a startled cry, "Evie?" She looks down at the ground in recognition of her surroundings.

It is at this moment that I can feel another hand wrap around my own and Estelle's. I glance over and see an amber eye gleam in my periphery.

Simultaneously, Ian and I pull Estelle back up and over the balcony's rail.

When my feet finally make contact with the ground beneath me, Estelle tumbles over next to me, and I lose my balance. Ian lets out a breath, which forms into a cloud escaping his lips. I know my own nose and ears must be red with the bite of cold air.

Estelle scrambles to a sitting position as I sit forward as well, the rush of blood pounding into my ears.

"Wh-what—?" Estelle stutters as she looks over at us and the small crowd that has formed, keeping a respectful distance, whispering in shock. "Evie, what happened?"

Glancing at the crowd, I can't tell if anyone saw what really happened. From the angle that we were hanging over the railing, though, it would've been difficult to see anything. Even Ian would've only seen my hand wrapped around Estelle's, the silver web of threads gone at that time.

Looking back at Estelle, I immediately go into my doctor mode and scan her for any injuries, assessing her startled look and fast breathing. It's strange, but I can already tell that the confusion is genuine and that she's clear of any illicit substances that might have been slipped into a drink.

Already knowing the answer, I ask her anyway, "Do you remember what happened?"

Estelle shakes her head, and she chokes in fright. "No. I just remember being at the front of the stage with you and then...I'm hanging over the railing of a balcony!" She swipes the sheen of sweat from her forehead, her hand shaking.

Ian leans over her, his brow furrowed, and I can tell that he's scanning her for injuries, too. "Do you remember being with anyone? Accepting a drink from someone?"

Frowning, Estelle again shakes her head. "No! I would never accept a drink from a stranger...rules!"

Relief washes over me as Estelle starts regaining her normal mentation, her head clearing. I smile despite the situation. And then I see a flash of green and skin covered in flowering tattoos as someone rushes over to us.

"Are you okay?" Dean is hauling over a large box with a red cross on it. "Do you need assistance?" Dean breaks open the first aid kit and brandishes an enormous roll of gauze and bandages. He's hovering over Estelle, his face screwed up in concern as he lifts her arm as if trying to discover a bloody wound under her armpit.

Estelle indulges him with a pained expression, but he actually takes this for some horrible injury. "Oh god! What's wrong? Do you need me to call nine-one-one?" He whips out a shockingly pink cell phone. Seeing this, a look of affection lights up Estelle's face—obviously she appreciates his taste in cell phone accessories.

I roll my eyes but am reluctant to leave Estelle's side. Although she is now animated and gesturing to Dean, I can't help but remember how blank Estelle's eyes were, standing there on the railing of the balcony—an expression on her face that I've never seen before, even compared to the dazed look she develops when she's daydreaming about Kiran's cooking.

The crowd disperses as Estelle and Dean somehow get on the topic of a local bakery down the street.

"I know! Their strawberry cheesecake bonbons are to die for." Dean waves the roll of gauze enthusiastically.

I realize then that Ian is still standing there, observing the spectacle with a concerned expression. As if reading my mind, he simply shrugs his shoulders as a way to reiterate how strange the last few moments have been, unable to express himself any other way.

I stand up and brush my knees unnecessarily, since they're pretty clean from the newly floored balcony. Looking over at Ian, I can see that he's walked closer to the balcony, his gaze pointed down at the street.

"It looks like the show is over," he observes quietly as I join him and notice that the street below us is slowly flowing with a steady trickle of people reluctantly exiting the club. Some are lingering on the street corner, waiting for their rides or someone still in the club. I can see clouds of vaporized air and cigarette smoke. Some people are jumping up and down and rubbing their bare arms, apparently unprepared and poorly dressed for the bite of a fast-approaching winter.

"I should probably locate my sister now." A cloud of air escapes his mouth, but he doesn't seem to be particularly cold, even though his own arms are bare in a black T-shirt with a pale gray design on the chest, which I immediately recognize as the insignia printed outside on the club's door.

I am curious how he was able to obtain a shirt for a club having its grand opening tonight, but before I can inquire, I see Estelle spring up with Dean's help as she effortlessly regains balance on her three-inch heels. He smiles up and waves at us as he closes his enormous first aid kit and hauls it away.

"Dr. Nakano and Dr. Hashimoto." Estelle grins mischievously as she sees us standing next to each other on the balcony. I immediately take a step sideways to distance myself from Ian, who just shoves his hands in his pockets and smiles boyishly. I glare at Estelle. She just raises her eyebrows in an expectant way as she rocks onto one heel, and her tone of voice changes suddenly, "By the way, thank you for saving me from…well, from apparently trying to throw myself over the balcony."

For the first time, Estelle seems to acknowledge the danger she was in. However, it seems that she is trying hard not to let any fear escape her voice with Ian there.

Ian stops smiling, the concern returning to his face, but before he can ask Estelle anything more about what happened, Estelle turns around. "It is *freezing* by the way!" She practically runs over to the door and disappears behind it, the door closing with a snap.

Again, the feeling of not wanting to leave Estelle by herself comes back, and I move to run after her. I step forward but feel a hand on my arm.

I frown down at it, surprised at the firmness of the grip.

Ian looks at me apologetically and releases my arm. "I just…wanted to make sure that you were okay."

He glances quickly at the door Estelle disappeared behind, and then his amber and blue eyes return to mine, his brow furrowed.

I feel blood rushing up my neck, and I'm suddenly warm in the bite of the cool, still air. The events of the past few minutes flash rapidly in my mind. Remembering the strange silver web, I can't help but feel a strange sensation in my fingers and resist looking at them.

"I think so." I smile cautiously at Ian and make my way to the door. "I'll see you later, Ian."

He smiles as I say his name. I realize that it's the first time I have used it.

CHAPTER TWENTY
DEAREST SISTER

"*CERIN!*"

Startled, Neko whipped around to his sister, who had been sitting tensely on her obsidian throne. The smooth, inky black surface of her seat gleamed in the dim light of the room. Auriel's long fingers gripped the sharp blade-like armrests tightly. Although her hands were remarkably unscathed, Neko found himself surprised that she hadn't sliced through her skin with the amount of pressure she was applying to those armrests.

"*Cerin!*"

Neko couldn't resist wincing slightly. It wasn't so much the volume of Auriel's voice, which wasn't terribly loud at all, but the fact that it seemed to roar through his own head in what could only be described as a thousand whispering voices pounding against his ear drums.

A heavy smoke-like shadow appeared between them, which gradually took the form of his older brother.

Even in the dim light of the room, Neko was surprised to notice that Cerin looked less than his best. His brown hair, normally messy as if constantly being caught up in a windstorm, hung loosely around his ears and forehead. His cheekbones were sharper than usual and his colorless eyes seemed to have a cloudy gray sheen to them.

"You look horrible." Neko did not hesitate to express his observations as astutely as possible.

Cerin had barely inclined his head toward Neko before Auriel stood up from her obsidian throne, the heavy golden strands of her hair flashing and glittering dangerously as they caught the light.

"You called, sister?" Cerin's voice filled the room, which despite the impressively high ceilings did not echo at all. Cerin hated how any sound in this room seemed to sink heavily into a pool of murky water. He felt stifled, the tall walls and expansive rooms doing nothing to allay his feeling of being closed in. Of suffocating.

Auriel seemed barely able to contain her frustration. She took a deep breath, her eyes unblinking as they narrowed.

"You lied to us." When Auriel finally spoke, her voice was just above a whisper.

Cerin matched her unblinking stare, and Neko suddenly felt uncomfortable. He hated sibling arguments, but he somehow knew it wasn't the time to comment on this fact.

As Cerin remained silent, Auriel threw up her hands in a completely uncharacteristic gesture, unable to maintain her normally statuesque and controlled state.

"She is not just a child of Maluna," Auriel's voice was breathless as she squeezed her hands into fists, the skin pulled tight against the knuckles.

Neko raised his eyebrows. "Wait…what? Not just a child of Maluna? Don't you think that's putting it rather lightly? There hasn't been one in the mortal realm for centuries."

"Unless they were being hidden." Auriel's expression remained remarkably blank, even as her chest heaved. Cerin seemed to become even paler, his eyes clouding over more as he lowered his chin in a reluctant gesture of confirmation.

"Father cannot know."

Auriel's eyes widened.

"Okay, what?" Neko, who had meandered to the opposite side of the room, suddenly appeared in between his siblings, a cloud of black and heavy smoke sliding down from his shoulders and sinking into the ground.

Neko turned his face toward his brother and then his sister, before finally resting back on Cerin's.

"What is this about? What do you mean 'father cannot know'?" Neko paused incredulously and threw his hands up into the air, nearly mimicking his sister's gesture just moments before. "He knows everything! So, what if there were a few born of Maluna? What significance are they to father's rule?"

Neko cringed at the thought of hiding anything from their father. The consequences had always been terrible.

"Apparently, he doesn't." Auriel frowned, her gaze fixed on Cerin, as if willing herself to catch any subtle movement or blink of an eye. "Apparently father doesn't know what Cerin has been hiding. It's why he sent us."

"But…" Neko snapped his head back to his sister. "What has he been hiding?"

"Nothing," Cerin finally spoke. His voice was quiet but surprisingly raspy. Neko was shocked again at how ill he looked. "Nothing that father wouldn't have knowledge of already."

Neko rolled his eyes. "You never disappoint with your abilities to be as vague as possible, Cerin. Of course, father would know. He's been around…well, a very long time."

"What are you hiding, Cerin?" Auriel's jaw clenched as she ignored Neko. The room appeared to dim, the windows now letting in a dull gray light.

"Wait, I thought you knew." Neko felt furious with annoyance at this point, but at least he wasn't the only one in the room who didn't know what was going on, besides Cerin.

Cerin closed his eyes, trying to focus on anything other than the heavy quietness in the room while his brother and sister both stared at him expectantly.

"I don't know." He opened his eyes as his sister sank back down into her smooth obsidian throne, hands grasping at the armrests tightly.

"I'm…" Pausing, Cerin's gaze shifted toward the window. Clouds could be seen passing by. He had the sudden desire to brush his fingers through them. "I'm trying to gather more information. It's true that I know more than both of you, but I need more time.

"But father cannot know," Cerin repeated again and took a step toward his sister, who lowered her eyes, wide with disbelief. "When the time comes, I will be the one to tell him everything. Please."

A heavy quietness filled the room. Even Neko could not seem to find any words to respond to his older brother's plea. A plea to keep a secret from their father. A dangerous request, and they all knew it. The words did not need to be spoken, because it was echoing through all their ears.

"You need not beg, brother," Auriel finally said. Her fingers had found their way to a golden strand in her hair, which she was now spinning around her fingers; the gold glittered and flashed as it slid against her skin.

Cerin did not respond, continuing to gaze out the window.

"We will give you time, Cerin," Auriel whispered. "But you will not be alone."

Inclining his head once again, Cerin turned slowly around as a cloud of inky black smoke enveloped his body and he disappeared. The last thing Neko saw before his brother vanished were his gray, cloudy eyes closing slowly.

Neko walked quickly toward his sister, his voice rising just slightly. "That's all? We didn't find out a single thing. Father will be furious."

Auriel leaned back into her throne, continuing to twirl the golden strand around her fingers.

"Cerin will not be alone," she repeated in the same quiet whisper.

"Well, he will definitely not be pleased about that." Neko recalled the message they had received earlier; the little brown bird's wing pinned to a tree trunk before unfurling into a warning with rather concise wording.

"We know more than he thinks."

"The man with the heart attack on the streets and the incident at the club." Neko's voice calmed in a tone of agreement. "It was, indeed, remarkable."

"Yes, it was." Auriel, agreed, narrowing her eyes again.

Neko sat down in the identical throne of obsidian next to his sister. Strands of silver light forming into a glowing web slithered across his thoughts.

CHAPTER TWENTY-ONE
BETWEEN THE PAGES

Estelle is uncharacteristically quiet on the walk back to the apartment, which is at a brisk pace, given the bite of the winter night's chilly air.

We are hardly through the door of the apartment and Estelle has already slipped out of her gladiator heels and tossed them onto the shoe mat. She then grabs a chunky sweater lying on the couch and immediately pulls its hood up and over her head before burrowing down into the cushions behind her, her knees drawn up toward her chest.

Pulling off my own boots and setting them next to Estelle's strappy sandals, I sit down in the recliner across from her and wait. I somehow know that Estelle will speak first without any cues.

She looks up at me and shakes her head. "I just...I can't remember anything."

I stare down at my hands, which are clasped in my lap, and nod. "I didn't think you would." I pause, then look up and catch Estelle's wide eyes. The green in them seems to stand out more than usual. "Your eyes. You didn't seem to be you." I try recalling the feeling I got looking into Estelle's empty stare as she stood on the balcony railing.

"The last thing I remember was Ness singing on stage." Estelle stares at the coffee table as if trying to reimagine the events on its grainy brown surface. "And then you, Evie."

She unfolds her legs from her chest. "Evie. You saved my life."

I try to shrug my shoulders in nonchalance but feel the nervousness in my body tense up. I can't help but wonder if Estelle saw the web of silver light at all—the tendrils that wrapped themselves around her hand and practically lifted her toward me.

However, Estelle doesn't mention this at all. She continues to shake her head in gratefulness. "Thank you, Evie."

I let out a breath of relief. She would have mentioned any other strange details of her experience at this point. The tension slowly starts to leave my body, and I allow myself to lean back into the soft recliner.

"Well, Ian definitely lent a much-needed hand there." I grin, and Estelle grimaces painfully at what I think is a brilliant pun.

The grimace is then immediately replaced by her characteristic smile of mischievousness. "So…'Ian' is it?"

My grin is immediately replaced by a frown. "Yes. Just Ian. Or Dr. Nakano," I find myself sputtering out rather ineloquently. "Er…ran into him at work. Like…literally."

Estelle just continues to smile. I then raise my eyebrows in disbelief. "That's why you ran out on us on the balcony. You were trying to get me alone with him!" I huff and throw up my hands. "What about not leaving your friend alone in a club with a stranger?"

"Oh, whatever. You knew him from work. He was a coworker!"

"Wait, how did you know that?"

"I ran into him at the club," Estelle suddenly recalls, but this time her tone sounds a little confused. "I'm not sure at what point, though. I think it was when we got separated in the crowd. He ended up next to me at some point and recognized me, so I formally introduced myself." She nods as if the details are now forming into a complete picture. "He…sort of casually inquired if you were with me." Estelle's smile returns.

I stand up from the recliner and look pointedly for my messenger bag, which I had actually been leaning up against in the recliner. I think longingly of my soft bed and try to distract myself from thinking of Ian's uneven smirk, interesting eyes, and curious accent.

"I need a shower," I say suddenly, and pivot toward the bathroom.

I hear a loud, dramatic sigh coming from Estelle.

"Don't try to drown yourself in denial in there," she calls out after me. "I need some of that hot water, too."

Freshly showered and already pulling out a book from my messenger bag, I surprisingly don't feel very tired as I enter my bedroom and turn on the light.

I freeze. I vaguely hear a door close and the shower start in the background as Estelle replaces me in the bathroom.

Atop my soft white bedspread, its black rippled cover

standing out starkly, is the strange sketchbook. I can't help but glance back at the bookshelf, but then I remember that it actually should have been in my messenger bag. My eyes flit around the room futilely, my thoughts scattered into confusion—this book somehow got out of my messenger bag and is now lying atop my bedspread as if waiting for me.

Closing the door behind me and setting my small paperback book aside, I stand at the foot of my bed and pick the black book up. Honestly, I haven't looked through it except for those two times. For some odd reason, I've taken to carrying it with me to work, hidden between my other books and notes of my messenger bag.

I sit on the bed, and with determination, I steel myself to simply flip through every page of this mysterious book.

When I finally open the book, I'm surprised that the drawings appear scattered, as if the person who created the drawings had simply opened the book haphazardly to any page that was blank. The black, gray, and white style of charcoal media is consistent throughout, with silver dripping across the pages either messily or in clean, sweeping lines.

I stop at one particular drawing. For some reason. it seems to pull at my attention.

It's of the shadowy figure, its long, thin body hunched over a pool of water. Its long claw-like fingers are reaching toward the smooth, glassy surface. Rather than looking at a reflection of itself in the water, there is something looking up at it. Floating just under the water's surface is the silver-haired figure, tendrils of silver wrapping and flowing around her. The strands almost appear to be moving, as if swirling in the pool of water. I strain to make out the features of their faces, but they are clouded over by shadowy strokes of black smudges. It almost seems too purposeful, as if the person drawing it hid their faces as a frustrated afterthought.

My heart grips tightly, and a strange feeling of understanding fills my chest. It seems impossible, but I know that the individual who created these drawings did so out of frustration, anger, and…something else. Longing?

I close my eyes tightly and will myself to remember my own frantic drawings as a child. The helplessness that I felt to validate what seemed impossible, to understand through the strokes of a pen, paint, or whatever I could manage to get my hands on. I remember the feeling of reprieve and then fear when I realized that it was futile. That no one could understand.

I was alone.

I open my eyes and stare back down at the drawing. I slide my fingers over the silver tendrils of hair. The very recent memory of a dying elderly woman comes back to me, the faintest reflection of silver glinting in her glazed eyes as she closes them for the last time.

Suddenly I see something flickering at the edge of the book. I gasp as I realize that it's a small wing, pressed down between the pages of the book. I flip to the page quickly, and I can see that the wing belongs to a small butterfly lying at this page's very edge. Its wings are black, and it is barely moving.

I can't understand how it got there—how it had not been completely smashed or how it survived this long in the pages of a book.

I stare at the butterfly and slowly reach out a single finger to touch its delicate wing. I imagine snow melting against the heat of my skin, but instead I know my touch will be cool. I gently maneuver the small butterfly onto the tip of my finger, its wings barely moving anymore. I stand up from my bed, the black book gently sliding out of my lap and onto the soft fabric of my blanket.

I open my bedroom window and the cold night air bites at my skin. I resist the urge to immediately close it, but instead, I lift my finger. The butterfly's wings have gone still.

A cool sensation fills my body and I can feel it traveling from my chest and down into my fingertips.

The butterfly's wings move and start to flutter. It lifts its tiny body from my finger, and before I can blink an eye, it flies away, moving its wings without any resistance into the cool night air.

CHAPTER TWENTY-TWO
THE TOWER IN THE MOUNTAINS

CERIN GAZED OUT of the window. Lately, he found himself doing this more and more. This time, though, his body was poised as if waiting for something.

"Oh, Cerin."

A soft, musical voice filled his ears, and he reluctantly tore his gaze from the window. He hardly noticed his reflection in the window's dark glass, but he caught a glimpse of his opaque, sick-looking eyes staring back out at him.

"So much time in the mortal world…it has not suited you." The musical voice belonged to a tall and beautiful woman. Her eyes were a clear crystalline color, her hair pure white, and her skin the color of glowing black pearls. She was clothed in gold silk, which flowed around her in a light that was bright and luminous. Cerin felt a warmth, not so much on his skin, which was freezing cold, but in his chest, as if the sun were peering behind cloudy skies and it somehow found its way into his heart.

It was almost painful.

"And yet, it suits you. It has always suited you, mother."

Her glittering eyes filled with sadness, and tears appeared at their very corners.

"My child." She reached out her slender hand and touched his face. "You're causing yourself so much suffering. I have not seen you smile in so long."

Cerin leaned his cheek into his mother's hand, willing her warmth to somehow embed itself into his freezing cold skin. He then lifted it away, gently and sadly. His mother's hand fell to her side.

"Mother…" Cerin walked over to a towering bookcase. "I think…I think something has happened that could have a massive impact on our world. On the Obsidian Throne."

His mother nodded without hesitation. "Yes, Cerin." She walked over to stand by him at the bookcase. Reaching out, she brushed her fingers across the bindings of ancient books, the spines of some worn and fragile, and some others encased in hard metal bindings.

"Your father suspects, but he is unable to comprehend anything beyond his own chair, his walls of obsidian and burning hellfire."

Cerin was amazed at how his mother's voice was so calm, devoid of bitterness. In fact, the words seemed to come out forced, with a sadness that caught at her throat.

She then folded her hands into the depths of her dress and motioned for Cerin to follow her. The room was small, but above them spiraled winding staircases that appeared endless, reaching to an incomprehensible height. Distracted for just a moment, Cerin couldn't help but be overwhelmed by the limitlessness of this building that his mother lived in, and yet, it still enclosed them tightly.

"This belonged to Kana Akihira." His mother's hands rested upon a heavy and yet very small book, its size perfect for being packed and carried away easily. Its cover and binding were of hammered metal, and the ripples in its surface caught the light in such a way that made it both beautiful and intimidating at the same time. "She was the greatest general in the war. She was also my greatest friend."

His mother let the last words trail away in a soft note of reverence and fondness.

Cerin looked down at the book, his focus settling on its surface, his fingers replacing her own.

His mother always found herself aching at the soft and kind tone of her son's voice as she gazed at him. She thought longingly of her other children, how they were so easily taken away by shadows and unfeeling, icy indifference.

But for some reason, Cerin was always different. He had always found his way back to her, no matter the difficulty, and he had suffered greatly for it.

"I want you to have it."

Cerin looked at her, his eyes tired as he took his hand away from the book. "I can't. It is dear to you."

"Yes, it is. Which is why I want you to have it." His mother picked up the book that she had held in her hands so many times over so many years. "Please. You…will be able to learn from it. Many things."

Cerin hesitated before reaching for the book, and it transferred to him as a heavy and comfortable weight in his hands. Before he could utter the words to thank his mother, his eyes snapped toward the window, and he saw it.

It was a small, black, and flitting thing. It fluttered against the window's glass frantically. His mother simply watched as her son walked over to the window—it had no way of opening at all, which was the case for all the windows in this tower-like building. But he still reached out a finger to touch the glass, and as if by some magnetic force, the flitting object appeared on the opposite side of the glass to land on his fingertip. That small spot on the window's surface rippled like water as Cerin pulled his hand away.

On his fingertip was a small black butterfly.

His mother couldn't help but pull herself toward him as he stared at the small, delicate butterfly; his look of childlike amazement filled her heart. She felt a smile begin to warm the corners of her mouth, but then the butterfly stopped moving. The smile slipped away; she could hardly take in the desolate look on her son's face.

Devastated, Cerin watched as the butterfly ceased to move its wings. He winced as frigid cold engulfed his hand, and his eyes caught his mother's, clear and glittering. As she watched, she could see Cerin's cloudy gray eyes become less opaque, now colorless, like brushing fog from a glass of water. Even the color of his skin seemed to brighten slightly.

And yet, when he looked down at the butterfly, it lay dead and still. He transferred it to the palm of his hand and closed his eyes tightly. A small blue flame appeared from his skin and rolled over the small insect. It then vanished into a small tendril of flickering ash.

Cerin turned from his mother, barely feeling the weight of her hand resting on his shoulder. He stepped away from her and toward the window. Then he found himself on the other side of the window, looking at his mother behind golden bars that glowed in incredible brilliance. It was terrible and mesmerizing at the same time.

Her hand was still outstretched where his shoulder had been. She lowered it slowly and nodded at her son. Black smoke started to wrap around him, and he clutched the silver metal-covered book tightly in his hands.

He imagined his mother standing on the other side of those bars where she was finally free. The last image he saw as he was carried away was his mother's towering prison spiraling up endlessly into the sky.

CHAPTER TWENTY-THREE
A COMPOSITION OF TRUTH

JUNE REACHED FOR her nose and felt slightly panicked when she realized that the familiar plastic nose prongs that carried her oxygen was missing. Her heart skipped a beat, but she quickly realized that it wasn't because of lack of oxygen. She took a deep breath through her nose and felt her heartbeat slow down comfortably. She felt like crying for what had to be the thousandth time. Just a few days ago, she had been dying in a hospital bed, and now…now she wasn't.

She looked around her and noticed that another girl had entered the room. She was young and small. Her head was covered in a sparkly knitted hat. Her parents followed close behind, and after noticing June sitting across the room, they smiled at her.

"Sylvia, we'll be in the cafeteria while you're meeting with Dr. Mendez." Her father looked down at her, and the expression of happiness was identical to that of his wife standing next to him.

"Okay, I'll come find you when Dr. Mendez is done,"

Sylvia said with a serious tone of voice, showing a maturity that impressed June for someone so young. June herself had just turned sixteen this month, and she somehow felt that she would easily be able to have a conversation with this young girl even though she had not spoken a word to her yet.

Sylvia waved to her parents, and as they left the room, she carefully removed the knitted cap from her head, which had the beginnings of an even coat of short curls growing close to her skull.

"Hi." Sylvia walked over to June and smiled. June couldn't help but find her smile infectious. Sylvia held out her small hand. June took it and was met with a nice, firm handshake. "My name is Sylvia Plait."

"Hello, Sylvia Plait," June responded. "My name is June Reese."

"Hi, June." Sylvia sat in a chair next to her, and just as she settled down, another person walked into the room. This time a young boy strolled in as his parents peeked inside. They gave Sylvia and June a smile. His dad patted him between the shoulders and his mother kissed him on the cheek

"See you soon," he said, holding a glossy book with the illustrated cover of a green dragon on it.

He turned to Sylvia and June, his expression and body language shy. Sylvia immediately stood up and pointed to an empty chair next to June.

"You should take that chair." Sylvia's tone was instructive and helpful as she held out her small hand the same way she had done for June. "Also, hi! My name is Sylvia Plait."

The young boy looked taken aback by Sylvia's

friendliness but shifted the book into his other hand to take hers. "My name is Ivan Kovalchuk."

"This is June Reese," Sylvia promptly introduced June, who nodded her head indulgently. Ivan responded with a shy smile and sat down on June's other side.

It was at this moment that Dr. Mendez stepped into the room. He was not wearing his usual white coat. Instead, he wore a checkered blue dress shirt and gray slacks, his sharp glasses perched on the bridge of his nose. He stood in front of them across the room and peered over at them from the frames of his glasses, his thick eyebrows raised slightly.

"Thank you for joining us today," he said, his firm and deep voice surprisingly warm—something that always comforted his patients and families, who were usually intimidated at first by his serious and unsmiling demeanor. He held out his hand, like Sylvia had earlier, and shook each of their hands individually.

"No studies today." Dr. Mendez pulled up a chair so he was sitting across from them. By "studies" he was referring to blood tests or other types of medical exams that he had discussed with each of them individually while with their parents. "I just wanted you three to meet each other. Your parents already told you what this is about, so I don't want to bore you with all those details." The corner of his mouth twitched slightly in a grin. June, Sylvia, and Ivan smiled back appreciatively. "All three of you have responded to your treatments in a way that...well, although was hoped for, was—miraculous. We need to carry out more studies to understand how we can help more young people like you."

All three of them nod in unison. Although young, they all had the lingering and haunted look of the dying.

"I think getting to know each other will be a good thing since you will be running into each other often. You'll be seeing me and my partner, Dr. Hashi—"

"Evie?" Sylvia slid to the front of her seat excitedly, her toes barely brushing the floor.

"Yes. Evie." Dr. Mendez raised his eyebrows and nodded at Sylvia. His look was affectionate and warm—June imagined he was a wonderful father. She found herself thinking about these things more often when she was around people. She wondered if their interactions with the people they loved were meaningful. June remembered her father being by her side all the time throughout her treatments and couldn't imagine not having him there. Every moment she gasped for breath, she only wished for more time with the people she loved.

"I'll be leaving you three to get to know each other. I'll be back in forty-five minutes with some materials for you to take home. It's kind of like homework, but not graded." Dr. Mendez raised up his hands in defense, and they all laughed a little nervously, curious about what the homework-like materials would be.

He then stood up, dipped his head, and gave them a small wink before leaving the room.

They all looked at each other, not exactly sure how to begin.

Sylvia stood up and looked at the two of them, now suddenly shy. She walked over to her coat, which she had hung carefully by the door. Standing on the tips of her toes, she pulled out a slim tube of paper from one of the inner pockets. Walking back over to them, she unrolled the paper, which revealed a slender instrument.

"When I was getting my treatments and staying at the hospital, I started to write music." Sylvia eagerly unrolled the piece of paper and although clumsily drawn, there were indeed musical notes scrolling across it.

June leaned in and was immediately impressed that Sylvia was able to do this at such a young age, but then she remembered learning that Mozart had only been five years old when he started to compose music. June remembered trying to learn how to play the oboe when she was twelve years old—it ended up being a disaster. Her dad even admitted, very gently, that the musical talent may have skipped a generation. (Her grandparents played a variety of instruments.) Although she had accepted that she was not musically inclined, she was hoping and eager to start playing softball again.

"I actually wanted a drum set so that I can start a rock band, but my parents said that I should 'explore my options' first and 'ease myself into the musical art form.'" Sylvia said these words with an indulgent tone, but then proudly displayed her flute-like instrument. "They gave me this. It's called a shinobue flute, and it's made of—"

"Bamboo," Ivan seemed startled to hear himself speak and immediately displayed an apologetic look for interrupting her. "One of the main characters in the book series I'm reading plays it." Ivan's face began to flush and June could tell that he was resisting the urge to relate more information about the book that he was reading. Sylvia nodded in confirmation, but her young eyes were bright with eagerness. Her eyes flitted back and forth between the two of them. "Would you mind if I played something?"

Immediately June nodded and saw that Ivan did, too. He even set the book down on the floor behind his chair.

Sylvia grinned nervously and after a brief pause started to play a simple and pretty melody on her flute; her fingers slowly lifting up and down. The hallowed sounds of the bamboo were hard to describe. June imagined that this was what the sound of wind and water would be if it were made of music.

Ivan seemed entranced, though June and Sylvia were too occupied to notice the strange expression on his face. He felt his heartbeat slow down in a steady rhythm, like when he was catching his breath after a strenuous lacrosse practice or after sliding the bow gently over his violin strings.

But he felt something else. It felt like something that had been hiding just out of sight in the shadows, pulling gently at his memories. He stared at the very end of Sylvia's shinobue flute, and for some reason, he remembered a sensation of cool water washing over him and the soft movement of silvery hair that glimmered like light reflecting off water.

Ivan felt his eyes widen and his heart beat faster. He couldn't quite explain it, but he knew that he had somehow remembered something that was important.

Just as Ivan was beginning to explore his brain for more details, Sylvia removed the flute from her lips—the last note pierced his eardrums in a hollow, low note.

It was at this moment that Dr. Mendez walked into the room, as if he had been waiting for Sylvia to finish playing. They all looked at each other guiltily, not sure if they had used the time the way they were supposed to, but Dr.

Mendez hardly seemed too concerned and didn't ask them any questions.

Instead, he handed them each one of three slim navy-colored moleskin journals. Each was the size that could easily fit in a jacket pocket.

"This is your homework," Dr. Mendez explained in his typical serious voice. "Treat it like an activity log. Maybe make a single entry in the morning when you wake up and one when you're about to fall asleep. Record any strange feelings or interesting thoughts that you might have. We're curious to see if the treatments have any side-effects, which may not be apparent immediately."

Each of them nodded. Sylvia seemed absolutely delighted at her little journal. Dr. Mendez shook their hands and they all got ready to meet their parents in the cafeteria, which Sylvia was eager to lead them to.

As Ivan clutched the book in his hand a little more tightly than he might have meant to, he glanced at Sylvia's flute, which she had rolled back into her paper of music notes. He couldn't help but think that he had forgotten something.

CHAPTER TWENTY-FOUR
A MOMENT CAPTURED

CERIN HELD THE book in his two hands, admiring its weight and the smoothness of the metal binding and cover. He slid his pale fingers across the hammered metal surface, and it reminded him of rolling ocean waves.

A luminous glow caught what little light surrounded him and reflected off his colorless eyes. He carefully opened the cover of the book, where a small square of parchment pressed into the book's first few pages slid down into his open hand. The letters on the note scrolled out into a beautiful inky script that looked almost like it was brushed onto the parchment. The message was short and addressed to his mother:

To Ayesha, my closest friend,

Please forgive the brevity of this letter. Time is short and this battle approaches. Although my body is prepared, my spirit is weary, and my heart unsure. I deliver this small journal to you for safekeeping. It is precious to me, for in its pages are the history of my family, and among these pages lay many secrets. I hope to return to it someday. I entrust it to you in the meantime, my greatest friend.

May the light guide you, by the moon and by the sun, always, Kana

Cerin stared at the script that had been written so very long ago and could imagine tears trailing down from his mother's eyes as she read it. This battle was a long and old one, and Cerin already knew the outcome of the war.

Kana did not return, and soon after, his mother gave birth to him.

Pressing the fragile piece of parchment back into the pages, Cerin began to read, his eyes skimming over letters that formed an unfamiliar language. His brow furrowed slightly, and he felt his vision blur and refocus as if looking through a foggy telescope. Gradually he could see the letters forming into words that he could recognize in his mind. It was as if he were swiping away thick layers of dust from his memory.

The pages were filled with perfect script, some of which were recollections of battles and strategies. Cerin struggled to remember the names of individuals and places that were prominent in this little book, but historical records like this had been destroyed many millennia ago. He could barely recall any stories of this war. Even the name Kana Akihira seemed obscure, hardly an echo that whispered into his ears of something that was meant to be forgotten.

Cerin felt the familiar sense of hopelessness that seemed to cloud his every thought; a heaviness filled his chest, and he

clutched the book in his hands tightly. He closed his eyes and the fleeting image of a small butterfly fluttered across his thoughts.

When he opened his eyes, he was staring at the image of a crescent, which covered most of the page. The crescent was filled with a flowing design of silver filigree, painted with what looked like ink that dripped off and slid down to form a black pool beneath it. Under this design was a brief inscription:

And she was born under the darkness of the moon's shadow.

Cerin brushed a finger over the symbol, and he felt something sharp slide across his finger tip as if a needle-thin blade had slid against it. When he brought his finger to his eyes, he saw a fine drop of silvery blood blossom from where it touched the symbol on the paper.

The drop of silver slid off his fingertip. Cerin stared as it fell to the very corner of the page beneath it and began to turn black before his eyes.

The corners of his mouth lifted into a smile.

It's a crisp morning on a day that I happen to have off from work. After spending a couple of hours curled up in bed reading about the fascinating histories of various chicken breeds, I suddenly become restless.

After setting aside my book and neatly folding the cover of my comforter back, I slide a small box out from under my bed. Inside is a camera that belonged to my grandfather. The weight of the camera sits comfortably in my hands.

Without a second thought, I'm getting dressed and heading out of my bedroom. I can hear Estelle's snores faintly behind her door. Even when we work the same days, we always end up leaving for the hospital at different times. Estelle is not a morning person. She insists that five minutes is an adequate amount of time to get ready for work. This also allows her to get her daily cardio in at the same time, since she's usually running to work the moment she rolls out of bed.

When I push the door open to our apartment, the sudden burst of cool morning air almost takes my breath away. After adjusting the camera strap over my shoulder and heaving my messenger bag over the other one simultaneously, I shove my hands back into the depths of my winter coat just as the cold air starts to nip at my bare skin.

Closing the door behind me, I then make my way to the local park.

A cloud of vaporized air escapes my lips. I am startled by how quickly the cold season has rushed in.

Once I reach the city park, I can feel the crunch of frosted dew beneath my shoes as I make my trek. The park is quiet except for the morning trail runners and dog walkers moving at a brisker pace than usual in the cool air.

I pause at a small clearing away from the main trail of the park. There is a bench nestled in the copse of trees, which could easily be missed if you weren't looking for it. I set my messenger bag down on this bench before sitting down myself. I then busy myself with my camera, twisting lenses off and on, refocusing them, and then snapping random pictures to test the lighting of the crisp morning.

A brown bird lands in front of me just as I am about to put the camera to my eye again. Chirping at me for a possible treat that I'm sure it is hoping for, I snap a few pictures of it looking at me curiously. It seems entertained by the click-ing of the camera and flies to various low-hanging branches around the clearing, staying at a close distance. I feel a grin spread across my face, and just as I am about to snap the last picture of my feathery companion, I hear a rustle as someone enters the clearing.

The crunch of feet on frosty grass seems a little louder in the still air of the clearing. A figure emerges from the trees just as the shutter snaps closed.

I lower the camera.

"Clark?"

Clark looks up at me, surprise on his face. His eyes had been fixed on the ground, his hands hanging loosely at his sides. I can't help but notice that he's wearing a rather thin and worn-looking racer jacket, and nothing but a white T-shirt under it. However, he hardly looks cold, whereas I am already feeling the tips of my fingers going numb.

"Oh, uh, Evie. I-I wasn't expecting…" He trails off a lit-tle awkwardly as he shoves his hands into the pockets of his jacket and glances around the clearing. "I'm sorry, did I inter-rupt anything?"

I set my camera down on my lap and shake my head. "Nope. Just photographing some friendly, local city wildlife. Um, you wouldn't happen to have a pocket full of bread-crumbs, would you?"

Clark pulls his hands from his pockets in an exaggerated look of disappointment. "My supply of bread crumbs has been low lately."

Reaching for my messenger bag, I start to stand up. "Do you need the space?"

"No, not at all," Clark answers quickly. "I was on my way

to meet someone actually, but they canceled on me. I usually like to stop by here when I walk through the park though."

His words trail off again. It is at this moment that I notice dark shadows under his eyes, and his cheekbones seem a bit sharper compared to the last time I had seen him, which had been just a day or two ago. I wonder if he has been sick, which is likely given the fact that we are just at the beginning stages of flu season (the hospital likes to remind us about this at least every other hour of the day).

I am about to voice this question and concern for his health, when he says, "It looks like rain."

He is peering up where the peaks of the trees form a small opening. Gray clouds pass by, throwing a shadow across the clearing. A small and very cold drop of rain splashes right into my eye. I blink rapidly as the raindrop slides down my cheek.

I catch Clark's eye, but he breaks away just as rain starts to splash down on his own face. He doesn't bother to wipe it away though; instead he walks a little closer to the bench that I'm sitting on, where there are more tree branches overhead to shield him from the steady drizzle.

It is at this moment that the little brown bird begins to chirp a little more enthusiastically on a low-hanging branch. I am surprised by how much louder the chirping seems, but then I realize it is because more birds have joined the first one. At least a dozen birds are now scattered throughout the small clearing, which seems a little strange. I've always felt that I had to search for wildlife within the city limits, even within the park itself.

Clark notices this as well. "Maybe they're trying to stay dry because of an impending downpour?"

I smirk a bit. "There's always an impending rain-related event in the Pacific Northwest."

A big smile lifts the corners of Clark's mouth, and he nods in agreement. He then pauses as something catches his eyes behind me. I follow his gaze as he walks closer to the bench and kneels down. He gently pushes aside the leaves of a small bush and pulls something out.

His eyes scan the object, which is some sort of small book covered in what looks like silver metal.

"Did you drop this?" He turns it over in his hands, brushing off a small amount of dirt that easily slides off its surface. He then stands up and holds it out to me.

I immediately shake my head, a little more vigorously than intended. "I have more than enough books in my life," I try to joke as I glance down at my messenger bag, but my mind goes straight to the strange black book that I have taken to carrying with me now, its slim velvety binding always catches my eye every time I open my bag.

I can't help but notice the glinting silver metal flashing in the dim light of the clearing even as the clouds rolling overhead cast a shadow across us.

I reach out for the book, and Clark transfers it to my hand. The book is small but surprisingly heavy. The metal ripples in soft waves across the surface. I frown, as it reminds me of the strange rippling surface of the black book with all the drawings in it.

"Are you sure its not yours?" Clark tilts his head as he sits down on the bench next to me. A drop of rain lands on the cover of the metal, and rather than sliding down its smooth surface, the water rests there as if frozen. A few more drops of rain form nearly perfect little spheres like the first one.

"Evie?"

Startled and mesmerized by the strange behavior of the beading raindrops, and remembering that Clark is with me, I quickly run my hand across the cover of the book as if drying it off, and the beads of rain water wipe away cleanly. I wonder if Clark noticed, but when I look at him, I realize that he isn't looking at the book at all, but at me. He has a concerned look, his brow furrowed slightly.

"Are you okay?"

I nod and hand the book back to him. "This looks valuable. I wonder who lost it."

Clark opens the book and squints his eyes. "It's written in a different language."

Curious, I lean over and unexpectedly feel my eyes widen. The language is different, but for some reason, it looks familiar. Other than some Japanese phrases that my grandfather relayed to Kiran and myself growing up, I don't speak any other language besides English, so I can't explain how I recognize the words written across this book's pages.

Noticing my expression, Clark raises the book closer to me. "You can read this?"

Without saying anything, I mechanically reach for the book again, feeling its weight rest comfortably into my hands. My eyes skim quickly over the page, and I find myself nodding without meaning to.

"It's a story about some…battle over a crown made of black rock… or glass. Obsidian." I am shocked to find myself saying these words out loud. The comprehension of this language feels like a jolt to the neurons already firing frantically in my brain.

I tear my eyes from the pages of the book and see Clark's

eyes lock on mine. "I don't understand. I've never seen this language before."

Clark looks down at the book and then back at me. "Are you sure? You seem to be able to read it just fine." He smiles but then stops when he sees the look on my face.

I squeeze my eyes shut and try to remember ever seeing this book or this language before, but nothing comes up. My mind is literally flashing with images of the letters that somehow appeared out of nowhere in my brain. The letters are forming themselves into ideas that I can't seem to stop. It's as if it has always been there, like a memory that has been long forgotten.

I snap the book shut, overwhelmed. The feeling is almost as great as seeing Estelle hanging from a web of silver threads somehow coming from my own hands.

"I need to go," I say suddenly and stand up. The book slides from my hands and lands at my feet.

Startled and confused, Clark stands up with me and at the same time reaches for the book. "Are you sure you're okay?" He makes to hand me the book again, but I avoid looking at it.

"Yes. I'll see you at work, Clark." I swing my messenger bag across my shoulder. The rain is suddenly coming down in a steady shower, and the birds continue to chirp around us. I can't help but feel that their chirps sound urgent. The rush of blood pounds in my ears, and I feel just a little lightheaded.

Before Clark can say anything else, I hurry out of the clearing, and as I glance back just once, I can see the cover of the silver book in his hands, shining in the rain.

CHAPTER TWENTY-FIVE

TWO TOO MANY BOOKS

MY EYES CATCH the glittering light scattering down from the surface of the water, which is such a clear color that I feel like I'm looking through a glass that has just been swept clean. I'm surrounded by water, but I'm suspended in it without needing to tread at all. My arms float at my sides and I feel light; a warmth is wrapped around me like I'm curled into a soft blanket.

I can see my hair float up around me, waving like seaweed in the still water. It shines in a dazzling silver color, but rather than the light reflecting off it, the glow seems to come from the strands of hair themselves.

A shadow appears above me. For some reason, it fills my chest with a heaviness and a feeling that I can't explain. I rise slightly as I float closer to the surface. At the same time, the shadow pauses as if hesitating, but then it gradually descends closer.

And then I see it. A large, black, claw-like hand breaks the surface of the water above me. It's covered in inky black smoke, which falls away and sinks down like heavy stones. The tips of the claws are a beautiful silver, which reminds me of my own hair.

I reach my hand upward toward this black, clawed hand, dripping with heavy black smoke. My fingers graze the pointed claws just barely, and I feel it flinch as if wanting to pull away. I extend my hand further and feel the claws tense, gripping my fingers gradually, hesitatingly.

I gasp. A bitter coldness fills my chest and rises up into my mouth, and I realize that water is filling my lungs. Air bubbles blow out of my mouth as I cry out.

The clawed hand encircles my own firmly as I rise further up toward the surface of the water. But it's at this very moment that I feel something jerk at my ankles. I don't even look down because I know already that it's a golden chain pulling itself taut. I cry out again, but only more bubbles appear before my face.

The clawed hand then releases mine, pulling its fingers away from me. I feel my hand still reaching upward as my lungs somehow empty of water and I can breathe normally again. The water surrounding me returns to a crystalline stillness.

I see the shadow move above me. It stops abruptly, and something drops into the water off to my side. I slowly float over to it, my arms already outstretched. I catch it as it descends.

It's a slender black book filled with drawings.

I open my eyes and sit up straight in bed. I can feel something wet on my cheeks, and brushing it away with my hands, I realize that they're tears.

A hard edge presses against my side, and I realize that it's the black book. I must have fallen asleep with it next to me. I rest a hand on its now-familiar surface. The rippling texture of the book is comforting, and I am reminded of the water gently rolling above me in the dream.

I close my eyes and try to remember more details—I'm surprised because I don't have to try very hard. I sigh and open my eyes again just as the digital numbers of the clock at my bedside change to 4:59. I swing my legs out of bed and switch the alarm off before it can screech at me to wake up. I grab the black book and gently slide it into my messenger bag, which is always at the foot of my nightstand.

Standing up and raising my arms above me in a gentle stretch, I head out of my bedroom.

Just as I'm about to turn into the bathroom, I hear a gentle knock at the front door. I pause, thinking that this is a very odd and early time in the morning to be receiving visitors (or even a delivery of some sort). It's sure to still be dark outside.

I walk over to the front door and crack it open just a bit.

"Clark?"

Clark is wearing his dark blue hospital scrubs with a puffy winter coat over them. I can't help but be a little relieved that he's wearing something more substantial than the racer jacket from the day before.

Clark ducks his head a bit sheepishly, clouds of air appearing from his lips. "Sorry, Evie. I just felt bad about yesterday. You looked a little shaken up and I just…well…"

I swing the door open, surprised. I guess I did look a bit shell-shocked when leaving the clearing. Actually, thinking back on it, I'm pretty sure I looked like someone trying to run away from a fiery explosion.

"Yeah, I'm sorry about that, Clark." I rub my arms as I feel the sharp air bite at my skin. "I'm not sure why I reacted that way." I try to brush off my odd behavior, but then realizing that I am starting to shiver and Clark is still standing out in the cold, I grab his arm and pull him inside, throwing the door shut.

Clark stumbles slightly in the doorway as I explain to him that he shouldn't be standing out in the cold like that. "It's flu season." I stop short of asking him if he has been well. He still looks like someone who needs about sixteen hours of sleep.

I gesture for him to take a seat. I then fly into the kitchen and within a few minutes, I'm out of the kitchen and passing Clark a large mug of steaming hot chocolate into his hands.

Before Clark can respond, I hear a loud yawn as Estelle enters the living room, having obviously just rolled out of bed. I feel my eyes widen with disbelief when I see her. On the one day that she decides to be a morning person, I have a boy sitting in our living room at a questionable hour of said morning.

"I thought I smelled hot chocolate." She pauses mid-yawn as her eyes flit between me and Clark. "Hm?" She raises her eyebrows, and before a large grin can make its appearance on her face, I interrupt before she can get any amorous ideas of why Clark is present in our living room so early in the morning.

"Clark was on his way to the hospital and realized that he had one of my books that he wanted to drop off."

I reach my hand out. Clark, immediately understanding, starts rummaging through his backpack and pulls out the small silver book, which he dutifully drops into my hand.

"Well, that must be some important book." Estelle swings her hips to one side as her hands rest on them and smirks as she jaunts over to the kitchen.

"Of course," I say to her defensively. "It's a *book*!"

I then glance at Clark. "One minute."

I rush back to my bedroom, toss the small book onto my bed, change clothes, grab my messenger bag, and then after hurriedly brushing my teeth and splashing cold water on my face, I'm about to go back to the living room when I stop abruptly in the hallway.

I walk back into my bedroom and stare down at the metal-covered book lying nestled in my blankets. I hardly realize that I'm about to leave my bed unmade and reach for the silver book instead.

Blinking once and hardly thinking another second, I shove it down into my messenger bag. I have the vaguest thought that it might be getting a little crowded in there.

Clark is in mid-sip of his hot chocolate when I clamp my hand down on his arm and rush him out the door. Estelle is rummaging in the kitchen. Grimacing at all the funny ideas she might be getting about "a boy" appearing in our living room, I lock the front door behind us. I hardly notice that Clark is still holding his steaming mug of hot chocolate.

He swings his backpack over his shoulders and follows me as I rush down the stairs and onto the Seattle streets, which are lit faintly with orange lights. The sky is still dark above us, and the winter air is sharp and crisp as it hits me in full force. I pause for Clark to catch up with me.

"Sorry." I steady my stride and glance over at Clark, who is casually sipping his hot chocolate. "Estelle has some notion that you might be a sexy vampire from one of her romantic sitcoms."

Clark sputters into his mug, his face turning a little pink. "A—a what?"

"Exactly."

I watch as Clark mechanically raises his mug-free hand and touches one of his canines in his mouth. I raise my eyebrows at him. Catching my expression, he immediately lowers his arm.

"Ahh…just checking." His cheeks look just a little pinker as he says this, but he gives me his characteristic sheepish grin and looks away quickly.

I sigh and think back to Estelle, who will definitely be wanting some type of explanation of my nonexistent love-life. I glance up at Clark, still drinking from his mug of hot chocolate, and for some strange reason I notice the shape of his ears, which are a little bit on the larger side and just a little tapered at the top. His brown hair, which is usually messy, brushes the tips.

"…and I think he's been having better days lately. What do you think?"

Clark looks at me, and I look back at him in alarm, just now realizing that the entire time I was staring at his ears, he was talking to me.

I feel the strap of my messenger bag slide down my shoulder, and I scramble to hoist it back to a comfortable position. "Er…I'm sorry, Clark. Can you repeat that?"

Nodding indulgently and with a slight look of amusement in his eyes, he begins again, "Dr. Mendez. I feel that he has been having better days lately. Happier. I'm not sure why. It's hard to tell with him sometimes."

"Hm, he has been a little more expressive lately." I think back and realize that our meetings have been on the lighter side. "He tends to use more than one- or two-word phrases to address me nowadays, at least." It still amazes me that Dr. Mendez was the one to offer me my first job fresh out of school. He has been described as nothing less than the bane of my fellow colleagues' medical school experience. I still remember all the shocked expressions on their faces when I told them that he personally offered *me* a job.

"It might be the treatments. He seems frustrated that other doctors are not getting the same results, but at the same time, he's happy that there has been any positive results at all."

I feel myself nod distractedly and look down at the ground in front of me. Clark is still sipping his hot chocolate with a satisfied slurping sound.

"I mean, it *is* incredible, right? The treatment results?"

I feel Clark looking at me expectantly, but I purposefully avoid his gaze as the hospital looms up before us. "It is. I think he's encouraged. The focus group was a great idea of his. He wants to study June, Ivan, and Sylvia to see why the treatments worked and what we can do to improve them more…so that more patients can have similar results."

My hands, buried in my pockets, involuntarily squeeze tightly, my fingernails poking into the skin of my palms.

"Thanks, Evie."

I jerk my head back to Clark, who is holding his now empty mug of hot chocolate out toward me. I look at the mug and notice that we're now standing in the hospital lobby. I reach out for the mug, and Clark transfers it into my hands.

"I really needed that," Clark murmurs as he begins to adjust the straps of his backpack. I again notice how tired he looks. The gray shadows under his eyes are still there, and he seems paler, even with the warmer temperature of being indoors.

"I'll see you upstairs then." Clark waves at me as he rushes over to the elevators, ready to relieve the night shift nurses.

CHAPTER TWENTY-SIX
THE OBSIDIAN BLADE

DEAN HUDDLED HIS chin into the collar of his jacket as he bounced back and forth on the balls of his heels. His usually green and spiky hair lay flat and straight, long enough to be swept to the side. Peeking out of his collar and twining their way up his neck were his tattoos of vibrant, colored flowers.

He flipped a bright and shining pink cell phone out of his pocket to check the time. He had just arrived outside of the Thorny Heart, the doors currently locked since it was so early in the morning.

"Hello, Dean."

Surprised into nearly dropping his cell phone, Dean twirled around to see a slight figure dressed in a clean white suit, her pale blonde hair pulled up into a tight bun, sharp black-framed glasses framing her eyes. He almost didn't recognize her as the lead singer of Lenore's Wings, but he smiled anyway. "Hi, Ness! I got your message." He waved his pink cell phone at her. "On your way to work?"

Ness nodded as she lifted the case carrying her instrument. "To the hospital. Music therapist," she said plainly, but she smiled back. Dean couldn't really say if he was necessarily attracted to her, since she was definitely very pretty, but there was something that made him uneasy. However, he brushed it off, his impish grin never leaving his face.

Sliding her fingers into her pants pocket, Ness pulled out a single key and proceeded to open the door to the club.

Dean gasped. "A key? You have a key to the club?" Practically bursting with excitement, Dean clapped his hands together, his eyes widening in amazement. "Oh-my-gosh. Are you the oh-so-mysterious owner that, like, everyone is talking about? And by everyone, I mean the staff. Everyone was wondering about that because we had all responded to the same ad and none of us had met the owner except for a phone interview! Not that I have anything to complain about...I mean, working at the Thorny Heart is amazing! I love it. Especially the hours. I have classes during the day, so it's perfect."

Ness was already walking into the club, holding the door for Dean to follow her as he took a breath in between his excited stream of words.

"Part owner with my brother," Ness said and then set her music case down, walking purposefully to where a tall desk and stool were set. This also happened to be where Dean met people as they entered the club.

The door closed quietly behind them, and they were immediately closed off from the morning stirring of the city streets.

"Joseph Dean Manuel Thompson." Ness placed herself on the stool, her hands folded neatly into her lap.

"Um, that's my name…like, my actual name." Dean frowned. Not many people knew his whole birth name. He usually just went by 'Dean Thompson' on most documents and even within his social network. "How did you…?"

Ness lifted her hand as if to wave the question away. Intricate black tattoos of twisting vines, leaves, and flowers were just visible on her wrists as she did this.

"I have a special job for you." Ness slid open the top drawer of the desk and pulled out a tarnished, gold-plated box. She tapped the box with one finger.

Dean could feel his eyes lock onto the box uncomfortably. The sound of her fingernail tapping on the box was dull and flat, as if whatever was in the box was heavy and dense at the same time. Without realizing it, Dean found himself standing across from Ness, the box between them on the surface of the desk.

"Go ahead." Ness gestured toward the box, a smirk lifting the corners of her mouth, but her eyebrows were straight, her eyes blank and dark.

Dean touched the corner of the box and slid his finger down where he could lift the lid. There was no latch or lock; the box looked nearly seamless, and yet somehow, he knew exactly where to put his finger to open it.

Inside the box was something that looked neither heavy nor dense. Instead it looked like a slender sliver of glass. Without hesitating, as if mesmerized, Dean picked it up. When he held it up to the dull light of the room, it was so dark in color that it looked like ink. Smooth and sharp, it tapered to deadly points on both ends. No light reflected off its shining black surface.

Ness pushed the lid of the box closed, and Dean looked

at her, his eyebrows raised in question, but before he could say anything, he saw her fingers reach toward the base of her neck where she touched something in her hair.

Before he could blink, gold flashed before him, and he felt something cold and sharp pierce his chest. Dean fell to his knees, the black shard falling flatly on the ground in front of him. He held a hand to his chest, and as he breathed in, a sensation of cold heaviness filled his lungs. The feeling then seemed to flow into his blood, pushed along with his heartbeat.

When he looked up, Dean saw Ness stand and place a stack of dark purple flyers onto the desk. She then walked over to her instrument case and picked it up, as if not noticing Dean still kneeling on the ground.

"Your good work is appreciated, Dean." Ness headed to the door, about to push it open. "Call this a type of promotion." She paused, waiting patiently.

Dean breathed again, and this time it came a little easier. He looked down at the black shard in front of him and picked it up as if it were a pen that he had simply dropped. He stood up and slid it carefully into a pocket on the inside of his jacket. He then walked over to the stack of purple flyers and placed them into his bag, which had fallen from his shoulders when he had fallen to his knees.

He walked over to Ness, who pushed the door open to let them out of the Thorny Heart. Without another glance at each other, they both walked away in opposite directions.

CHAPTER TWENTY-SEVEN

SONGS OF THE DYING

IT WAS EARLY in the morning, but Ivan felt wide awake. He was reading his book in the backseat of his parents' car. His lips moved silently as he followed the words, his eyes flitting over the illustrations of the book. He flipped the pages slowly, almost reluctantly, lingering on each one to make sure he wasn't missing any details.

He felt a nudge at his side as his violin case bumped into him. His parents were driving him to the hospital for a quick checkup, and then he would be heading to his first day of class since he had been admitted and discharged from the hospital. He was eager to be back in school, for things to be back to normal. After he turned each page, he immediately returned his hand to rest on the violin without realizing it.

After a few minutes longer, they parked the car at the hospital. Ivan slid a bookmark carefully into his book to save his place. He walked in between his parents, zipping up his jacket all the way to his chin as the cool air hit his face. Holding his book at his side, Ivan waved his free hand at the receptionist, who waved back at him enthusiastically. He followed his parents as they led him to the special research part of the hospital.

After checking in at the front desk with a different receptionist, his parents took seats in the lobby, and Ivan was led to an office-like room with some hospital equipment tucked neatly away in the corner of the room.

The door closed behind him, and Ivan took a seat in his chair. He was barely turning the first page of his book when he heard a faint click from the door opening. Anticipating that someone would be entering the room, Ivan closed his book, but after a few seconds passed, he realized that no one was coming in. He stood up and walked over to the door, thinking that maybe the receptionist who had led him to the room hadn't closed it all the way.

He was about to close the door when he felt the handle bump against his hand unexpectedly, as if someone were trying to push the door open from the other side. Ivan furrowed his brow slightly and pulled the door open to look out into the hallway, but no one was there. He could hear the faint clack of the person at the front desk typing away at their keyboard.

Ivan started to close the door again when he heard it— the familiar sound of a string instrument. Curious, Ivan pushed the door open wider. He scanned the hallway more thoroughly, trying to find the source of the music, which seemed to grow a little louder but pleasantly so. The sound was deeper than a violin, played in a slow and sonorous melody. Ivan was reminded of the feeling he had when Sylvia played on her bamboo flute.

He felt the blood rush through his ears and his heartbeat slow down. He closed his eyes for a moment, and when he opened them, he realized that he was walking down the hallway toward the source of the music.

He came to a sudden stop outside of a door that was open slightly. Ivan peered into the room and could make out the profile of a woman in a white suit, her ear flashing with gold piercings. She stood up straight, her gaze fixed on a point in front of her, her fingers moving over the strings of a dark-colored viola as she slid the bow in a flowing motion with her other hand.

Ivan couldn't help but nudge the door just a little wider; the sound of the music resonated within him, and he felt his heartbeat slow down even more. The light before his eyes seem to dim as he felt his breath grow heavier.

Suddenly he felt something grip his upper arm. Startled, he blinked once and felt his heartbeat pick up rapidly. He swayed a bit, feeling surprisingly light-headed as the lights became brighter again. The door slammed shut in front of him, and he swore he could hear the soft laugh of the woman inside as the music stopped sharply. The sound was so deep and haunting, he was almost convinced he imagined it.

"Hey, Ivan?"

Looking up, Ivan recognized Clark, who was smiling down at him, but his eyes were creased in concern. He was gripping the doorknob in front of him. He released it quickly, and gripped Ivan's arm a little more firmly as if readying himself to push him out of the way of an oncoming bus.

"You all right?"

Ivan blinked, the music still echoing in his ears. He looked down at Clark's hand as if surprised to feel its weight there. Nodding slowly, he looked back up at Clark. "Yeah."

Clark still seemed concerned, and for the first time since Ivan had met him, he looked frustrated; his eyes narrowing slightly as they flitted back to the closed door.

They walked back to the office, where a familiar person stood waiting for him. Her hair was now a soft blue color, and she was waiting patiently by the window.

"Well, hello, Ivan! We thought we had the wrong room for a second." Evie grinned as she walked over to him. "Well, until we saw this." She held out his book and handed it to him appreciatively. "By the way, I can recommend a ton of riveting books on a number of chicken breeds…fascinating stuff!"

Ivan laughed but then immediately stopped when he realized that his doctor wasn't joking. Clark raised his eyebrows, a smile turning up the corners of his mouth as he caught Ivan's startled look. He then pointedly started to rummage through the hospital equipment drawer behind Evie.

"Oh, uh…chickens?" Ivan was worried that he might've hurt Evie's feelings with his laugh, but she hardly seemed to notice as she recounted her latest foray into such "riveting" titles as *The Chicken: The Greatest Domesticated Animal of the Human Era* and *Chickens: Fowl or Prehistoric Marvel?* Clark was taking his vital signs as Evie talked. She was also doing her own assessment, running her hands under his chin and throat, and pressing them gently down onto his collarbone. Occasionally, between her chicken musings, she would ask him to cough, breathe deeper, and move different parts of his body. She then paused for a few moments to listen to his heart and lungs, pressing a stethoscope at different points onto his chest and back.

Evie then asked him questions about how he was feeling at home, and if anything seemed out of the ordinary. Ivan paused as Evie and Clark were moving around him, Clark getting ready to draw blood and Evie typing on her tablet as Ivan answered her questions.

"Anything seem wrong or out of the ordinary since you left the hospital?" Evie repeated, this time in a gentler and quieter tone.

Ivan hesitated as he fidgeted with the corner of his book cover. He didn't know if having the same dream about someone standing over his bed with what looked like silver, glowing hair was something that he was supposed to relay to them. He looked up, catching Evie's eye. He then automatically shook his head from side-to-side. "No. I feel great. I can't wait to get back to school, too."

Evie nodded and continued to type on her tablet. Clark then tied a blue rubber band around Ivan's arm and quickly inserted a small needle into the crease of his elbow to draw his blood. After a second passed, he placed a bandage over the puncture quickly and carefully as he withdrew the needle.

After a few more comments about the many various and worthy titles of books related to chickens, Evie waved her hand at Ivan, wishing him a good day back in classes. Then Ivan followed Clark back into the lobby, where his parents were waiting for him. After checking out with the receptionist and setting up his next appointment, he tucked his book against his side and walked out of the hospital with his parents on either side of him.

Back in the car, he felt a little distracted as his parents asked him how his appointment went. He thought it was nerves related to returning back to class, but he kept on looking down at his violin case as he answered their questions.

When they finally reached his school, students were just beginning to flow steadily into the building. He gripped the violin case with one hand while he climbed out of the backseat of the car. His parents hugged him as if this were his first day of school, his mother smoothing out the collar of his coat and his father gripping his shoulder in pride and what looked to be relief at the good health of his son, whose cheeks were pink rather than pale and dusky.

He watched for a moment as his parents drove off. Then hoisting his backpack across his shoulders and feeling his knuckles turn white with how tightly he was gripping the handle of his violin, Ivan rushed into the school. He could hear the greetings of his friends, most from his lacrosse team, who were the most familiar with his illness. He waved at them, giving them a big smile, but his mind was already fixated on his first class period.

When he reached the band room, he pushed the door open and was relieved to find it completely empty; the lights were not even on. The teachers were still finishing up their morning coffees and students were eating breakfast or mingling with friends before the first class bell rang for the day.

Ivan flipped the switch on in the room and sat in his usual seat. Swinging his backpack off, he flipped open his violin case. He felt his fingers start to buzz in anticipation of the familiar vibrations of running his bow against the strings. He flung the violin up and under his chin, and without a single thought of what song or notes he was about to play, he began to slide the bow across the strings in a purposeful rhythm.

He wasn't sure where he had heard the song before, but he recognized similar notes strung together from Sylvia's composition and that of the haunting melody he had heard at the hospital just that morning.

It was as if a light had been turned on.

He could suddenly see fleeting images of what he had thought were dreams, but now he knew were memories. He could remember waking up at the hospital and seeing the figure of a silver-haired person standing in front of him. He could remember his illness leaving his body the very moment this person had placed their hand against his skin.

When the school bell rang, he froze, his bow paused in mid-note. His muscles felt warm, his heartbeat steady and strong.

Just as the door opened, the first group of students hauling in their own musical instruments, Ivan looked down at the bandage sitting in the crease of his arm. Without knowing exactly why, he peeled the bandage off and stared down at the skin underneath.

Rather than revealing a small bruise, puncture, or any sign that the vein had been pierced with a needle, it was completely unblemished and smooth.

CHAPTER TWENTY-EIGHT
SILVER LINES

CERIN WALKED TO the very edge of the building's roof. The winter sky was already darkening even though it was early in the day. The clouds made it appear as though the sun was already setting while the frigid air blew in sharp snaps.

His eyes scanned the street below him as if searching for something in the steady rush of people flowing in all directions around the hospital. Even if someone were to look up, they would be unable to see anything but a shadow perched at the very top of the hospital roof's ledge.

There was movement and a blur of green hair as his eyes locked on an individual. Even at this distance, he was able to make out the finest detail of flowering tattoos showing from the collar of the young man's jacket.

He was handing out dark purple flyers as people walked around him, a steady spot of green in the stream of moving bodies.

Cerin lifted his hand and twitched the fingers just slightly. A dark purple flyer escaped the fingers of a man who had just *received it. He made an effort to reach up as the flyer whisked up and over his head, seemingly caught in a breeze, but realizing it was probably gone, he shrugged his shoulders and proceeded to walk ahead.*

The single dark purple flyer fluttered and dipped gracefully as it traveled upward.

Cerin watched its progress patiently until it was at a short enough distance that he could reach out and grasp it between his fingers.

His eyes traced the shining gold calligraphy of an advertisement for the Thorny Heart Nightclub. An emblem of thorns wrapping around an anatomical heart emblazoned across it. Under that was the name of the band, Lenore's Wings, with a black feather sketched beneath it. There was also the message that Everline Hospital staff would be receiving a cover charge waiver for attending.

Cerin's colorless eyes clouded over. He frowned, and creeping blue flames appeared from his hands, covering the piece of paper until it disappeared in a cloud of black smoke.

"Evie!" A familiar voice shouts my name and I jump. The cup of coffee (thankfully, lukewarm) that I am holding at my computer slops over and spills into my lap. Pulling the sleeve of my coat down, I reflexively dab at the brown liquid stain on my upper thigh but immediately regret this when I remember that the sleeve of my coat happens to be white.

"Evie!" I spin around as I hear my name again, my chair stopping at the expected ninety degrees, but rather than having to spin the rest of my way around to complete a half circle, Estelle is already flinging a dark purple piece of paper at my face.

"Estelle!" I grab the piece of paper and glare at her. "Shouldn't you be saving lives and/or body parts right now?"

Scooting a chair close to me, Estelle rolls her eyes. "I had some downtime…and all my lives and at-risk body parts are secured at the moment."

I lean back into my chair, and remembering the paper in my hand, I skim over it, instantly recognizing the emblem arrayed across the top. It is a flyer for another event at the Thorny Heart.

"No," I say, handing the paper back to Estelle. I make to spin my chair back toward my computer screen. "But—but why?" Estelle holds the paper, which flops limply over her hand.

"It's a Monday night!"

"Yeah, but we're not on-call Monday nights." Estelle waves the paper back at me.

"We work Tuesday morning, though."

Estelle gasps dramatically. "Our lives should not be dictated by the constraints of the human body's circadian rhythm."

"The body needs a regulated sleep pattern," I say.

Estelle then tries a different approach, pulling her two hands together and giving me puppy dog eyes, her lower lip quivering slightly.

This time I roll my eyes. "Estelle, this method doesn't work on me."

"I know. Your emotional threshold is restrictive at this time of day."

I glance at her in disbelief. "I thought you would be more than a little reluctant to go back to this place. You almost flung yourself off the roof!"

Nodding carefully and shrugging, Estelle hardly seems to acknowledge what I'm saying. "Well, the odds of that happening again are extremely low."

I open my mouth to make a counterargument, but Estelle raises her hand and starts again before I can even form a single word. "Okay, okay. What if I made you an incredibly delicious German chocolate coffee cake? Or personally bedazzle your pager for you? Or both!" Estelle claps her hands enthusiastically.

"Er…" I twiddle my thumbs as if thinking extremely hard about this offer.

I'm about to refuse again when for some reason I pause. I glance back at the dark purple paper that Estelle has placed on her lap, my eyes landing on the sketch of the feather drawn under the band name of Lenore's Wings. My eyes focus on something silvery. Reaching for the paper, I hold it in my hands, my eyes catching the silver ink-like pattern creating a subtle outline on the feather. I'm not exactly sure why, and maybe it is just a coincidence, but my mind goes right to the silvery details of the black book with all the drawings in it.

I pull my gaze away from the flyer and look at Estelle. Her big grayish-green eyes are staring back at me hopefully.

"Okay. But I'm leaving at exactly eleven forty-five." I hand the flyer back to her, my eyes lingering for just a second on the black feather.

Estelle leaps up happily from her chair and nearly

prances out of the room, the purple flyer fluttering in her hand.

"And I want that German chocolate coffee cake ASAP…and don't touch my pager!" I call after Estelle as she exits the Hole of Optimism.

CHAPTER TWENTY-NINE
CAGED IN

Neko observed his surroundings. He was in a loft-like room divided into two sections. A ladder led up to the sleeping area, and below, Neko stood in a large, open area that was void of any furniture or electronic devices.

A large window filled the entire wall of this room. The window looked out into the cityscape, tall skyscrapers towered over the park trees, which could be seen below. In the very distance was the outline of a mountain range silhouetted in a darkening sky, the sun beginning to set.

Neko grimaced at the thought of so much light filling this small living space; though it was now cast in a dusky shadow, it still seemed to have too much lingering daylight.

However, it would be necessary, since the room was nearly filled with plants of all shapes and sizes. They grew in pots and vases, sat on tables and pedestals, and even hung from the ceiling. Long leafy tendrils brushed the fabric of his black garment, which rippled out behind him with his movements. The air in the room was still.

Curiously, though, the room wasn't quiet. The soft, muffled sounds of chirping came from all over the room, the source of which were small birds held captive in large, delicate, spherical and bell-shaped glass containers. With brown twine, these containers hung around the room at varying lengths, nestled in between the foliage.

Neko found himself entranced by these hanging glass containers with their feathery occupants. He walked up to one, which happened to be at eye level. He brushed aside the leaves of a bushy plant that had small white flowers scattered all over it.

Reaching out a long-nailed finger, he tapped the glass. The little bird tilted its speckled brown head and repositioned itself on a thick brown rope strung across the inside of the cage.

Neko caught his gaze in the glass. His colorless eyes barely reflected in its pristine surface. His eyes shifted slightly as he caught the subtle movement behind him, a wisp of air lifting the thin fabric of his sleeve.

"Brother, you have a very interesting taste in décor." Neko didn't turn around as he tapped his fingernail against the glass again.

"Why are you here?"

Neko turned around this time, a smile lifting one corner of his mouth.

"To bring you a gift." Neko waved his hand, the fabric of his garment lifting up in the breeze that he created. It billowed out as a cloud of inky black smoke appeared and gathered at their feet. As it sank into the ground, there appeared a medium-sized cage with a white dove beating its wings against the metal bars.

"I know how fond you are of our feathery friends here." Neko's voice carried a slightly teasing tone.

Cerin ignored the cage and bird, though his eyes seemed to glaze over. Their colorless depths appeared murky, like looking down into muddy water.

"You really have been looking awful, Cerin." The smile disappeared from Neko's face as he observed his older brother. *"How can you stand to take care of your pets here"*—Neko waved a hand lazily at the room around him—*"and neglect yourself. You're causing yourself undue suffering by playing this caregiver role. It's unnatural."*

Cerin stayed silent.

Neko frowned in annoyance, but his mouth soon gave way to his customary smirk. His canines, which were slightly longer than an average human's, glinted in the dimming light of the room.

"Cerin, we're trying to help you."

"Then leave." Cerin's voice was flat as he stared, unblinking, at his brother.

"Unfortunately, that is impossible. Things have become a lot more interesting lately…and it has been quite some time since things have been this interesting." Neko continued to grin, his teeth shining. *"But in the meantime, you're welcome to assist us. I'm sure you're aware of the show that Auriel has planned for tonight."*

Cerin blinked, and as if taking this as some sort of signal, Neko began to walk past him and toward the window-filled wall of the loft. *"You're invited. As you always are, beloved brother."*

With a whisper of moving fabric, Neko turned, walking

through the glass of the window, a shadow disappearing on the other side.

Cerin stared ahead and very slowly turned his gaze downward. The dove was still flitting around the metal cage. He felt his chest clench with pain, and suddenly a great and gnawing hunger burned through his body. His gaze caught the glass containers holding his other birds. His only comfort was that they were safe.

But this dove...

As if his muscles were contracting involuntarily, his arm reached out in front of him, toward the cage. His finger touched a single metal bar. Then his whole hand was gripping it, and without even blinking, he clenched his fist, and the metal bar screeched as it was wrenched away. Laying the bar down beside him, his eyes followed the frantic movements of the dove in the cage as it tried to fly to the opposite end, its wings beating against the metal dully.

Cerin felt cold as he reached his fingers through the wider gap he had made between the bars. A thick and heavy sensation, like wet sand, seemed to leech its way out from his fingers. It formed into thick black tendrils of inky smoke, which snaked their way toward the white dove. The dove continued to beat its wings, trying futilely to fly away as the black tendrils wrapped themselves around its body.

Cerin breathed out a heavy sigh as the dove became still, its wings pinned against the tendrils, which seemed to cling to its feathers like an inky stain. He pulled the bird toward him, wrapping his fingers carefully around it. It blinked up at him, and Cerin closed his eyes as he felt the bird shudder.

He felt his skin grow colder, but the sensation was almost a relief as it washed away the pain burning through his veins.

The murky shade of his eyes suddenly gleamed silver, then turned clear; becoming a colorless pool of glass.

When he looked back down at the white bird, it lay limply in his pale hand. The black tendrils slid down from his fingers, sinking into the ground. He felt the beating of his heart against his chest as he lay the bird gently back down at the bottom of the cage.

CHAPTER THIRTY
CHOCOLATES AND SHADOWS

I STARE AT myself in the mirror. I have just showered and dried my hair, which has already faded to a powder-blue color. Peering closer, I can see a very fine white stripe along the part in my hair. The white color is so subtle that I doubt anyone else would notice. Maybe if they did, they would pass it off as some sort of early-onset, stress-induced aging thing related to my job (or something along those lines).

Except, *I* know it's there. I close my eyes and see an image of my younger self, looking into the mirror in the same way that I am doing right now. My small, frantic fingers discovering shocks of white in the darkness of my straight hair.

I jump as I hear a loud knock from behind me. With just another glance at the mirror, I quickly run my hands through my hair, trying to mess it up enough that my part will be less noticeable.

"I hope you're fully dressed." Estelle gingerly pushes the door open and peeks inside. I turn toward her, and in fact, I'm already dressed in a slouchy black sweater and black leggings.

Estelle, on the other hand, is wearing a gold sequined skirt with a flattering ivory-colored blazer. She has colored gemstones pinned throughout her long black braids; they catch the light and sparkle in a subtle way.

"Pink socks?"

I look down to inspect my feet, wiggling my toes, which are indeed covered in a comfortable pair of pink polka-dotted socks.

"I'm wearing boots."

Pursing her lips to resist saying anything, since I agreed to accompany her to the Thorny Heart (and the German coffee cake is still in process), she holds something out to me.

I reach out my hand and Estelle drops a large, round pendant into it. I can tell that the white glittering stone is an opal, which is framed on one side by a piece of silver in the shape of a crescent. It hangs on a long silvery chain.

I look at Estelle, and she places a hand on a sparkly gold hip. "Something to break up the soul-crushing blackness of your wardrobe."

My mouth falls open in offense as I gesture at my pink polka-dotted feet. But before I can say anything, she holds something else out, and I immediately recognize it as my cell phone.

I take it frantically, inspecting it thoroughly. Reassured that it hasn't been bedazzled, I slide it into my messenger bag, which is waiting right outside the bathroom for me.

"Cell phones on us at all times." Estelle smiles, and I can't help but smile back hesitantly. I haul my messenger bag over my shoulder. We already had a conversation earlier that the messenger bag would be non-negotiable. I had discreetly removed two or three hardcover books. Along with the additional mysterious items that I've taken to carrying with me at all times, I've definitely started to feel a little strain on my shoulders lately. Of course, I don't feel the need to admit this to her.

I then gently bring the pendant's chain over my head.

"Are you sure you want me to wear this?" I can't help but run my fingers over the opal, admiring its smoothness that pairs extremely well with the silky silver crescent.

Estelle shrugs as she grabs a small clutch and slides her own impressively bedazzled phone into it. "I almost forgot I had it. My mother gave it to me when I started premedicine."

I glance back at Estelle, who is now sliding some modestly pointed two-inch heels on. Following suit, I quickly lace up my boots. While doing this, I suddenly realize that Estelle never really talks much about her family. The one or two times that Estelle has brought up her parents, a rare look of serious quietness crosses her face. She then either changes the subject, or mentions something about dinner.

I try remembering what her parents look like. The first and only time that I have ever met them was after our graduation ceremony. I recalled two individuals, the same height as Estelle. Both had serious faces. Her father was in a crisp navy-blue suit, wearing sharp-framed glasses, and her mother in a flowing red dress, her long, braided hair like Estelle's was bound in a neat headband of the same color as her dress.

However, this one image of her parents standing close to her, talking seriously to each other, is the only one I have of Estelle and her family.

My boots now laced, I stand up, heaving my messenger bag strap securely over my shoulder. I can hear a sharp crackling sound as Estelle unwraps a piece of chocolate in green foil and then quickly tosses the small creamy cube into her mouth. She gives me a wide grin, and we head out of the apartment.

"Remember, I'm leaving at eleven forty-five sharp," I remind her as the night air hits our faces.

Estelle nods and tosses me a chocolate, which I catch in my hand easily even with my messenger bag slung across my shoulder. I sigh as I start to unwrap it, grateful for the taste that seems to warm me up in a pleasant way.

I can feel the opal pendant hanging from my neck. The weight, rather than burdensome, is actually comforting. The chain is long enough that it hangs almost to the middle of my stomach. I wonder if the necklace length was meant for someone taller, and I think of Estelle, who is much taller than I am.

Estelle is already popping another chocolate into her mouth as we walk the few blocks to the Thorny Heart. When we approach a familiar corner, I see without needing to search for it the dark door with the nightclub's emblem gleaming subtly in the street lights. The thorns that wrap around the heart seem sharper in the shadows cast over it.

With Estelle leading the way and pushing the door open, we find ourselves face-to-face with a smiling green-haired and flowery-tattooed individual.

"Hello there, Dr. Kagwe and Dr. Hashimoto!" Dean greets us with familiarity, already holding out a small wooden stamp, which he firmly presses onto the inner parts of our wrists, leaving the image of a heart with thorns.

I am about to pull out my wallet, but he holds up his hands with a look of exaggerated offense. He shakes his head and gestures down to a sign hanging in front of the podium he is sitting at. "Promotional night for Everline Hospital employees! The owners wanted to boost their local clientele since we're so new."

"Oh." I suddenly remember this information on the purple flyer and nod sheepishly. Estelle flashes Dean an enthusiastic smile and claps her hands together as we both walk toward the opposite side of the antechamber where we can hear the murmurings of people talking behind the other door.

As we enter into the club area, I expect to see and hear a surge of people and loud music. Instead the large room is filled with people sitting at numerous round tables made of dark polished wood. The stage is in the same place, and the band with the red-haired singer that I recognize from our first night at the Thorny Heart, is sitting at its center; his dark skin sparkles fiercely with glitter even in the soft lighting. His voice has taken on a different cadence compared to the previous show. It is a slow, crooning sound that pairs attractively with the gentle beat of drums and electric guitar strings.

A space created in front of the stage serves as the dance area, which is already packed with people pressing into each other to get closer to the music.

My eyes continue to scan the room, which is lit by large tapered candles along the mosaic walls and around the tables. I vaguely wonder if this might be considered a type of fire hazard, but before I can think more about it, we are already being greeted by another familiar face.

"Well, what a pleasure." Ian stands in front of us wearing jeans and the black T-shirt with the Thorny Heart insignia across the chest. He smiles at Estelle and myself. The amber of his eye seems to stand out more than the blue in the candlelight, reflecting it in a startling way.

Estelle's customary wide-eyed stare lasts for nearly thirty seconds before she finally clears her throat. "The pleasure is ours! I think I'll be deferring any impromptu base jumping attempts this time."

I frown at Estelle's lighthearted tone regarding what I consider to be a pretty serious occurrence. Ian catches my eyes as this thought crosses my mind; his mouth turns up in a curious smirk, and I look away to continue scanning the room.

"Hm, Everline Hospital is definitely represented well here…and on a weeknight," I state plainly, trying to hide the surprise that I feel.

Ian shrugs, his eyes glinting as he lazily follows my gaze over his shoulder. "We can't fault good, hard-working people for wanting to have some quality leisure time…even if it *is* a weeknight."

At that moment, it seems the tone of the music picks up. The red-haired singer stands as he grabs the microphone and swings it closer to him. The voices in the room also seem to surge with laughter and conversation as people lean in closer to each other, holding their drinks or biting into the small snacks they ordered.

Estelle stands up even straighter, as if tingling with electricity, and before I can say another word to her, she has tossed a chocolate my way and is practically skipping over to the small crowd growing on the dance floor. I catch the green-packaged chocolate, which crinkles between my fingers. I anxiously watch her disappear into the crowd of moving bodies.

Sighing, I looked down at the chocolate. "I have no idea where she has the room to carry these things." I think of her small clutch, which hangs on a chain slung over her body.

"You mean, you don't carry a pound of chocolate with you in that bag of yours?" Ian raises his eyebrows as he refers to my messenger bag still slung over my shoulder.

"Of course not." I hand the chocolate to him. "Why would I do that?" I think fondly of all the books that I have wedged in there as Ian inspects the chocolate after unwrapping it.

"Hm, I've always been fond of sweets." Ian grins as he pops it into his mouth.

"So, don't tell me that you plan on a bit of light reading at a place like this?" Ian raises one of his eyebrows as he chews his chocolate thoughtfully.

I frown. "Well, that is kind of the intention. I was promised a German chocolate coffee cake or a bedazzled cell phone if I accompanied my good friend here."

"And?"

"I picked the German chocolate coffee cake."

Ian laughs, and I can't help but notice how deep and pleasant the sound is. The tips of my ears grow warm, and I find myself trying to avoid staring at his dual-colored eyes.

"So, are you here with your sister again?" I ask, remembering this from our last conversation, but heat immediately starts creeping down my neck. "Er—not that I'm trying to be nosy or anything. I'm sure you could have been here with anyone else!"

Ian just smiles. "Actually, it was the right assumption."

Suddenly there is a flurry of purposeful movement on stage as the red-haired singer and his band are replaced by a team of people in black shirts with the club's emblem emblazoned across their chests. They quickly start to change the equipment in a quiet and efficient manner.

It is only when a young woman appears in front of me that I realize I've become distracted with watching the group of people working. She holds out a tray with two glasses of iced water. I notice that she is wearing the same black T-shirt as Ian and the people on stage.

"Dr. Nakano." She inclines her head toward Ian and then toward me as well. Confused for just a moment, I realize that the second glass is for me.

"Oh. Th-thank you!" I grab the glass of water, spilling it just slightly onto the tray as the young serving woman nods politely and walks away.

I watch her walk away and then look back at Ian. "Um, you seem to be well-recognized around here for such a new establishment."

Ian takes a sip of his water, his eyes raised over the rim with a look that I can only describe as mischievous. "Well, that would be appropriate, since I am part owner of this new establishment."

Sputtering, I lower my own glass of water from my mouth. "What? Really? You're part owner of the Thorny Heart?"

"Yes." Ian takes another drink. "With my sister."

After he says this, the lighting on the stage dims, casting a shadow across the room. With the candles flickering in the background, it's easy to appreciate the colored glass making up the mosaic on the walls. It gleams and shines, creating the illusion of water scattering a rainbow of lights.

Even on the darkened stage, I can already recognize the shadowy figure of Ness. Her slender shape stands out among the larger ones of her bandmates. As she positions herself at the center of the stage, I can just see a glint of gold flash from her nose and ears.

When the lights turn on again, Ness is sitting on the same stool the previous singer with red hair occupied. Her light blonde hair falls straight down to her waist. She is wearing a long white dress, the fabric hanging down heavily on her small frame while her black shoes peek out from the dress's hem. The black tattoos that are visible up and down her arms and chest stand in stark contrast to her pale skin and white dress.

Her eyes are turned down, her hands clasped firmly in her lap. Standing across the room, I can see that her fingers are covered in shining gold jewelry. Per her last routine with her bandmates, she sits still and silent as they tune their instruments. The deep pulse of a bass guitar and the thrum of electric strings are accented by the occasional tap of sticks against a drum or cymbal.

Mesmerized, I find myself anticipating the start of the performance. When the music finally starts, the sound of Ness's voice fills the entire room with a startling fullness that seems surprising from such a slim and small person. Her voice is both deep and soft, perfectly paired to the haunting music that accompanies her.

I close my eyes and my brows furrow slightly. The sound is oddly familiar and not just because this is my second time hearing Ness perform with Lenore's Wings.

My eyes shoot open as I feel a rustle of movement, and a cold sharp breeze hits my skin. I turn my head, embarrassed because I forgot Ian was standing next to me. But when my gaze falls to where he should be, he is no longer there. I look in the opposite direction reflexively, but I don't see him. I realize I'm still holding the glass of water, my fingers wrapped loosely around the rim. I transfer it to my other hand and then gently place it on a vacant table next to me.

It's then that I see it. I blink, squeezing my eyes shut for just a moment before opening them again.

It is an unnaturally tall shadow, wrapped in black smoke that falls away from it, slowly sinking to the ground before disappearing. Its claws are the most defining characteristic, sharpened to tapered points and gleaming with a silver luminosity.

The shadow glides heavily to the staircase that spirals toward the upper level of the building. Its claws are raised to the black railing, barely touching it as it ascends. It seems to slide unknowingly between the distracted people surrounding it, weaving carefully between their bodies as they continue their conversations or stare mesmerized at the stage.

Without thinking twice, I start toward the staircase.

CHAPTER THIRTY-ONE
THE APPROACHING DARKNESS

DEAN WAS ON his knees, his teeth chattering with a cold, burning sensation that spread directly from the center of his chest. He resisted the urge to cry out even though he was pretty sure no one would be able to hear him, since he had just locked himself behind the heavy bathroom door just seconds before.

He crawled over to the sink and somehow dragged himself to a standing position. When he raised his eyes up to his reflection in the mirror, he couldn't resist crying out this time, but from surprise rather than the pain, which seemed to worsen with each agonizing second.

His reflection was his, but he felt as if he were looking at a stranger. His skin had turned ashen, and black veins started to spread gradually from his eyes, extending down along his cheekbones.

Another stabbing sensation pierced through his chest. He automatically clawed at the collar of his T-shirt, pulling it down. Heavy black veins similar to the ones that leached out from his eyes were now spreading from the center of his chest, creeping slowly up his neck.

He cried out as he scratched at his skin frantically, as if he could grasp the black veins and pull them off like spiders.

Dean let out a final gasp when he suddenly felt a horrible tearing sensation rip through his chest. He became still as his body sank to the ground.

After a few moments had passed, there was a flicker of muscles and twitches of movement as Dean stirred. He gradually pulled himself up by the sink again. He felt cold, but the burning pain had subsided.

When he looked at his reflection in the mirror, the black veins were still there. But his usually brown-colored eyes had turned black all the way to the whites of the sclera.

He hardly seemed to notice as he mechanically turned around; his black eyes found his coat lying in a pile on the ground where he had pulled it off in a panic when the pains started. He picked it up and carefully put it back on.

When he reached into his coat's inner pocket, he felt the sharp point of the black obsidian shard brush his fingertips.

When I reach the spiraling metal staircase, the tall shadow has already reached the top. I quickly ascend, weaving through a number of people as my eyes stare ahead, not wanting to lose the shadow. My eyes strain as I try not to blink too much, afraid that the tall black shadow will somehow disappear behind the darkness of my eyelids at any second.

The image of silver-tipped claws pulling the wings off a white butterfly suddenly flashes before my eyes. I feel the bones and muscles of my hands flex as they tighten on my messenger bag where I know the black and metal-covered books are tucked away. I feel drawn to the shadow, as if it has somehow emerged from the pages of the sketchbook to become something tangible and real.

When I reach the top of the staircase, a frown creases at my brows as I look for the shadow. My eyes dart around, flitting across the twisted metal art pieces hanging on the walls and scanning the people walking in pairs or groups standing at the bar. The sound of voices, punctuated by a laugh, seem like far-off waves crashing along a beach.

For some reason, I walk toward the door that leads to the balcony where Estelle nearly fell to the cold, paved street below. I push the door open and am met by the still and frigid winter air. I inhale sharply—it feels like I've walked into a wall of ice. I step out, and the balcony door closes tightly behind me.

Probably because of the bone-shattering cold, the balcony is unsurprisingly empty. People have understandably opted for the warmth of a crowd preoccupied with the steady beat of music.

I look up and notice that I can make out a few stars and a sliver of the moon in the blackness of the sky. I find myself distracted for just a moment, almost forgetting the tall shadow completely. The soft pulsing of Lenore's Wings plays in the background. I find that if I focus enough, I can still hear Ness's lilting and haunting voice.

When my gaze finally breaks away from the sky, I see that someone else is now standing across from me on the balcony. I draw in a sharp breath that causes an ache in my lungs.

"Dean?" The name leaves my lips uncertainly, my heart skipping a beat. The green hair and flowering tattoos that peek out from the collar of his jacket are unmistakable. But it is his eyes that I can't quite register. The whites of his eyes are shot through with an inky blackness that stretches down and across his cheekbones and temples in spidery tendrils. Something is definitely not right.

"A-are you okay?" I ask, and at the same time, I slide my foot back, my hand reaching up and behind me as I try to find the doorknob. The cold metal brushes my fingers, and I cling to it, giving it a sharp twist. But it's stuck. Locked. Dean is suddenly standing right in front of me, moving in a way that is impossibly fast. I hardly have any time to blink. My mouth opens to say something, but I stop myself. Instead, I find myself simply staring into the black pools of his eyes.

He raises his right arm, and in his hand I can see that he was clutching a long, black sliver of something that looks almost like glass. It is the color of his eyes. It shines dully, catching the dim light that surrounds us.

The next few moments seem to slow as I watch him bring down his arm and shove the black shard of glass into my chest.

Ivan sat up in bed, breathing heavily, his skin slick with a sheen of sweat. His hand was clenched to his chest. His gut twisted as he remembered the waves of nausea that would hit him when he was undergoing treatments at the hospital. He was relieved when he realized that this was something entirely different, but the relief quickly dissipated as he continued to feel a sense of something that was terribly wrong.

He squeezed his eyes shut, trying to remember the dream that woke him. All he could remember were fleeting images that were hard to string together. He caught flashes of a long jagged piece of rock flying at him, piercing him through the chest.

Opening his eyes and looking down, all he could see was his hand twisted into the fabric of his T-shirt. He slowly relaxed his fingers, letting go. He then swung his legs out of bed, kicking the covers off, and stood up.

He felt strange, unsure of what he was doing. Although he had woken up from a deep sleep, he was wide awake, his heart still beating fast. He resolutely made his way to his window, pushing the fabric of his curtains aside. Looking up, Ivan immediately found the sliver of a crescent moon illuminating a tiny portion of the black night sky. Another image from his dream flashed across his vision.

It was of a woman with silver hair that fell down to her waist. He couldn't make out any facial features or even what she was wearing, except that it was long and flowing. She was completely surrounded by a bright shimmering light. Her fingers reached up overhead to brush the sliver of the crescent moon. Ivan had the bizarre feeling that he knew her somehow.

Ivan blinked, and the image vanished. He reached down and touched his chest again, feeling exhausted in a way that he never had before, even when he was at the height of his illness. He found steadiness and calm in his heartbeat, which was strong beneath his fingertips.

Even though he was convinced that he had been dreaming, he couldn't explain the feeling that he was having. The feeling that had woken him. Then it hit him—the feeling was fear. Not for himself, but for the silvery-haired woman. Ivan realized that the black shard of rock wasn't aimed at him but at her.

He stared back up at the night sky, his blue eyes reflecting the slim light of the moon. He imagined spears tipped with that slim crescent and he was not afraid anymore.

I stare down at the black shard protruding from my chest, my fingers reaching up to brush it gently. I am surprised that I feel nothing. No pain or feelings of terror. I'm sure that I am experiencing a sort of shock, but all I can really take in are the details of the object embedded into my chest. It is a beautiful black color, soft like a cloud of velvety smoke, and yet its edges are sharp enough to pierce through my heart.

I suddenly come to the realization that it is actually a piece of volcanic glass. Obsidian. My eyes focus sharply as I try to remember something that I must have forgotten.

I then look up and see Dean staring down at me, his gaze black and blank.

Time picks up rapidly at this point. Dean lifts his foot to take a step closer to me when a sudden shudder in the air around us whispers and swirls into one dark shadow.

I can make out the flash of silver claws glinting, and then Dean is on his back, pushed down by the dark shadow that has appeared before us.

I lean against the door, my body sliding to the ground, my eyes closing.

CHAPTER THIRTY-TWO
THE SECOND WAR

I am standing in a wide open area. A field. And it is burning.

In the distance I can see the ocean waves crashing against a jetty of jagged rocks. When I turn to look behind me, a mountain range towers up toward a sky tinged red, like the color of blood. Thick black clouds of smoke billow up and stain the sky with darkness.

When I look down at my feet, I gasp and step back, almost tripping over the bodies of men and women of all ages. I know they are all dead. They form a blanket across the field surrounding me.

I cry out as my hair whips and swirls around me. I spin around in one spot, staring at the countless number of bodies that lay in all manner of horrific death. Most are pierced through with weapons or burnt with some sort of blue fire that ripples across their bodies, devouring their flesh as it blackens to a charred mess.

Some sort of battle has taken place here. And these are the bodies of soldiers.

I fall to my knees, my hands flying to my face and coming away wet with tears.

I look down at the body closest to me—a young woman with eyes that stare empty at the blood-tinged sky above us. She is wearing armor that is sleek and fits her like a satin sheath. The metal gleams even in the burning darkness of the field of bodies.

At least a dozen black and smoking arrows pierce her chest. I reach down and touch her face, but she lies still as stone. Her flesh is cold and hard as cement. I brush my fingertips to her eyelids to close them, feeling my breath catch and shudder in my own chest.

It is then that I notice she is wearing a collar, which gleams with a beautiful and familiar pendant of opal, framed with the sliver of a crescent moon. My eyes widen, and I frantically reach down, placing a hand at my chest.

But instead of finding the pendant that Estelle let me wear, I stare down at a black shard piercing my heart.

"Evie? Evie! Evie, please!"

My eyes flutter open. I take in a breath as something hollow fills my ears. My vision focuses sharply, and I find that I am staring at someone with dark brown eyes shot through with amber flecks, and brown, wavy hair falling across his forehead.

"Clark?" I am shocked at how ragged I sound as I breathe out his name.

Clark's eyes widen and relief floods his features. I am confused, but any questions I have are wiped away as I remember the obsidian shard piercing my chest.

"Evie...don't move." Clark is also staring at the black shard. His hands are on my shoulders to steady me.

I roll my head back and am about to close my eyes again when I feel Clark squeeze my shoulders firmly but gently. "Evie, you need to stay awake."

My eyes shoot open. A sensation of cool water seems to flow over my skin. Clark releases his hands as if he has been shocked. He doesn't move back from me but stays kneeling in the same position.

"Evie?"

His voice seems distant as I close my eyes and reach a hand toward the black shard. My fingers wrap around it loosely. I then begin to pull, and the cool sensation rushes through me faster, somehow concentrating at the point that the shard has entered my chest. The soft light of thin threads appear as they wrap around the black shard and my hand.

Air flows through my lungs. My heart fills up with a comforting coolness, and I finally open my eyes. When I look down, I am holding the obsidian shard in my hand. I find myself distracted by how slender and delicate it is. It looks like it could be broken in half with the pressure of two hands, but I know otherwise.

When I look down at my chest, there is nothing there, but at the very tip of the shard is a drop of silvery liquid that shines as it slides down the glass.

Clark stares at the piece of obsidian in my hand. His eyes close and open again.

I suddenly feel the edges of my vision blur. The shard slips from my fingers, my muscles collapsing with exhaustion. And then everything goes completely dark.

Auriel sat in her throne of black obsidian, the edges sharp and deadly. She was still, statuesque, her colorless eyes staring ahead. Her arms lay loosely across the armrests.

In front of her knelt a young man with green hair. His eyes, which were black pools throughout, were still cloudy and dark and now streaked with red, the shapes of his irises visible and his skin less pale but still veined with black.

"I was unsuccessful," Dean stated, his voice flat and toneless. Even in this room, with such high ceilings and emptiness, there were no echoes. The air was heavy and still.

"Well, technically not." Neko leaned forward in his own throne that matched his sister's, his hands pressed together under his chin. His eyes narrowed lazily as he listened to Dean recount what had happened on the balcony of the Thorny Heart. "You accomplished what you were intended to accomplish. Which was to place the Obsidian Blade into the heart of the designated target."

Auriel continued to stare ahead, but her fingers flexed and gripped the armrests tightly. "Yes, and she…survived."

Neko kept his lips pressed together, but he could feel an unfamiliar sense of uncertainty creep at the very edges of his thoughts.

Dean lowered his eyes to confirm what Auriel had said.

"I had hoped that wouldn't be the case." Auriel blinked slowly. "She is not just a curiosity now. She is dangerous."

"Do you think our brother knew this?"

Auriel twitched her gaze sharply toward her twin brother. "Yes…and if he didn't know for certain before tonight, now he does."

"*Something forced me away from her on the balcony,*" Dean stated.

"*We know,*" Neko replied.

"*Cerin.*" *Auriel said their brother's name in a soft whisper tinged with disappointment and bitterness.*

Neko's face was blank as he tried to understand what this could all mean. He thought of his brother, Cerin, and what role he was playing in all of this. He leaned back when a sudden thought occurred to him. A thought that had been playing at the very corners of his mind and was now blossoming to the forefront like a spot of blood spreading out in a pool of water.

"*We need to talk to our dear brother.*" *Auriel lifted a hand and at the same time Dean stood up from his position of kneeling, his back straightening and his shoulders pulled back. "I think he may have knowledge of what's about to come.*"

Neko's eyes glinted dully. "You mean, the Second War."

I open my eyes. I'm lying down, and after a dazed moment of trying to reorient myself, I realize I'm actually in my own bed. I sit up slowly, involuntarily pressing a hand to my chest. Had the whole event at the Thorny Heart been a dream? But then my hand closes around a heavy pendant hanging off of a silver chain. I look down at the opal and silver crescent, the image of a dead woman wearing a version of the same pendant stares back up at me.

When I break my gaze away from the pendant, I realize that I am not alone in my room.

Clark is sitting on a stool by the window. His eyes are shadowed and he looks exhausted. He is leaning forward, resting his forehead on his hands, as if trying to stay awake.

He startles as he hears me stir in bed and quickly sits up straighter on the stool.

"I'm sorry, Evie," he begins quickly. "I brought you home, and you hadn't woken up yet. I just wanted to stay and make sure...that you were..."

I interrupt him before he can finish, "Thank you, Clark." My voice feels strange in my own ears, as if I haven't used it in a long time. My throat is raspy.

Before I can think of anything else to say, there is a mug in front of me. It smells sweetly of hot chocolate. I breathe it in gratefully as Clark passes it into my hands.

"I hope you don't mind. I helped myself to one as well." Clark holds up his own empty mug and smiles sheepishly.

I nod, and can't remember ever being more grateful for a cup of powdered Swiss Miss stirred into hot water.

It is quiet for a moment as I take a few sips. I chance glances at Clark, who was staring out of the window, his hands folded loosely into his lap. I remember his wide eyes filling with relief on the balcony at the nightclub, and I have trouble sorting through all the questions I want to ask him. About Dean, about the obsidian shard, about how he got me home all by himself when I was apparently unconscious.

Then I realize that this last question is probably the easiest to answer. No doubt the taxi driver or whoever he called just thought that I was another club-goer who may have had one too many alcoholic beverages of some sort.

"Did you—" I hesitate as I clutch the hot mug in my hands. "Did you see it all?" I know that the question is pointless, but I can't stop myself from asking.

Clark turns his head quickly in my direction and nods.

"I saw everything." Clark's own voice is hesitant. It seems like he is about to say something else but stops himself.

My thoughts start to jumble together as I try to come up with something that I can say to explain it all away. However, all my reasons and excuses I'm imagining (including something about the earth and moon alignments causing delusions of strange happenings and healing properties) seem just as bizarre as the actual truth of what happened.

Instead I look down at the mug. "How did you get on the balcony?" I vividly recall the only entrance to the balcony being locked.

Clark appears just as uncomfortable as I feel. He avoids my gaze, but before he can say anything, I hear a door slam and the frantic rush of feet barreling through the hallway.

My bedroom door flings open as Estelle flies into my room.

"Oh my god, Evie!" Estelle looks almost hysterical, her eyes shining with tears that I can tell she is trying to hold back. "Evie, I thought something…I was looking for you. I waited outside the club until midnight and realized that something was wrong. I looked everywhere and couldn't find you, and you wouldn't pick up your phone, and then I found this on the balcony." Estelle swings my messenger bag up in front of her. "I thought something—!" She drops the messenger bag at her feet and presses the palms of her hands to her eyes. "Okay, we never have to go back to that club again, and I'll make you TWO German chocolate coffee cakes."

"I'm okay, Estelle." I glance at Clark. "I wasn't feeling too well, and Clark helped me home."

Estelle sniffs loudly and her face springs up out of

her hands as she finally realizes that Clark is sitting by the window.

"Oh." Estelle's eyes widen and brighten at the same time. Her head goes back and forth to him and me. Rather than try to explain anything else, I lean back into my pillows and sip my hot chocolate.

"Oh," Estelle repeats conspiratorially. She then makes an exaggerated pirouette toward the door and raises her eyebrows at me. Fluttering her fingers at Clark, she dramatically closes the door behind her.

Clark's own eyes are wide with nervousness. "She doesn't think I—"

I shake my head vigorously. "I can assure you, Estelle is always thinking of something."

Clark looks down at his mug, obviously confused, but decides against pursuing the matter further.

"Um…" I start to grip the mug even more tightly in my hands, inviting the distraction that the straining bones and muscles bring. "Clark. You can't…no one knows about… me." I frown and resist a wince as I realize how helpless I sound. "No one can know."

"The cancer treatments," Clark begins just above a whisper.

I immediately turn my head away, already knowing what is about to come.

"Sylvia, Ivan, June…Mrs. Mickelson," Clark says the words resolutely, but with a certain tone of gentleness that makes me look back at him, our eyes connecting.

I feel something pressing into my throat as I fight the tears that are threatening to choke me. "I didn't know that would happen. I mean…" I suddenly stop as a realization that I have been trying to suppress for so long finally emerges. "Maybe I always knew though."

A silence presses down heavily before I break my gaze with Clark.

"You can heal yourself and others?" Clark says carefully, as if he wants to create something concrete and comprehensible by forming words.

I continue to avoid his gaze as I remember the little white butterfly that died in my grandfather's hands. When I touched it, it started to move. It started to live. "Evie."

The sound of his voice and the strange way he says my name makes me snap my gaze back to him. The full extent of his exhaustion somehow seems to lift from his features as he holds my gaze for a just a second, before looking away and standing abruptly.

"Evie, you need to read it."

I watch Clark questioningly as he walks over to the messenger bag Estelle dropped by my door. Without even needing to search through the bag, his hand emerges with a book bound in hammered metal.

I am confused at the direction of the conversation because I had assumed there would be a little more in the form of exclamations or inquiries regarding my abilities to pull a lethal object from my chest—and surviving it.

Instead, Clark seems content with the fact that I am alive and still able to read. He hands me the small metal book and it strikes me for the first time that it looks very much like a diary. I hesitate for just a moment before setting my cup of hot chocolate on my nightstand. Clark then passes it into my hands.

"Clark..." I look at him, my eyebrows raising. "Do you

know something about this book?" I realize that it must be a strange question, since we discovered it at the same time in a secluded area. I remember the sound of little brown birds chirping all around us, the air wet with the promise of rain.

Clark's face becomes blank. It is this lack of expression that has me even more curious.

"I can't tell you that right now."

I sit up straighter, the metal book clenched in between my two hands. "Why?" And then before he can say anything else, my mind starts to reel back, something falling into place. My mind turns slowly, like the key in a rusty lock, fingers hesitant, as if waiting to see if it will actually open. "The Obsidian Blade."

Clark frowns, this time raising his own eyebrows in confusion. He automatically reaches into his coat pocket and pulls out the long, black shard. He holds it in his hands and then looks back up at me. "How did you know?"

"Know what?" I find myself staring at the blade, mesmerized by this object that Dean used to try and kill me with.

"The name, 'The Obsidian Blade'?" Without asking me, as if he knows what I am thinking, Clark hands me the thin object glinting in the orange light of my bedside lamp.

"I'm not sure." I lay the metal-covered book down in my lap, pulling my legs up to a cross-legged position under the covers. "It was like when I knew what the writing in the book said—even though I've never seen the language before."

I am now holding the blade in my hands. I am surprised to see that the silver blood-like fluid that appeared from my wound is somehow dried onto the black obsidian. A single streak of silver shines and glimmers in a distracting way. It almost looks as if the silver has become a part of the black glass.

I gingerly touch the tips of the blade, my fingers just grazing over both ends, which are sharpened to deadly points.

"Broken," I murmur quietly to myself, almost forgetting that Clark is standing there. "It's part of something that has been broken." I hear the words come out of my mouth without really knowing why I am saying them, even though I am certain I'm right. I scan the subtle edges that jut out from one end of the shard.

"It's been broken for a very long time."

I look up at Clark as he says this. His voice is tentative, but even so, I can tell that he wants to say more. I stay quiet as a hundred questions start flying through my brain.

Clark's eyes flit to the window almost longingly. "I need some more time to really understand what's going on, but the thing you're holding right now should not be here." His voice grows deeper, his tone changing in a way that I have never heard it sound before.

I resist the urge to ask more about what he knows and how he knows it. My mind moves slowly, something under the surface trying to break through. Even though someone tried unsuccessfully to kill me less than ninety minutes ago, I feel more frustrated than scared.

"What happened to Dean?" His eyes, like pools of black, and his vibrant tattoos of flowers stained with inky black veins seem to linger unpleasantly in my already confused thoughts.

"I'm not sure." Clark looks even more exhausted. "He vanished when I found you."

"There was something…" I lean back into my pillows, the Obsidian Blade lying in my hand, my fingertips cradling it. "Something that pushed him back from me right after he stabbed me." *A shadow flashing with silver-tipped claws.* "Something…or someone?"

Clark makes his way to the window, looking out with tired eyes, his hands hanging loosely at his sides. "I didn't see anyone else."

I blink slowly, realizing how heavy the weight of my eyelids feel. I am so tired.

"You should sleep." Clark is at my bedside again.

"You should sleep, too," I mumble groggily. "You look like you need it."

Even as sleep starts to drift over my thoughts, I can see him grin, the amber in his brown eyes standing out a little more.

"You're right."

My eyes close and I fall into a deep and dreamless sleep.

CHAPTER THIRTY-THREE
A MOTHER'S LOVE

THE NEXT MORNING, my eyes snap open at the first chirp of my alarm clock. I sit up quickly, amazed at how deep my sleep was. I haven't even moved from the position I fell asleep in, but surprisingly, I don't feel any stiffness. My hand is resting on the metal-covered book, and the Obsidian Blade is gone.

Clark.

Without even thinking twice about it, I know that he has it. For some reason, this doesn't seem so strange to me. A number of other strange things seem eager to take its place as my thoughts race.

I swing my legs out of bed, setting the metal book next to a mug still half full of now cold hot chocolate.

Turning off the alarm clock, I notice a small yellow Post-it note by the mug. Small lettering is written carefully across it.

Evie,

I know you still have questions. I have them as well. I might not see you over the next few days. When I return, I'll find you as soon as possible. In the meantime, stay safe. Please.

Clark

I set the note down, my level of confusion now elevated from what it was even before reading the note.

For the first time since deciding to pursue medicine, I actually consider calling in sick. I really think I'd be able to make a fair argument given the fact that I somehow survived my heart being skewered just hours ago.

Remembering what Clark said last night, I grab the metal-covered book, brushing my fingers across the smooth, rippling surface. I wish that I could go to my secluded area in the park and sit there bundled up in a sweater and raincoat reading it.

I sigh and walk over to my messenger bag, sliding it carefully in next to the larger and slimmer black sketchbook.

What's happening? I think this over and over again as I stare at these two books in my bag. Images of the events of the past few weeks flood my brain.

I realize that I am still clutching Clark's Post-it note in my hand. His involvement in this whole thing doesn't make any sense to me, and I find myself looking forward to his return—not just for my sake and the alleviation of all my frustration and confusion, but for his safety as well. The pointed edges of the black shard keep reappearing at the forefront of my thoughts.

Carefully, I place the Post-it note into a random spot between the pages of the black sketchbook. I then stand up, stretching my shoulders and lower back. The heavy weight of the silver and opal pendant hangs down around my neck. I carefully lift the chain up and over my head. I feel strangely naked without its weight.

I walk out of my room, and instead of heading straight to the bathroom like I normally do as part of my usual morning routine, I head toward the opposite end of the hall. Holding the pendant in my hand, I stand in front of Estelle's bedroom door. I can hear her soft snoring through the closed door.

I quietly hang the silver chain and pendant on her doorknob, my gaze lingering over the flecks of color that flash in the soft whiteness of the opal.

Ayesha glanced up from the large tome that she had laid out in front of her, long and elegant fingers sliding down a page as she stood up slowly. The golden fabric of her gown flowed down from her shoulders, pooling like a shimmering lake at her feet.

She made her way to the center of the circular chamber, which was surrounded by books reaching to the very heights of her towering prison, a stairway spiraling up to dizzying heights.

When she finally reached the center of the chamber, she folded her hands into the depths of her billowing sleeves.

She then lowered her gaze and waited.

She didn't have to wait for long.

The air in the chamber shuddered. The pages of some open books rustled as the air swirled around her. The light of tapered candles flickered but did not go out as shadows passed over them.

Then the rustling stopped abruptly and the air became still.

A heavy cloud of inky black smoke descended in front of her. As the smoke fell away and sank into the ground, two individuals were revealed.

"My children." Ayesha raised her clear crystalline eyes, her straight white hair brushing the dark skin of her shoulders and high cheekbones.

"Mother," Neko and Auriel said in unison, their voices echoing around them.

Ayesha blinked slowly, feeling a tightness clench at her heart as she let the echo of their voices fade.

"To what do I owe the pleasure?" Ayesha asked gently but firmly.

"No need for the formality mother." Neko smirked, his canines more visible than usual as his eyes scanned the books surrounding him. "We would forgive the intrusion—however, you don't seem too surprised to see us."

Auriel remained still, her colorless eyes staring blankly at her mother, whose gaze lowered to the floor. "It is because she knew we were coming."

"Of course." Neko's eyes clouded over, his smirk leaving his face. "Courtesies of Cerin, our dearest brother."

Ayesha raised her eyes and took a step forward. Her gown rippled out behind her with even the slightest of movements.

"Yes," Ayesha said, her tone unchanged. "Your brother was here. Just moments ago actually." With a swift and graceful movement, she revealed something from the folds of her sleeves.

"He wanted me to return this to you." Something whistled through the air, aimed at the empty space between Auriel and Neko.

Reflexively, Auriel raised her hand before the object could pass between them completely. It froze in the air and gently spun toward her outstretched hand.

The Obsidian Blade.

Auriel inspected the blade, her eyes flitting quickly over the object, taking in the silver streak of blood that now stained it.

Neko's own eyes widened as he observed the black shard in his sister's hands. The gray almost colorless irises of his eyes gleamed with the reflection of the silver striking through the blackness of the blade. "What could this mean?"

Ayesha's eyes were on her two children as they inspected the piece of volcanic glass. If they were to look up, they would have seen unshed tears glistening in the beautiful mirrors of their mother's eyes as she looked upon them. She blinked them away before they could fall, her face serene and quiet as she tilted her chin up.

"You know where the Obsidian Blade came from." She brushed her hands back into the folds of her golden-sleeved gown. "It means the world is turning and the moon is full."

Neko rolled his eyes, his hands flying up. "Enough with the riddles and this prophetical talk. It's just so vague.

Auriel flung the slender black shard at her mother's feet. It slid to a stop before it could touch the hem of Ayesha's gown.

"It means war." The words left Auriel's lips in a hiss as she spun around in the very spot she was standing in. The heavy blackened hem of her white dress twisted around her legs; the black crept up as it enveloped her in shadow. She disappeared, wisps of black smoke sinking down to the floor in her wake.

Neko hesitated as he caught his mother's gaze. He then lowered his own eyes and swept the sleeves of his garment back before disappearing in kind.

Even after many minutes had passed, Ayesha remained standing where she was, staring at the spot where her two twin children had been standing. The shard still lay at her feet.

A single tear slid down her cheek.

CHAPTER THIRTY-FOUR
A BROTHER'S LIE

"Evie!" A loud and very familiar voice shouts out from behind me.

Although not drinking any coffee at the moment, I'm sure that I would've spilled it if I had been. Instead, I am sitting in the Hole of Optimism typing furiously away at some notes regarding my current patient cases for the day. This is pretty much what I have been doing since the moment Dr. Mendez greeted me this morning. I welcomed the distraction to completely immerse myself in research documents and other such related materials—normal and familiar things.

I turn around and come face-to-face with a very annoyed-looking Estelle Kagwe, her hands on her hips and her mouth pursed into a pout.

"Well?"

"Well, what?" Although I know what she is waiting for, I can't resist prolonging what is definitely going to be a very anticlimactic recollection of what happened last night with a particular male in my bedroom.

Estelle huffs as she crosses the room in an impressive amount of time, even given the length of her long legs. Swinging a chair over to me, she resolutely takes a seat and crosses her arms over her chest. She hardly acknowledges the fact that her stethoscope is hanging precariously over one shoulder.

"You know what."

Sighing with resignation, I shuffle my feet in my beleaguered rotating chair so that I am now completely facing her.

"Nothing happened, Estelle…" I find myself hesitating. Even though I have been able to keep myself from thinking about it for the last few hours, the events of the night before come flooding back to me all at once. Estelle sits forward in her chair, assuming my hesitation is related to something more provocative than drinking hot chocolate and discussing strange healing abilities and mysterious pieces of pointy rocks with a particularly handsome coworker.

This last thought catches me off guard a bit, as I remember Clark's concerned look, sheepish smile, and the first time that I realized his brown eyes are flecked with bits of amber that almost look golden at times.

"Evie, you're lying." Estelle tilts her chin as she observes me, but her eyes widen in delight. "Your ears are turning red!"

"What?" I immediately ruffle the sides of my hair to hide my ears, which doesn't do anything to assuage Estelle's suspicions.

"His name is Clark, right?" Estelle attempts to whisper his name discreetly, but her whisper can probably be heard by anyone passing maybe eight feet down the hall outside of a closed door.

"Yes," I confirm reluctantly. "Clark Aeron. But before you go all sexy sitcom theory on me… no, there's nothing but a professional relationship between us."

"But he made you hot chocolate!" Estelle clasps her hands together in enthusiasm. "And it's *not* a sitcom."

"Packaged hot chocolate. It's not necessarily a well-known sign of infatuation." I place my hands in my lap and twiddle my thumbs in a purposeful schoolmarm impression.

Despite my lack of relevant information, Estelle continues on rather impressively. "He definitely reminds me of the dark and oh-so-handsome type. He's mysterious, too."

"I work with him. And see him nearly five days out of the week." I roll my eyes at any outlying thoughts regarding Clark and his life out of work, which could be perceived as a reflection of something somewhat normal. However, I immediately shut this line of thought down, realizing that Clark is indeed gone to take care of some task of mysterious origins. My brow furrows a bit, but rather than say anything else to affirm Estelle's theory, I remain silent.

Fortunately, there is a very loud beeping unmistakably coming from Estelle's scrub pocket. She hauls out her bedazzled pink pager and immediately hops up out of the chair. "You owe me some more details tonight."

"Wait, I thought *you* owed me a German chocolate coffee cake." I begin the feat of rotating my chair with my shuffling feet as Estelle makes her way out of the room. "Two of them actually."

"Oh, speaking of delicious food," Estelle says as she drops her pager back into her pocket. "Your brother invited us to dinner tonight."

"He did?" I shove a stack of papers aside on the desk looking for my cell phone. "He didn't message me about that."

"I got the message this morning." Estelle whips out her pink bedazzled cell phone. She waves at me and is out the door before I have completely rotated my computer chair around to face my work area.

I stare at the computer screen, my hands poised over the keyboard, when I realize that I'm not typing anything. I lean back in my chair and rub my temples with my fingertips. I am officially distracted from Estelle's interruption, unable to think of anything else but the little yellow Post-it note in my messenger bag.

While the restaurant is clearing out and Kiran prepares our own meal in the kitchen, I sit at a table that has been made with three table settings.

There is a whooshing noise as the kitchen doors swing open and Kiran walks out, pulling his apron off over his head. I have always been a little envious of my older brother's build. Where I am short, petite, and slender, he is taller, leaner, and in general much more athletically built than I am. Besides cooking, which is his single greatest passion, he has always been extremely fond of basketball. Something that I never could quite grasp even though I had attempted to participate on numerous occasions growing up, simply for the sake of allowing him a little more practice before a game out of sisterly devotion.

"Eggplant casserole with a side of honeyed potatoes." Kiran's face is slightly flushed from working in the heat of the stove and ovens, but he seems pleased with the effort. His eyes shine brightly as he smiles down at me. "Should be ready by the time Estelle arrives."

He seems even more pleased with his last statement. He pulls out a chair next to me as he relaxes, leaning back into his chair to stretch the muscles in his neck and legs.

"She's already on her way. She got caught up in a few complicated cases in the emergency department."

Kiran nods in his customary fashion whenever I bring up the work that Estelle and I do. Rather than needing me to elaborate, Kiran already knows that "complicated cases" in the hospital usually have something to do with a patient actively dying to a certain extent, which usually leads to complicated plans of action—which eventually results in staying later than the usual twelve-hour shift.

Kiran leans forward as his eyes focus on something laying on the table in front of me.

"What's that? A diary?"

My gaze trails downward until it lands on the small metal-covered book in front of me. I am surprised to see it there, even though I remember pulling it out of my bag and setting it in front of me with the intention of reading it before dinner was to begin. Instead, I just continued to let it sit there. My mind has been trying to focus on too many things and at the same time nothing. I feel my thoughts blur at the edges like the charcoal smudges of a sketched drawing. I suddenly feel a tingling in my fingertips and a familiar ache to draw something.

I frown slightly and look back at Kiran. "A diary? Why do you think it's a diary?" I vaguely remember thinking the same thing when Clark handed it to me last night.

Kiran's brows tilt downward in the same way as mine, the corners of his mouth doing the same thing very subtly. Even though different in almost every other aspect of character and mannerisms, it is moments like this that my parents like to point out how similar we are, our expressions almost mirroring each other.

"I'm not sure. It just looks like one." Kiran leans in a little further, his eyes staring at the ripples of silvery metal.

Impulsively and without knowing why, I push the surprisingly heavy little book toward him. Without even glancing back up at me, Kiran picks the book up and hefts its weight carefully in both his hands. He then lifts the cover open to the first page.

I can't read the expression on his face, his eyes just barely narrowing as they skim the page in front of him.

"Kiran," I begin quietly. "Can you read it?"

Kiran's eyes stop moving, and in one quick motion, he snaps the book shut. "No." He lays the book back on the table and pushes it toward me. "It looks like some sort of ancient language...or alien language. Are you sure you can't read it?" Kiran's face lights up in a joking grin.

I look at him, getting a strange feeling that I have never had around my brother. He continues to smile and stands up, his eyes darting to the clock.

"I need to check on that casserole." He rubs his hands together and begins to make his way to the kitchen.

My eyes flit toward the book and then back to the kitchen doors, which are still swinging after Kiran pushed through them.

The strange feeling still clings at me before I finally recognize what it is.

It is the feeling of being lied to. Something that Kiran has never been good at and has always resisted doing unless it is to avoid hurting someone's feelings...or to hide something for someone.

I suddenly remember Kiran handing me the folded up drawing that had somehow been torn from the black sketchbook.

"It reminds me of your drawings from when we were younger."

His voice echoes in my brain and I'm remembering Kiran as a little boy. His voice always so gentle and even, his small hand on my shoulder when he found me sitting on the floor of my bedroom crying silently.

"It's okay, Evie," he would say as he picked up the drawings that I had flung across the floor, my hands black from markers, paint, and pastels as I drew the same image over and over again.

"Don't tell mommy and daddy," I would whisper as Kiran knelt down to put the drawings into a neat stack.

Kiran looked at me. His eyes had the same serious look as when he told me that Grandpa Takeo passed away. I was sleeping at the time, and he gently woke me up after he had awoken himself; hearing stirrings from downstairs where he said he overheard our parents talking about our grandfather dying. The next morning our parents told us as we sat at the kitchen table. Kiran and I both nodded sadly. They were both a little surprised after realizing that we already knew.

I remember Kiran holding all the drawings in his small hands. He nodded and walked over to a big box in my closet. He placed the drawings carefully inside the box, closing the lid tightly.

To this day, whenever my parents ponder about my choices in career and my sudden disregard for my artistic talents, Kiran comes up with excuses for me and avoids telling them the truth about my proclivity to drawing monsters. He lies to our parents to keep my secret.

As I watch the kitchen doors swing slowly back and forth, the image of Kiran snapping the book closed replays in my mind over and over again.

My heart skips a beat. Kiran is lying.

CHAPTER THIRTY-FIVE
DISTANT LANDS

CERIN COULD FEEL the darkness wrapping around him. Inviting him in, grasping at his hands and arms. He ignored the sensation as he observed his surroundings.

He stood on a plain leading out to black jagged rocks, which struck up and out toward the crashing ocean waves. Gliding over the terrain toward the jagged rocks ahead, he could feel his feet brush the hardened dirt beneath him.

As he approached, he could hear what he thought was the ocean spray shooting up as it hit the rocks. However, as he listened more carefully, the spray seemed to dissolve into faint and ghostly whispering in the roar of the crashing ocean waves.

Leaning down, Cerin brushed a finger over the surface of one of the rocks. He breathed in cold, bitter air as the rock-like surface started to ripple, pulsing as if trying to rid itself of its thick, earthy coating. The rock then flashed and glistened, revealing its obsidian surface.

He put his hand in his pocket, hesitating for just a second before finally taking his hand out. He opened his palm, and resting in the center was a shining black ring the same texture and color of the obsidian at his feet. He placed the ring on one of his fingers. Even as it slid on perfectly, Cerin had to resist the urge to remove it. It rested heavily against his skin.

Its weight burdened him.

His brow furrowed in concentration, Cerin set his hand with the ring upon the obsidian surface before him. As he did this, the ocean waves crashed higher and with more force all along the jagged rocks that bordered the vast plain surrounding him, as if serving as a terminal demarcation of the land and sea.

A dark shadow appeared from his hand. The shadow twined itself around his fingers, creeping up his arm and extending toward his chest before gradually receding down to his fingertips and into the obsidian surface beneath his hand.

The obsidian rippled again and seemed to melt into a blue fire, burning away at the black glass so that it sunk toward the ocean to form a steaming and roiling mass at the base of the jetty. It was at this single point that the ocean suddenly became still, the ocean waves rocking back until the water rippled quietly.

The black mass continued to move thickly until it hardened into a smooth and glistening platform made of obsidian at the base of the rocks where the ocean waves touched it almost hesitantly.

Cerin straightened up and waited.

"…blood just started pouring out of every orifice. And splattered all over the floors. I literally considered throwing my shoes into the biohazard container, but then realized that I didn't have a spare pair in my locker, and then how would I have made it to dinner?" Estelle waves her fork dramatically as she recounts her trauma-filled day at work, her mouth always slightly filled with either a bite of eggplant casserole or honeyed potatoes. Indeed, she has not thrown her blood-splattered shoes away, instead reporting to the oncoming physician team while pulling on a pair of blue hospital shoe covers so that she would be just in time for Kiran to take dinner out of the oven.

Kiran and I both listen to her, grimacing as we chew our own bites of food while Estelle continues to treat us with all the gory and interesting details of the day's emergency department cases.

"Positively gruesome," I say a little half-heartedly as I see my brother nod subtly, the corners of his mouth lifting just a bit.

"Oh, by the way, Ian was looking for you."

"Hm?" I reply a bit distractedly as I spear a particularly juicy potato onto the end of my fork.

"You know, Dr. Nakano? A.k.a. Dr. Beautiful Eyes?"

Kiran's eyes widen, his gaze whipping over to me in apparent recognition of the name. "Ian Nakano? You work with him?"

I meet his look with confusion. "He's a cardiologist. He's new, from some distant land. Wait, how do you know him?"

"Distant land?" Estelle chews happily, her eyes glazing over in what I am sure is some romantic fantasy.

"Oh, you know. I think from some place in Europe."

Kiran rolls his eyes. "Plovdiv."

"What is that? A type of dumpling?" Estelle's eyes refocus as she gazes at Kiran longingly.

Kiran's face turns a rosy complexion, even though he has been far away from the kitchen for almost thirty minutes.

"Plovdiv," he repeats plainly. "It's in Bulgaria."

"He's Bulgarian?" I raise my eyebrows in confusion, remembering his slight accent and the almond shape of his amber- and blue-colored eyes. "His last name sounds—"

"Japanese," Kiran finishes, tilting his chin thoughtfully. "He said he was adopted with his twin sister. Traveled a lot but lived in Bulgaria."

"Have you met his sister?" I ask curiously.

"Nope." Kiran takes a bite of his casserole. "He's actually a relatively private person. I didn't know he was a doctor."

"Sooo…how is it that you are somehow acquainted with this prince charming?" Estelle leans in, her whole body shifting grandly as she winks at me.

Kiran looks at me in confusion but shrugs. "He's been a regular here since I've had my grand opening. He's also asked me to open a contract with him to supply his own business with some small food items."

"Business?" This time Estelle is confused. "He works at the hospital though."

"He's part owner of the Thorny Heart with his sister," I recall. Kiran confirms this with a nod.

"Mm." Estelle raises her fork in a grand gesture of acknowledgement. "I thought I had tasted those rosemary sweet potato fries before! No one can make them as good as Kiran, so they had to be Kiran's!" Nodding firmly at this revelation, she seems less than interested at the knowledge that one of the doctors we work with owns a trendy night club.

Kiran's flush returns, his ears turning as red as mine do when embarrassed. "Yeah, it was a generous contract. Its pretty much allowed me to hire two new helpers for the restaurant." Kiran turns to me, his eyes bright with curiosity. "Why was he looking for you? You said he's a cardiologist, right?"

I avoid his gaze, happy that my ears are hidden behind a curtain of blue hair. "Maybe for a consult?"

"Well, Evie has suddenly discovered that her aloofness, intelligence, and absolutely perfect facial features and amazing hair are somehow magnets for attractive healthcare professionals." Estelle pauses while she takes a sip of her mango-flavored iced tea. "It's either that—or her messenger bag is the magnet."

Kiran twirls his fork and shakes his head, continuing Estelle's lead. "Most definitely the messenger bag."

"A very attractive messenger bag." Estelle smiles.

I roll my eyes at them both and sit back in my chair, crossing my arms in exaggerated defense. "Don't bring my messenger bag into some odd plot of romantic fetishes."

Kiran chokes and sputters into his plate of food. "I didn't say that!"

"I only implied it." Estelle finishes her casserole and potatoes with a flourish of her fork. "Anyway, Dr. Beautiful Eyes wanted to invite us to a small concert by Lenore's Wings. Exclusive. As in by invitation only."

I start shaking my head, about to open my mouth to recount all the life-threatening events that seem to happen at the Thorny Heart—then I remember that I haven't told Kiran anything and Estelle suspects nothing about why I left the club before her other than it having something to do with Clark—I press my lips together and set the fork down.

"No," I state firmly.

Kiran seems more than a little amused by my simple-worded resolve. "Why not, Evie? Ian seems all right. He invited me to the concert, too. I'm actually really looking forward to it. I haven't had much time to go out since the grand opening…we could all go together!"

I can't help but notice how Kiran avoids looking at me, his eyes flickering toward Estelle as she takes another sip of her drink. His face is just slightly flushed again, and he's starting to fidget with the end of his napkin, a look of shy hopefulness on his face.

My heart fills with sisterly affection, and I finally say, "Okay, I'll go."

CHAPTER THIRTY-SIX
TANI OF THE FIVE OCEANS

GRADUALLY THE WATER started to shift, a movement like fine silk being pulled back.

Something slowly broke through the surface near the obsidian platform.

A hand. Slender fingers grasped the edge of the platform. Another appeared, and after a brief pause, the water whispered and surged gently upward.

Emerging from the swell of ocean water was a woman, who stood with her eyes raised up to the sky as the water gently receded back and off the glassy black platform. Her whole figure seemed to be surrounded by an ethereal light.

Her skin was the color of dark sand, wet from the tides flowing over it. Her face was square, while at the same time soft. Her round eyes were the color of green sea glass, and her hair the dark shade of seaweed.

While obviously beautiful—hers was the type of beauty sharpened like the blade of a knife. Her body was covered in dark blue-green armor designed like fish scales. Around her neck hung a necklace of silver daggers the length of her fingers, with slashes of opalescent white, streaking the blades. One hand gripped a rope of sleek silver coiled next to her hip.

"It has been thousands of years since I, and my people, have stepped on land," her words rang upward over the jagged cliffs. The hint of the roaring ocean surged just beneath her echoing voice. Her eyes never left the sky.

"I never thought it would be a child of the frozen hells that would bring me this moment." Her hand flexed as her fingers tightened around the silver rope at her hip.

Cerin stepped off the jagged rocks. Before he could begin to fall, his body became wrapped in heavy black smoke. This black cloud sank toward the obsidian platform, until it landed softly and fell away.

"Foolish child," the woman's voice became deadly, the ocean waves licking at the edges of the platform as if preparing to break it in half.

Cerin, his colorless gray eyes never leaving the woman's face, immediately lowered down to one knee. "I address you, Tani, Queen of the Five Oceans."

Tani laughed darkly. "I am no queen. I am a prisoner, child. A prisoner of your father. A prisoner of these infernal waters where my people have been trapped since the war that froze the tides."

"The tides are not frozen," Cerin stated quietly.

"No. The oceans are too great. It is the tide of light and freedom. Of the world's warriors who fought for our good Kana Akihira… Our friend."

Tani's voice seethed as the ocean roiled, the waves crashing at Cerin's feet. His hands were getting wet as he remained kneeling upon bent knee.

"No. The tides are not frozen," Cerin repeated again, his voice unwavering and even.

Tani's chest rose and fell as she remained silent, staring unblinkingly down at Cerin, her sea-green eyes piercing him with anger.

"I have found her descendant." Cerin paused, the black ring on his finger seeming to weigh even heavier, as if a rock had been set on top of it.

"Descendant. This means nothing. Kana has been dead thousands of years. Kana may have descendants. But there was only one Queen of the Moon. Only one general of the Crescent Warriors. Only one who was feared by the God of Death himself. There was only one. And that was she—she of the silver hair." Tani flexed her fingers at her hip and the silver rope slithered out in a brilliant burst of shining light. Its tip lashed out, sliding across Cerin's pale and ashen cheek.

He didn't flinch or move. Even as the skin broke, dripping a silvery liquid that quickly darkened to an inky black color. His eyes never left Tani's as her own burned into his.

Instead Cerin reached into his pocket; he then slowly extended this hand out to Tani.

"Thousands of years have passed, Queen of the Five Oceans. I am not here to waste your time."

Tani's eyes widened. "What is this?" She grasped the object in his hand. It was a small lock of hair tied with a thin strand of string. The lock of hair was a light blue color, shot through with bits of white. But as she brought it closer to her eyes, it started to gleam and shine before turning the color of silver, its brilliance even greater than the rope lying at her feet.

"Impossible," Tani murmured as she looked down at

Cerin. "Tricks." However, even as she said these words, the ocean waves began to recede from Cerin's feet and hands.

Cerin straightened his torso a bit, but remained silent, waiting.

"I believe you," Tani finally said as she gripped the lock of hair tightly in her fist. "But why bring this to me? What does your father want from me? He must know that I would spend an eternity in these infernal waters before serving him."

"He doesn't know." Cerin finally stands, straightening his legs. "I came here alone." Squaring his shoulders, Cerin pointed at the obsidian platform beneath him. "My father sits upon his obsidian throne, as do my twin siblings. I refuse to sit next to them. My mother is in a prison in the distant mountain towers, chained behind golden bars." Cerin paused, his breath ragged but quiet and even. "The war is nearing, and Kana's descendant will lead the Crescent Warriors against my father and his frozen hell."

Tani narrowed her eyes and raised her face toward Cerin in defiance. "You mean to take the Obsidian Crown then? To replace your father upon his throne of death and ice?"

Cerin frowned, clenching his fists to his side. "No. I want a new queen to sit upon the throne."

This time, Tani's sea-green eyes widened in surprise. She looked down at her hand, the lock of hair shining silver and beautiful in her palm.

"I understand." Tani flexed her fingers, the silver rope slithering back into a loose coil at her hip. "However, child of the frozen heart"—she took a step toward him, her arm extended wide to take in the vastness of the jagged rocks lining the ocean—"like your dear mother of the Crystal Sight, I am a prisoner."

Cerin's gray eyes shone dully, but the corners of his mouth lifted into a stony smile. He held out his hand where the black ring rested on his finger. He slid it off and then extended it out to Tani. She hesitated, staring at the ring and then at Cerin before reaching out. The ring gently dropped into the palm of her hand.

"The key to my prison. The key to the prison of my people for many millennia."

Cerin nodded, but his eyes were cold and blank. "It's just a ring."

Tani, who was staring at the ring with unbelieving fascination, suddenly darted her eyes back at Cerin. She smiled fiercely and with a flick of her wrist tossed the black ring into the ocean's depths. The ocean roared as if anticipating this moment; the waves rose all around the platform they stood upon, but they remained dry, as if in the eye of the storm. The jagged rocks of black obsidian discarded their earthy coats before sinking and completely disappearing under the weight of the ocean's waters, which rose and crashed up even higher.

Cerin stood frozen as Tani's eyes flashed in amusement.

"I owe you a favor, death's shadow." She stepped forward. "I will honor this moment. But your fate is tied to your father's. Whatever the outcome may be in the Second War, your fate is sealed."

Cerin lowered his eyes as Tani began to turn around, but before she could step off the platform and sink into the swirling waters beneath her, she faced Cerin again.

"My son is alive," she said.

Cerin raised his eyes. The fierce look faded from Tani's face, softening her features; her eyes clouded over in sadness.

"Your brother should know. My son would want him to know."

Tani then turned away and stepped off the platform, the water enclosing around her before she disappeared into the fathoms of the ocean.

CHAPTER THIRTY-SEVEN
WHEN IT RAINS

JUNE LEANED FORWARD, her hands on her knees. Her neck was moist with rainy mist, and clouds of air puffed from her lips as she breathed in and out, her heart beating to a steady pace.

"Whoa, just under five minutes on your first ever mile on the track?" Mr. Han, wearing a bright blue raincoat and holding out a stopwatch, let out an impressed whistle between his teeth.

June looked behind her, the rest of her PE class was still completing their mile-long sprint; their faces flushed pink with the effort. She couldn't help but be surprised. A couple weeks ago, she would've hardly been able to make it halfway around the track before collapsing in a faint, the tumors in her lungs blocking the oxygen from reaching her blood.

"Hey, Reese, have you thought about trying out for the track team?" Mr. Han eagerly suggested as she took a seat on the bleachers, waiting for the rest of her class to join her.

"I'd have to talk to my dad first." June smiled as she reached into her backpack and searched around until she found a small navy-blue notebook. It was the same notebook that Dr. Mendez had given her the first time she met Sylvia and Ivan. Since then, they'd met a few times, and each time Dr. Mendez had them share whatever they had decided to write.

Sylvia's notebook had been filled with musical compositions. She was becoming more adept, and June found herself looking forward to the small recitals on her bamboo flute. During their last meeting, Ivan actually joined her on his violin.

Ivan had a mix of entries about his day in his notebook, about how he was feeling, and sometimes he had written short stories—mostly about dragons and traveling atop them to distant lands throughout the sky.

June grabbed her pen, opening her notebook to write about her day. She had become fascinated by her athletic prowess. Although always fond of sports before getting sick and starting the treatments at Everline, she considered herself average when it came to most sports. She mostly pursued her place on the softball team as a hobby and a way to see her friends and have fun.

After finishing her entry about completing her one-mile sprint just now in under five minutes, she closed her notebook and carefully placed it back into her backpack. She then leaned back onto the bench and happily thought of Mr. Han's suggestion about joining the track team. June was already planning the conversation that she would have with her dad when she got home from school.

As she watched the rest of her class finishing their

sprint, her gaze drifted down to her hand. She froze as she noticed something strange.

A few small perfectly shaped spheres of water were sitting on the top of her hand. She looked up at the sky, and even though it was gray with clouds and the air was moist, it still wasn't wet enough to form raindrops. She stared at the little spheres and tilted her hand. They rolled a bit before stopping rather than falling apart or sliding completely off her skin. June's eyes widened as she looked around. Her classmates were sitting in the cool grass or talking to Mr. Han as they checked in with their times. No one was near her. She gently touched one of the water droplets. It rippled faintly but kept its spherical form. She then pinched the drop of water and it rolled between her fingers like a small round pearl.

"Hey, June!"

June jumped and dropped the pearl of water. It bounced on a blade of grass before falling apart into a little burst of water. She quickly brushed the rest of the water spheres from her hand and looked up, trying not to watch as they burst apart as they landed on the grass at her feet.

"Nice time, by the way." Devon jogged over and sat next to her on the bench. He was breathing heavily, and June was relieved that he didn't seem to notice anything.

"Geez, did you even break a sweat?" He laughed and leaned back, his legs stretched out in front of him.

"Just a little," June joked, but her mind was racing. She wondered if she sounded nervous. Devon didn't seem to notice as he continued to talk to her.

"You would love track. We need some new team members, too!" he encouraged enthusiastically. June wondered if

Mr. Han had sent him over to recruit her, and she couldn't help but laugh a little, relaxing.

"Yeah, I'm going to talk to my dad about it tonight. I just got out of the hospital, so I want to make sure if he thinks it's a good idea."

Devon bobbed his head before proceeding with the virtues of joining the school track team. June nodded appropriately, but she kept getting distracted, her eyes drifting up toward the sky, wondering when it was going to start raining.

Chapter Thirty-Eight
GORAN AND THE MAD OWL

*Neko glided over the forest floor. The ferns and branches sur-
rounding him brushed his silken cloak, sliding over everything
like a silent tide of black water.*

*The sky that could be seen above was lit with stars scat-
tered across it in a dazzling celestial display. Neko quietly wove
through the forest, occasionally brushing a finger across the leaf
of a tall plant or the trunk of a tree. Wherever he touched, a
black scorch mark that dripped with ice would be left.*

*As he approached a clearing of large thin trees, the star-
light glittering above, he saw a creature plodding before him
on four legs. Its antlered head turned slowly toward him, its
large round eyes blinking sadly.*

*"Hello, Goran, old friend," Neko smirked, his teeth glint-
ing sharply, almost like silver needles in the starlit clearing.*

*The stag turned its head away from him and continued to
trek through the trees, weaving through them in a languid and
lumbering pace.*

Neko raised his eyes in frustration. "For once, I would like to be on the receiving end of pleasurable conversation and suitable company." He sighed dramatically under his breath and began to make his way toward the stag.

He paused as something descended from the trees high above him. He could feel his silken cloak float in the stirring air. The creature swept back around, its large wings spread out silently, as it flew straight toward him, letting out a bone-chilling screech.

"Enough, Elaine," a deep and gruff voice filled the clearing. It seemed to come from all around Neko. The great horned owl that had flown at him suddenly reversed direction and glided over in the direction of the stag.

However, where Neko had expected the stag, he found instead a man, his arm outstretched as the owl landed atop it. The owl and the man both stared at Neko.

"Elaine? You call that vessel of feathery flying hell Elaine?" Neko threw up his hands in disbelief.

Elaine's feathers bristled. The man whispered something to the bird and, as if understanding him completely, she took off from his arm and flew up toward the high treetops.

"I was expecting you, young sprout. Although, I cannot say that I am pleased at all to see you."

"Sprout?" Neko repeated the word with some annoyance. "Well, you old...old goat...or elk...or whatever. I take it that you've been paid a visit already."

Goran nodded. His skin was coated in a light dusting of dirt, his body covered in a garment sewn together with round plates of stone and leather. His dirty beard and hair fell to his belt, which seemed to be the only clean thing about him—its silver loops radiated with a brilliant glow to rival the stars above. Despite his rugged appearance and his large build beneath the armored plates, which made him look as if he were a walking mountain, his copper-colored eyes shone with an unexpected gentleness.

"Your brother, the little shadow of death," Goran stated plainly.

"Only you Goran, Man of Mountains and furry things, can make that term sound so endearing." Neko rolled his eyes before gliding over to close the distance between them. He wearily glanced up at the trees above him, wondering if Elaine was gathering a flock of her friends to ambush him.

"I'm sure this may be a little pointless, but any chance that you may be able to relay details of his meeting with you?"

Crossing his arms, Goran nodded. "He said a war was fast approaching. And that it would be wise to prepare for it."

"Yes, yes. War. Destruction. An angry father. And something about the Obsidian Crown." The corners of Neko's mouth lifted. "Anything else?"

Goran was silent before he nodded again. "He told me the mountain tops are shining and the moon is bright."

Neko's mouth fell open slightly. "Unbelievable. Why does everyone speak in riddles and silly metaphors?"

"You would be wise, young sprout, to acknowledge the wisdom of the ancient words." Goran's dirt covered hands rested on his belt. Neko noticed that the loops were actually large rings that could be removed. He wondered what use Goran had for these large, silver rings. He expected something grander for a great warrior's weapon.

"Stories," Neko muttered impatiently. "Stories belonging to those who died before they ever knew the outcome of the war that would lead to their deaths."

Neko made to turn around but froze in place. He stared at Goran as if seeing him for the first time.

"There's one more thing, Man of Mountains."

Goran rested a hand on one of the rings on his belt; he seemed reluctant to do so, though. His eyes locked onto Neko's in a tired way.

"You've been freed." It wasn't a question—and before Neko could take another step forward, Goran seemed to fade as a haze enveloped him.

Where he had stood, a large black raven had appeared. Its black wings spread out wide, and it spiraled at a remarkable and graceful speed up to disappear somewhere in the treetops.

Elaine fluttered down, resting on a low-hanging branch above Neko's head. Her round eyes almost appeared to be glaring at him, the feathers on her neck ruffled and her wings lifted just over her torso as her talons grasped at the branch lightly.

Neko lifted his hand in surrender, sighing wearily. "No need to worry your feathery head. I'm not much for chasing after things."

As Elaine's gaze followed him suspiciously, Neko walked over to where Goran had once stood.

On the ground, amidst the rocks, leaves, and dirt of the forest floor lay the remnants of chain links. They gleamed with the black sheen of obsidian.

For thousands of years, the Man of Mountains, nature's greatest friend and guardian, had been a prisoner of this very forest, trailing black chains behind him as he roamed his prison among his forest-dwelling companions, unable to leave.

Until now.

Neko's colorless eyes stared unblinking and cold down at the broken chains. "Oh, dear brother, what have you done?"

CHAPTER THIRTY-NINE
KANA

AFTER DINNER WITH Kiran and Estelle, I successfully dodge any further questions about "The Bedroom Incident" with Clark, which is what she's taken to referring to it as. I just nod in acknowledgement of all the romantic fantasies that Estelle has impressively concocted over the past thirty minutes.

My mind keeps going back to the image of Kiran's eyes scanning the page of the metal-covered book—the snap of the cover echoing through my ears as he quickly closed it.

When we finally reach our apartment, I am eager to shut the door of my bedroom behind me. Estelle is already humming and skipping down the hallway back to her room, all the way gushing about Kiran's amazing rosemary French fries.

I stop at the kitchen and pour a glass of cold water. Bringing it to my bedroom, I sit on my bed, my legs curled beneath me as I slide the metal book out of my messenger bag so that it rests on my bedspread, shining with a soft metallic gleam. I remember the raindrops that behaved so strangely on its silver cover the first time I encountered this book in the clearing where little brown birds surrounded me. As I bring the cool glass of water down from my lips, something seems to grip and pull at the edges of my thoughts.

Then, as if it were a reflex, I dump the glass of water onto the small metal book. Although startled, I find myself almost expecting to see what is now visible before me.

Instead of the water sliding off the soft metal cover, it forms a perfect spherical pool of water that ripples on its surface. I reach a finger out, and after hesitating for just a second, I gently touch the sphere of water. It ripples more intensely where I touch it, a small ring spreading from the point of my finger.

I pull my finger back, replacing it with both of my hands, reaching out to hold the ball of water, which is just a bit bigger than the palm of my hand. I breathe in sharply when the water does not burst, but retains its round form. I bring the ball of water up to my face and then rotate my hands slowly so that they rest on the top and bottom of the sphere rather than the sides. I notice that somehow the weight of the water, or whatever force is keeping it in the form of a ball, has shifted, and now I find the ball suspended in front of me. Its as if magnets from both my hands are somehow floating the ball between them.

I blink quickly, mesmerized by what is happening. Gently, I rotate my hands so that they are both under the ball of water. It lowers down gently to rest in my palms. I then shift the ball of water to one hand and transfer it back to the empty glass, where it splashes down, a couple of drops actually hitting me in the eye as it ricochets off the glass forcefully.

My heart starts to pound in my ears as I look back down at the book. I lift the cover, and once again I'm astonished at how quickly the strange shapes of letters and words—symbols I have never seen before—can form a barrage of understanding and recognition in my brain. It feels like being struck by lightning.

I recognize the description of battles from when I first opened the book briefly. Battle strategies, outcomes, and the many names of people and locations are detailed throughout. I read page after page of painstaking details of a world that seems too impossible to have ever existed. A world of warriors who wielded spears of crescent-shaped blades and other strange weapons. There are also descriptions of exotic creatures that I can't help but picture in my mind as mythological illustrations from stories of the ancient histories of the world I know.

Some of these entries are even separated by small beautiful drawings of these creatures and sleek, silvery weapons. I'm surprised to recognize an image of armor and even some of the weapons.

The image of fields burning in blue fire, spiraling up into black clouds, suddenly appears in my memory—the dead eyes of a female soldier wearing this very armor staring up at me blankly.

I quickly turn the page, my heart skipping a beat. This next page is completely filled with the meticulous drawing of a smooth, scaly creature the deep blue color of the sky. Even in the illustration, parts of its body somehow appears to glow with a shining white color, and I can imagine it disappearing as it weaves through the clouds, its wings reflecting the sunlight.

However, it's the eyes—both piercing and gentle—that holds my attention the longest. They are a pale, beautiful blue. It finally dawns on me that this has to be a dragon. Under this image are words written in careful script: *Ha-Neul of the Blue Kingdoms.*

Pausing in disbelief and amazement, I reluctantly turn the page. The next page is different than the other page; something about the softness of the writing makes me realize that this isn't about battles, victories, alliances, and casualties.

The entry scrawled out almost appears careless compared to the neat and detailed script of the entries before it:

Day 17 of the Month of Cassiopeia's Sky Reign

I received a hastily written letter today from my dearest friend, Ayesha. She is with child. Her words are filled with delight, and despite the present circumstance that takes me away from her side, I cannot help but share in her happiness.

I do not have the heart, though, to tell her what she wills herself not to see. I wish I did. Her husband has locked her away to keep her safe from the war's destruction. Even my letters only make it to her by the golden sight and wings of our phoenix friends, the only ones who can cross the mountain range and know of any single individual's whereabouts.

Forgive me for having fleeting thoughts of cursing the stars and moon, because I cannot cast off these horrible images they give me. I have visions of death in her unborn child's eyes. I have visions of a world heavily veiled by creeping black tides of smoke and obsidian encasements.

I see darkness surrounding this child at the center of it all. A jagged crown of terrible beauty, of obsidian, resting in his hands.

My fingers tremble even as I write these words. As the war carries on, I grow wearier as every day passes me by. Every day I see the lands and people of my kingdoms burn away from me, and I feel coldness settle into my bones.

And yet, I am their queen, their general of the Crescent Army. I fear much, but not for myself.

The moon and stars will raise the skies even when I am gone.

I frown as I read the last words. My brow creases as I close my eyes. I can almost hear the words being spoken in a far off voice.

"The moon and stars will raise the skies even when I am gone."

I strain through the muddy waters of my thoughts and memories, trying to recognize the voice saying those words. However, it is all in vain.

I open my eyes again, staring at the entry. After carefully turning a few more pages, reading more about the descriptions of battles, I find myself vividly imagining them in my mind. A silver-clad army marching in waves against opponents cloaked in darkness and sharp spears, knives, and swords of black obsidian blades.

These detailed imaginings are suddenly swept from my mind when my eyes rest on one particular page. Like the blue-white dragon, this image takes up the entire page. Its lines are sharp and clear. I can't help but compare it to the charcoal drawings of the black sketchbook, with its rippling cover.

It is of a crescent filled in with swirling and flowering silver filigree. It is rising out of a black pool of water, which drips off its surface wetly. Under the drawing are carefully written words in neat script:

And she was born under the darkness of the moon's shadow.

I feel my breath steady as I reread this line over and over again until my eyes focus on a spot at the very corner of the page. It almost looks like a smudge of black ink, an imperfection that confuses and surprises me at the same time.

Lifting my finger, I run it gently over the smudge mark. It smears like charcoal or wet ash. Raising my finger to my eyes, I see that it shimmers slightly before disappearing from my skin. When I look down at the smudge mark on the page with the filigreed silver crescent, I notice that it looks as if a brush has been taken across it. With one swipe of my hand, the ashy mark shimmers away, leaving the page unmarred.

I'm not sure how long I sit here, the book still laying open in my lap, the page's silver crescent shining up at me.

Eventually, I fall asleep, dreaming of skies filled with blue-white dragons and shining soldiers marching across black fields burning with blue fires.

CHAPTER FORTY

THE CURSE OF LOVE

"Dr. Mendez?"

Turning around, Dr. Mendez nodded in acknowledgement of his name being called. His eyebrows raised over his sharp-rimmed glasses in his customary way as a nurse walked over to him.

"Yes, Chandra?"

Even though her curly brown hair was pulled back in a ponytail, it still somehow got itself wrapped around the stethoscope draped over her neck. As she distractedly tried to disentangle a strand of her hair from the stethoscope, she addressed Dr. Mendez.

"There's a gentleman in the waiting room. He was actually looking for Evie, but she's off today. He said he really needed to talk to her about something. Said he was a patient of hers. I told him to wait while I got you instead."

Before Dr. Mendez could inquire further, Chandra turned around, successfully disentangling her hair from her stethoscope, and then briskly walked into a patient's room behind him.

Sighing, Dr. Mendez straightened the sleeves of his coat, glancing down at his wrist where his watch was secured. His eyes paused over the silver ring on his finger, lingering on the brown topaz for just a second before making his way to the patient waiting area.

The waiting room was quiet. There were usually not very many people at this early hour of the day, most people deferring to a late morning commute so as not to get stuck in the traffic-locked grid of the city during rush hour.

Only two people were in the waiting room, an elderly woman dozing off in her chair, a magazine laid out across her lap, and another person standing by the window, looking down at the street below. When he heard Dr. Mendez enter the room, he quickly turned around.

Dr. Mendez didn't recognize him but immediately walked over, his hand outstretched.

"Hello, I'm Dr. Julian Mendez. Dr. Hashimoto is out of the office today, but maybe I can assist you."

The man shook his hand. He looked to be in his thirties or forties, his face young but sharply shadowed with stubble. The hair on his temples was just slightly gray. He wore dark slacks and a neat blue shirt and tie. He looked like a businessman, his eyes friendly enough but carrying an edge of shrewdness.

"I apologize for the pretense." The man placed his hands in his pockets, his face sincere but his voice hesitant. "I told the nurse that I was a patient here, which I technically am, but Dr. Hashimoto isn't my doctor. I thought if I said I was a patient, she would be more likely to meet with me than a total stranger."

Dr. Mendez raised his eyebrows in curiosity, folding his hands in front of him as he waited for the man to continue.

Taking Dr. Mendez's silence as encouragement, the man quickly held out an Everline Hospital pamphlet. Dr. Mendez recognized that it was the one that introduced the hematology-oncology providers among its folded pages.

"I saw this pamphlet on a cafeteria table while I was waiting to meet with my cardiologist." He pointed at a picture. "She saved my life. I recognized her immediately." The man seemed surprised and confused at the same time.

Dr. Mendez's eyes followed his finger, and he immediately recognized Dr. Evelyn Hashimoto, her hair an extravagant orange color, which she insisted at the time was "a peachy coral." She further insisted that this was appropriate for a professional photograph that would be available for hospital-wide publication. Suppressing a huff of exasperation when remembering this particular conversation, Dr. Mendez just tilted his eyes back up over his glasses to look at the man again.

"Only, her hair was a different color...silver or white." The man looked down at the picture briefly and then back at Dr. Mendez. "I-I wanted to thank her. She had a friend with her, too. I think another doctor. I wanted to thank them both. They happened to be on the same street when I had a massive heart attack."

The man shrugged helplessly. "I had no idea...I never went to the doctor. I never needed to before."

Dr. Mendez's eyes scanned the man who looked, by all means, to be a healthy and fit person; his torso lean and his shoulders broad.

"I had a congenital heart defect. I felt like my heart was being torn apart inside my chest. It was something I was born with that I didn't know I had. The doctors said that I should've died that day. I was lucky."

The man stood straighter as Dr. Mendez carefully took the pamphlet. He had written his name and cell phone number on the pamphlet in neat permanent marker. "My name is Raymond Green. I-I need to talk to Dr. Hashimoto."

Looking back up at the man, Dr. Mendez could recognize a look of desperation on his face, which struck him as being out of place. This man seemed like the type who was proud and confident, rarely given to moments of helplessness or requests for assistance.

"I will let Dr. Hashimoto know of your visit, and I will give this to her." He raised the pamphlet.

Raymond seemed relieved, breathing out as tension left the muscles in his shoulders. "Thank you." He quickly grabbed his coat, which hung over the back of a chair, and with one more look back at Dr. Mendez, he left the waiting room.

Dr. Mendez slowly turned around after a brief pause as he looked at the name written across the pamphlet again. Then he walked back to his office.

Dean knelt down at the foot of Auriel's obsidian throne. The one next to her was empty. Her twin brother, who usually occupied it, was gone on a mission.

Dean's usually vibrant green hair had turned a darker, mossy shade tinged at the roots and ends with black. His skin was pale, and the blackened veins had faded to a dark blue color that seemed to tint his lips as well. He looked cold, as if submerged in a pool of icy water.

Auriel shifted her weight forward, sitting closer to the edge of her seat. Her fingers wrapped around a slithering gold thread embedded into her pale yellow hair. She lifted her other hand up, bringing with it a shining dagger. Its blade was of black obsidian, and its handle of dark polished gunmetal that looked to be scorched by fire.

"Take this."

Dean lifted his face and reached for the dagger. When his skin touched the handle of the blade, he felt the skin of his fingers burn with heat and cold at the same time.

"Its name is Tanwen." Auriel watched as Dean rotated the blade in his hands, admiring its weight before lowering it and raising his eyes upward.

"It was forged many millennia ago and saw many battles among my father's armies. Its wielder has always served him well. It is a blade that will always return to you even when lost. However, it will eventually be the death of you. It is a powerful and cursed weapon."

Dean tightened his hand around the handle of Tanwen. He felt a distant feeling of surprise at the cold emptiness that seemed to fill his chest as he breathed in. Sometimes he wondered if his heart still beat and if blood still flowed under the flowers inked onto his skin. Even those flowers seemed dull compared to their original bright colors. His skin was cold.

"An army will rise soon," Auriel said quietly. Her colorless eyes stared past him as she wrapped and unwrapped the golden thread tied to her hair over and over in between her slender fingers. "You will help me and my brother lead them."

Auriel raised her now empty free hand. Dean stood as if she were pulling him by invisible ropes hanging above him.

"The army is frozen in my father's hell lands. They need life to wake them up."

The golden thread in her fingers continued to slip and slither around her finger. The metal glinted as she trailed her eyes lazily over to Dean.

"You will be tasked in helping us to accomplish this." Auriel stood and pivoted slightly to stand next to a thin pedestal between the two obsidian thrones. On the pedestal sat a medium-sized golden chest. It was wrought with engravings of people in all manners of suffering, their golden features frozen in grimaces of pain, their bodies engulfed in flames or pierced with spears, swords, or arrows.

Auriel laid her hand over the chest carefully, almost reverently, as the lid shifted and slid open. She then lowered both hands into the shining chest and lifted out what looked like a bandolier of sleek black leather. Hanging off the leather at ten intervals were small rings of obsidian and nothing else.

Turning around, Auriel walked over to Dean. Dean immediately lowered his head as Auriel snapped the bandolier across his chest. It fit perfectly. Straightening up, Dean looked down at his chest, the hand that wasn't holding Tanwen brushing the obsidian rings.

Auriel lifted the corners of her mouth bitterly as she stood back, observing Dean and remembering a time when she had equipped another soldier in this same manner with the same bandolier. For a moment, she allowed the image to flit across her thoughts before she brushed it aside, her face once again going blank.

Dean spun Tanwen in his hand, admiring its weight and

how it seemed to balance his entire body. A tingling sensation shot through his chest like pins and needles. He welcomed the feeling. When he moved his thumb across a certain part of the handle, the blade retracted and he was able cleave the dagger to a loop on the bandolier.

"You will do well." She waved her hand carelessly behind her, and the golden chest snapped shut with a dull thud.

CHAPTER FORTY-ONE

FIRE AND ICE

Estelle taps the toes of her shoe impatiently as we stand waiting in line of a small local film and photo developing shop. I insisted on the detour on our way to the Thorny Heart.

We are both dressed for a night out, although Estelle is a little more so with her smart slacks and pretty blue blouse. I have my usual messenger bag accessory and dark sweater on, only this time I decided to fling a scarf woven with bronze thread around my neck. Although simple, I feel particularly put-together, my hair a fresh color of magenta. Estelle is taken by it, saying that it reminds her of Kiran's rhubarb pie. Any compliment related to food is at the height of Estelle's approval scale, so 'rhubarb' seems an acceptable description to me.

"Well, this is quite the prelude to a fun-filled night of entertainment and fine company." Estelle sighs dramatically as the line creeps forward. Personally, I am surprised at the popularity of this small shop, but I shrug as I sip a coffee that

I insisted we stop for on the way to our fun-filled night at the Thorny Heart. I try to push away the feeling of anxiety creeping at the corners of my thoughts as I imagine returning to the place where I almost died. I wonder if Dean, his eyes veined and shot through with black, will be there.

At the same time, I can't help but remember the black shadow. Its claws alight with a vibrant silver. I know that it was what had saved me.

"Hi, Evie!"

"Hey, Beck," I greet the cashier when we finally make it to the counter.

Beck grins shyly, her freckled face going red as she looks up and greets Estelle as well. Estelle insists that Beck has a crush on me, and before she can reference the romantic magnetism of my messenger bag, I shoot her a look, my eyebrows raised.

"I-it's been a while since you've been in. We were worried that you forgot about your photos," Beck stutters as she quickly runs to the drawers that are alphabetized by the client's last name. When she reaches the *H*s, she carefully pulls out a small manila envelope and sets it in front of me.

"I love your hair, by the way!" Beck blurts out, immediately going redder in the face. She looks at Estelle. "You both look beautiful. You must be going out tonight?"

"Thank you, Beck." I smile at her and pull out my wallet to lay money out for my photos. "We're actually heading to a concert at the Thorny Heart."

Beck rings the cash register open and grabs my change. "Wow. Really? Everyone has been talking about that place! Almost all my customers have heard about it."

Estelle springs in enthusiastically, "It's amazing. You

have to make your way there sometime! One of the doctors we work with is part-owner of the place. And our music therapist is the lead singer of the headlining band."

"I don't know about that. We've had some questionable experiences there, personally," I state plainly.

"Isolated incidences," Estelle chimes in nonchalantly, ignoring my look of incredulity.

"Oh." Beck hands me my change thoughtfully. "I guess I should check it out at some point."

"Definitely," Estelle responds as I grab my envelope of photos, sliding them into my messenger bag.

"At your own discretion," I say pointedly.

"Well, have fun you two." Beck waves as we head out of the shop.

"Thanks, Beck." I wave back at her, and just as the shop door closes behind us, I twirl toward Estelle.

"I don't know if we should be encouraging patronage at a place that you almost experienced an early demise in, as well as—" I quickly cut myself off, remembering that Estelle knows nothing of my experience with Dean. However, she doesn't seem to notice, instead digging around in her clutch until she pulls out a piece of chocolate.

After unwrapping it, she pops the chocolate into her mouth. "It was just that one time. I haven't had any lingering urges to jump off any more balconies lately," she says rather cheerfully.

Shaking my head, I toss my now-empty cup of coffee into a trash can we pass by. We continue walking for a few more blocks, our breaths becoming clouds as the sun begins to sink farther, and twilight starts to shadow the city, lit by orange lights that gradually turn on as we pass them.

I try to ignore the anxiety that creeps up and tenses around my shoulders. I am almost surprised when we finally face the nondescript door of the Thorny Heart. Shifting my messenger bag over my shoulders nervously, I follow Estelle through the door. We are immediately greeted by Kiran, who has been waiting for us in the ante-chamber that serves as the entryway to the club. He seems to be in a happy discussion with a noticeably new person sitting where Dean had greeted us previously when we had come to the Thorny Heart.

The greeter, a large man with equally large muscles, stands up. "Welcome. You must be guests of Mr. Ian Nakano," his voice booms in what sounds like a South African accent that carries impressively around the room with very little effort. "I am Edward."

"Hi, Edward," Estelle and I find ourselves saying at the same time.

"Edward is a huge fan of my stuffed bell peppers," Kiran says enthusiastically as Edward nods in approval.

"They are wondrous, my friend," Edward reiterates Kiran's statement, his face serious, arms crossed over his chest stoically.

"Stuffed bell peppers! Kiran makes the best stuffed bell peppers. And eggplant casserole, chocolate cheesecake, spicy tuna rolls with avocado, and—"

"Everything else edible," I cut Estelle off in a mean-ingfully bright tone before she can list nearly every item that she has ever consumed with the Hashimotos, courtesy of Kiran.

Estelle simply nods. "Pretty much!"

There is no doubt in my mind that even in the dimly

lit entryway, Kiran's face is flushed as he tries to avoid making eye contact with anyone.

"Proceed." Edward tilts his chin up toward the door ahead, his arms still crossed over his broad and very muscular chest.

Kiran leads the way. I can't help but notice the comfortable ease with which he does so. Obviously, he has become well acquainted with the Thorny Heart, even after a short period of time, due to his business relationship with the owners.

As he holds the door open, we are met with the sight of a decent crowd of people, but noticeably smaller than what Estelle and I have experienced before. The room is familiar, the stage at the far end, though, is dark and quiet.

There are two small stools and a single microphone pole seated at its center.

I don't distinguish anyone in the crowd at first, but then I find myself recognizing Ian rather quickly. My gaze falls on him, his dark hair a little longer than I recall it being before. It falls down to his neck and flows out in a way that I can't describe as anything other than pretty.

He stands a foot taller than the person he is talking to, his face serious, but the corners of his mouth are turned up in that familiar smirk of his. It hardly takes me a moment to realize that this person he is talking to is our hospital's music therapist and lead singer of Lenore's Wings, her hair tucked behind her gold-pierced ears, her black tattoos visible where there is skin showing.

Ian's eyes suddenly lock on us, both blue and amber lighting up in pleasure to see us. Ness also turns, a smile quirking up at the corners of her mouth as she recognizes us. Her smile strikes me as being extremely familiar for some reason.

Walking forward, Ian shakes hands with Kiran in an accustomed gesture of companionship.

"I see you were able to convince a special appearance by our guests here," Ian says, his tone light as he grins at me and Estelle.

After a moment, Ness joins us.

"I guess we have all met at some point." Ian waves a hand around the small group. "But a proper welcome wouldn't be too much of a waste of time. Thank you for joining us at the Thorny Heart, Seattle's up-and-coming nightclub of trendy dealings and humble origins."

Ness rolls her eyes, an indulgent smile on her face as Ian continues.

"As I'm sure you're well aware, this is Ness Rose," Ian says, exaggerating a tone of nonchalance. "Lead singer of our premier headlining band, Lenore's Wings. And also, part-owner of this fine establishment."

Estelle gapes as she suddenly comes to the same realization as Kiran and myself. "So, that must mean that Ness is your sister?"

Ness nods. "Your conclusion is correct."

There is a moment's pause as we stare at the two of them. It is at that moment that I realize why I found Ness's smile so familiar. It is the same as Ian's—a corner of her mouth lifting up slightly before the other one soon follows.

"We get that same reaction all the time," Ness assures us as she places a hand on her slender hip, the fabric of her long white blouse flowing down her arms as she does so. "Would you believe that we're actually fraternal twins?"

Ian laughs, jokingly placing his own hand on his hip to mirror his sister's posture. "Obviously. Like yin and yang."

I definitely agree as I shake off my initial surprise. Where Ian is dark, his sister is light and fair, with the exception of her tattoos; however, the pale blue of her eyes seems to match the exact blue one of Ian's.

"So, I never get the chance to ask, but what made you do all of this?" Kiran spreads his arms wide toward the nightclub, his face alight with intrigue. "Not busy enough as health-care workers, I take it?" Kiran eyes me in a teasing brotherly way. I find myself resisting an eye roll similar to Ness's.

"Oh, I'm plenty busy enough." Ian shrugs. "But I always find that it's good to have a healthy balance of work and play. Right, Nessie?"

Ness grimaces at the use of her name in this fashion, but eventually nods in agreement. "Indeed. We try to make use of our talents. Ian has great intuition regarding 'trendy' business ventures. Oh, and talking."

We all laugh at this, Ian included. His laugh comes so easily. I am annoyed at myself for the effort it takes to avoid looking at him. His heterochromatic eyes are just as distracting as when I first ran into him on the street.

I am grateful when Ian motions for us to sit down at a table specifically set for us. The crowd of patrons begin doing the same as they take their respective seats. We soon find out that these are potential vendors and some performers that Ian hopes to attract to the Thorny Heart.

Instead of joining us, Ness walks over to the simple makeshift stage consisting of the stool and microphone. Emerging from the crowd is the androgynous red-haired singer who opens for Lenore's Wings. He is without his multi-colored garments, but his eyes and dark skin are covered in silver glitter. Small clouds of it sparkle and catch the light with any small movement.

He takes the stool next to Ness and gently lifts up a set of panpipes that he's carrying. His red hair falls in loose curls on one side of his face. His smile is contagious, and I can see why he opens for Lenore's Wings. He sets the tone and pace for a night filled with entertainment.

"Marcus Strong." Ian leans in toward me, his head close to mine as he whispers the name. I am startled to realize that, somehow, we ended up sitting next to each other while Kiran and Estelle sit opposite us on the other side of the table. He hardly seems to notice my alarm as I reposition my glass of water for the sake of having something to do.

"My sister has a good instinct for talent. Marcus was the first one she had brought into the Thorny Heart."

"Where did she meet him?" I ask distractedly as Ian brushes back a strand of his hair that has fallen across his cheekbone.

"Marcus is a talent for hire. We've been acquainted with him for *quite* some time." Ian grins as he says this.

It is at this point that Marcus brings the panpipes up to his lips. The fingers holding the instrument are long and graceful. Hanging on both of his wrists are beautiful bracelets made of some green stones shaped as leaves. He starts to breathe into the panpipes and suddenly the room hushes, along with the rustling of clothing and quiet clinking of silverware or glasses.

Ness's voice soon accompanies the sound, but I can't

tell when she actually started to sing—her voice seems to naturally become part of the low, hollow, and windy notes of Marcus's panpipes. After a few moments, I can make out the familiar words of her song from a poem I distantly recall:

> *Some say the world will end in fire,*
> *Some say in ice.*
> *From what I've tasted of desire,*
> *I hold with those who favor fire.*
> *But if it had to perish twice,*
> *I think I know enough of hate*
> *To say that for destruction ice*
> *Is also great*
> *And would suffice.*

As the song comes to an end, the name of the poem by Robert Frost echoes from my lips. "'Fire and Ice.'"

Ian glances over at me, the look of mischievousness gone for a second. I can see him in profile as his amber eye focuses on me.

"An avid reader of more than chickens, quahogs, and exotic foods?" Ian smiles as he joins in the exuberant applause.

Bringing my hands together, I feel the redness creep up and around my ears. "Estelle must've informed you of my reading habits?"

Ian shrugs. "Perhaps, but I gathered so much on my own. You are rarely without a dozen books at any given time."

"It's more like three or four at a time, depending on the quality of the cover. If it's paperback verses a hardcover for instance."

Laughing, Ian seems only a little surprised by my answer. Perhaps he expected more of a defensive response about my book-carrying habits.

"It would almost seem as if you're trying to distract yourself with more interesting things…like quahogs," Ian teases, and I can't help smiling in response.

"Quahogs are interesting creatures. They are considered immortal."

"No one or creature is immortal." As if surprised by his own comment, he leans back quickly, but not before I see the look of sadness flash across his sharp and smiling features.

I find myself looking at him fully now, my earlier attempts to avoid eye contact with him forgotten. He genuinely looks surprised and troubled after saying this, when a waiter whisks by and sets plates of food down in front of us. Ness soon joins us, Marcus no longer at her side; instead trailing glitter in his wake as he greets guests at different tables.

"That was beautiful Ness." Estelle takes a pause from the conversation she's having with Kiran. I suddenly feel bad, realizing that I have not been interacting with them— but since they are talking easily and enthusiastically with each other, I feel forgiven for being distracted on the other side of the table.

Ness nods her head in modesty as she takes her seat, her plate of food waiting for her.

"Yeah, wow, that was really something." Kiran seemed preoccupied by the performance, as we all did when we heard Ness sing in Lenore's Wings for the first time.

Ian grabs his fork almost reluctantly as he looks down at his food. "What *is* something might be this particular chef." Ian glances over at Kiran apologetically. "My sister and I are looking to expand our dining options for this place. Unfortunately, nothing seems to compare to what Kiran has provided us."

Kiran smiles graciously, grabbing his fork and quickly taking a bite of the chicken entree in front of him. Chewing thoughtfully, Kiran nods. "Well, it could use a little more of my touch."

Estelle laughs, already having taken a few bites of her meal. "Yeah, this definitely doesn't compare to Kiran's chicken spicy marsala and teriyaki artichoke hearts."

This time I can't help but roll my eyes as everyone starts to eat their food and continue with different threads of conversations. Ness picks at her food, taking small bites and answering questions politely. Ian is more inclined to pick up the loose ends of conversation that his sister leaves. I start to pick up on subtle mannerisms and similarities between them, despite how physically different they appear.

"We traveled quite a bit, but mostly preferred Bulgaria," Ian answers Estelle's question about their traveling, referring to what Kiran had told us earlier. "My sister and I are somewhat nomadic. We've been…to many different places all over the world."

I find myself genuinely curious about how Ian and his sister were so well-traveled. They look to be closer to our age, and I personally would've found it hard to find the time and resources to travel with my studies and career choice. I wonder at least how Ian has been able to do this but don't feel comfortable asking.

Instead I opt for a simpler question, "What brought you here to the Pacific Northwest?"

Ian pauses before answering, spinning the tip of his fork in the middle of his plate, which still has quite a bit of food on it. "We wanted to be closer to family."

"Family?" Kiran lowers his glass of water. "That's a good reason. Evie and I grew up south of Seattle. Our entire family is here."

"Yes, it is a good reason," Ness states plainly, raising her dark eyebrows sharply at her twin brother.

Ian sighs. "Yes. Our parents separated when we were younger, but our older brother always was more of the consistent type. He decided to settle here recently."

Estelle chimes in enthusiastically, "This is definitely a wonderful place to be! I've traveled between Kenya and New York with my parents. My dad had extensive business trips and always tried to have us accompany him as much as possible. Eventually, I decided to be a doctor, and although I spent most of my time in New York and Kenya, I wanted to go to school somewhere else and just decided on Seattle."

"Well, this does seem to be the city for it," Ian comments, referring to Seattle's status as a hub for travelers because of the growing industry of technology and other business-related operations.

At this point, there is a sudden hush of anticipation in the small crowd as Marcus makes his way to the center of the stage where the stools and mic are. His face tilts in our direction as Ness gradually rises from her seat, her food barely touched. She pardons herself and makes her way to Marcus. As they meet, they both take their seats. This time, instead of holding the panpipes, Marcus has two slender pipe-like instruments, which he carefully places between his lips. Without much fanfare, he begins playing, deftly moving his fingers on either hand for each pipe as he plays both melody and harmony. When Ness begins singing, her voice carries a higher tone mixed with a strange, almost chanting tune. The sound of her voice seems to carry as if we were sitting in a cathedral with ceilings that extended upward endlessly.

When the song ends, everyone appears surprised but pleased as they applaud.

"Do you play an instrument or sing?" I ask Ian as the applause gently subsides.

Ian shakes his head. "Sadly, I do not. I never took to the arts like my twin sister or brother."

"The brother you were talking about who lives here?"

Nodding, Ian brings his hands down just as Marcus shifts in his seat, setting one of the pipe-like instruments down and holding just a single one. "My brother is a fantastic artist. A regular da Vinci."

Before I can ask any more questions, another song starts to play, Ness's voice filling the room once again.

I soon find that although time seems to slow down when the music plays, nearly three hours have passed and the night is ending before we know it. Our plates have long been taken away, replaced by hot mugs of velvety coffee, which we all sip gratefully.

"Wow, this has been wonderful," Estelle gushes as she holds the mug in both her hands. "And without any incident."

I choke on my coffee as Estelle says this, but no one else hears her. Estelle looks at me over her mug, a sweet smile and look of innocence on her face. Although slightly annoyed, I can't help but agree with her. With no strange occurrences of any sort, this has been a very pleasant evening at the Thorny Heart.

As we all begin to stand, the crowd of people stir restlessly, trying to greet Ian or compliment Ness and Marcus. I wander to another part of the open club area where it has been carefully lit with candles. I once again notice the mosaic of colored glass that decorates the walls. I raise my hands to brush my fingertips against the glass, feeling the crevices where each individual piece is separated from the other.

"Trying to find a secluded place to muse about the wondrous quahog?"

I jump at the sound of Ian's voice and turn around to notice him standing just a little way behind me. Rather than acknowledge that he startled me, Ian simply takes a few steps to stand next to me and gazes at the mosaic wall. I wonder if we look strange to anyone else, staring at a wall—although a very detailed and pretty wall.

"Maybe just a little." I tilt my face up to look at him. My magenta-colored hair brushes my cheek. I push it aside, tucking it behind my ear. "I also spend some time thinking about different chicken breeds, too."

Ian nods in mock seriousness. "Indeed. You never know when one will need to participate in the mysterious business of recalling the history of a particular chicken breed."

I laugh, a sudden lightness filling me for the first time tonight. Some of the remaining tension that I feel about returning to the Thorny Heart leaves me at that very moment.

The corners of his mouth lift, and his blue and amber eyes also seem to brighten slightly. "I was actually sent here from across the room to bring you back to the club's entrance. Your brother and good friend are waiting for you there. I volunteered to accompany you back in a timely manner while they wait. No doubt, they are enjoying the company of our lovely customer service representative, Edward." He seems reluctant to lead me out of the main club area, measuring out his paces slowly.

"Well, thank you, Ian. This has been a nice evening."

"It has been my pleasure."

There is a moment of silence as we approach the door that leads to the entryway of the club. Before we get to the door though, I feel a gentle pressure on my shoulder. I turn around, surprised to see that Ian's hand is resting there. He also seems surprised, and he quickly removes it.

"I'm sorry, Evie, but…" He opens his mouth as if to ask me something. Instead his blue and amber eyes lock onto my mine for just a second before breaking away uncomfortably. "I hope to see you again. If not sooner— then maybe for a cardiology consultation?" Ian jokes in what I have come to associate with his baseline mannerism.

"Maybe." I grin and push through the door to join Estelle and Kiran, who have indeed been waiting for me while having another enthusiastic conversation about Kiran's cooking with Edward. Ian pokes his head through to thank everyone humbly before waving, the door closing behind me.

I join everyone as we said goodbye to Edward and leave the Thorny Heart.

CHAPTER FORTY-TWO
THE BLACK RINGS

As Ian turned around, Evie now on the other side of the door, he was immediately face-to-face with his sister. Ian found his thoughts still lingering on Evie. His sister, who was a whole foot shorter, was perhaps the same height as her.

She raised her dark eyebrows as if realizing what, or in this case who, he had been thinking of. "You seem fond."

Ian narrowed his eyes slightly, but a corner of his mouth remained turned up in a smile.

"Sure, dear sister. I'm quite fond of many things. Besides her curious literary tastes, I'm also fond of understanding what it is our brother knows about her."

Ness frowned. "It is enough to know that she is dangerous."

"Which is why we need to know more." Ian pulled his shoulders back. "Tani and Goran are both free. There is something about her that even our own brother is willing to raise our father's ire and armies over."

Suddenly there was a hush in the club area, the only

remaining guests a young couple both dressed in business attire. They both seemed to be waiting for this opportunity to be alone with Ian and Ness.

"We were hoping to schedule a meeting with you two regarding some business matters," the man said enthusiastically.

"We love your vision and would like to help with any expansions you have in mind," his wife and business partner added, the metallic frames of her glasses glinting in the candlelight.

Ian and Ness both glance at each other.

"How lovely. Why don't we have that meeting now then?" Ness's voice lowered as the candles flickered and a shadow suddenly fell from the ceiling.

Dean stood before them, a cloak of black smoke falling from his shoulders. His black eyes were shot with red, faint spidery veins spreading down his cheeks. He was outfitted in black gear of leather-like material. It was so dark that the only thing that seemed to stand out were the obsidian rings that shone like glass across the bandolier fitted over his chest.

"What—what is this?" The man's eyes darted from Dean to Ian and Ness standing behind him.

"Just a business matter. We're eager for your cooperation as well." Ness regarded him coolly as Dean approached the young couple, who stood closer together.

Before they could say or do anything else, Dean—his face blank and his actions strangely smooth and mechanical at the same time—pulled off two rings from his bandolier and flung them.

The small rings flashed and split apart as they rippled

and expanded. The rings closed around the necks of the man and woman, snapping together as they both fell to their knees. They frantically closed their fingers around their individual rings, trying to pry them apart, their mouths opening as they tried to yell for help but unable to make a sound.

Suddenly they became still, hunching forward before disappearing in a flash of light that was somehow black, crackling with a distant sound. The rings fell to the ground heavily, neither rolling or bouncing. They now glowed with a flickering blue light.

Dean silently stalked over to the rings and picked them up, carefully snapping them back to his bandolier and turning toward Ness and Ian.

"Good," Ness commented on the event in a tone that was dismissive, as if she had just watched someone clear a table of a mess satisfactorily.

Ian yawned, his canines extending as he did so, catching the light and flashing slightly.

"And boring. Your last ring-throwing person was a little more interesting to watch," Ian stated lazily, ignoring his sister's glaring stare.

"This is not some circus show, dear brother," Ness's voice hissed as Dean walked over and knelt on his knee, his head bowed.

"Of course, neither is war," Ian replied flippantly.

"I fear the worst."

"I fear nothing." Ian smiled as his sister looked away.

CHAPTER FORTY-THREE
WHAT DEATH FEARS

THE NEXT DAY, I feel refreshed. Even after taking a seat for my usual morning meeting with a stern-faced Dr. Mendez, memories of the night before still flash through my thoughts. The hollow and beautiful haunting sound of Marcus's music and Ness's voice still played in my ears even when I woke up to the blaring sound of my alarm clock.

Aherm.

I jump, realizing that Dr. Mendez has pointedly cleared his throat when he realized that I hadn't been listening to what he was saying.

"I'm sorry, Dr. Mendez," I reply sheepishly. "Could you repeat that?"

Sighing loudly, Dr. Mendez slides a pamphlet across his desk toward me. "You had a visitor yesterday. He wanted me to give you this."

Looking down, I realize that the pamphlet is one of the standard distribution ones given out by the oncology-hematology department offices to introduce the providers to new patients. I look up at Dr. Mendez questioningly, but realize that the pamphlet is folded open to my coral-colored hair profile. A name and cell phone number are written neatly next to it with black sharpie.

"Raymond Green," I mutter, trying to place the name but unable to. "Um. Hm. A patient?"

Dr. Mendez looks up from a document that he is reading, his eyes peering sharply over his glasses.

"In a manner of speaking. He's under the impression that you and a friend of yours saved his life during a massive cardiac event."

"Oh!" The image of a man on the street and Estelle doing chest compressions, suddenly comes back to me. It also happened to be the day that I met Ian for the first time. I'm embarrassed that I recall this particular detail so quickly. It doesn't seem to be the appropriate time. "He— he remembered us?"

I am slightly shocked that someone who had just had a cardiac event would remember these details. "Estelle must've been giving good enough compressions to oxygenate his brain," I joked lightheartedly, but Dr. Mendez just glances back up from his document with a look of seriousness.

"He seemed to have something important to tell you." Curious, I tuck the pamphlet back into my coat pocket. "Maybe he needs a cardiology recommendation?" I say a little distractedly, but Dr. Mendez shakes his head.

"He already sees one here."

"Oh," I say again, feeling my ears redden under my hair.

There is a polite knock outside the door.

Dr. Mendez sets his document down and looks up,

his eyebrows raised over the tops of his glasses. "Welcome back," he states matter-of-factly.

I turn around, and there is Clark. He ducks his head as if trying to minimize his interruption.

"Thank you, Dr. Mendez." He waves and then quickly addresses me. "Hey, Evie. Sorry to bug you right now, but I was wondering if you could help me with a particular issue?"

Before he can even finish his question, I am already clumsily pushing my chair back and standing up.

Dr. Mendez waves his hand as if to dismiss me and returns to his work. I follow Clark out the door and to an empty corridor. My heart beats rapidly as I restrain myself from pummeling him with a barrage of questions. But once we are safely out of hearing distance from the reception area, nurses' station, and other areas with heavy traffic, I realize that all the questions I want to ask him disappear for a moment.

"Clark." I look up at him and notice that although he still has dark shadows under his eyes and his skin is pale, he looks slightly more rested. "How are you?" The question is a little anticlimactic, and Clark seems surprised at first, but a sheepish smile spreads across his face.

"Better, I think," he says, then turns his head in either direction as if to make sure the hallway is clear. However, when he turns his head to the right, I notice a long scratch extending from just behind his ear to his collarbone. It looks shallow enough, but I am startled to see it.

"What happened to your neck?"

Clark turns his face back to me and shakes his head. "A

little run in with a pet bird belonging to an acquaintance of mine. Apparently, she wasn't too fond of me."

I raise my eyebrows but press my lips together, waiting for Clark to say more.

"Evie, I need to talk to you," he says, which I feel is a little unnecessary. I am already standing in an empty hallway with him, hoping he will have something to tell me.

"There's a lot though. I was hoping to talk to you after work. Can you meet me here?" He holds out a small square of paper, which I slowly unfold; written in his careful handwriting is an address unfamiliar to me.

Without asking for any more details, I fold the note back up and place it in the pocket with the pamphlet. "Okay."

Clark sighs with relief and then straightens his shoulders back. "Also, I just saw Ivan for his usual appointment."

My eyebrows furrow a bit in surprise at the sudden turn in conversation, but a twinge of worry pulls at me. Ivan has been doing so well, and the look of concern on Clark's face makes my heart stutter a bit.

"Is he okay?"

"Yes." Clark steps just slightly closer toward me. I can see the amber flecks in his eyes a little more clearly. "It's his dog, though."

"His…dog?" This time the twinge of worry is replaced with confusion. I would smile if it weren't for the look on Clark's face, which is still worried.

"Maido. His parents got him a puppy after he went into…remission," Clark says the last word with hesitancy, as if he wants to use a different word, but I suppose his health-care professionalism won't let him refer to Ivan's sudden perfect health, with all traces of the blood cancer ravaging his body completely gone, as anything else. "He named it after a character in the books he's been reading." At this, I can just make out a faint smile lifting the corners of his mouth, before it is once again replaced by a serious expression.

"Maido," I repeat the name of Ivan's dog, but I'm sure the look of confusion on my face is even more pronounced.

"He got hit by a car."

Before I can form any thoughts or words related to this, Clark immediately continues. "Ivan seemed shaken up when I brought him back for his check up, so I asked him and that's how I found out. He said Maido saw something and ran off so quickly that he lost hold of his leash. He ran right in front of a truck and it struck him at full speed. Ivan said that he carried the dog away and expected him to die. He was devastated."

I realize at this point that I am holding my breath, imagining Ivan carrying his battered dog to safety.

"But, Maido was fine."

I let out a breath but wait for Clark to continue, some-how knowing that there is more to this story than the sur-vival of a pet dog.

"Ivan said that it was as if he had no injuries at all. After he carried him home, Maido woke up and acted as if nothing had happened."

"How, though?" I find myself questioning, my mind going blank as I absorb all this information. "He must've had some sort of injury."

Clark nods. "Ivan thought so, too. He is grateful, but he doesn't understand. He was still shaken up. He—"

Clark's voice catches a bit, as if he isn't sure he should continue.

"Ivan told me a while ago that he thinks someone helped cure him. That he thought it was a dream at the time. He said he has been having the same dreams that feel like memories. They're dreams of someone helping him when he was sick."

I shake my head, feeling my heart beat faster.

"He thinks that somehow that same person helped his dog through him," Clark worded this last sentence carefully.

"He thinks the dog was healed by me," I rephrase Clark's words as he slowly nods. "But that's impossible. I've never been able to—Clark, I was nowhere near..." I stop myself, an overwhelming feeling enveloping me as I think of Ivan holding his dog and somehow being able to heal him. It is unbelievable. Impossible. But then everything that has been happening can be described as such.

"I don't understand."

Clark hesitates before carefully touching my shoulder. I look up at him, but before he can rest his whole hand's weight on it, he lifts it away.

"I—I think I do. I think I might understand."

I remember the folded piece of paper in my pocket. I look at Clark and simply nod.

"Is Ivan still here?"

"No. Dr. Mendez saw him. But Ivan didn't say anything to him. I'm not sure why." Clark seems genuinely confused. "He hasn't told anyone else. Not even his parents."

"It's because he trusts you."

Clark is startled when I say this, his mouth opening

but no words coming out. He looks away from me, his expression darkening as he glances down at the ground. I am surprised at his reaction, but when Clark looks back up at me, all I can make out from his expression are his tired eyes and his mouth pressed into a straight line.

"I'll see you soon, Evie." He turns and walks away.

CHAPTER FORTY-FOUR
SONGS OF THE LIVING

IVAN SET HIS book down, the page of a green dragon soaring through the sky displayed in front of him. Even the respite of his newfound interest was not enough to keep his mind from wandering and thinking of things that troubled or confused him. Instead his gaze fell to the foot of his bed where a golden-haired dog lay. It was still small and gangly, the age where puppies were all big paws and clumsiness.

He leaned forward and pet his dog on the ruff of the neck. Maido lifted his head, long ears flopping over before happily falling back to sleep again.

Ivan then placed his hand on his cheek, his blue eyes unfocused as he recalled the incidents of what happened earlier that day for what had to be the one-hundredth time already.

The sound of screeching tires and a sharp yelp of pain echoed in his ears. The image of Maido collapsed and bleeding, barely breathing, kept on flickering across his thoughts.

Closing his eyes tightly, Ivan remembered the feeling of carrying his small dog's body, limp in his arms. He'd felt as if time were slowing down even as he ran back home frantically—the pulse of blood pounding in his ears as he felt something cool flow down into his arms. For a moment when this happened, he was horrified, thinking it was Maido's blood pouring out of him. But it would've been warm. This sensation was calm and cooling. A sensation that felt familiar to him. Like water flowing over a river bed, gliding over smooth rocks.

Opening his eyes, he watched his dog lying at the foot of his bed, perfectly happy and oblivious to the fact that he had somehow survived an injury that should've killed him hours earlier.

Ivan raised his hands to his face, folding his fingers open and closed over his palms. He leaned back onto his pillow and buried his fingers into the nest of blond hair on his head.

He suddenly felt restless.

Sliding off his bed, he grabbed his violin case, his movements quick, impulsive, and almost reckless. Unsnapping the case, he took out his violin and grabbed it forcefully. Wrenching the bow tightly between his fingers, he flung the cool wooden instrument under his chin.

Remaining as he was on his knees, he started to play.

The sound coming from his violin was rapid, careless, frantic, but a melody could just be heard beneath it all. He tore the bow over the strings, willing some kind of thoughts, memories, or revelations to appear as they sometimes did when he played or listened to Sylvia play her wooden flute.

He willed anything to come to him, images of the silver-haired woman who he knew had somehow cured him, as crazy as it seemed—and he did fear that perhaps a slow madness had come over him.

In the discord of his playing, he heard a faint knock on his bedroom door. The bow came to a screeching halt. The sound reminded him of tires skidding on pavement. The bow slipped from his fingers. Somehow, he had created a fracture in the slim piece of wood, which shot up and slid smoothly across the palm of his hand.

"Vanya," he heard his mother call him softly behind the door. She was the only one to call him by this name. Her voice seemed hesitant, as if she wanted to ask him about his haphazard playing, but instead she said, "Dinner is ready."

"Okay, I'll be out soon, mom." Ivan glanced down at his hand as he heard his mother turn from his door and walk down the hall, her steps receding in the opposite direction.

His palm had a clean cut right down the center. He saw his blood pushing up from the skin, red oozing out and sliding down his wrist. He was about to stand and grab something to wrap it in when he felt something like cold water ripple down his neck and toward his chest. He gasped as if someone had thrown ice cold water down the back of his neck. The cold sensation flowed down and toward his fingertips, creating a pooling sensation at the center of his injured palm.

Fine and luminous threads of silver appeared, wrapping his hand in what looked like a glove. His blue eyes widened as they reflected the silver light.

He blinked and suddenly the silver threads were gone.

And his hand was healed. Not a single mark remained.

He touched his palm with the fingers of his other hand. A rustling of movement caught his attention as Maido hopped down from his bed and approached him. Maido looked at him curiously and then lowered his nose to sniff the broken bow.

Ivan quickly moved the bow away from his dog, worried that he would hurt himself on its jagged and splintered edge.

Maido wagged his tail and plodded over into his lap, placing his head conveniently under Ivan's now-healed hand. Ivan absently started to pet his dog as he stared at the broken bow.

CHAPTER FORTY-FIVE
THE CITY IN THE SEA

UNFOLDING AND FOLDING the paper with the address that Clark gave me tightly between my fingers, I walk briskly through the city streets, busy with traffic as people travel home. Most people have their heads down, their chins buried into the collar of their coats as a cold and frigid wind blows against them. My own hair flies up and around my face.

I soon find myself looking up at a nondescript building. It is an older building for the standards of Seattle's more modern and metropolitan landscape. It looms up but has the stunted look of a tall building quickly being overshadowed by its towering skyscraper neighbors. Made of darkening bricks and shaded windows, I am puzzled that a building like this still exists at the epicenter of a rapidly growing city.

I look down at the now wrinkled piece of paper in my hands and tentatively walk up the sturdy cement steps to the front door. Placing the paper in my pocket, I reach for the bronze door handle that is perhaps the only bright point of the building. It stands out startlingly against its dark backdrop.

Before turning the doorknob, my eyes land on a scratched-up and faded plaque just at my eye level. It would've been easily missed, since its original brassy surface seems to have eroded over time, now as dark as the door that it is attached to.

"The City in the Sea," I murmur under my breath, reading the words on the small and slim plaque. I turn my head to look over my shoulder as the wind roars in my ears, my hair snapping me across my face. I notice the people walking past never seem to look up, as I did, at this strange building. Maybe it is the wind forcing their faces down and away. I also can't help but wonder if this building has just become forgotten.

Turning the doorknob in front of me and expecting at least some resistance, or for the door to simply be locked, I find that it opens easily. Entering the building, I step into an area that is largely vacant and dimly lit by the light that is able to escape the windows, which are cloudy with age and time. As the door shuts behind me, a final gust of wind rustles my clothing and hair. The stillness of the quiet and dark building catches me off guard after walking with the swirling wind surrounding me outside.

The building seems to be well-insulated. No sounds from the streets outside can be heard and no drafts leak out from the windows. I'm not sure what I was expecting though. Maybe loud shutters banging against the windows or drafty hollowed sounds blowing through the corridors?

Instead the building, apart from appearing vacant and abandoned, is just that. Empty.

As I take a few more steps, the wood paneled floors make no sounds beneath my feet. No creaking or loud snapping of the old boards, but rather the soft plodding of the soles of my shoes.

The walls are pure white, pristine even, as if freshly painted. Built into the walls are rows upon rows of empty shelves. Walking over to one of the shelves, curious, I run a hand over its smooth surface and am surprised to see that not even a speck of dust lifts away.

"Hey, Evie."

I turn around so quickly that my hair flies up and hits the side of my cheek. Quickly brushing it away, I see that Clark is standing some distance behind me. When or how he got there, I have no idea. It surprises me, though, since it had been so still and quiet.

He has changed out of his dark blue hospital scrubs and is wearing a pair of old jeans and a thin leather jacket over a white shirt. His hands are in his pockets as I slowly make my way toward him. Even though he is looking at me, his eyes seem unfocused, as if actually seeing something else.

"I guess I'm in the right place then?" I am just close enough that I can see the scratch creeping up above the collar of his jacket. It's darker than the first time I saw it. Though maybe it's just the dim lighting of this building compared to the fluorescence of the hospital, but it appears dusky and deeper in color. I can't help but wonder if it's inflamed in some way, but then I would expect it to be slightly reddened at least.

"Your neck." I frown as I walk just a bit closer to Clark.

His eyes refocus suddenly and he absently places a hand over the scratch. I wince, wondering if it hurts him at all. Instead, he lowers his hand and smiles.

"Just a scratch," he says and then walks past me a bit to stand closer to the book shelves. "It looks worse than it feels."

There is a moment of quiet and I feel the urge to suppress all my questions, thoughts, and concerns, waiting for Clark to say more. I am also just not sure where to start. So many questions revolve around seemingly impossible circumstances, but somehow I know without really knowing why that Clark will have answers to some of it. But how does he know these answers?

"Did you read it?" His voice is quiet and calm; however, I recognize an underlying tone of apprehension.

My hand lowers to the messenger bag hanging off my shoulder. I nod and carefully pull the small metal-covered book out so that it rests in both my hands. As I raise it out of my bag, the skin of my knuckles brushes against the rough rippling texture of the black sketchbook. I hesitate, looking at Clark and wondering if I should show him this book, too. I realize that I have not shared it with anyone. Kiran may be closest to knowing of its existence, having unknowingly given me a sketch that belonged to it.

Before I can think on this anymore, though, Clark lets out a breath as if he had been holding it.

"Maybe half of it," I admit. The book, for its compact size, is remarkably dense. There are so many pages that I have yet to read.

"And she was born under the darkness of the moon's

shadow." He looks at me, and I can just make out the amber color of his eyes, but they seem darker, shadowed by gray circles against his pale skin.

"You can read it?" My voice catches with an over-whelming relief, knowing that someone else can read the strange language of the book—at least someone who will admit to it. I again see the image of my brother snapping the book closed, the sound echoing in my ears ever since.

But then this feeling almost immediately becomes overshadowed by more confusion.

"Then, you knew how to read it back in the clearing." I recall the day that I had been photographing the little brown birds in the park. I remember Clark reaching down into the clearing's brush and pulling the metal-covered book out. "But how...how did you know how to read it when you've never seen it before?"

Clark breaks his gaze away from me for a moment, his eyes glancing over at the white shelves before returning back to mine. "It's because it wasn't the first time that I've seen it."

I freeze as I stare at Clark, his brown hair falling into his eyes. I have the sudden urge to reach up and brush the hair away. Surprised by this thought, I clutch the book tighter in my hands and chalk it all up to my instincts as a health-care provider to take care of someone who is injured, which Clark obviously is with his scratched-up neck.

"The book was given to me." Clark hesitates before continuing, "But I needed to get the book to you some-how. So I—I put the book in the clearing to be found."

"Why didn't you just hand me the book?" I counter Clark's explanation. "I would've read it without question. I rarely hesitate to read anything. I mean, I read books about *chickens*!" I sigh heavily, feeling frustrated at the strange look Clark is giving me—and pretty much everything else that I can think of. "And how did you know to place it in *that* particular clearing in the park?"

This time Clark is definitely trying to avoid my eyes as he looks over at the shelves. "I go there a lot by myself. I like that small clearing quite a bit. I have gone there many times to get away from the city or after a rough day at the hospital."

"Sometimes, you would be there, too. I would of course try not to disrupt anything you were doing and go about my way. But there was that one time that I needed to get the book to you." Clark's voice, which has been even and calm this whole time, picks up in a worried tone at the end of this explanation.

"And, well, it didn't feel right just *handing* you a strange book with this strange language in it." Clark throws his hands up a little helplessly.

I open my mouth to say something but then close it. I find that I sort of agree with Clark. I guess it would've been a little strange to hand someone a book covered in silver metal with a language that doesn't seem to exist anywhere except for the strange book.

"The language in the book," I begin as I look down at the book in my hands. "What is it?"

"*Maluna*." There is something musical and filled with sadness in the sound of his voice as he says this word.

"It's an ancient language that died out thousands of years ago." The hesitancy in his voice seems to disappear as he continues on. "It is the language of a people that have been forgotten, thought to have vanished from the worlds. It is the language of healing and of great power."

"You say 'worlds' as if there were more than one." Images of burning fields of blue fire and dragons whose scales flashed as if camouflaged in the sky flew through my thoughts.

Impossible, I think to myself, but the word is quiet in my mind as I remember dead eyes looking up at me from a battle that scorched the grounds and bodies black—the eyes that belonged to a soldier clothed in luminescent and silvery armor. I see a web of silver appear from my fingertips as Estelle falls away from me, grasping at her own fingers to pull her closer to me.

Clark has stepped closer to me, pointing to the book. "This belonged to Kana Akihira. She was the writer of this book. She was also a great person who lived thousands of years ago. Kana was a friend to many and ruled as a queen among many kingdoms who loved and respected her. She was also a general, a leader of a great army."

"She's dead," I say. Black and shining weapons piercing the bodies of many soldiers flicker in and out across my field of vision. It is as if the white walls of shelves have turned black, melting away in blue fires. I try to shake this vision from me, my heart beating a little faster.

Clark nods. "Yes."

"How did she die?" The question leaves my lips before I can even assess whatever else Clark has told me.

"In a war. The Great War, but it has been called many things. Now it's being called The First War." I feel a vague sense of surprise at the bitterness that bites at his words. Clark seems to notice it, too, because his tone immediately softens when he continues. "She was killed by a blade forged from the same fires that would create her enemy's crown."

"The Obsidian Crown." I remember one of the first words from the language that I recognized when first opening this book.

A dark shadow passes over Clark's face as he frowns, but he continues. "The Obsidian Crown belongs to a cold and cruel person. He sits on a throne of molten fire that has frozen into blackened ice."

I can't help but notice that Clark uses the present tense to refer to this person. "This battle was thousands of years ago. What do you mean? This person couldn't possibly still be alive. How…?"

"Evie," Clark interrupts me, the frown leaving his face. A look of contained sympathy softens his features, his brow smoothing out. "This is a world of gods and great powers. It's a beautiful and terrible world."

I involuntarily lift a hand to my chest, where days before I had pulled a black blade from my heart. I blink, and this same hand shoots out to grasp Clark's forearm. He seems surprised, wincing just slightly.

"Who was she?" The words are strained as I say them. "Clark, who was she?"

For the first time, Clark looks at me in confusion. "Evie, what—?"

"No." I pull myself closer to him, looking up at his widened eyes. His explanation of Kana Akihira echoes in my mind, but I realize that something is missing. Something in the explanation is empty. Something hidden just beneath the still surface of a pool of water. Something that is rolling and churning beneath the calm.

Clark seems to realize at that very moment what I mean, my fingers gripping into the fabric of his sleeve.

"She was a great and good queen. She was gifted with powers. Powers of the celestial…of healing."

"Of healing," I repeat the words, my eyes unfocused as my heart skips a beat.

Even with my mind reeling at the new and impossible realizations, I find Clark's quiet voice calming in a way that I can't quite explain.

"Many millennia have passed, and it has been said that the people of Maluna have vanished. But sometimes someone will appear with the ability to heal or alleviate the suffering across worlds. *You* are Maluna, but more than that."

Clark breathes in sharply before saying, "You are directly descended from Kana herself."

My grip on Clark's arm loosens slightly.

"My family, though," I say, thinking of my grandfather as he held the white butterfly in his hands.

"Thousands of years hid it within your family," Clark explains, the sadness returning to his voice. "Sometimes, these powers never appear. Time has a way of hiding things. Of forgetting things."

My hand slips from his arm as more emotions sweep over me, this time, a sense of loss that I haven't felt since my grandfather passed away.

"I have these dreams," I say just above a whisper. "They feel like memories, but I didn't understand."

The look of confusion returns to Clark's face, his brow furrowing. "Memories?"

My gaze becomes unfocused as my thoughts start to scatter in hundreds of directions. I look back up at Clark and nod. "Yes. At least they feel like memories."

Clark remains silent, as if trying to understand what I am saying.

"How do you know all this?" I finally ask the question that has been burning away at me since waking up after pulling the Obsidian Blade from my chest.

A blank look appears on his face. Expressionless, Clark shakes his head. "I can't tell you that now, Evie."

"Why?" A flashback of when I was in my bedroom, holding the Obsidian Blade in my hand and drinking hot chocolate with Clark, comes to me while standing here with him now. I would laugh at the thought of discussing this all over mugs of powdered hot chocolate again if I weren't concentrating so hard on what Clark has just told me. "You've said this before, but why not tell me now?"

Closing his eyes, a pained look crosses his face. He opens his eyes again, but the blank look has returned. "I think you'll find out soon."

Suddenly Clark goes a shade paler, his face almost white as he stumbles back a bit.

"Clark?" I step forward and reach out to steady him, the small book slipping from my fingers and falling heavily to the floor. I position myself at his side, using my lower center of gravity to push him up, my arm around his torso. He reaches out his arm to rest on the shelf closest to him. He quickly pulls himself up, and I feel the tension of his weight lift away as he finds his footing again.

"Are you okay?" I pull away from him, finding that I have to steady myself slightly as well.

Still looking paler than he normally does, Clark smiles awkwardly, as if we were in the hospital and he was delivering a message to me from Dr. Mendez. "Yeah. Just really tired."

I feel the wave of questions that I still want to ask recede a bit. He looks exhausted, and I feel guilty for not noticing right away. I am just about to say as much when Clark stoops down to pick up the book, which has fallen open. He takes a shuddering breath as he stares down at the open pages before him.

I realize that the book has fallen open to a section that I haven't seen yet.

The page is filled with the image of a person wrapped in tendrils of black shadow, which fall away from his shoulders like a cloak. His gaze is focused downward, his eyes a pale gray color. He wears a beautiful crown that shines a gleaming black, its tips long and pointed like the talons from a bird of prey. In front of him, pointing straight down, is a horribly long and deadly blade, which I know already, like the crown, to be made of black obsidian all the way to the hilt.

However, it is his hands or lack thereof that catch my eyes. Where hands should be are long black claws that extend into points dripping with what looks like silvery fluid—blood. These claws are wrapped around the hilt in a loose, almost lazy way.

There is no other written description on the page. It is as if Kana could barely bring herself to draw this particular image. Even the page that lay open next to it was left blank.

Clark seems frozen as he looks down at the drawing. I stand waiting for him, wondering if he will say something about what he is thinking, or anything really, but instead he gently closes the book and stands up, pulling his shoulders back as he straightens his spine. He hands the book to me without a word, my fingers brushing his lightly. I realize how cold his skin is with even that brief amount of contact.

"You really should get some sleep," I say gently, trying to take off the edge from my usual professional tone of voice. "You look like you haven't slept in days."

"It feels like longer," Clark says absently, but with a smile to quickly follow his words.

My brow creases again as another thought creeps its way forward.

"You mentioned a war," I say slowly. "Called The *First* War. Does that mean that there's…?"

I break off before I can finish my question, as Clark is already nodding.

"Yes, another war. And it's already begun."

CHAPTER FORTY-SIX

CHILDHOOD VOICES

AT SOME POINT, I leave Clark in the tall brick building with its walls of white bookshelves. I glance over my shoulder as I descend the stairs. The bronze-colored door knob shines against the drab and dark exterior of the building, the slim plaque with the words, "The City in the Sea," pretty much invisible even from a short distance. You wouldn't even know it was there if you didn't walk up to the door.

The wind, which hasn't receded into the twilit night, is a chilling snap against the skin as I make my way home.

I stare blankly ahead, my eyes fixated on no single point as people hurry past me trying to get out of the wind and indoors where it is warm. It feels strange leaving the quiet calm of the building and returning to the bustling city streets where everyone rushes about. I think of a war going on between beings with strange powers and how separate I feel realizing that I am part of this strange world that this is happening in.

At the same time, I feel as if I don't belong in either

reality, that I hang between these worlds, balanced on a rope and trying not to fall.

Clark's words echo through my thoughts. Especially a single name:

Kana Akihira.

I try so hard to attach some meaning to the name. Even with the book of writings and drawings by her own hand lying in my messenger bag, I can't help but feel that any meaning that this great name has been attached to has died with her thousands of years ago.

Clark explained to me that her name was erased from all records of their histories, that great healers have appeared across worlds but have essentially been eradicated, along with the original people of Maluna. Even people of this different world that I somehow came from do not remember the name Kana Akihira.

Somehow, I am descended from her, which explains my powers to heal, but not everything.

Clark explained to me again that there are many things he doesn't understand himself. My ability to heal is one thing, but my ability to survive a mortal wound, which should have killed me, is a completely different thing that carries no precedent in any of the research or histories that he was able to obtain.

Where he researched all this information is a point that he was unwilling to share. While vaguely frustrated, I also realize that he has given me answers to all my other questions. Kana herself was killed by this king of the Obsidian Crown, who had pierced her heart with his own blade.

His explanation of the king who wore the Obsidian Crown was clipped and strained, as if he wanted to tell me more but was unsure of how much. I hardly knew what questions to ask for the most part. I gathered from Clark that this king led armies against Kana and her kingdoms and allies who supported her in the war that would claim her life and curse them all. He said that many had been killed slowly over thousands of years, or simply imprisoned.

When I asked about the king's name and whereabouts, Clark just shook his head, which I took for his ignorance of this particular detail. It was at this point that the conversation really seemed to come to an end. Clark's face was cast in a dusky pallor, his eyes appearing to cloud over with exhaustion.

I am relieved when I finally reach my apartment. As I begin to pull my keys from my coat pocket, though, the door flings wide open. Estelle stands in the doorway, smiling and sporting a deep red apron, which looks curiously like the ones that Kiran uses at his restaurant.

Before I can process any further information from my already overloaded brain, Estelle has already thrown a warm plate of cake—which smells of espresso and chocolate—into my arms.

"Voila." She places her hands on her hips and looks spectacularly pleased with herself despite being covered in flour and smudges of chocolate pretty much from the top of her head to the very toes of her socks. "German chocolate coffee cake."

Looking down at the cake, I have to force my face into a smile of gratitude. The cake looks delicious, but my mouth goes dry at the thought of eating at this very second.

"This looks incredible," I say enthusiastically, hoping that she won't notice the strain in my voice as I say it. I follow Estelle into the apartment, impressively kicking my shoes off with my messenger bag still hanging across my body and the plate of cake balanced in my hands.

I trail Estelle into the kitchen as she treks floury footprints across the carpet and linoleum. When I peek into the kitchen, I restrain a gasp. It literally looks like a floury tornado has made its way through, while at the same time flinging chocolate cake batter as well. Estelle pulls the apron off and over her head, although what use this actually was is questionable to say the least, since Estelle is still somehow covered in cake and flour under the apron as well. I sigh as I take my customary seat in the living room.

Plopping a slice of coffee cake on a plate of her own, Estelle eagerly sits on the couch across from me, already spearing a piece of cake into her mouth before sitting down completely.

Taking a bite of the cake, I can't help but smile. Even though I don't have much of an appetite, the cake is delicious. For some reason, my thoughts flash back to Clark and sipping mugs of hot chocolate.

Before I can feel the warmth creep from my neck to the tips of my ears, I brush the thought away. The time and many revelations that I have had with him are obviously the reason why I am having these thoughts in the first place.

At least, that's what I try to convince myself of.

Looking at Estelle, I can't help but be impressed by how quickly she has consumed most of her chocolate cake. I am still on my second bite.

"Are you close to your family, Estelle?" I am surprised to hear myself ask her this.

Maybe it is to distract my mind from strange thoughts and imaginings of worlds that are hidden from each other, but for some reason, I choose this moment to learn more about Estelle's life outside of our professional lives—other than meals or recent nightclub outings, I know next to nothing about her family.

It seems that I never truly had any close friends growing up, choosing to keep to myself; throwing myself into my artistic pursuits, studies, and books. For me this had always been a more comfortable place to be in. I was never lonely, but rather relieved that I could limit the number of people that I had to keep secrets from.

However, with Estelle, the effort is minimal. She is outgoing, with a sense of humor that balances out my own dry and sarcastic one.

But then there was the moment on the balcony at the Thorny Heart, and the opal pendant that I have somehow come to recognize. Could it be just a coincidence? Maybe opals are in fashion now, I think vaguely. Estelle is easily more fashionable than I am on any given day of the year.

Estelle looks up from her plate. She seems just as surprised as I am by my question. She pauses, her forkful of cake raised halfway to her mouth. She slowly sets it down on the plate, her face puzzled, before shrugging her shoulders nonchalantly.

"As close as I can be." She gives me a strange look, her eyebrows raised slightly. "I mean, they *do* live in New York."

"Right." I feel slightly awkward, but continue anyway. "That's not really what I meant though."

This time Estelle sighs, but not impatiently. Her gray-green eyes lower as she looks down at her plate. "I wouldn't describe my family as very close. There was a time when I was a kid that I would've described us as close in that way. Like your family is."

Estelle's fork hangs loosely between her fingers as she continues on in a quiet and uncharacteristically restrained voice, "I had an older brother, he probably would've been the same age as Kiran is now."

"A brother?" I stare at Estelle. I always assumed she was an only child, but then she just now mentions her brother in the past-tense.

"Yeah, his name was Kyle." Estelle drifts off for a moment, lost in her thoughts. I'm not sure if I should interrupt her, but I don't need to wait too long on this before Estelle lifts her eyes up and toward me. "He's gone now."

Gone. The word lingers between the small space that separates us in the living room. There seems to be something clinging to that word, though, even as Estelle said it. The word is an odd choice. As if something is missing.

"Well, maybe not physically gone. It's hard to explain," Estelle falters over her words, which is something that I have never heard her do in the years that I have known her. She usually carries herself with so much self-assurance and confidence (well, in matters not having to do with boys of a particular quality).

"Something happened to him when we were younger. My first memories of it were when I was seven years old. We would be walking home from school and he would start muttering stuff under his breath. I was young and thought it was weird. I would ask him what he was saying, but he would look at me like he didn't know what I was talking about. Soon my parents started to notice. They thought it was a phase that would pass, so they left him alone, but then it would continue. Sometimes they would stand outside of his bedroom and listen to him through the door. They started to worry. He was talking to himself constantly, and started to isolate himself." Estelle looks at me as if surprised to hear herself say all of this. I wonder if she has ever talked to anyone about this before.

"My parents started taking him to doctors, therapists, psychiatrists. Everyone you could think of. At some point, he had to stay home from school. We were a little older at this time. I think I was thirteen and he had turned sixteen. One day, he just stopped talking to anyone, even us. The only time we would hear his voice was behind closed doors. He was just talking nonsense. Nothing but nonsense." A sad bitterness falls across her face as she closes her eyes and then opens them back up slowly.

"I'm sorry, Evie. I totally went off just now." Estelle laughs, but it doesn't reach her eyes as she picks her fork back up.

"What happened to him?" I ask. *Gone.* The word repeats in my head as Estelle spears a bite of chocolate cake back onto her fork.

"My parents institutionalized him," Estelle states, her tone blunt. "I see him with my parents every so often. But it's like he's not even there anymore. He's just a shell staring at the wall."

I honestly have no idea what to say at this point. Estelle has set her plate down, the bite of cake still speared onto the tines of her fork. Sighing, she sits back into her seat heavily.

I look down at my plate of chocolate cake, an

overwhelming guilt floods over me with the knowledge that I never knew this about Estelle.

As if sensing my thoughts as I sit silently, Estelle leans forward and gives me a reassuring smile. "Honestly, I try not to think about it too often," she says faintly. "My parents changed after that. Became more distant. I did, too. It was easier to interact with each other that way. So that we never had to mention the fact that we missed Kyle, but in a way, I'm not sure if it was right to. I didn't really get to know him that long."

I immediately think of my grandfather and the brief time that I got to spend with him as a very young child. "You don't really have to know someone that long for them to matter to you though."

Smiling sadly, Estelle just nods.

CHAPTER FORTY-SEVEN
CRACKS

NEKO FOUND HIS brother standing in the midst of foliage at the very center of his living quarters. The night cast long shadows through the windowed wall and onto the glass spheres hanging from the ceiling. Green plants filled nearly every available space to the point that Neko actually had to brush his own sleek and flowing garment away from the leaves.

There were occasional flickers of movement from the small brown birds perched in the glass spheres. They eyed him curiously as he passed by. Reminded of a particularly aggressive breed of feathery animal by the name of Elaine, he avoided any further eye contact with the small creatures.

"Have I mentioned lately how awful you've been looking?" Neko stated but couldn't restrain a slight tone of surprise as he approached Cerin, who indeed looked terrible. His eyes were so completely clouded over that Neko wondered if it was possible for him to see, and his skin was ashen even in the darkness of the moonlit room.

Swaying just slightly where he stood, Cerin simply held

up a glass pitcher of water and poured it into one of the hanging plants.

"Brother," Neko said with a frown, his teeth gritting, canines flashing sharply. "Stop this foolishness."

He walked closer to Cerin. They were nearly the same height and build, Neko just slightly more slender where Cerin was leaner, with arm muscles that tensed even as the pitcher hung precariously in his fingers.

"What foolishness, Neko?" Cerin murmured just under his breath, lowering the pitcher and allowing it to hang at his side, but turning to directly face his younger brother.

"Stop it." Neko suppressed his frustration, the corner of his mouth curling into a sneer. "You are terrible at hiding secrets. Thousands of years as your brother and nothing changes that which I know of you."

"But what of the changes that you know nothing of?" Coldness dripped off of Cerin's voice, his breath ragged and his fingers tightening on the slender glass handle of the pitcher.

Neko clenched his own fingers into tight fists. "I have no idea what you're talking about."

Cerin stepped closer to his brother. "The war has begun."

"This fact has been made clear to me over and over again." Neko dropped something at Cerin's feet, where it unraveled itself into a loose heap. They were chain links made of obsidian.

"Is this the change that you speak of?" Neko locked eyes with Cerin, his own clear colorless ones reflecting the milky gray of his brother's. "What of the stirring in the oceans?"

Cerin continued to lock gazes with his brother, not even glancing once at the broken chains at his feet.

"What do you seek to accomplish here, brother?" Neko's eyes

narrowed, his fingers releasing slightly, but his palms imprinted with the trace of his long nails.

"A new purpose," Cerin stated in an unwavering voice.

Neko rolled his eyes toward the ceiling and flung his hands up in the ar. "Is this some sort of mid-millennia crisis or something?"

Without waiting for a response, Neko waved his hand carelessly. "Never mind. You're so like our father when it comes to conversation topics. Speaking of whom. Our father has risen Tanwen, and Auriel has brought back her rings of the hell armies."

Tanwen.

Cerin recalled a great dagger that had been encased in the black ice of their father's hell lands. The last time a soldier had wielded it, a great battle had been won for their father, and many of the opposing had died. Although this was concerning to him, for the time being, it was the mention of Auriel's doings that concerned him more.

"She did not hesitate to bring her rings back." Cerin frowned, realizing that his hand now gripped the glass pitcher so hard, he was creating small fractures in the delicate handle. He released some pressure, his fingers loosening, but the muscles remained flexed, as tense as the rest of his body.

"Our sister has never been a patient one," Neko stated cheerfully, but his eyes flashed as sharply as his teeth. "You on the other hand. I feel that you, dear brother, have been enacting a plan long in the making."

In Cerin's silence, Neko confirmed this suspicion, but instead of feeling triumphant, he grabbed his brother's shoulders, a hand gripping him on either side.

"Please. Cerin. Stop this now," Neko implored, his eyes searching his brother's blank ones.

"Why, Neko? I thought you feared nothing." A voice echoed around the room, stirring the birds in their spheres nervously.

Neko let go of his brother, removing his hands as if they had been burned. Cerin turned his head to gaze upon the source of the voice.

Auriel walked toward them, the blackened hem of her dress brushing heavily against the floor and any leaves that hung low from potted plants. She seemed to appear from the very shadows of the room, as if they had been standing in a makeshift clearing in the middle of a park or forest.

"It is not fear, sister," Neko responded airily, his eyes still on Cerin. *"It is concern for the foolish actions of someone who is dear to us. Foolish actions that could lead to one very unnecessary war and one very unhappy father."*

"He is lost." Auriel stood by her twin brother's side, her eyes as colorless as his. *"But he will return to us."* She smiled, her lips curved cruelly. *"He has no choice. It is his fate."*

For the first time, Cerin's blank expression gave way to a hard glare, and he once again tightened his grip on the glass handle of the pitcher. He felt a vague sense of security holding it, as if clinging to something solid would keep him from stumbling and betraying the exhaustion he felt.

"Be warned, Cerin," the sound of Auriel's voice was as steady and flat as the expression on her face. She looked like a statue carved in marble, her hair shining with golden metal threads and her neck veined with black that crept up and toward her jawline. *"Father will not wait for his army to rise. He will come for her personally."*

"So why raise the armies, Auriel?" Cerin felt a crack as the glass pitcher handle started to give under the pressure of his hand again.

She blinked slowly, tilting her chin toward her shoulder. As if taking this as his cue, Dean appeared, stepping into the dim light of the moon filtering into the darkening room.

Cerin assessed him, a blank expression once again on his face as he took in the bandolier of black obsidian rings strapped across his chest. Near his belt was the unmistakable scorched hilt of Tanwen.

"Cursed," Cerin whispered. "Have you no heart? To curse another with the same fate as one you once loved?"

Auriel's jaw locked as her colorless eyes shone dangerously. "Cursed are the ones who fall in love, dear brother."

Neko twitched his face toward his sister as if to say something, but then seemed to change his mind at the last second.

Instead it was Cerin, his voice quiet and calm, who said, "I can stop him."

Auriel smiled as if expecting him to say this. "But you won't. You had the opportunity once. You have grown weak." The smile vanished as she said the last word, her eyes trailing lazily away from Cerin as she took in her surroundings. Her gaze slid over the green leaves of the plants and birds ruffling their feathers in their glass spheres hanging from the ceiling.

"This role you play…" She slid a long fingernail sharpened to a fine tip gilded with gold over a leaf by her hand. Where her nail touched it, the leaf started to burn with a dripping blue fire, which slowly turned the green to a scorched black. "It is a farce. You fool yourself into believing that you can deny who you are."

Auriel watched as the leaf dissolved into ash and then without another word turned around, Dean following her. Her words lingered in Cerin's ears as they both disappeared into a cloud of heavy black smoke.

Neko hardly seemed to notice his twin sister's departure.

"You are trying to protect her," Neko stated plainly, trying to read his brother's cloudy eyes. He couldn't help but wonder if he had truly gone blind, but Cerin locked his gaze with his. "On the balcony of the club, Cerin. We know it was you."

Once again, a tone of concern and almost pleading underlying his voice, Neko repeated, "You must stop this. Nothing good will come of this war." Cerin's eyebrows rose in surprise at this last sentence. The realization that his brother may not hold Auriel's impatience to prepare for war struck him. Neko smiled at his brother sadly, the sneer on his face gone before a cloak of black smoke enveloped him and he disappeared.

Cerin felt his body shudder, his muscles finally collapsing from the effort of masking its exhaustion and weakness from his siblings. He lowered onto his knees, the pitcher with its cracked handle still remarkably intact as he finally set it down on the floor.

Pressing his hands onto the tops of his thighs, he felt a pain burn through him. He felt as if his body were passing through a shower of flames.

Right at the moment that he felt as though the flames would tear through his chest, a cracking noise sounded above him. A silence filled his ears as if a pillow had been placed over them. He took in shallow breaths, suppressing the pain as he realized that the sound had come from one of the glass spheres nearest to him.

He slowly pushed himself up into a standing position, now eye level with the sphere. His expression was one of terrible sadness as he saw that a crack had appeared in the glass, a bird looking at it curiously.

Chapter Forty-Eight
SHADOWS REVEALED

Ivan had just walked out of his meeting with Sylvia and June. It was surprisingly more subdued than previous meetings. Their awkward shyness when meeting for the first time had long been forgotten as they got to know each other better.

However, Ivan felt that everyone, including himself, had been quieter. The only reprieve was Sylvia talking enthusiastically about her parents agreeing to her first set of drums. Ivan and June had both expressed their happiness over this, but the conversation soon faded away. The only sound eventually came from Sylvia playing her shinobue.

The pretty hollow sounds of the wooden flute seemed to comfort Ivan's troubled thoughts. Even June, who seemed a little more tense than usual, relaxed at the sound, her eyes closing as she sat near the window.

At the end of the meeting, they had left their navy-blue notebooks on the table in the room for Dr. Mendez, who said that he would finally be collecting them.

They were each a little reluctant to do so, though. Ivan found that he was the last to set his down, wondering if the repetitive dreams and random stories that he had written in his book would concern Evie and Dr. Mendez at all. He felt his fingers linger over the cover as he clenched his fist gently. He hadn't written about Maido or his hand. Maybe they would think it was some strange side effect of the medications that had saved his life. Maybe they would simply think that he had gone crazy.

He couldn't help but have a clinging fear that maybe he was.

He followed June, who had pretty much jogged out of the hospital to meet her father waiting for her in the parking lot, while Sylvia's parents were standing in the lobby waiting for her. They both smiled at him as they met their daughter. Waving to the Plaits as they left the hospital, Ivan scanned the lobby looking for his parents. He wasn't surprised not to see them there, since they sometimes went to the cafeteria for a quick breakfast. It became a routine for them as Ivan became a regular visitor to the hospital.

Ivan walked to the cafeteria, his hands in the jacket of his coat and his eyes following the trek of his feet on the floor ahead of him. When he reached the cafeteria, his blue eyes looked up, seeking out the familiar figures of his parents. His eyes skimmed over the familiar dark blue scrubs of a few nurses or other hospital staff members, the white coats of doctors, and some patients or family members sitting as they ate their breakfasts.

He caught sight of a person with magenta-colored hair approaching him, a smile on her face.

"Good morning, Ivan! Looking for your parents?" Evie

had her white coat slung over her arm and her messenger bag hanging over her shoulder. A cup of steaming hot coffee was balanced precariously on top of a book that looked as if it had a picture of a rooster on it.

Ivan returned her smile, realizing that he was pretty much eye-level with her now. He vaguely wondered if he'd had a growth spurt. He had always been a little on the shorter side. Dr. Mendez said that it may have had something to do with the cancer.

As if just realizing that she was at risk of causing a serious crisis related to spilling her coffee, Evie immediately grabbed it in her freehand while scanning the cafeteria as well.

"Hm, I haven't seen them actually. Maybe they're back at the waiting room or main lobby?"

Ivan nodded in agreement. "Yeah, you're probably right. I should—"

Ivan froze. He stood still, his eyes widening slightly. He started to turn his head from side-to-side, his eyes troubled.

"Ivan?" Evie looked at him. "Is something the matter? Maybe caught a whiff of someone burning toast again? Or most likely a whiff of something else…it *is* the hospital." She smiled jokingly but then stopped when Ivan didn't acknowledge her.

"Do you hear that?" Ivan touched his ear, his hand shaking slightly.

Evie set her coffee, book, coat, and messenger bag down on an empty table next to them. "Hear what, Ivan?" He vaguely felt it as Evie placed a hand gently on his shoulder.

Ivan closed his eyes and then opened them slowly, reluctant to say anything. "It's music. It's so loud."

Familiar music, he recalled. He remembered the strange woman with the golden piercings wearing a white suit and playing a viola. Her laugh echoed through his ears as the sound of the music tore through them.

I frown, trying to listen harder to the sounds around me, even brushing my hair back behind my ears.

"I need to know where it's coming from." Ivan turns slowly around before stopping like the arrow of a compass. He walks briskly away without saying another word.

"Ivan?" I find myself rushing to follow him as his pace starts to pick up ahead of me.

I hardly have to dodge any people, since it is so early in the morning. He is walking quickly, occasionally brushing his ear as if something were clinging to it. I try harder to hear the music that Ivan was referring to, but all I can hear is the steady pounding of blood in my ears.

Suddenly, Ivan stops, his gaze staring ahead as if he has seen something.

He then starts to run.

It was her.

She looked different, though. Instead of her light-colored hair pulled back in a neat bun and the dark-rimmed glasses on her face, her hair hung loose and it looked like gold pieces of metal were threaded through the length of the strands. Her eyes were a strange color that looked almost like glass reflecting dark rain clouds, hiding the pupils behind them. Black veins spidered their way from her chest and up her neck. She wore a flowing dress that seemed soaked in black ink at the hem.

She stood in the middle of the hallway, not too far from him. It was as if no one but Ivan could see her. People walked past her, sipping their coffees or glancing down at their phones.

The music was loud in his ears. The sound reminded him of a storm—mesmerizing and terrible.

The woman smiled at him. The corners of her mouth curled up, but her eyes remained blank as she locked gazes with him.

She then turned as if floating, the hem of her dress twisting heavily around her ankles. She started to glide away, and Ivan, without knowing why, knew that he needed to follow her.

I follow Ivan, pacing myself as I run and ignoring the brief stares around me. I hear the occasional chitter as someone jokes about me being late for a meeting or a code (the type of thing that you shouldn't be late to).

I realize that he is heading toward the stairway. My breath catches as the door ahead flings open as if blown out by a gust of wind, but that would be impossible. Although drafty, there just isn't any way that door could open the way it did.

It was as if someone opened the door for Ivan.

Without a moment's hesitation, Ivan goes through it, the door slamming closed behind him.

My heart stutters as I reach the door. I have a second of fear, wondering if it will be locked. I push it open, relieved.

The pattering of feet echoes overhead and I'm shocked to realize that Ivan is already a few flights ahead of me.

I frantically try to catch up. For some reason my body feels lighter, my feet barely touching down on a step before I bring the other foot up. I vaguely wonder if this has something to do with adrenaline fueled by fear for Ivan… or something else.

I follow him up flight after flight of stairs. Not once do I hear Ivan pause or stumble. I can hear his breath and my own as we climb upward.

When I finally catch up, Ivan is facing a closed door. It is the last flight of stairs, and it leads to the hospital's rooftop.

Ivan glances over his shoulder at me, his blue eyes bright. His hand shaking as he raises it toward the door handle.

"Ivan, wait," I hear myself say, but my voice is faint in my ears as I watch him push the door open; a gust of wind sweeps past me, blowing my hair back. I follow him as quickly as I can.

We are standing on the rooftop now. It is raining, a steady shower that falls heavily; it is a matter of moments before we are drenched.

I am about to call out to Ivan again when the words freeze in my throat.

Standing at the other end of the roof is Dean.

Ivan ignored the rain pouring into his eyes and stared straight ahead. The piercing sound of music was fading in his ears, but he hardly felt relieved. He found himself face-to-face with a person clothed in black, a bandolier of gleaming rings of the same color strapped across his chest. His hair was a dull green, and tattoos of flowers peaked out from the tall collar of his outfit.

He held a dagger, its blade curved and black.

"Mom! Dad!" Ivan felt his voice break. He hardly recognized it as his own.

Kneeling, their hands pulled behind them, his parents stared back at him. The man holding the dagger stood between them, the dagger's blade pointed at the base of the back of his father's neck and his other hand wrapped tightly around the base of his mother's neck. They looked dazed, but the fear on their faces clenched at Ivan's heart. He felt his hands tighten into fists at his side.

"Vanya," his mother shouted out in fear. "You must run away! Please!"

Ivan's father, unable to move for fear that the blade would pierce his neck, looked at his only son, his eyes imploring him to do as his mother said.

"That would be counterproductive." Another man suddenly appeared. He walked lazily over to Ivan's parents. "Such gallant advice, though." He sighed admiringly at the two kneeling before him.

Ivan could hear Evie as she stopped next to him, positioned slightly ahead, as if to place herself between him and the two dangerous-looking men.

"Ian?"

CHAPTER FORTY-NINE
THE CRYSTAL SIGHT

His blue and amber eyes are unmistakable, even in the shower of rain and the clouds that darken the skies gray.

He looks at me apologetically, but one corner of his mouth is quirked up into a smile.

Standing next to him is his sister. But it almost seems harder to focus on her for some reason. I feel as if I am staring at something behind the hazy glass of a window, the rain sliding down and obscuring it. The outline of her figure fades slightly before I can finally see her clearly. It is Ness, but at the same time, everything about her is different.

"Who are you?" I can feel Ivan stir behind me. His eyes widen in my periphery, and I realize that he has seen the same thing I have. It is as if Ness has cast off a disguise.

"Auriel." The woman's voice is cold, the sound of haunting melodies underlying it. For some reason it reminds me of stories of shipwrecked sailors. I can imagine their dying cries as they listen to the song of the sirens.

In the single blink of an eye, she is standing in front of me. Heavy black shadows curl and fall from her shoulders to disappear at the hem of her dress.

She gazes at me, her glassy eyes flickering back and forth as if scanning my face, trying to recognize something. Auriel then curls a finger around a golden thread from her hair; it glints and slips around her finger like a serpent's tongue, falling away from her hair and into her palm. The whole time she stares at me, her expression blank and her lips pressed together.

A split second passes where my muscles respond reflexively, but before I can back away completely, she has already twitched her wrist, the golden thread straightening itself into a fine point. It pierces the air between us.

It skims across my cheek, sliding across the skin like a sharpened knife. A glimmer of gold flashes in the corner of my eye before disappearing. I continue to back away from her, moving closer to Ivan, my eyes flitting over my shoulder to make sure he had not been harmed. At the same time, I can feel something slide down my cheek, heavier and thicker than the rain.

It is my blood. I bring my fingers up to brush it away. When I bring my fingers down, I can see the tips flash a bright and shining silver.

Auriel's eyes widen, her mouth twisting in a sneer. "It is true then."

Ian walks up to stand next to Auriel, a look of shock on his face as he stares at me.

"Take her," Auriel whispers.

Dean moves immediately, his actions sharp but mechanical at the same time. He slips his dagger toward his belt, and within seconds he has a black ring from his bandolier in each hand. When he draws his hands away from his chest, two black rings fly forward.

Ivan cries out as the black rings expand and split apart, snapping around the necks of his parents. They bring their hands to their necks, the whites of their eyes turning black as they struggle to pull the rings away.

Dodging past me, Ivan runs toward his parents, not noticing that Dean has the dagger in his hand again, raised and ready.

"Ivan!" I start to push past Auriel when a shadow blows past me. It feels like ice washing over my skin. The shadow shoots toward Dean, knocking him backward.

Ian spins around, the outline of his figure blurring as smoke curls up from his fingers and slides up his arms, wrapping itself around him before falling away slightly. Just as with his sister, Ian is himself but not at the same time. His black hair grows longer, falling in a straight veil down his back, now the color of gray smoke streaked with black. His irises glint dully with the same clear glassiness as his sister's. His mouth is set in a frown, his canines shining.

He seems to float in midair, the black smoke loosely wrapped around him as he barrels toward the shadow that has appeared. Dean is already rolling back up on his feet, the dagger raised, as Ian makes contact with the shadow, which is starting to take the form of another figure. I can see the flash of silver-tipped claws as they tear at Ian's black cloak, but this image lasts for only a second. The rain pulses down more heavily, and the shadowy figure disappears, spiraling up and around Ian before landing back down, knocking him to the ground.

All sound is muted. I can feel a pounding in my ears as I see who is standing there now. He stands over Ian, his breath ragged and his face pale as he looks down. Dark shadows under his eyes make the amber in his irises stand out more. A long scratch marks his neck.

Clark.

"Well, I may have underestimated you, dear brother," Ian drawls sarcastically from his position on the ground.

"Clark!" I shout as Dean, moving impossibly fast, aims his dagger at Clark's back.

Twitching his face toward my voice, he quickly spins around and shoots his hand out. It connects with Dean's chest. He huffs in surprise, but the dagger is no longer pointing toward Clark. It is at this moment that Auriel laughs, a cold unfeeling sound.

Before Clark can turn around, Ian wraps himself in black smoke. Auriel's fingers stretch out as a gold dart pierces the air. Before Clark can take in another breath, the gold dart pierces his chest, but rather than stumble or cry out, he stands up straighter, his hands clenched tightly at his side as if nothing has happened.

There is a single moment's pause when Ivan shouts again. His parents have slumped over, their bodies lying next to each other. He rushes over to them, ignoring everyone else, but before he can reach them, they vanish, disappearing into a blast of crackling black light. The black rings, gleaming blue, are all that remain.

"No." Ivan's legs give out from under him. Falling to his knees, tears slide down his already rain-soaked face. But he quickly struggles back up and faces Dean, who has picked up the rings, securing them carefully across the bandolier on his chest.

"What did you do to them?" he shouts, his blue eyes bright with anger.

Auriel smiles coldly. "You will find out soon enough."

Dean starts toward Ivan this time, lifting another ring from a different part of his bandolier. I can feel my own legs moving forward, frantically trying to reach him before Dean.

Clark calls out, his voice hoarse in a throat that sounds raw and dry. His lips are cracked, his face bruised and scratched from his altercation with Ian. He looks exhausted as he wrenches the gold dart from his chest and flings it at Dean, who dodges while at the same time throwing the black ring in his hand at Ivan.

Ivan backs away, closing his eyes tightly. My eyes widen, horrified. Everything grows still, but before the ring can close around Ivan's neck, it shudders to a stop in mid-air, as if hitting an invisible wall. Ivan opens his eyes as the black ring falls heavily to the ground.

The rain parts, like a curtain being pulled back. Emerging from it is a tall woman, her skin the same color and luminescence of black pearls, her hair falling straight down her back, pure white— her eyes are startlingly clear, reminding me of the iridescence of crystals. She is clothed in gold fabric that shines so bright it hurts to look at, like staring at the sun even behind the clouds.

Auriel's eyes widen. "It can't be."

"Mother," Ian gasps in surprise. "How—?"

"I freed her." Clark remains where he is, his eyes not leaving Ian or Auriel.

"Impossible. Father would never—" Auriel hisses unbelievingly, but before she can finish the thought, the woman turns toward me.

I hold my breath as she scans my face, her crystal eyes so clear that I can almost see my own reflection in them.

"He doesn't know." She gazes at me, a look of sadness on her face. "My name is Ayesha."

I let my breath out, feeling lightheaded as she addresses me. She walks toward me, the fabric of the gold cloth gliding over the rain puddles like air.

"I know." The words leave my lips before I can think of where I have heard the name before, but as I look upon her, I feel like I have always known her.

"I am known as the Mother of Fates, and at one time, I was the One with the Crystal Sight before I lost that ability of my own doing." She reaches a finger toward me. "But I can still see some things."

I don't move as she touches the place where Auriel's dart glided over my cheek, but it has already healed, leaving a streak of silver blood shining there. Her finger is soft and gentle as she slides it across my cheek and into my hairline, brushing a strand of my magenta hair behind my ear. I close my eyes and feel a calm settle over me.

When I open my eyes, she is still looking at me, and I can somehow see silver reflected in the crystal mirrors of her eyes. When I look down, I realize my hair has somehow turned silver, falling down my shoulders and rippling like light reflecting on the surface of water.

A faint but sad smile appears on her lips as she faces Ian and Auriel again.

"You have betrayed us," Auriel's voice shakes as Clark stands next to Ayesha. Ian looks frozen in shock.

Clark remains silent as Auriel twists her hands into her hair as if she is going mad with disbelief. Instead, she is wrapping her fingers around the golden threads, and when she lowers her hands, she holds a glinting bouquet of golden darts. Without saying anything, she flings them out toward us.

The familiar cooling sensation washes over me, the shower of rain wrapping around me. Lifting my hands out in front of me, I can feel the rain ripple and flash, forming a silvery translucent shield that is large enough to protect us all against the shower of gold darts.

As the darts flicker and bounce off the surface of the shield, Ayesha glances at Clark, who nods. Ayesha then walks over to Ivan, her hands resting on his shoulders. He seems frozen in fear and disbelief. She kneels down, her long white hair brushing his face. She whispers something in his ear. Ivan blinks slowly and nods. When she straightens up, he seems calm. He looks at me, and just as Ayesha is about to swing her long golden sleeves up and over him, he mouths the words, "Thank you."

I feel my heart stutter a bit as he and Ayesha disappear. Somehow, though, I know that he will be safe. As the last of the darts fade away, I can see Auriel and Ian standing side-by-side through the shield that I raised.

I lower the shield, and it falls away in a shower of raindrops splashing at our feet.

Auriel looks at me, her face blank. She turns slowly as a cloud of black smoke appears, wrapping her, Dean, and finally Ian into its dark folds.

The last thing I see is Ian as he catches my gaze. He blinks, and his once colorless eyes are now blue and amber. Too afraid to look away, in case they change again, I can't help but notice a great sadness—a sadness that matches his mother's—reflected in his own eyes.

"Evie." Clark turns toward me, a smile of relief on his face. But before I can return it, he begins to fall.

CHAPTER FIFTY
ASHES

"CLARK!" I THROW myself under him, his torso slamming into me as I bring my arms up and around him. I stumble from the force and effort it takes to hold him up, but somehow I feel my footing stabilize, and I am able to lower him easily to the cold rain-drenched ground of the roof.

His eyes are closed, and I realize that he is unconscious. I touch my fingers to his neck to search for a pulse but immediately jerk my hand back. His skin is so cold.

His eyes fly open and he tries sitting up.

"No, you need to lie down, Clark!" I lay my hand across his chest to push him back as gently as I can, but he flinches away from me. When I look down at my fingers, they come away silver, but it seems to darken before my eyes and flake away like ash. I stare at it for a second, the rain falling down my face.

Clark seems delirious. "Evie, go away. Please."

I shake my head automatically, the ash washing away from my fingers in the rain.

"I need to get you help." I start to panic, searching the roof around me and for the first time not knowing what to do even though we are literally at the top of a hospital's roof. I kneel down closer to him. I try bringing my hands to any part of his skin, but he winces every time I try touching him. He grabs his chest in pain, his breathing becoming more shallow.

Suddenly, a black cloud descends over us. I gasp, my eyes widening as darkness wraps around me. My lungs feel as if they are filling with water rather than smoke, though. The feeling is familiar, and fear closes over me, but when I think I will start to suffocate, the sensation falls away.

Already on my knees, I stumble forward onto my hands. I quickly push myself up when I realize that I can breathe normally now.

My eyes take in our surroundings. We are no longer on the roof.

We are in a covered space now, and for a moment I think we are in a forested area, surrounded by green plants. I can see rain falling outside, an entire wall of the room is a window. Hanging above us are numerous glass spheres suspended from ropes. Small brown birds flit around.

I look down, and Clark is lying in front of me, but he has grown still.

"Clark?" I whisper, reaching out a hand hesitantly and letting it hover over the space above his chest. I then lower my hand, resting it gently over the area where a large black stain spotted with silver is spreading. When I realize that he is truly unconscious and unable to flinch away from me, I grab his shirt front, finding the surprisingly tiny hole through which Auriel's golden dart had pierced him. It seems to be at the dead center of his chest. Reflexively and without blinking, I rip this section of the shirt open.

It is then that I can see what damage the small dart has made. The wound is small, but oozes silver blood in a steady stream, which then turns to black ash. Not really paying attention to proper hygiene practices, I immediately pull my jacket off and swipe it over his chest to clear the ash away. I try to ignore this strange occurrence, wondering if it is possibly poison causing this weird reaction. But it still doesn't explain how his blood is silver to begin with.

Silver. Like mine.

I shake my head to clear myself of these thoughts. Bringing my hands over his chest, I rest them there. His skin is so cold that it almost hurts to touch him. I grimace slightly even as I feel a familiar cool and calming sensation flow from my own chest and down my fingertips.

Clark's chest rises up slightly, and his eyelids flicker. Encouraged by this, I continue to clear my thoughts, when Clark's body starts to shudder. His eyes still closed, he raises his arm slowly and lays a hand over his chest, the tips of his fingers settling on my own. His breathing seems to relax, but only for a moment.

His eyes then shoot open, and I can feel an odd pressure of somehow being forced back. He scrambles up to a sitting position. His face looks gray and his eyes are clouded over, the irises milky. He raises his hands as if to hide his face from me.

I find myself pressed up against the glass window as I stare at him. The sound of glass breaking surrounds me, and I lean away from the windowed wall, but when I glance over my shoulder to look, I realize that it is intact.

The sound is coming from the spheres hanging from the ceiling.

I look up and see the small brown birds fluttering frantically as they realize their glass walls are cracking. The sound fills the room and suddenly everything shatters at the same time.

Clark ducks his head into his knees, but I sit there, still and mesmerized, as a shower of glass rains down on us. The plants that are nearest to Clark start to blacken and shrivel, as if a winter chill has touched them; ice drips and curls the leaves. But it is the sudden quiet of the room that feels like it is choking me. The faint twittering of birds is silent.

When the glass spheres shattered, somehow the birds disappeared—and now ash rains down all around us.

CHAPTER FIFTY-ONE

THE OBSIDIAN CROWN

HE WAS SHROUDED *in black smoke that fell heavily off his shoulders and coiled at his feet. When he moved, the smoke flared and flowed outward before wrapping around him loosely again.*

Walking slowly, he inspected the circular room around him, eventually making his way toward the curved walls covered in shelves of books. It was easily noticeable that large numbers of the books were missing, as if quickly and purposefully removed in a short period of time.

Twitching a long black sleeve aside, the fabric of which shimmered slightly with a dull blue iridescence, he lifted a horribly clawed and cruel hand. Where fingers should have been, instead were long tapered points that were both smooth and lined with ridges. What looked like stains of silver streaked the appendages' black surface.

Extending one of the fingers of this clawed hand, he ran it slowly over the books' spines.

His features were heavily shadowed in the room, with very little light flickering from tapers on the walls, long since extinguished by the wind that gusted through the room, creating hollow echoes that climbed up and wrapped around the now vacant tower.

The wind spiraled into the tower from a single window in the circular room with the books. Splinters of gold and shards of glass from the ravaged bars that had sealed the window lay scattered throughout the room.

A room of a tower that had been sealed for thousands of years.

Continuing to drag his clawed finger over the spines of the books, he made his way to the opposite end of the circular room, where there was a desk with many books opened across its surface; a high-backed chair appeared hastily pushed back.

However, at the center of the desk, a single lantern with an ever-burning flame encased in a small glass box sat as if carefully placed there. Next to it was the Obsidian Blade.

When he opened his clawed hand, the black and gleaming blade floated into the center of his palm.

He raised it carefully between the tapered points of his claws. The gray of his eyes shone dully as he saw the silver blood that had dried onto the surface of the blade. The blade almost seemed to disappear against the backdrop of his own clawed hand, the silver streaks standing out even more.

Turning around and holding the blade loosely between his claws, he crossed the threshold of the circular room. In a large broken shard of glass that still clung to the window's frame, he could see his own reflection shrouded in black shadows.

On his head, shining and smooth, was a black crown that, despite its glassy appearance of opaque obsidian, seemed to swallow light like a pool of tar.

As he left the tower nestled into the mountains, it slowly started to dissolve into a torrent of rising blue flames.

"Clark?" I whisper hesitantly from across the room. Ash spirals around me, landing on the ground and dusting the leaves of the green plants.

I sit with my back lightly pressed up against the windowed wall. I can almost feel the rain pouring down on the other side of the glass.

Even though I am certain that Clark did not hear me, he raises his head from his knees. I can make out the amber flecks in the brown of his irises. Rather than look the worse for wear or even slightly injured, his skin is less pale and the shadows under his eyes and the scratches and bruises on his face are gone. His brown wavy hair falls across his eyes and curls loosely around the base of his neck, no longer marred by the scratch that had streaked it just moments earlier.

He hardly seems to want to move, though, his arms are still wrapped loosely around his knees.

I stand up slowly. Ash floats off my shoulders and hair, which I notice is still the strange silvery color that ripples like water. Walking over to him, I kneel down, feeling my caretaker instincts kick in.

"Can I see?"

Without needing to elaborate more, Clark straightens his back, lowering his knees slightly. I can see the tear that I made in the front of his shirt. At the center of his chest, where there had been oozing silver blood and ash moments earlier, there is now nothing but clean unbroken skin underneath.

"You healed yourself?"

A blank expression, hauntingly reminiscent of Auriel's, appears on his face.

"I am incapable of healing anything," Clark states bluntly. "I take what I need to survive."

As he says this, ash continues to fall around us, but it is gradually slowing down. The sound of shattering glass and bird wings fluttering frantically flash across my thoughts. My heartbeat quickens.

"I don't understand. You work at a hospital, though." I can't help the horrified tone as I utter this comment.

Clark shakes his head. "Please." He leans forward, his eyes filled with sadness. "I have never—I would never hurt anyone there."

Despite myself, images of Clark flash across my thoughts. Clark with bags of medicine piled into his arms. Clark caring for patients. Clark reading a book with Ivan. Clark appearing at the balcony and taking me home. Clark handing me a mug of hot chocolate.

"I believe you." The words leave my lips even as Clark is about to say more, perhaps to defend himself.

Clark's expression relaxes in surprised relief, but he seems confused at the same time. "You don't seem…surprised."

I reach into my coat pocket and pull out a small and slightly battered manila envelope. It is the envelope with the photos that I picked up prior to my last encounter at the Thorny Heart. I take a photo out and carefully slide it over to him across the space between us, at the same time brushing ash away.

"I am surprised, but I already knew that there had to be something about you. I went through these pictures this morning before coming in to work. I wasn't looking for anything, just something to do—keep my mind off of... everything. I was going to ask you about it, but then I got distracted." A smile quirks up ironically at the corners of my mouth for the first time as flashes of the events that just happened ripple through my thoughts. "I took this the day that we were in the park and we crossed paths."

Clark reaches down and picks up the photo. It is of him coming through the brush, gently pushing away a branch as he looks up, surprised to see me while I am photographing pictures of birds. Although nothing appears abnormal in the photo upon first glance—it is his eyes.

At first I had thought it was a trick of the lighting that day or an error when the photo was developed, but the photo is too clear, and rather than any sort of red-eye or glare, there is no mistaking the fact that Clark's eyes are a different color than their usual brown. In fact, they look perfectly colorless, just slightly cloudy, the pupils completely invisible.

"Ness and Ian," I say their names as Clark lowers the photo. Disbelief and confusion flood back to me. "They have the same color eyes."

"That's because they are my brother and sister," Clark states plainly. "Those are not their real names. Their names are Auriel and Neko."

"What's yours?"

Clark frowns, and for a moment, he looks pained in the same way that he did when injured with his chest bleeding. "Cerin."

"Cerin," I repeat. The name feels strange as I try to associate it with Clark, this person sitting across from me.

"We disguise ourselves and spend most of our time traveling. Never settling for too long at any given time."

"Ayesha is your mother," I recall the details that I learned on the hospital's rooftop.

Clark—Cerin—nods but doesn't elaborate on this fact. Rather than press it, I continue on.

"Cl—I mean, Cerin, why are you here?"

Cerin looks at me, and I can see Ayesha's sadness reflected in his eyes. "To help you."

"Why?"

"You are in danger from the king of frozen lands and fire." Cerin looks away from me as he continues on mechanically. "The wearer of the Obsidian Crown."

The image of the shadowed figure with gray eyes illustrated so realistically and terribly in Kana's journal comes back to me. Claws gripping a black sword and a beautiful crown sitting on his head. I feel as if Cerin is withholding some important detail, but I'm already overwhelmed by the events of the day, and exhausted as well, so I ignore it.

"Your brother and sister work for him?"

"Yes. I did, too. For a long time."

My eyes flicker back up to Cerin, who continues to avoid my gaze.

"Why not anymore?"

This time Cerin looks at me, his features set like stone, his brows furrowed. "He's a tyrant, holding the world hostage, imprisoning his enemies, entire kingdoms, and killing them cruelly. Kana was his greatest adversary. He feared her."

"So he killed her."

Cerin just looks at me, his expression smoothing out

so that it appears blank again. I wonder how he can do this so easily.

"Your mother." I recall Ayesha's beautiful face, her crystalline eyes gazing at me sadly. "He was the one imprisoning her? For being Kana's friend?" *Mother of Fates.* Her words ring once again through my ears.

"For betraying him," Cerin's voice seems to catch, as if wanting to stop himself from saying anything more. "She was his wife, and she tried to escape with their firstborn son soon after giving birth, which was right after he had killed Kana."

My eyes widen as a realization hits me.

Even though I don't need him to, Cerin states it anyway.

"Auriel and Neko…and me. We're his children."

I stare at him, unable to say anything. For the first time, it feels like a white sheet has blanketed my mind. Everything is completely blank and empty of thoughts. The moment is perhaps seconds, but it feels like hours.

Mother of Fates. Ayesha's title whispers in the distant corners of my mind as I look at Cerin. A dark edge of fear creeps up around me, my gaze unable to leave his face. He looks absolutely miserable at that moment, staring at what I assume is a point on the floor past his own feet—or perhaps he is looking at nothing at all.

And still. I trust him.

"What was it about Kana that made your father fear her so much?"

Without saying anything, Cerin reaches toward the

plant closest to him. Its leaves are black where it had been green moments before the glass spheres shattered. Placing his hands into the pot, he pulls out one of the leaves, a charred root dangling at the end. He then extends this dead thing toward me.

"Well, I never expected this to be the situation leading to my first social gesture involving a plant. Not that I had any romantic expectations or anything," I joke flatly as I reach for it. I'm not sure, but I think I see a brief flicker of a smile appear at the corner of his mouth; his face, though, remains serious.

Closing my fingers gingerly around the plant, I almost expect it to crumble into ash. Instead, a coolness flows down my hand—and even though I expect it, I still feel my heart quicken in surprise as the plant, starting from its root, begins to extend and grow, the charred and blackened leaves somehow flaking off and revealing a new growth of deep and vibrant green underneath.

Even though I'm sure he expected it as well, when I look back at Cerin, his eyes are wide. Something about this expression seems almost childlike. His fingers twitch as if he wants to reach for the plant, but instead he quietly starts to speak.

"My father rules his kingdoms with death's touch. His kingdom and crown were forged from blue fires, which melted everything into black glass. Years passed, and the burning hells froze into something that nothing, not even the light of the sun, could warm. He craved greater powers and a wider reach, but Kana had the love and rule of the sky, sea, and forest realms. She also had the love and friendship of those that carry the light- and the Crystal Sight, Ayesha.

Who my father, even with his frozen heart, also loved. He feared Kana Akihira because of this—her powers to grow things greater than fear. But most of all, she had the ability to heal and bring life back to what death had touched."

Brushing my fingers absently over the surface of the plant's leaves, I listen to Cerin continue. "There is no greater fear than death, except for what Kana could do to it. That's why he waged a terrible war against her. That's why he killed her."

"Were you close to your father?"

Cerin's hands hang loosely in front of him. "Yes."

"What happened?" I almost don't want to ask, but I recall clearly the look of hurt and anger that never seemed to leave Auriel and Neko's faces throughout their encounter on the rooftop.

"I-I can't," Cerin stumbles over his words, a pained expression on his face. "I can't tell you right now, Evie. I owe you the answer at some point, but I want to tell you when the right time comes."

I find myself nodding despite my confusion. I'm so tired, but I still have so many questions. The most pressing question, though, burns away at me slowly, an ache that has always been there like a chronic wound festering since I was a child.

"What will happen now?"

Cerin closes his eyes for a moment as if thinking carefully of what words to say. When he opens them back up, his eyes reflect my own—tired, rundown. The amber flecks seem even brighter in the brown of his irises.

"The kingdoms are rising up, and my father is stirring. There will be a war. A war to take his crown." Cerin breathes in slowly, his gaze steady as he looks at me. "Evie. You are the one to lead this war. You have abilities that Kana herself never had or ever predicted. It has been thousands of years, and the time has finally come. Many look to you. *You* will be the one to end death's reign."

CHAPTER FIFTY-TWO
THE SHADOW OF HOPE

I DON'T KNOW how long I sit there, the plant still in my hand. Although not much time has passed, the plant continues to grow.

Memories flash slowly through my mind. An overwhelming feeling of drowning, of being submerged under so many revelations and even more questions, makes a pressure rise in my chest that feels like it will burst at any moment. My mind, for some reason, lands on the details of my messenger bag. I feel silly thinking about something as insignificant as that old bag carrying all my books, but then there is one more thing that I need to know...

"The sketchbook." I can almost feel the rippling textures of its black cover even as I recall it at that very moment.

Cerin raises his head in surprise, looking almost embarrassed.

"It's mine," he states quickly. "I mean, it was mine. I wanted you to have it."

I frown, wanting to ask why, but before I can, Cerin

looks at me apologetically. "I had to learn about you. You had so many similarities to Kana, not just the obvious ones either. Kana loved to draw. It was almost an impulse, something that she couldn't help."

"I stopped doing that a long time ago." I stare at a point over Cerin's shoulder, a sadness coming over me. I wonder if Kana thought of her proclivity to draw as a gift rather than a curse, like I did.

"I know," Cerin states, a gentleness to his voice that I recognize in everything that I have associated with Clark. Focusing on him, I realize that I am starting to find a sort of comfort in this. Cerin is still Clark—but at the same time, not. Maybe it is because he's the first person I have ever been able to talk to in this way, about myself, as if I have nothing to hide or avoid saying. Maybe there are other reasons, but I'm not sure what they were.

"I thought maybe you could start again. Maybe—maybe it'll be easier." There is something like hope in Cerin's voice as he says this. I wonder if he himself has found comfort in something as simple as creating art. The child, whose father is death.

Despite myself and everything that has happened, I smile even as ash continues to settle around us.

EPILOGUE

ESTELLE FELT A vibration in her scrub pocket and started to dig around for her pager. After a moment, she realized that her pager was actually sitting in front of the nurses' station, which was at the center of the emergency department—and, in fact, it was not vibrating for once.

She sighed when she realized it was her cell phone; she always seemed to confuse the two, grabbing the wrong one.

Walking over and grabbing her pager while at the same time pulling her cell phone out of her pocket, she took a seat at the nurses' station. She welcomed the moment that she got to relieve the pressure on her feet. She couldn't remember the last time that she had actually sat.

Answering her cell phone without checking the ID, she leaned back into the chair luxuriously. "Hello, this is indeed Estelle Kagwe."

"Stella? This is your father."

Estelle nodded a little impatiently even though her father wouldn't be able to see her. The introduction was really unnecessary, though. The only people who ever called her "Stella" were her father, mother, and her brother when he was still young. She couldn't help but feel a twinge of sadness whenever she thought about him.

Without waiting for a response, her father continued. "Kyle is missing."

Estelle leaned forward, almost propelling herself off the chair in surprise.

"What? Are they sure? But the institution is locked down. Besides, Kyle wouldn't even leave his bedroom. Even if the door was left wide open." Estelle heard the words leave her mouth even though she knew that they were redundant. Obviously if they reported him missing, he was no longer in his room.

Before her father could say this, Estelle continued. "Do I need to come home?" Estelle tapped the computer in front of her. When the internet browser opened up, she started searching for flights to New York.

"No," Estelle's father stated simply. Estelle leaned back from the computer screen, surprised but also expecting this.

"Your mother and I have done everything that can be done. There is nothing more except to wait."

"Right." Although hating the sharp and matter-of-fact tone, Estelle knew that her father was right.

"We will keep you updated. I must attend to your mother now, Stella. She is beside herself."

As if hearing Estelle's silent nod over the phone, he ended the call.

Estelle set the cell phone down in front of her and before she even had a moment to register her thoughts any further, Dylan, an enthusiastic emergency room technician breezed by, greeting her and depositing an envelope in front of her.

"Came with the pizza delivery for some reason." Dylan grinned. "Also, your favorite anchovy and pineapple awaits."

Estelle nodded, and Dylan walked away, a look of confusion on his face at her uncharacteristic behavior. It was a very strange and unheard of occurrence for Dr. Kagwe to not jump up in seconds with any mention of food entering the department.

Grabbing the envelope hesitantly, she saw that her name was indeed scrawled across it, but nothing more. Thinking it vaguely strange that someone would send her a message with a pizza delivery, she broke the envelope open. Inside, there was a single piece of folded up and lined paper. It looked like it had been torn from a spiral notebook. Sliding the paper out, she unfolded it and gasped.

All across the paper were scrawled strange shapes—shapes she could only assume were characters to an unrecognizable language. They were drawn messily across the paper, but at the center was a crudely drawn image of something that she did recognize.

It looked like the crescent and round opal pendant that she had lying in a box in her bedroom.

Her eyes widened as a few of the letters amidst all other strange characters came into focus.

Help Evie.

Estelle mouthed the words silently.

Without understanding how, Estelle somehow knew that this was a message from her brother.

Continue the Story of

The Obsidian Crown

in book two of the series:

Frozen Flowers

COMING IN 2019

Acknowledgements

THANK YOU TO my ancestors and generations that preceded me, for bringing me to this moment in time, because *wow*. I feel so fortunate to have been born during a time when I am able to share what I love most about life. (Besides human interactions, of course... which is mostly okay when I think about it.) But what I am really referring to is books—and writing them.

So, I would like to thank you, my dear reader. You have no idea what dreams you have made come true for me by just opening this book.

And a special thanks to everyone in my life who has encouraged me. My parents and my brother for always believing in me—and indulging my book collecting. And my husband, who really was the one who gave me that final nudge after a lifetime of uncertainty when it came to sharing my stories. To my oldest friend and her mother for reading my story in its rawest form! (And for all the furry critter .gifs along the way!)

Thank you to my editor, Kelley Frodel for helping me make my story better. Thank you for guiding me through my writing journey.

Oh, and DFTBA.

About the Author

Louisa Gene Moriyama is a reader, book collector, and writer. She lives in Puyallup, Washington with her husband, cat, and son. She can be found at: LGMoriyama. com, LGMoriyama@ gmail.com, and @LGMoriyama on Instagram.